# THE
# EXILED

ALSO BY POSIE GRAEME-EVANS

*The Innocent*

# THE
# EXILED

*A Novel*

POSIE GRAEME-EVANS

**ATRIA** BOOKS

NEW YORK   LONDON   TORONTO   SYDNEY

ATRIA BOOKS
1230 Avenue of the Americas
New York, NY 10020

Originally published in Australia in 2003 by Simon & Schuster
(Australia) Pty Limited

Library of Congress Cataloging-in-Publication Data

Graeme-Evans, Posie.
    The exiled : a novel / by Posie Graeme-Evans.—1st Atria Books trade pbk. ed.
        p. cm.
    ISBN 0-7434-4373-X
        1. Great Britain—History—Lancaster and York, 1399–1485—Fiction.
    2. British—Belgium—Fiction. 3. Brugge (Belgium)—Fiction. 4. Young women—
    Fiction. 5. Exiles—Fiction. I. Title.

PR9619.4.G73E95 2005
823'.92—dc22
                                                                    2004060752
First Atria Books trade paperback edition June 2005

10  9  8  7  6  5  4  3  2  1

ATRIA BOOKS is a trademark of Simon & Schuster, Inc.

Manufactured in the United States of America

For information regarding special discounts for bulk purchases,
please contact Simon & Schuster Special Sales at 1-800-456-6798
or business@simonandschuster.com

*To my loving, kind, funny and
patient husband, Andrew Blaxland.
Thank you for understanding
my obsessional need to write,
for making the winters so cozy
and for the good red wine.
I am blessed by your care of me.*

# THE
# EXILED

# Prologue

The storm came down like God's hammer.

The wind, violent servant of the bruise-black sky, sucked and churned the sea until it flung mountains onto the shore, saltwater mountains that heaved and broke and shattered; rock is stronger than cold sea.

"I see it!"

There were two of them riding ahead of the storm searching for shelter—a cave in the cliff wall ahead.

"There! There it is!"

Neither brother heard the other, words taken by the rain, but the horses knew where to go, scrambling up the wet, slick shingle, closer, closer.

"Hold up, hold up!"

Did the big man call to his brother, his horse, or himself as the hooves struck sparks from the rain-black scree?

"Yes! Sweet Mary, yes! Up now!" One last clambering rush, but the smaller of the two reached the cave mouth first, ducking under the sea-made lintel with perfect timing as he brought his horse, Hautboys, to a stop with steel wrists. The cave was vast, dark, and the rain-gray light from the opening was soon lost inside.

"Thanks be." The young man shook himself like a dog or a seal as his brother—bigger, wetter, and annoyed at not having won the race—made the same faultless entrance, neatly turning

*I*

his stallion, Mallon, to one side at the last moment. Now the two horses, flanks heaving, heads down, were neatly ranged side by side as if stabled for the night.

Richard grinned. "So, Edward, you let me win, did you?"

"I was looking after Mallon's legs." A virtuous response, but Richard snorted as he slid down from his saddle. "Liar. I outrode you; be a man, admit it."

Edward, King of England, the fourth of that name, choked on laughter and annoyance. It was true this time; his youngest brother had outridden him, but he'd been honest: he didn't like running Mallon over broken ground, least of all wet shingle.

"Think it'll last long?"

Tossing Hautboys's reins to the king, Richard, Duke of Gloucester, sauntered toward the cave mouth, the opening veiled by a temporary waterfall from the tons of water falling down the cliff face.

"I hope so." Edward spoke without thought as he patted Mallon's neck, jumping down to the clean, sanded floor of the cave.

Richard turned to look at his brother. "What did you say?"

"Never mind." The king joined the duke and together they looked out through the falling water at the violent sea.

People seeing them together for the first time were always surprised they were brothers; Edward was taller by half a sword's length and so fairheaded that in summer his hair was barley-straw white; and his was a long, strong, open face with the beauty of an avenging angel—or so a girl had once told him, long, so long ago, it seemed. He shook the sadness away as he saw her face, unsummoned.

No one had yet compared Richard to an angel, of any kind.

He was watchful and dark: dark eyed, dark skinned, dark haired, and whipcord slight where his brother was big and massive armed. However, both had the strength of men who fought from horseback: strong backs, strong thighs.

The young duke looked at his brother. Edward was brooding again, eyes so far away he might be in another country.

Richard shrugged, impatient. The king had been gloomy for

far too long; it was part of the reason he'd suggested they go riding, just the two of them, to get away from the courtiers and the tedium of the "Progress" as Edward's court moved south toward London and the Palace of Westminster.

The duke smiled faintly. They'd know both brothers were missing by now and there would be great alarm, especially from the queen. She'd be furious that Edward had slipped his noose.

Richard looked around him with interest. This cave was famous, famous enough to have a name, Loki's Hall: Loki, the old god of shape shifters, of fire, of sorcerers.

It was big enough to be a hall, certainly, and, yes, there were columnlike rock formations marching back into the belly of the cliff, similar to what you saw in Westminster, for instance; curiously carved by something, too—some shaping force. They couldn't be the work of human hands, could they? Perhaps a sorcerer, servant of the old gods, had made them.

Richard shivered and quickly crossed himself, touching the seal ring on his left hand. Under the carved onyx there was concealed a tiny but assuredly powerful relic, one of the milk-teeth of Saint George. The duke wasn't frightened of old magic, of course, but—

*Boom!* The cave shuddered and both men leaped to hold the horses as an enormous grinding groan shivered the air and jangled their heads, shaking their very teeth.

Dust filled the cave and light blinked out; sudden darkness, grit as they tried to breathe and a deep, bowel-loosening thunder beneath their feet, all around them, in the cave with them!

"Brother!" Richard couldn't help himself. He was gripped by terror, a shameful thing.

"I'm here, I'm here. All's well." Yes, it would be, Richard knew that. It was his brother's greatest strength—his calm—when the world shook loose and became a fearful place. He'd learned that skill early, at Towton, Palm Sunday, when he'd used his battle-ax in combat for the first time and the snow ran rich red, rose-red, and the order of the world was remade.

The shuddering stopped. Suddenly. All four, men and horses,

took deep, urgent breaths in the instant quiet, sucking at a stream of clean, pure air where there was none before. Richard coughed explosively and spat grit.

"What was that?"

The raging wind was gone, and with it the veil of water over the cave mouth turned to breaking dribbles. Light returned.

"Let's see." Edward gave Mallon one last pat and stepped cautiously toward the light.

Much had changed. Whole sections of the headland had come away and the shingle was littered with crushed rock and uprooted, broken trees from the missing clifftop.

But the mouth of the cave was open, open enough, though they would need care leading the horses out among the storm wreckage. No race home for them.

The king laughed. A harsh laugh. His luck had held. Again. "Edward?"

The duke was a pale shape behind him, a white, indistinct pillar from the dust; the king's right hand reached for the pommel of his sword—he'd heard the fear. Silently, quickly, the king moved toward his brother, one pace, two, three, and then he saw . . .

"Is this sorcerer's work, Edward?"

Richard nearly controlled his voice—it was low, which was good, and steady, but "work" came out as a squeak. Edward often forgot how young he was.

In the depths of the cave, a curtain wall of rock had fallen away to reveal a man lying on a rock ledge. In the gloom, he could have been asleep, but as Edward bent down he saw . . . a naked corpse. A black, naked corpse.

Cured and darkened by the salt air, perhaps, the skin of the man was the color of sea coal, but it lay in strange inhuman folds; muscle had dissolved from beneath leaving an outline, an approximation, of the collapsed shape of a man. That was repellent enough in its sucked-out strangeness, but this death had been a cruel one.

The man's throat had an old, profound wound, a gash just beneath the jaw that was deep enough to show the spine's junction with the skull. There were blade marks on the white bone and a stiff noose of animal sinew had dropped into the tear as the flesh of the throat decayed around it, a noose that had once been brutally tight.

"Look." Richard had his voice steady now. In the uncertain light, he pointed and Edward just made out, black on black, a thin, leaf-shaped blade between the dead man's ribs. It had been rammed into the chest with such force that several of the ribs were broken. A strange thing for such a small blade.

Edward reached down to take it.

"Don't! Don't touch it. It could be cursed. He could be cursed." Richard's voice shook but the king ignored the subtle, fearful breath of old magic, old beliefs.

"No, brother. See? It's just a kind of knife, I think." The king held the black thing up: it was beautiful, fitting his hand so well it might have been his own, yet he was puzzled. It was made from no metal he knew and the cutting edge was slightly scalloped, though lethally sharp. Perhaps it was stone, but stone such as he had never seen before, more like black glass, and very cold.

The man-thing lay silent before them, curled up like a sleeping child. A slow, unwilling shiver touched the king's spine.

"Edward, I think we should go. They'll be looking for us, after the storm. The queen will be unhappy." Richard laughed nervously. He really wanted to leave this strange place, right now, but thinking of Elizabeth Wydeville's certain rage was a bracing thing, a human thing that helped somehow. He made a move toward the horses.

"Wait. Richard, what did you mean, cursed?"

Richard was suddenly very busy with the girths of both horses; he spoke over his shoulder.

"Well, the triple death. You know: drowned, or burned, or buried after hanging and cutting the throat. There were different ways of doing it when they wanted to make a sacrifice or . . ."

"Or what?" The king was almost conversational as he bent down and carefully left the nasty little black knife, if knife it was, lying near one of the dead man's hands.

"Or to prevent an evil man walking after death. Sometimes

they buried them at crossroads. Just old stories, I expect, but . . . Edward, what are you doing?" Richard's voice was sharp with nerves.

"There, my friend. Sleep well." If the dead fingers were ever to reach out, ever to uncurl, they would touch the murderer's final weapon. Did the dead have need to defend themselves? Edward shook his head at the strange fantasy.

The brothers walked their horses out of the cave and away between the crushed rock, over the new landscape as the sea slowly quieted, slumping back, hissing softly on the shingled sand.

Gratefully, Richard snuffled the salt on the air as he mounted and crossed himself, kissing the relic ring. "Thanks be to Our Lady, and Saint George! That old Loki didn't get us! Lucky again, brother—we might have been companions to his friend back there for all time. No one would have found us."

But Edward, once more on Mallon's back, riding toward duty, toward responsibility, took no notice of his brother's words. Luck? Once, when he'd really needed it, his luck had run dry. And thinking of that time, unwillingly, nearly a year ago, he heard only one thing, the sound of sea birds calling, and only saw one thing, Anne's face.

From a distance he'd watched her go, hadn't prevented it as she and Deborah sailed away from Dover's harbor. And now, as Mallon stretched out to a gallop on hard sand at the sea's edge, the pain came again, fresh, clear, and almost sweet; the pain under his ribs that was there when he saw her face, as if he, too, had been sliced open with that black knife, sliced to the quick. And died. Died for her.

Where was she? Where was she?

PART ONE

# The Apprentice

# Chapter One

"Enough. Rest now. You must be stiff."

The girl kneeling in front of the casement window stretched and sighed, easing her clenched muscles. It was true she was stiff, and cold also, from holding the pose. The charcoal braziers had burned out long ago and the room was frigid.

"We have worked well today, you and I." The painter, oblivious to the temperature and happy to chat as he ground pigment in his mortar—it would yield rich scarlet when bound with boiled linseed oil and powdered gum arabica—spoke truthfully, for the girl had knelt uncomplainingly for several hours. That was unusual among his clients, and he was grateful.

Satisfied, finally, with the consistency of the bloody paint he'd now mixed in an oyster shell, he took some to the tip of his brush and smiled apologetically.

"If you are ready, I must use this light, mistress; perhaps a little more padding for the knees?" He smiled encouragingly as she knelt again, but then frowned as he leaned toward his canvas, lost once more in catching that annoyingly elusive highlight on one small fold of the velvet that was giving him trouble, such trouble . . .

Sound traveled well in that still, icy dusk. The shouts of children playing on the frozen canal outside the painter's narrow house bounced off the walls inside the studio when, finally, the man put his brush down and stood back from the picture.

He flicked a glance toward his sitter, obediently kneeling still. She was rimmed by the last of the light outside his casement and he could barely see her face, for the red sky in the west was darkening; soon the oil lamps, the tallow dips, and the candles would be lit against shadows all over his city.

"That is all for today, mistress. The light is gone."

Gratefully, Anne de Bohun sat back on her heels, allowing her body to slump, as she flexed stiffened fingers one by one.

"Maestro? May I look?"

"Not yet, mistress. Bad luck to look on it unfinished. Perhaps tomorrow."

She understood his reluctance perfectly. It would be hard letting something out into the world, even when it was finished, if you'd brought it into being. Very well, she could wait a little longer.

Without fuss, Anne picked up a winter cloak and draped it around her shoulders. Best to cover the garnet-red velvet of the dress she was wearing, for it was the most valuable thing she owned and there were strangers on the streets this winter. She did not want to invite robbery—or worse.

"Lotta! Bring light!" The painter's voice was shockingly loud as he yelled for his servant, not even bothering to open the door and call down the stairs. She would hear him.

As they waited, Hans Memlinc, the German painter, watched Anne covertly while he cleaned his brushes—those ivory hands with their long, capable fingers pinning her cloak together, smoothing the folds of the stiffened veiling surmounting the embroidered cap that hid her hair. He'd never seen her hair. He was sad about that.

Anne de Bohun was a mystery. His paintings cost a great deal of money, but she'd not balked at the price when they'd struck the contract. Yet, if gossip was correct, she was not, herself, personally wealthy, even if her guardian, Mathew Cuttifer, the English merchant, was. Perhaps he had paid.

There was a timid little thump at the door. Suppressing irritation, Memlinc leaned over and flicked the iron latch up. The door swung into the room, revealing the anxious face of his servant, Lotta. She was holding a branch of lit candles in one hand, a small, sputtering oil lamp in the other. She was very young and flustered, and her anxiety to please her master made her clumsy. She dripped oil from the lamp onto her kirtle as she curtsied to her master and his guest.

"Set the candles down, girl. Not there!" Lotta had hurried to comply, putting the branched lights down on the first available surface, his worktable cluttered with mortars for grinding pigment and pots full of brushes. "How many times? No! Put the candles in front of the mirror; it will double the light."

Anne took pity on the harried child. It had been only so little time since she, too, had been a servant. "There, Lotta, give me the lamp for your master. And please let Ivan know I am ready to go home."

Gratefully, Lotta scuttled out of the studio, and Anne glanced at the painter as he dropped a fine muslin cloth over the face of his work. The material was held away from the surface by a delicate wire prop. Delicate things pleased them both. They smiled at each other.

"Thank you, Maestro. Today was a good day. I shall look forward to our final session together tomorrow." Such a subtle stress on the word "final," but the painter heard her, heard what she meant, and surprised himself by nodding. Yes, they would finish tomorrow.

Anne reached up and carefully placed the little terra-cotta lamp on a shelf above his worktable, where the uncertain light spilled down to the painter's best advantage, then began fastening iron-shod wooden pattens over her soft shoes.

"Until tomorrow, then."

She was grateful that tomorrow would bring completion, for it had been a lengthy process, sitting for the painter, and she was impatient to have the picture home.

Hans Memlinc had no idea how important his work was to Anne. It was only paint, canvas, and the skill of his hands, but this picture was Anne's private, tangible symbol of hope, hope for her future, and her future success in this city, and as such was worth every one of the carefully hoarded gold angels she would pay.

Anne's pattens clicked on the painter's tiled floor as she left his studio smiling happily. Belated conscience struck him and he called after her, "I've kept you late, mistress. You must be careful going home. There are too many mercenaries in town this winter. Wild and silly, most of them, but no one is safe after the curfew bell."

She laughed. "I'm not worried. The Watch'll have chained the streets by now. Soldiers all drink too much anyway. I can out-run them, Maestro!" He heard her giggle as she clattered happily down his staircase and he found himself grinning.

Anne was still smiling as Ivan, her guardian's Magyar manservant, closed the front door of the painter's house behind them. He'd been waiting in Master Memlinc's warm kitchen, quite happy to while away another winter's day chaffing little, shy Lotta and flirting with Eva, the cook-housekeeper. She was substantial, Eva, with an abundance of good flesh packed tightly into a pretty skin. He liked that. She liked him. They had been pleasant times.

"The picture will be finished tomorrow, Ivan, so no more happy days with Eva." Spooked by Anne's prescience, the man nearly dropped his flambeau. He crossed himself quickly, but she saw it.

"What's this, Ivan? A prayer? Who for? Eva?"

Her laughter was so unforced, so clear in the dark, sharp air that Ivan was ashamed. She was not a witch, this girl, just clever—for a woman. Cautiously he smiled, and held the light higher.

Anne pulled on her one winter indulgence—fleece-lined mit-tens—as she breathed deeply of the wood-smoke air. A few min-utes' brisk walk beside the frozen canal and she would reach her guardian's new house with its warehouse near the Kruispoort— one of the nine fortified gates of the city of Brugge—but Ivan would have his hand on the hilt of a short stabbing sword the whole way.

It was a good feeling, if she was honest, that he was her pro-tector, for the town was filled with outlanders this winter: mostly mercenaries in the service of the Duke of Burgundy who roamed the streets waiting for the end of winter and the certainty of the coming spring campaigns. The Lowlands were still restless and their new duke had much to do to secure his duchy, let alone deal with the French. Mercenaries are only ever half tame, everyone knew that, and winter made them dangerous: too much time on their hands and too much blood from rich food and good beer.

Ivan understood. As a very young man he, too, had been dangerous—still was, in a more controlled way—which was why he'd been hired by Sir Mathew Cuttifer, Anne's patron and guardian, to help protect his interests in this city. Anne fell into that category for reasons Ivan was not paid to understand.

Brugge, this Venice of the North, was booming and there were rich pickings to be had, and not just for English merchants with interests outside Britain, like Sir Mathew. Young, landless men are always attracted to wealth, and many here had more ambition than a short lifetime's service as one of the Duke of Burgundy's paid fighters.

And it was hard to be poor in such a place, hard not to be envious of other people's good fortune—if you had none yourself—for wool, spices, and jewels arrived daily in barges down the Zwijn from the coast. More wealth to add to that already stuffed in behind the sturdy walls of this dynamic city—and Sir Mathew and his friends, the English Merchant Adventurers, commanded much of it.

Thus it was Ivan's job to see that his master, and his master's ward, Lady Anne de Bohun, lived in peace, the peace he could help give them in dangerous times when so many coveted Sir Mathew's rich possessions, this girl included. He took the office seriously as a matter of professional pride.

Anne was a realist, too, for all the joking with Meinheer Memlinc. It was the darkest time of the year and she was grateful to have this short, powerfully squat man pacing at her side, alert as a hunting dog.

Cold air breathed up from the ice of the canal as she walked. Anne shivered, though she and Ivan were moving briskly, her pattens clicking on the cobbles, he pacing beside her in good leather boots, matching his stride to hers.

Around them, houses crowded thick and tight, and warm light bloomed from some proud windows, though much of the town was dark. It was the wealthy who kept lights burning on into the night: the merchants, nobles, and priests who thronged around the new Duke of Burgundy as his court formed, eager for advancement.

Sensible people went to bed even before the curfew bell, however, for heat and light were expensive in winter and it was easier, and cheaper, to stay warm under the covers. You didn't need light in bed.

Nearly there now, nearly there. Anne could see Mathew's house on the other side of the frozen canal just past the bridge. It was well lit for her homecoming and that was good: her toes were burning, tingling with the cold, pattens or no pattens to keep them out of the muck.

"Mistress?"

Ivan had slowed his pace and spoke softly.

"Hold the light, lady."

He was always calm in a crisis, Ivan, for he'd survived far too many bloody turns to get excited, but even he, now, was tense, because ahead of them, blocking the narrow bridge across the canal that led to Sir Mathew's house, was a compact group of silent men. Faint light from the stars caught the movement as they silently drew swords.

"Behind me. Drop the light when I tell you." Ivan breathed the words and Anne slid quietly into his shadow.

"Now!"

The flambeau's light hissed out into the dirty, banked snow at the lane's edge, but as it died, the flame showed Anne another three men behind them.

"Ivan, behind us. Three more!"

"The canal. Jump when I yell." It was the only choice and so, as he sprang toward the men on the bridge screaming, "A moi, Sainte George!" Anne kicked off her pattens, scooped up her skirts, and ran to the edge of the canal.

Too late to think, too late to judge the drop from bank to ice, she half fell, half dropped down, and though she rolled as soon as she hit the hard surface, to cushion the jolt, she knew she'd soon feel the shock in her muscles—if she survived.

Above her there were shouts from the bridge as Ivan fought his way into the midst of the attackers. The men had seen her drop and someone was yelling, "Get the girl, get the girl!" but Anne still had an advantage of seconds, though she was encumbered by long skirts.

Breathing raggedly, heart jolting, she scrabbled to her feet and blessed the lessons of moving over the ice that Ivan had made her practice this winter—one foot, next foot, striving for balance. Then fear turned to panicked acid in her throat: she had to cross the fragile, new ice in the center of the canal if she was to reach Sir Mathew's frozen water gate ahead of her attackers. On the bridge, Ivan was fighting with the fury of his berserk ancestors, but he could not, single-handedly, hold them all away from her. She must do it, must move on.

With a yell, two men dropped down off the center of the bridge, but the freeze was only two days old and the ice was not as thick as it soon would be. Their yells changed to screams as they fell through into the frigid black waters of the Zwijn.

Anne saw the cracks in the ice shoot out from the hole they'd made as she slid on toward the farther side of the canal, but she was far enough away from them, and so much lighter, that the ice held together under her soft shoes. Breathing hard, she reached the other bank and scrambled toward Sir Mathew's water gate—it was frozen shut but it was close, closer. Perhaps she could climb it.

Now she was yelling, too, "Help us, help us!" as lights flared in houses above the canal. No one liked another's dispute, especially if it was just a fight among drunken mercenaries, but they had heard her calling out and a woman's voice stirred the conscience—a little.

Blessedly, torchlight suddenly shone down and willing hands reached out to haul her up—Sir Mathew's steward, Maxim, and two of the stable boys. "Help Ivan! There, the bridge." She could hardly gasp the words as her arms were wrenched above her head, but then they had her onto the roadway and Maxim was hurrying her inside, into the warm hall, while he shouted for more men.

It was over very soon. Maxim and Sir Mathew's servants rushed the bridge where Ivan was viciously defending the honor of his master's house. Two assailants, lethally slashed, were groaning at his feet and one man was dead, his blood a black steaming puddle in the snow. Of the two who had jumped from the bridge, one was lying on the cracked ice half drowned and gasping, while his companion hadn't surfaced. The other men, the followers, had disappeared.

Now Anne stood in front of the expensive new fireplace in Sir Mathew's hallhouse under a painted panel of Saint George destroying the dragon; it was an apt expression of her life: she must slay the dragon of fear here, tonight. Holding out her hands to the flames, she swallowed hard, trying to control her breathing, trying to banish the burning vomit in her throat.

It was a shock. All she had been warned about was true. And if this was more than it seemed—a kidnap for ransom—then she had enemies and it was time to face these facts, time to think her way through her situation very carefully.

"Mistress? Are you harmed?" It was her foster mother's anguished voice Anne heard now and she turned slowly, giving herself enough time to gather a smile to her face.

"Not at all, Deborah. As you see. Where's Edward?" She must not give in to the fear; must not. Shakily she forced herself to breathe slowly and deeply as she tried to unfasten her cloak with suddenly useless fingers.

Deborah answered the unasked question. "He's fine. Just fine. Here. Let me." Deborah hurried to help, gently detaching the cloak from Anne's shoulders and unpinning the crushed and distorted headdress. "He's asleep, bless him. We've got his cradle near the fire in the kitchen. He fed well again tonight—I'm very pleased with the new nurse; she's a fine strong girl, abundant milk."

Routine. Reassuring, safe routine. All was well—Deborah could always do that for her. Anne summoned another smile and carefully smoothed the folds of her expensive red dress. She grimaced. It would never be the same. The hem was dragged and dirty and there were dark wet patches where she'd fallen on her knees; it would have to be carefully dried and brushed if the fabric was not to be completely ruined. Hans Memlinc would see her in another dress tomorrow.

"I shall see how my nephew fares." She needed to see the baby, needed to hold him. Deborah smiled at her, touched her hand gently. "Yes, it's nice and cozy in the kitchen. I'll see to warming the solar."

Anne was calmer now, soothed as always by Deborah's care of her. Tremulously the girl smiled in return and would have leaned against her foster mother for strength, except that Maxim or one of the other servants might see the moment of weakness and be curious.

She was too new to Brugge, too new to the role she'd been given—that of Mathew Cuttifer's ward—to be anything but careful; too much was at stake. She and Deborah must always retain the appearance of servant and mistress in front of the household, yet both women found the constant role-playing a strain, especially now. They'd get used to it, they had to. For the moment, it was their only safety for they had nowhere else to go.

Anne sighed, then consciously relaxing her rigid shoulders, folded her hands at her waist, and stepped down the wooden staircase to the kitchens without fuss, breathing deeply as the peace of being home and safe clothed her softly as a cloak.

The kitchen was always busy in a large household, especially now as it was close to suppertime, but as Anne appeared, all work stopped. She was well liked, their master's ward.

"Lady, are you harmed?" The Flemish cook, Maître Flaireau, hurried forward. "Please, please, sit here by the warmth."

Anne nodded brightly in return for the relieved smiles from Ralph, the filthy scullion; Henri, the spit boy; and Herve, the Maître's meat man. She allowed herself to be led to the ingle seat beside the largest of the cooking fires. She must not let them know how strange she still felt or let them see how hard it was to keep her tightly clasped hands from shaking. She had one aim now.

"Is Edward . . . where is he?" As Maître Flaireau pressed her to sit. "There, mistress, do you see?"

They had moved his cradle into the shadows, out of the light of the cooking fires into a warm corner of the cheerful tiled room. And he slept on, oblivious to all the bustle around him in the busy kitchen.

Anne yearned to pick him up, to kiss him awake, to hug him tightly to her breasts—the breasts that had never fed this child, but she restrained herself. Time for that later, when she was alone again with Deborah, the baby safely in the little annex of her solar.

"Wine! Hot wine for our mistress. Herve, hurry now!" Anne smiled slightly at the courtesy title "Mistress." Lady Margaret Cuttifer, Mathew's wife, was mistress in this house, even though she was so rarely here.

Four months since Edward's birth, four months of lies. She sipped the hot, rich wine; they'd spiced it with honey and nutmeg and beaten an egg yolk into it for strength. She was tired now, and aching. Leaning into the ingle seat, she closed her eyes, just closed them and . . .

"Sssh! Herve, move quietly!" The cook hissed at his assistant as he pantomimed creeping silently around the girl, who seemed to have fallen into a deep sleep. Chastened, Herve took care to sharpen the wicked boning knife as quietly as he could. He would be mortified to wake her, poor lady.

But Anne was not asleep. She smelled the blood again; it was animal blood from the carcass Herve was butchering, but it was enough, she was back there. . . .

His birth, Edward's birth. Four months ago and a long, long way from Brugge. A tiny, suffocatingly hot room in the convent she'd been sent to by Sir Mathew to await the labor well away from prying eyes, away from gossip.

Blood. Blood everywhere. On the straw-stuffed mattress, the whitewashed wall beside the bed, all over her. But he'd been born, alive and strong. Deborah had taken him from her belly and given him to a woman who'd been hired to suckle him, immediately, not even wiping the wax and the blood off his little body.

It was best this way, said Deborah, best that Anne never suckled him for if she did, to give him to another would be unbearable. It would be easier with time. These words were muttered as a prayer by her foster mother as she bound Anne's breasts with bruised arnica and mallow to help with the pain when her milk let down, the milk that would not be given to her child.

And now she and the Cuttifers called the baby her sister's son. Her dear dead "sister," Aveline.

Anne frowned in the strange half sleep as the light from the fire flickered on her face, her eyelids. Aveline . . . her name was a breath, not even a sound. For Aveline was indeed dead, and she, too, had borne a child named Edward. Yet she was never a sister of Anne's, although, in the end, in that other life lived as the Cuttifers' servant in London, Anne had loved her like one.

Aveline, who'd served in the Cuttifer household as Lady Margaret's maid; Aveline, raped and made pregnant by Piers, Mathew Cuttifer's only son; Aveline, who'd endured a forced and dreadful marriage to Piers Cuttifer, finally killing both her repellent husband, then herself, and leaving her own child an orphan to be raised by his grandparents Sir Mathew and Lady Margaret.

The tears were genuine when Anne spoke of the sadness of Aveline's life and death, and perhaps it was easier to believe, for others, that Anne's baby was Aveline's son for he was not much like his "aunt;" his skin was olive and he had speedwell-blue eyes, his father's eyes in truth, where her own were some strange amalgam of green and blue. Jewels, he'd called them, sea topaz, kingfisher bright.

Anne remembered too well every word they'd spoken, every moment they'd ever had together. But it was useless to dream. Dreaming would not bring Edward's father to Brugge and she had her own way to make in life without him—an aching, lonely thought.

But then Anne's courage rose a little as she dismissed the image of her lover's face. She had much, so much, to be thankful for in comparison to many others. She'd been left a small estate in Somerset, gifted to her mother, Alyce de Bohun, and that provided a small income faithfully accounted to her each quarter day. She had good, warm clothes, a house to live in—even if it was not hers—and a small number of jewels, if all else failed her: a topaz brooch, a great ruby ring (a precious keepsake given her by Edward's father), and the little pearl-and-garnet cross presented to her by the Cuttifers when she'd left their house for the Court of Edward IV and his queen, Elizabeth Wydeville.

Anne shifted uneasily in her chair, frowning as, unbidden, the images came; pictures from that time as Elizabeth Wydeville's body servant when dread and joy were her constant companions.

For it was at court she'd fallen in love with Edward the King, and it was at court she'd found out who she really was: the natural daughter of the old king, Henry VI. Thus the man she loved, adulterously, had usurped her father's throne.

That knowledge had brought fear, and sudden clarity. Yes, Anne was illegitimate, but she was the illegitimate daughter of a king. Sighing, almost groaning, Anne shook her head. It hurt, it still hurt like a deep, deep burn, the choice she'd made: self-exile to Brugge rather than remain in England. For if she'd stayed, she'd have to have chosen a side, eventually, as the old king's daughter.

A terrible choice, for how could she support her father's natural enemy, the man who'd taken his throne, driven him into hiding, even if she loved him?

But then, she'd not known she was pregnant when she'd sailed from Dover into exile. Perhaps Edward might have wanted her to stay if she could have told him, even with the risk to his throne. He'd had only daughters with Elizabeth Wydeville, the queen—but she, Anne, had a son. England desperately needed a male heir if Edward was to consolidate his reign. Perhaps he'd have forgiven Anne her ancestry for the sake of their child—this combination of York and Lancaster.

Forgive her? Better she should think of forgiving him! He was her father's usurper! And how could she allow herself to contemplate, for even one moment, allowing her own child to be engulfed by the vicious game of English politics just because she loved his father still?

Anne's eyes snapped open with the turmoil of her anguished thoughts and she sat up. England was in her past forever, and life must continue if she, little Edward, and Deborah were to find a real home for themselves, a place not dependent on the kindness of others. There was a lesson in this attack—she must plan, seriously, for their future. If she did not, others would do it for her. Perhaps after she had eaten, clarity of thought might return and the tide of emotion recede. For now, though, she was tired, very tired, and her knees ached, for the ice on the canal had been hard and jagged as thorns in places.

"Thank you, Maître." Courteously she sipped a little more of the wine he had prepared for her. "Delicious. I shall enjoy this with supper."

Gently, Anne kissed the sleeping baby in his cradle, tucking one small hand under the velvet counterpane. How much she yearned to pick him up, but his sleep was so peaceful, it would not be kind.

"Please call me when he wakes, Maître Flaireau."

"Of course, lady. This so dear baby delights us all, but truly, his heart is in his aunt's keeping." The cook bowed gallantly, understanding how much Anne loved the little boy. Fear touched her heart for a moment. Perhaps he knew, perhaps they all knew that he was truly her son.

She must be careful, and go on being careful, if they were all to survive.

Tonight was the tolling of a bell: a tocsin, a warning. From her brief time in Brugge, Anne had begun to believe that she could make a new life for herself here—and for little Edward. The Cuttifers had been very kind in their support, but she was a guest in their house; she would not, could not, allow herself to live on their goodwill forever. She had a choice. She must find a way to make her own living independently or . . . marry.

But if she was to have a husband, let him be one of her own choosing, not someone who came at the point of a sword.

Anne shivered as she stopped near the top of the stairs outside her solar; dark images from the attack forced themselves behind her eyes. Breathing faster, she let the pictures come, trying to understand. Perhaps a calculating young bravo had been watching her—the ward of a powerful, wealthy man—and decided to improve his fortune. She wouldn't be the first.

But was there another explanation?

Had someone paid to have her killed? Someone eager to remove her from the board of European politics? Someone who knew about her—her relationship with Edward, King of England—and, perhaps, also, knew about her son?

Anne's hand shook as she pushed open the door into her own private solar—yet another kindness from the Cuttifers. The pretty room was softly lit by a hanging brass candelabrum whose six fat wax candles burned clear and bright, a very great extravagance, but one she was happy to pay for from her own modest means; the smell of burning tallow made her sick.

She entered the solar with gratitude; it was peaceful and beautiful, a well of calm in a mad world. The room faced the canal at the front of the house, and the windows were so extravagantly large that they took up the entire width of the central gable. Thus her room was never dark during the day, no matter how sullen the skies might be; and sometimes, on the night of a full moon, Anne slept with her shutters drawn back and the casements flung open, a practice opposed by Deborah. It was common knowledge that the moonlight had power to strike the unwary. It was unhealthy to lie within that treacherous silver glimmer, breathing night air—in itself, profoundly harmful—for bad dreams and bad luck came from Luna's light, especially for women at the time of their monthly flow.

Anne had kissed Deborah softly on the brow when the older woman first voiced her fears—kissed her, but ignored her. The moon was her friend. It had been on a moon-flooded night that her son had been conceived and for that she would always welcome the brightest nights.

On this dark evening, Deborah had had a fire lit so the room was warm and cozy, though a wind was rising off the canal now, moaning around her casements and rattling the fastenings with spectral fingers. Despite the warmth, Anne shivered. How close had she just come to other cold hands tonight? Without Ivan she might have been a prisoner now in a very different room, among rapacious strangers. Or she might be a corpse.

Wearily, Anne slumped down onto the chair set ready for her

by the fire as a quiet voice called her. "Mistress, may I come in? I have water for you."

"Yes, Jenna. You are welcome." It was not like Anne to allow others to sense when she was tired or frightened, she'd learned that in the last few years, but tonight, shock brought her defenses down.

The other girl, open faced, a silvery blonde, entered the room silently carrying a brass bowl and a ewer filled with hot water from the kitchen.

"Would you like me to help you with the gown, lady?" Anne shook her head.

"No. Deborah will be here very soon, I expect. But I do need to clean my hands, Jenna."

Anne inspected her palms, and then her nails, dispassionately. She had grazed the heels of her hands when she'd dropped down onto the icy canal and broken several nails as she'd been hauled up the brick wall on the other side. Ordinarily she was proud of her hands, and now that she did not have to work with them, as once she'd had to, they were soft and white, the calluses at the base of each finger nearly gone. The broken nails would need trimming and cleaning, though—best to soak them first.

Jenna was a sensible girl. It was one of the reasons Deborah, as Lady Margaret's recently appointed housekeeper in Brugge, had given her a post in this house, so she didn't wince or fuss when she saw the blood on Anne's hands; she poured warm water in a steady, gentle stream, not even commenting as it turned rose-red.

"I'll get some more water for you, mistress."

"Yes, do that, Jenna. There's a large cauldron on the fire in the kitchen; it should be hot by now." Deborah had entered the room unseen as Jenna opened a casement and threw the dirty water into the canal, then paused for a moment to tidy the room as the older woman bustled forward.

"Here, mistress. Let me dry your hands. I've brought some fresh woundwort salve; it will help the healing."

Without protest, Anne let Deborah lift each of her hands and gently dry them on the linen towel she'd spread across her lap.

"Where is Ivan, Deborah?"

Deborah coughed to hide the chuckle that had risen unbidden. Fear did that to her sometimes. "I left him down in the kitchen, throwing back good Gruuthuse beer and boasting. He has a slash through his sleeve on one arm, but that's all. Luck of the Devil—or protected by him." Deborah did not approve of Ivan; he distracted the women of the house too much.

The older woman's astringent tone roused Anne from exhaustion. She was grateful to Ivan and it was important to voice that. "He did his job, and he did it well. When I am changed I shall thank him." Deborah kept silent, though she was hurt by Anne's sharp tone.

Anne felt the knife of guilt, but for now, in front of Jenna, she must play the role of their master's ward.

"Jenna, will you get the water, please, while Deborah helps me off with this heavy thing?" The door of the solar opened, and then closed quietly. Jenna had left.

Anne rose out of the chair, allowing her foster mother to unlace the back of the red dress. She closed her eyes for a moment. All she could hear was the crackle of the flames and the buffeting wind outside her curtains. What she would not give to lie down on her bed and fall into a long, dark sleep.

"Mistress? The rose-pink or the blue?" How hard it was to open her eyes. "The blue kirtle, I think. And the French linen shift, if you please. I hate feeling wool next to my skin."

So tired, so tired, it was hard to talk.

"Would you still like your body washed before I dress you, lady?"

Deborah's tone was formal and correct. It made Anne grin, a blessed lightening of her spirit.

"Yes, Deborah. As you used to do when I was little," and she smiled warmly, fondly at the older woman. "It will be nice to be clean again." There was a genuine smile in return, and suddenly the women felt like friends again. Close and loving friends.

# Chapter Two

 Anne kept deliberate state in the hall during the evening of the canal incident. Sitting alone at Mathew's high table, she was waited on with some ceremony as the household sat below the dais, eating.

Deborah had restored Anne's appearance as well as she could, and the household was surprised by her calm as they ate the special delicacies prepared in thanksgiving for her survival. As the meal was finishing, Anne called Ivan up to the high board. The curious hum died down in the hall. Of course, news had flashed through the household as soon as Anne had been half carried through the doors of the house, but there was much wild speculation as to what, exactly, had happened and why.

As Ivan joined her, Anne rose slowly to her feet and smiled at the household below. "Ivan saved my honor tonight, and the honor of this house. I believe that without his fearless action I might never have tasted Maître Flaireau's famous pike fritters again!" She smiled, and it lightened the mood; there was even laughter. Ivan had dropped his head humbly, as was proper. This amused her—this fighting bear was the antithesis of humble.

"Ivan has protected us all tonight—perhaps none of us would be sitting here at Sir Mathew's board if he had not done what he did . . ." Anne saw them glance from face to face. Turned out of this comfortable hall by violent strangers? A stark fate in a hard northern winter. "And I believe that Sir Mathew, your master and my kind guardian, would want me to reward Ivan for his bravery. Therefore I have consulted with Maxim," she bowed to her guardian's steward, "and he has suggested a suitable token of the esteem of this house."

Anne beckoned to Ivan. Blushing fiercely, he left his seat, to the good-natured jibes of his friends, as Maxim handed a substantial chain of gold to his master's ward. Hanging from it was a brightly colored, enameled shield about the size of a small child's palm. On one side was the red bear of Brugge and on the other, the arms of England—the leopards and the lilies quartered by the cross of Saint George.

"Ivan, wear this proudly. Then all will know of your courage. Thank you, my friend." Anne dropped the gold collar over Ivan's head and carefully arranged it to lie pleasingly over his shoulders. The man bowed with all the grace of a courtier and backed away from her as if she had been royalty to resume his seat.

"Now I have news of interest for you. Sir Mathew Cuttifer will be with us very soon—we've been given word that he sailed from Southampton some days ago. He will be most pleased to know that you have all performed so well in defense of his house. Therefore now, to celebrate the deliverance that Holy Mary has been pleased to send me, and the news of my guardian's arrival, there is good honeyed wine."

She signaled to Maxim, and stoneware jugs of hot Burgundian wine were brought in from the buttery and distributed among the diners—a rare treat.

A happy buzz ran around the hall as the household helped themselves. They all liked Lady Anne, but she was a bit of a mystery. It was a scandal that she lived here in Brugge without a husband, ward or no ward of Sir Mathew's.

Tonight's attack would set sage heads nodding all over town; Anne was a prize coveted by many, since she was a girl with her own modest fortune, or so it was said. It was therefore foolish—possibly even blasphemous—for such a woman to live outside her father's house and expect to be left in peace. Certainly there would be gossip in the Markt and many questions asked, questions they would be glad to answer.

Anne hardly touched the wine that was poured first for her, beyond courteously lifting her green Waldglas beaker in salute to Ivan. A healthy and robust girl normally, she had a headache tonight that tightened across her forehead like a hot iron band. Sounds from the hall came to her as if she were underwater and she saw, from a distance, that her hands were still shaking when she put the beaker down.

Catching Deborah's glance, she rose and held up one hand for silence. "My friends, tonight I think I shall sleep well because I know I am safe. Please stay and drink to Ivan's health, and my own. With my thanks to you all."

Deborah hurried after her foster daughter as Anne left the hall, rushing to carry the tail of her blue dress as it swept over the tiles, holding her words until she was certain they would not be overheard.

"Anne, Maxim says tomorrow will be a foul day. Perhaps you should not go to Mass. Sleep in for just this once."

Anne shook her head. "No. Tomorrow of all days I must be seen. I want them all to know I'm untouched."

And when sleep came it was deep enough, but once in the night Anne woke and was surprised to find tears on her cheeks. Then she remembered. She'd been dreaming of his face again, dreaming that he and she, Edward and Anne, were together again and happy, and that he loved his son.

They had loved each other. He would not seek to have her raped and murdered, would he?

# Chapter Three

 It was very late as another long, glittering, and tedious feast in the great hall of Westminster wound toward its close. A gathering of great elegance—the court in full-dress splendor—it was silent, completely silent, by order of the chamberlain.

Earlier in the evening, the royal couple, Edward the King and Elizabeth Wydeville, his wife and queen, had processed to the dais placed across the head of the hall in silence. Silently they had been seated under their personal Cloths of Estate, and now, silently, they finished eating after fifteen courses, avidly watched by the entire court: relatives, courtiers, friends, and servants, ravenous to observe each fleeting expression, each formal courtesy that passed between the young king and his queen.

And it was a young court, Westminster, for most of the courtiers, friends, and supporters of the king were in their mid to late twenties, so it chafed to eat without permission to speak even to one's neighbor.

Things had changed in the last year and it was much commented on. Once, early in the king's reign, Westminster had been famous the length of Europe as a brilliant, joyous place to be, and to be seen at. A place of music, and entertainment, and jousts—and courtly, and not-so-courtly, love. And the king had always led the dance with or without his queen: the dance that was complex, tantalizing, and erotic.

Tall, a fearsome jouster, sighed over by half the women in England, Edward seemed a king from out of the legends of Arthur, a king well matched, moreover, with his glittering queen, Elizabeth Wydeville. The people were happy, for she looked just as a queen should look: a distant gossamer figure, as perfect as the Empress of Heaven, and yet now there were rumors swirling around the royal couple that disturbed the careful picture. Tonight, the queen's over-brilliant smile, and her husband's politely detached expression, added fat to the sulky fire.

"She's lost his favor; you can see it."

"There's not anyone else, is there?"

"Just because we don't know his fancy doesn't mean he hasn't got some plump doxy tucked away."

The courtiers might be silent during the evening, but the scullions were gossiping in the kitchens and laughing as the detritus, the slops from the feast, was scraped into bins for the breakfast of the poor at the palace gates tomorrow morning.

"Well, from the queen's expression it'll be a cold bedding if he tries his luck tonight!"

Distant bells woke Edward, groggy, tired, and alone, again. As sleep cleared, for one last moment he was back with Mallon at the tourney last year, the Valentine's Day tourney when Anne had ridden away from him on her little donkey. And he had not stopped her.

Behind the curtains of his richly tented bed he sat up, shaking his head savagely to banish the achingly sad dream he'd had too many times. It seemed he might never rest again unless he could clear this miserable fog of loss once and for all.

William Hastings, his chamberlain and closest friend, heard the king stir as he warmed Edward's shirt before the fire. The chamberlain was worried, very worried. The king had no current interest in sleeping with the queen. Perhaps it was natural after some years of marriage, though worrisome for the kingdom, since they had no male heir. Yet neither had he shown favor to the many willing women of the court for more than a year. In such a man as this king, it was unnatural behavior. The chamberlain cleared his throat deliberately.

"Yes, William?" The voice from behind the curtains was weary, truculent. William swallowed his anxiety, spoke up brightly.

"What, Your Majesty? I did not speak."

The king sighed impatiently as William drew the bed hangings aside. "Yes, you did—I heard you."

The chamberlain bowed but allowed himself to look surprised—a risk in the king's current mood. Unexpectedly, however, Edward suddenly laughed at the raised shoulders, the elaborately astonished expression, and Hastings smothered a sigh of relief. The king threw the covers back with some vigor and climbed down from his bed, naked. Energetically he strode to the fire, yawning and stretching arms and back as William hurried after him, proffering the shirt.

"Then, my liege, if I spoke, which I deny, what did I say?"

The king snorted. "A failing memory—the first sign of age, William! Come now, you told me . . ." The king held up three fingers. "One: that I must banish melancholy and look to the future. Two: you reminded me that today is the anniversary of the tourney we staged last year on Saint Valentine's Day where we most properly thrashed Warwick and his men; and, three: on this anniversary you counseled me, William, most carefully. About my health."

"Did I? You astonish me, sire. Was my counsel acceptable to Your Majesty?"

The king nodded as he held up his arms, allowing William to drop the clean linen over his head.

"Call them in, William, they'll enjoy what I have to say. About my health, on your prompting."

Praise be! Edward's mood had lifted, at last. Energized and optimistic for the first time in many weeks, William strode to the doors of the king's bedroom and threw them wide into the faces of the courtiers, who waited on the other side for the morning ritual of dressing the king. Hurriedly the tide of yawning men surged through into the Presence.

"Long winter nights are bad for us all, gentlemen—they sap

the vital spirits, make us dull and listless. I have a remedy to offer." His small suite was cheered to see the king so merry as he allowed himself to be dressed by three body servants and his valet, Belham. He'd had the shirt; now he was offered the breeches, the boots, the hunting doublet—and had his teeth cleaned with ground pumice on the ends of prechewed hawthorn twigs. "Tonight. A feast, a proper one, and a celebration—in honor of Saint Valentine and Saint Cupid."

One of the slower members of the court, a raffish second cousin of the queen, dared to call out, "Saint Cupid, sire? Is there such a saint?"

Hastings laughed. "Well, if the king says it, it must be so."

The dolt persisted, sniggering, "But if we learn to pray to him, sire, will we not neglect our duty to the other holy saints since he's such an effective little fellow?"

The king tolerated the sally, even smiled. "Well, Sir Nicholas, I'm pleased to agree with you that he is a most energetic saint, does well with intercession for those who honor him determinedly, as does Saint Valentine, of course . . . but Saint Cupid does not demand exclusive devotion—that would exhaust even the most devout." The men surrounding the king all laughed out loud; they liked seeing the light back in Edward's eye. "Though I for one intend to test his powers since we are old friends. Perhaps we should all pray together, my lords, on our knees tonight, that he send us his blessing."

William couldn't resist it. "And the ladies, sire, on their knees, too, tonight?"

Guffaws filled the room as the king smiled innocently. "We must do all we can to help our sinful sisters to salvation, chamberlain, and if that means assisting them to be especially devoted—to spend more time on their knees—well then, so be it!"

Laughter swept them from the room and out toward the king's great mews and the stables where the horses waited, saddled and patient in the winter dawn in case the king should need them. And each woman the rowdy group passed wondered why the king looked so happy at last, and why the courtiers around him were so fresh and cheeky, but universally they were glad, especially as word of the planned celebration leaked out. And suddenly Westminster was swept by gossip. The king was hunting. Hinds. He wanted hinds again.

Somehow they kept the gossip from the queen, but she, too, was pleased to hear about the feast planned for this evening; she saw the banquet in honor of Saint Valentine and Saint Cupid as a blessing. It had been too long; tonight she would rejoice with the king and, later, she would give him pleasure. She would rekindle the lustful spark between them and let it burn.

And that was exactly what each woman under forty in Westminster—and some yet older—thought as well.

# Chapter Four

Far away from Westminster, over the dark seas, the wind
had risen steadily through the night and Maxim's proph-
ecy proved true as the late-dawning day struggled to
bring light to a world lashed by flurries of sleet.

Anne had slept only fitfully after the dream of Edward's face
as, time after time, the wind threw hail against her windows, and
grotesque dream figures wove in and out of the darkness.
Screams, vicious pain, swords, and then blood, a pillar of blood
that resolved itself into the body of Aveline, buried these two
years and more. She'd sat up in her grave clothes and called out
Anne's name, though the pennies were still stuck over her eyes,
and the living girl was afraid, so afraid that Aveline would take
the pennies away and she would see what lay beneath the copper!

She awoke, heart hammering, mouth dry, as little Edward
cried in the annex to the solar, hungry to be fed.

Thus, Anne was very pale as she was dressed by Deborah and
Jenna while, by the fire, the baby was fed by his nurse, Anneke, a
stout, healthy girl who seemed to have abundant milk both for
Anne's "nephew" and her own child, Lily, whom Anne, most unusually, allowed to be kept in the house. Another small scandal to
be whispered about by the English merchants' wives.

Anne had chosen her second-best winter dress this morning—
for warmth, but also to remind her neighbors that she was a person of substance, someone not to be slighted easily without cost.

Two years after Aveline's death, Anne no longer wore full mourning for her "sister," but most often she still chose sober colors to wear, perhaps to take something from her youth. The red dress of yesterday was an aberration.

This dress was dark though elegant. An overskirt of smoke-gray velvet was slashed open and caught to a high belt revealing the underskirt of silvered brocade. The trailing hem was edged, like the sleeves, in the thickest white winter fur—rare arctic fox traded by Sir Mathew from the High East and given to Anne as a present.

Today Deborah had plaited Anne's heavy, glossy hair into a coronet and fastened a slender wrought-gold chain around her throat from which hung a filigree cross. As Deborah covered her hair with a stiffened gauze veil secured with silver pins, Anne touched the tiny jewels, the pearls and garnets, which formed the body of the cross; each one was a memory distilled. The cross had been a present from the Cuttifers when she'd left their house, still a servant, to go to the court of Edward and his queen. It had been a surprise, this gift—something a parent might expect to give a child when leaving home, rather than a token from an employer to a servant.

To feel the cool gold as it warmed on her skin was to see Blessing House again, the Cuttifer's dwelling and place of business, and Anne's first London home; and it was to smell the new rushes of the receiving hall, the good bread baking in the vast kitchen, and the sweet applewood fire in Lady Margaret's solar on a winter's day . . .

Anne was brought back to the present as her own fire sputtered and crackled, and Deborah finally stood back and surveyed her handiwork, walking around Anne so that she could see her foster daughter from every angle.

Anne's coloring was flattered by the rich fabric of the dress, and her body was graced by its simple cut, the smoke-gray velvet a lustrous contrast to the unlined ivory column of her throat. Anne's beauty was a joyous thing, but today it made Deborah frightened. Was she tempting fate, adorning this girl so richly—as richly as an idol of Mary dressed for Easter?

Anne smiled a little shakily at the earnest look on her foster mother's face. "Lamb to the slaughter? Or lion?" Deborah smiled too. She accepted the closeness of their minds, though it could still be unnerving sometimes.

"Lion, mistress. Never lamb."

Anne kissed Deborah and for one moment the two women clung to each other.

"Do you know what the day is, Deborah?" It was a whisper for her foster mother to hear, just a whisper.

"Yes. The Feast of Saint Valentine."

They both remembered. It was the anniversary of the day that Anne had turned her back on Edward at the Saint Valentine's Day tournament—and ridden into exile.

Anne closed her eyes to blink away sudden tears.

"Your nephew feeds well today, mistress." Placid Anneke burped the baby on her shoulder, then put him back to her other vast breast, touching Edward's cheek so that he renewed his hearty sucking.

Anne forced herself to smile. She should be grateful for his appetite, yet her own breasts still tingled when she watched him feed.

"A blessing, Anneke. He's doing very well—my sister would be so happy." Hard to lie but it must be done. "I am ready, Deborah. Would you see to the litter? We shall be late."

It had been a deliberate decision to take Sir Mathew's litter to the cathedral church of Saint Donaas. Anne had decided to visit the cathedral because it was there she would meet many of Mathew's trading colleagues and their families.

Due to the freezing weather, attendance at the service was expected to be down, but to get to the cathedral she would have to cross the Markt square and she had asked the household to join her, to give thanks at the Mass for her survival. They would form something of a little procession, and news would spread that she was alive and safe when the townspeople saw her.

People in the city would make what they liked of such a display. However, she intended that they see her confident, and well guarded too. Somehow she had to maintain that façade until Sir

Mathew arrived in Brugge. He would know what she should do then. Please God, let that be so . . .

Thus, into the frigid day trudged Sir Mathew's Brugge household, leaving only the cook and his staff in the house preparing the meal to be eaten on their return. Anne had asked Maxim to ensure that everyone dress in their livery of scarlet and gray to make a brave show on this gloomy morning, and she had instructed that the curtains of the litter be fastened back so that the townspeople would know it was she who was inside.

Marching at the head of her small procession was Maxim, carrying his steward's staff of office. He was followed by four men—outdoor servants from the stable, the byre, and the gardens—who carried her litter while beside her stalked Ivan, slung about with a sword and two daggers and wearing a steel cuirass adorned with glittering brass. Around his neck was the gold chain she had given him last night and he was scowling as he walked, swinging his fierce glance from side to side as if daring shadows to produce more abductors and assassins.

Behind the litter walked the women of the household and the remaining men led by Deborah, dressed plainly but in good English broadcloth. Each of those who followed her was warmly clothed and well shod, and they were healthy: no frail, rickety bodies, very few missing teeth. They made a satisfying display as servants of a rich, well-ordered household. It showed as they walked proudly, heads held high, across the vast square in front of the enormous belfry tower on top of its Cloth Hall.

Bells rang across the city, the wind buffeting the sound, as the people of the town were called to Mass on the Feast of Saint Valentine.

# Chapter Five

As usual in winter, the great space inside the Cathedral of Saint Donaas in Brugge was icy, and as folk whispered to one another before the service began, the mist from their breath hung in the air amid the incense smoke.

Anne walked in with Sir Mathew's household people and filed off to stand with the women on the left side of the aisle, while the men stood with other male parishioners on the right. In that piercing cold, she was grateful for the fur lining of her mittens. She was also grateful for the velvet-footed hose, tied under each knee with ribbon, and a silk underkirtle, but even then the layers of cloth were not quite enough to hold out the chill breathing from those ancient stone walls.

It was said this church was built over the remains of a much earlier building, perhaps even from the times when the Romans had lived in this place. Certainly Baldwin Iron Arm, one of the great original dukes of Burgundy and a fearsome man, had begun this building in more tumultuous times and a later descendant of his, Charles the Good, had been murdered in the choir. Now the early history of blood and struggle had been silently folded into the walls of this massive church with its forest of trunklike pillars, its interior so dark and full of shadows. Hundreds of years of incense-borne prayers and pleas for intercession had floated up into the blackened roof timbers and now, as the congregation around her kneeled while the priest prepared to elevate the precious host, Anne, too, sent up a prayer for help and strength to the Christian gods—for she was in their house.

The sonorous words of the Mass flowed over her and for this time, Anne forgot the fear that curled like a wakeful snake in her belly. If her prayers were heard, the intercession of the Holy Lady Mary, patron saint of this city, would help her see the way forward, would bring her light. And, later, when night fell, she would ask the other mother goddess, Aine, help of the dispossessed, the suffering, for guidance also.

Aine, goddess from her childhood in the forest; Aine, goddess of the disposed dark people of the West—she too had power, she too spoke to Anne in the dark quiet of the night when bad dreams tried to catch her.

Mary and Aine. They must be sisters? One dark, one light? Both the mothers of sons as she, Anne, was. They would understand her need, surely.

The bell near the high altar rang, once, twice, three times. Anne knew that if people outside the church heard it they would stop, remove their hats, and cross themselves devoutly because the priest inside was elevating the transformed host. It was comforting to think they all shared this same faith, this same belief that the Virgin Mother of Christ was their especial friend in times of trouble. Anne closed her eyes, the cold incense filling her nostrils, making her head swim.

Was it only yesterday, before she had sat for him, that Hans Memlinc had shown her another commission he had nearly finished—a Madonna and child commissioned by the English Merchant Adventurers in Brugge? Now as she meditated on the remembered image of that serene and beautiful face, she felt doubly certain she could ask for help from Mary because the Madonna seemed as natural and real as a friend. It was easier asking help from a friend than praying to an empress in Heaven.

But then other images flashed into her mind, images to be banished. Edward's face as he leaned down to kiss her, Edward's hands roaming her body as they had made love together in the crypt of another great cathedral, the anguish in his eyes as he turned to look at her for that last time in Dover.

Dear Virgin, would the pain never go away? The longing that breathed through every moment when she thought she would never see him again?

She felt a discreet tug at the sleeve of her gown and, opening her eyes, looked up to find the congregation standing around her. She'd been so far away that the service had ended while she was on her knees. Swallowing hard, breathing deeply to stop the tears she felt in her eyes and heart, she stood, waiting for the congregation to move down the aisle toward the western doors of the great church.

"Lady de Bohun, would you have a moment to spare later in the day?" She turned toward the familiar voice.

"Master Caxton, you are always welcome. Perhaps you would break your fast with us this morning?" She smiled brightly, confidently, up into the eyes of the man who had addressed her.

He was of some importance in this city of Brugge, William Caxton. An Englishman in his mid-forties, he'd lived here and in other Lowland countries for many years, instrumental in building trade between Flanders, Burgundy, and England. He was governor of the English Merchant Adventurers in Brugge, and it had been he who had led the English merchants en masse to Ghent and Antwerp when the previous Duke of Burgundy, Duke Philip, had tried to tax English trade at levels Caxton and his colleagues considered unfair.

It had only been in the last year that relations had been restored when Caxton had managed to persuade his fellow merchants of the advantages to be reaped from a return to Brugge.

He was a good-looking man, William Caxton—tall and still strong from a lifetime of hard work—and there was a little spark between them. Anne could not deny that, though he was married, very married, to the haughty Maud, a fellow English merchant's daughter intent on buying into court honors at home in England when William had made enough money in Brugge. Anne's invitation would not please his wife when she heard.

Perhaps the Devil made her do it? She giggled with the thought—definitely the lion, not the lamb today!

Caxton smiled, too, slightly puzzled. "Something amuses you, lady?"

"Oh, just a passing thought, Master Caxton. Deborah, can you see Maxim?"

It was hard to find the servants in the large throng inside the church because she wasn't tall enough to see over their heads. William Caxton, courteous and capable, had matters organized quickly. "Stay with your mistress, Deborah. I'll find him."

The bells from the belfry in the Markt were still ringing at the end of Mass as the slightly augmented party from the House of Cuttifer walked among the townspeople of Brugge only now beginning to fill the vast cobbled square.

The city was fully awake at last on this miserably cold winter morning, and Anne felt guilty that she'd insisted on so many of Mathew's people accompanying her to Saint Donaas's—they'd have a cold walk home while she was warm and snug. Courteously she'd offered Master Caxton a place in the litter, but she knew, as he did, that it would not be wise for him to take it.

To be seen reclining beside the Lady Anne de Bohun would create even more gossip, gossip that would reach the sanctimonious Maud Caxton in a flash. No, safest for him to walk beside the litter, respectably surrounded by the household of Anne's patron.

As always, though, when he was with Anne, Caxton found he forgot much of what he wanted to say as he strolled across the Markt square beside the litter. It was unnerving. It had to do with the unusual directness of the girl's glance, when she chose to employ it, and also, if he was feeling honest that day, the succulent quality of the skin on her throat. He wouldn't have been a man if such skin had left him unmoved. He'd confess his carnal thoughts later—tomorrow. For now, he felt warmer each time he permitted himself to look at her. No bad thing on such a freezing morning.

Caxton sighed. He would have to concentrate when they had their interview together shortly. She was clever and subtle for one so young, qualities that had caused disquiet among the cautious members of his guild when Sir Mathew introduced her into their comfortable, closed world as his ward; disquiet that now sent him, William Caxton, on this fool's errand!

Sometimes, Caxton disliked being English very much. When Anne had first arrived in Brugge, Sir Mathew had approached Caxton on her behalf saying Anne wished to invest in his trading house in Brugge, to become his joint-venture business partner.

Perhaps it was the girl's intelligence, perhaps her persuasiveness when she eventually talked to him herself about her plans to become a trader, but Caxton, as governor of the the Merchant Adventurers had promised that they would consider their joint request carefully, unusual though that request was; but in so doing, he had reaped the whirlwind.

Citing passages from the Bible, his affronted colleagues had declared it was, first, a scandal that Anne was setting up to be a merchant at all, even in partnership with her guardian; second, that no one might trade as part of their guild without first having been apprenticed through said guild—a clear impossibility in her case; and, third, that it was, of course, highly unsuitable that she wished to trade without a husband to guide her.

Thus, even though Mathew Cuttifer, her business partner and a man they all respected, had personally put forward Anne's case for special entry to the guild, his request was declined. She simply could not be admitted—for if they made an exception with her, where would it end?

Improper thoughts could be encouraged in their very wives, and that would challenge the nature of family structure as ordained by God. A woman should be subservient to her husband; it was his proper place to govern her and to provide for the household. The woman's place was to be a helpmeet, never more.

For a single girl such as Anne to work like a man, making money in trade, was a scandalous, even blasphemous, affront to all right-thinking Christian men.

Thus Master Caxton walked silently beside her litter, oppressed by his thoughts, as Anne bowed and smiled to the townsfolk she knew, who, like herself, were hurrying back to their warm homes from the Mass.

Of course, on his own way to Saint Donaas's this morning, Caxton had been stopped several times by friends, busy to tell him about the attack on Anne de Bohun the night before.

News of the attack had been another reason he'd wanted to speak to her. Perhaps, in one stroke, he had a solution to all the difficulties her unmarried state posed for his colleagues, and for her. He would help Mathew find his ward a husband. There'd been no shortage of candidates when he'd canvassed the idea among his colleagues; many of the English merchants had sons looking for a well-dowered wife, and some were widowers searching for their next spouse. Anne was more than welcome under these circumstances; each of them would be delighted to educate this girl and turn her away from such unsuitable, unfeminine notions as working for a living, while at the same time, the lucky husband could also secure more working capital. And there was the question of the girl's body, which, they had all noted—including their jealous wives—was very fair, another useful adjunct to any marriage.

Caxton grimaced. Snatching a quick glance down at Anne, he knew his own feelings for this girl were far from fatherly. Still, she'd listen to reason, he felt sure. He'd always found her reasonable.

# Chapter Six

"I thank you for your kind thoughts for my well-being, but I have no wish to marry at the moment, Master William."

Anne smiled pleasantly, but she was quite definite as she broke her fast with the English merchant after Mass in Sir Mathew's hall. She had no need to tell the merchant her own secret reasons for such a radical stance, but they were profound. After her experiences at Edward's court in London, she was deeply reluctant to trust any man to control her life—and that of her son—unless it was on her terms, an unlikely thing in most marriage contracts.

As they talked, William was slightly distracted at this, his first sight of Mathew Cuttifer's new house, for it was fine indeed. The hall smelt fragrantly of beeswax rubbed into the honey-colored oak furniture that had been brought from England; the colors too, were harmonious and simple, with walls either a rich sepia or washed with rose, and the great hall itself had a ceiling painted a dense, dark blue powdered with gilded stars. William noticed the pretty device for the first time as he leaned back and looked up, thinking of what he must next say to his hostess. He'd have to concentrate for he was more than replete and the excellent small beer added a pleasant, warm buzz of excitement increased by the girl sitting beside him. He'd always appreciated beauty.

He stole a glance at his hostess. Her composure told him nothing as she finished the last of the venison pasty she'd been served. William was impressed by that venison—she'd been personally sent a splendid haunch from Duke Charles's most recent kill in his game preserves around Brugge, and Maître Flaireau had made excellent use of every scrap of the generous gift.

Strange that a pie should represent so much. It testified to Anne's standing with the new duke as Sir Mathew's ward—he and Duke Charles's father, Duke Philip, had been friends of long standing—and, perhaps, it contained a message about her future because it was a most generous gift, a sign of great favor.

Anne must have served it to him with a purpose—perhaps she wanted him to spread the news to his colleagues that she was not without friends. And perhaps it meant that some of the rumors he'd heard about Charles and Anne really were true—he'd have to find a way to ask her tactfully. Though it was an odd thought, considering what he had to tell her shortly.

"Father, if you've eaten sufficient of what this house can offer, perhaps you would bless us all before we go about our work?"

Anne had one other guest this morning, an Italian Franciscan monk. Personally, Caxton regarded all friars and monks of the mendicant orders as pests, especially if they were Franciscans. For followers of the most humble of God's servants—as Saint Francis saw himself—they could be mighty arrogant and venal sometimes: parasites and corrupters of women.

Therefore he'd been surprised to find this Friar Giorgio waiting for Anne on their return and even more surprised to see the honor with which this unexpected guest was treated. He was a young man, too, and good-looking, if one favored the dark skin and brown eyes of the south.

His hostess would need to have a care—this man, his obviously familiar presence at Sir Mathew's table, would be yet another cause for scandal if it were generally known.

"Dear Lady Anne, you honor me, a poor friar." The merchant had difficulty in keeping the scorn from his face, for Friar Giorgio was hardly the picture of a poor man. His habit was made from the finest, most densely dyed black woolen cloth and he wore boots of fashionable soft leather instead of the customary sandals on his feet.

The friar stood and raised his right hand, slowly tracing the sign of the cross over the people below the dais where he'd been sitting. "May the good Lord look down upon our work this day and, at its end, may we sleep the peaceful sleep of the just and the worthy in God's sight. Amen."

William was surprised—he'd been expecting the priest to speak in Latin, but the blessing was well and gracefully made in French, with hardly a hint of an Italian accent. This was an educated man, plainly, not like some of the ignorant brigands who claimed the shelter of a cleric's robes.

"Amen," echoed Anne with the household and, after a moment for quiet reflection, she smiled warmly at her guests. "Father Giorgio, we are most grateful for your blessing. I shall look forward to our conversation later today, perhaps after None? You must be very tired after your long journey. I think Deborah has the guest chamber prepared—you must rest well before we speak."

William did not know, and Anne was not about to tell him, that Father Giorgio was part of a long-term plan she had. Before her son was born, they'd met at the convent where she'd been hidden, at which he regularly said Mass for the sisters. He knew her secret—but then she also knew his.

He was a worldly man, this priest, and yet devout, but his great weakness was a love of young men. He flogged himself for it but could not resist. Anne had once found him with a young shepherd who tended the sisters' flocks in the fields outside the convent. She could have destroyed him with what she saw, but though the Bible condemned his feelings for the beautiful young peasant boy, and the acts they had performed in the fields together, she could not blame another human being for seeking the comfort of love, wherever it was offered.

She, too, understood how hard it was to love what was forbidden in the eyes of the world. No, she was not shocked by his passions, but she was sorry for him, so sorry that he was trapped in a life that could not allow him to express who he truly was. And her compassion made her a friend for life—and a commercial ally—for the priest was a well traveled man.

Now, for the first time since her son was born, Friar Giorgio had come to visit Anne in Brugge with precious information:

news of fashions in Italy and Paris—even bringing her samples of fabrics with drawings of clothing and the ways women were dressing their hair. He was an amusing and adroit penman, among many other talents.

Since he was good-looking and personable, too, he had told Anne that many other fashionable, well-bred women in Rome, Venice, Florence, and Paris welcomed his occasional visits, inviting him to their houses and to their tables, and in return for saying Mass, they gave him news and amusing gossip. Giorgio's taste mirrored Anne's own, and they had much to offer one another if her plans to become a trader were realized. He could be her eyes and ears in the world—they could help each other to prosper.

Giorgio kissed Anne's hand like a courtier, with a deep flourishing bow, as Maxim escorted him from the hall, but phlegmatic Englishman that he was, Caxton found he deeply distrusted this priest who smelled very faintly of roses.

With a start, he remembered again that he must find a way to persuade his hostess for her own good, and his, that he had the key to her future happiness. And with some urgency, if his wife was not to be too displeased by his prolonged absence.

"Lady Anne, may I claim a little more of your time?"

Anne smiled as she led him from the hall. After cutting off the subject of her potential marriage, she was well aware that Master Caxton must be fretting. However, she'd learned commercial strategy from a master, Mathew Cuttifer. Speaking of rivals in trade, he'd always said to her, "Let them wait when they want something from you. Delay their access. That way you have the advantage when you finally allow them to speak in your presence—they'll blurt out more than they ever intended and you will learn more than they want you to know."

"Will you come to the workroom then, Master Caxton?" Mathew Cuttifer's parlor gave her a private meeting place while he was away, and was well furnished with a suite of handsome tapestries and simple chairs upholstered in gold-stamped leather. This room was where she would hang Hans Memlinc's painting until she made enough from trade to find a house of her own; and for that, she needed William Caxton's help with the guild.

It was a still, cold day, for now the early sleet had turned to snow, and as Steven, the household page, hurried to bank up the fire in its hooded embrasure in the corner of the room, a curtain of white fell silently outside the casement windows.

The room looked out into the walled heber at the back of the house—it was of a good size and in summer was a green bower murmurous with the sound of bees from the coiled straw bee skips in the kitchen garden. But now, as the snow fell, it was drained of color except for the red of the brick walls enclosing the space. Here and there some few yellow leaves still clung to the branches of es-paliered pear, quince, and medlar, but the life of the garden was hidden in the ground, waiting for spring.

Some people hated this time of year, the feeling that the earth had died, but Caxton loved nature in all its seasons, even winter, if one had the money to keep warm. He shivered suddenly, as an image of beggars in the Markt holding out hands reddened with chilblains, pleading for alms came into his mind. There, but for the Grace of God he went also.

"Are you cold, Master Caxton? Come, let us draw chairs closer to the fire. Thank you, Steven." The young page had hur-ried to draw two of the handsome Italian fruitwood chairs closer to the hearth. "Please ask Deborah to bring us some mulled wine when she has settled Father Giorgio."

But for the crackle of the fire there was silence for a moment as William Caxton collected his thoughts. Anne was content to wait—she would not begin this conversation.

"Lady Anne, I had news that you were attacked last night." He turned toward her earnestly, searching to see what effect his words had. Anne smoothed the velvet of her dress over her knees, half distracted by the luster of the pile as she turned it with her hand. Warm, dark silver flickered beneath her fingers. "Yes. But I was well protected."

Her expression was neutral and her words were calm, unsen-sational. William frowned.

"But do you know who it was?"

Anne controlled her breathing as her heartbeat ramped up with the memory. She allowed herself to sigh and shrug as if slightly impatient. "No. But certainly two of them died, perhaps more; we did not find all the bodies. Ivan . . ." Again she shrugged, this time philosophically ". . . Ivan is a good servant. Zealous. Still, they did not get what they came for."

There was a very slight quaver in her voice that she could not disguise. Caxton looked at her thoughtfully. "Lady Anne, I hope you will allow me to speak frankly to you."

"Again, Master Caxton?" She was smiling brightly now, but the raised eyebrows signaled he should be cautious; that what he needed to say might not be entirely welcome. Against the advice of a still, small inner voice, he continued.

"The fearful events of last night prove to me, and my fellows at the guild, that the wisdom of our stance is correct."

Anne sat very still and Caxton found the directness of her eyes disconcerting. He had a distinct urge to lean forward and take her hands in his, to soften the blow to come. He resisted— such a gesture might be misinterpreted.

"Lady, we cannot admit you to the guild. It would not be right, not correct."

Anne bit back a response. In her heart she had known it, but her throat closed over and she was shamed to feel tears gathering in her eyes.

William was mortified when he saw her distress.

"Sweet girl, surely this is a relief to you. How can it be anything else? As a woman it is not suitable for you to trade—you must see that. I suppose, because you're young, it seems exciting to you; I promise you it is not." Now he did reach forward, he could not help himself. If she would just let him take her hand . . .

But she shook her head brusquely, swallowing tears. There was a moment of painful silence, which Caxton tried to fill.

"I am sorry to make you sad. But there are other, more hopeful things to speak of. Your happiness."

Seizing the moment, William Caxton hurried on.

"Except for your guardian, a guardian who does not live in this city, you are a woman alone. Oh, I know," he held up his hand as if she had tried to interrupt him; she had not. That rattled her guest. "Ah, I know that you value independence, that you have Deborah and Maxim to guard you, and that you have some of the means to be independent."

Anne did not look at him, turning her attention to the snow as it fell, faster and faster. "But what happened last night will happen again—until you are settled. Safely, happily settled."

Under strict emotional control now, Anne leaned forward to stir the fire, one part of her seeing the snow had suddenly stopped; the world was white, unsullied. There was silence outside the window. That pleased her.

"But Master Caxton, I am settled. I am part of an excellent, well-run household, as you say, and I am surrounded by those who have an interest in seeing that my . . . independence . . . is safeguarded, as you know." There was truth in this; independence was deeply important to her. If she trusted only herself, then she would never be let down by the actions of others.

William bought a little time to think by walking over to the casements. After a moment he turned.

"You are a prize, lady, and as such, you are not safe. Last night showed us this. At present this city is full of lawless men and that will only become worse, as the year wears on."

Anne was cool. "I am uncertain what you mean, sir. If you refer to the mercenaries, well, Ivan has proved himself their match."

"Not the mercenaries, madam. Those who pay them."

Now Anne was genuinely puzzled. "But Duke Charles pays them. He would not harm me. Sir Mathew and Lady Margaret Cuttifer are especial friends of the Court of Burgundy, and through them, so am I. Who else?"

William bowed in acknowledgment before he chose to reply. Yes, it was true. She was favored by Duke Charles, witness the venison.

"The duke, yes. He, as I understand it, holds the House of Cuttifer in high regard. But there are others—surely you know."

Anne was finding it hard to maintain her calm. Her heart was beating faster—she had been badly frightened last night, though she was determined that the little world she lived in, personified by the man standing in front of her, would not know that.

"Master Caxton, if I listened to every little piece of malicious tittle-tattle from the Markt, I should be frightened of my own shadow."

Again she laughed, a little breathlessly this time. "As it is, I doubt that your Merchant Adventurers would be so upset should anything happen to me!"

"Ah lady, you do us a disservice. Many of our members are very worried about your situation, yet there is good news at this time also, especially for your guardian. And that, in turn, will be good news for you, I am certain."

He said it kindly, earnestly. Anne looked at him measuringly. "Now that is the second time you've hinted at something extraordinary, Master Caxton. Will you tell me this important news?"

William smiled broadly, happy to tell her. "News that we have long suspected is at last confirmed. Duke Charles is to marry again." He watched her closely as he spoke, but her face did not change. He was not a man who thought he understood women very well, but she seemed unaffected, emotionally, by the news.

"Well then, I wish him and his new duchess-to-be much happiness." Anne was quite calm. "When will the marriage be celebrated?"

"In the later summer, I understand."

Anne's breath was suddenly ragged; rage flushed through her as she understood. He was sharing remarkable trading information with her because it didn't matter. She would not be permitted to join their guild, so being told of the wedding was merely pleasant gossip. She'd never profit from it.

"And who is the bride, Master Caxton?" She was proud of how detached she sounded.

William Caxton was delighted to tell her. "The Lady Margaret of England—sister to the king." Even now he couldn't quite believe it—such remarkably good news! An English princess as the Duchess of Burgundy would massively strengthen the bonds of the English trading community to the court and all its wealth, its disposable wealth, in this previously hostile city.

"Mistress, are you ill?" All the color had washed from Anne's face. Her eyes were closed and she'd slumped against the embossed back of the chair. William, panicked, leaned forward to pat her hand. Another moment—and he stroked her brow, touched her cheek, was about to gather her from the chair and call out, when Anne spoke.

"No, no, please I, I must have eaten something putrid. It was just a wave of . . ." She swallowed hard and opened her eyes, forcing herself to smile "There, see, it's gone. Whatever it was."

Margaret of York. Edward's sister! Would Edward, King Edward—her Edward—come to Brugge to give his sister to Duke Charles in place of his dead father?

Would she see the king again?

"Lady, you're not well. Shall I ask for your maid?"

Anne laughed shakily. "No, Master Caxton. I am well, believe me. There, you see?" She stood, suddenly filled with energy.

Now she was desperate for William to leave so that she could think and make plans—such plans—in private.

Caxton was astonished—truly women were odd creatures. Here was this girl, one minute fainting, the next a pacing alaunt, a war hound. It was curious, too curious—William Caxton was no fool.

"Mistress, there is also the other matter of your personal happiness, as we began to discuss."

Anne was finding it hard to be polite now. "Master Caxton, perhaps we could meet to talk again, if you would like that, in a day or so?" She stopped pacing and looked at her guest, smiled at him, trying hard to soften the directness of her words.

"But, Lady Anne, allow me to repeat how concerned we've been, my colleagues and I, about the case you find yourself in?" Anne could not help it, she was sharp in response.

"Case, sir?"

He looked slightly embarrassed. He could hear the edge in her tone. "Mistress, as I said to you, plainly you need a husband to protect you."

"Sir, you are not my father." She was flushed, hot; the one thing she could not control, even if her voice was low and carefully steady as she spoke.

"No, mistress, that is true. But I speak as if I were since I am so much older than you." He laughed slightly to lighten the mood, so did she, to be polite. They both knew that in other circumstances—if his wife were not alive—he might have considered himself her suitor. That spark between them again.

"Unscrupulous men covet what you have. What you are." He was being very frank, though he kept his eyes firmly fixed on her face. "I am convinced that being a merchant would be most unnatural for you, that it would worry you greatly. As I said, allow a good man to take care of you and you can relax into your natural sphere of family and care of a fine house. You will be happier for it, I promise you. A good marriage is—"

"Yes, a good marriage, Master Caxton—and a good wife—is above the price of rubies. I know the text. It's just that I would prefer to trade in gems, rather than become one."

He shook his head, trying to reach her, trying to make her listen. "Please think on what I have said, Lady Anne. I believe, we believe, that you cannot go on living alone, or aspiring to trade. This city is plainly too dangerous for you now. Allow me to help you choose your destiny rather than have it forced upon you. There are good men within the English community here, men who are my friends and would like to be yours."

Anne said nothing for a moment, then sighed. What William Caxton said was the plain unvarnished truth in some respects; she did not want to live surrounded by drawn steel, and a young unmarried woman was not just a scandal, she was a prize, he was correct. She would speak of it to Mathew Cuttifer—he would give her sound advice because he always did. But for now, there was so much to think of! And dream about.

"Thank you, sir, you are very good to me. And I thank you for your care of my person. I shall think on what you have said, and take advice."

To his surprise, Caxton felt himself being walked to the door of her room without being aware she had taken him by the arm.

And as the door of that substantial house closed him outside in the white, still world, he shook his head.

Round one had ended, he rather thought. When would round two begin?

# Chapter Seven

Everything had changed, everything! This was the hinge point in her life and Anne recognized it. She measured the moment as if it were a solid thing—the moment when her life tipped from precarious stability into potential chaos, and she found herself detached, unmoved by the danger. The risk felt right, felt destined in some odd way.

The feeling of unruffled clarity remained with her as she hurried through the double cellar, which, underground, joined Sir Mathew's house to the warehouse next door—a clever security device, since his trading house had no other entrance—up to the counting floor under the eaves. She ran up the last few stair treads, arriving slightly breathless, and found Maxim, the steward, on the counting floor with Henry Fowler and John Aigret, the two young Englishmen who were Sir Mathew's apprentices in Brugge. All three were poring over ledgers with Hans Boter, the chief clerk, a canny Lowlander whom Sir Mathew had enticed to work for him some years before.

"Maxim, I must speak to Meinheer Boter for a moment, but can you come to the workroom soon and ask Deborah to join us, please? There is something important I must say to you both."

The warehouse was no less well built than the gabled house next door, because Mathew, careful to look to the welfare of his most valued servants, had made sure that the counting floor was warm, light, and dry even in freezing weather. People worked better if they had warm hands.

It was a matter of security too. Happy staff were slightly less likely to cheat him out of the trading capital kept in a locked, windowless inner room.

Maxim was startled and intrigued by Anne's passionate energy, but the pleading look in her eye convinced him.

"Very well, mistress. I shall join you a little later. Come, lads."

Anne could barely contain herself until the steward and the two apprentices had left the counting floor, though she was careful to drop the wooden door bolt into its keeper as the door closed behind them—to the chief clerk's bemused amazement.

"Meinheer, I have something urgent that needs doing and I have extraordinary news. If we move very fast, I will be able to take advantage of it."

Quickly she told him of the wedding that would soon be announced; now was the time to gamble whether she was an accredited merchant or not. Mathew Cuttifer would approve, she was sure of it.

"We must send to the Medici in Florence and arrange for credit letters to be honored. The first will be for one thousand florins; the second for three thousand florins—to be cashed in Venice. I intend to mortgage all I possess—my income from England and my mother's lands there—so that I can back the credit. I shall give you letters before Vespers tonight with orders for the goods that must be bought. And then I want what I have ordered to arrive before the Feast of Saint Michael and Saint George. I will take advice on whether we should have them sent by sea or by land."

The careful Dutchman did not allow his expression to change, but he was stunned by this boldness—and the risk. This girl was not an accredited merchant; if she deliberately brought trade goods into this city expecting to sell, the guilds would shut her down. And also, one, let alone two, precious cargoes on the sea well before the end of spring was a doubly enormous gamble. Instantly he calculated the odds. Perhaps the land route might be slightly safer, though, of course, the mountain passes at this time of the year were also very dangerous. If the snow did not close them, roaming companies of "wolves-heads"—brigands, soldiers, the murderous dross of late wars—who lurked on the trade routes must be repelled.

"Meinheer, please do as I ask. An opportunity like this is rare. And send Henry to Sluis for me also. He is to wait there until your master's cog, the *Lady Margaret,* is docked so that we can give Sir Mathew the news as soon as possible."

Meinheer Boter mildly asked if she had any more orders for him.

"None, my friend. But I should like your prayers. Such sober prayers on this hazardous undertaking would stand us well." She grinned at him and he smiled.

Hans Boter hardly ever smiled—perhaps it had something to do with the absurdity of his name. Boter meant "Butter," and he'd been much mocked for that as a child, especially as he was always afflicted with fatness. Now, on a day such as today, when this girl had risked all of the money she had, it seemed strange he did not despair at her folly.

"If my poor prayers can do some good for you, I shall be proud. As I will be when your cargoes land safely. You are right to be bold at such a time, and if there is much risk, the reward will be greater." It was the longest speech Anne had ever heard from him, and both he and she were amazed he'd uttered it.

Anne smiled. "Thank you, Meinheer. You shall have the commissioning letters as soon as I can write them—and one for your master."

Energized, she tried not to run back to the parlor where Maxim and Deborah were waiting as she'd requested.

She took one, two deep breaths as she sat in the chair that was proffered. It was hard, but she had to find strength and composure if she was to be effective now.

"Maxim, I have something very important to tell you—and you, Deborah." For the second time today she passed on William Caxton's remarkable information, and how she proposed to bargain with fate. If this gamble came off, she would be able to buy a home of her own, begin to build a truly independent life.

Maxim, like his colleague Hans Boter, was stunned by the boldness and risk of her plans. If the gamble failed she would be ruined and that worried him deeply, for he liked her. Also, even if she landed her goods, the guilds would surely stop her from trading them.

"I know what you're thinking, Maxim, it's on your face, but the guilds will not stop me—and yes, I could ruin myself, but I have the right to risk my own money. It will be Sir Mathew's choice to coinvest, if that's what he wants to do. Henry will give him my letter as soon as he lands."

Anne saw Maxim's surprise and some instinct made her say the one right thing that would bring him around to see the vision behind the risk.

"Ah, Maxim, you are my guardian's steward, but I think of you as my friend. I trust you. I ask for your help now. And your support."

Deborah, still stunned to hear of the Lady Margaret of England's marriage to the Duke of Burgundy—and what that would mean to Anne—said nothing, but she was warmed when she saw Maxim's wary correctness turn to something very like a smile.

"I want the cargoes here to Brugge before the feast of Saint Michael and Saint George." Little more than two and a half months, a ridiculously short time. Could it be done?

"And yes, before you ask, it can be done, but you must be there to do it. I want you, personally, to carry my letters of commission—and the requests for credit to Venice and Florence. And I want you to leave as soon as the *Lady Margaret* can be turned around—naturally, only if Sir Mathew agrees; you must help him to understand. Once you are in the city states, you must assess which will be the quickest way back to Brugge with the goods I'm ordering for the wedding. And bring them back yourself—under a guard that you arrange. And, Maxim, there's five percent of gross after the crews are paid as a bonus for you when all the landed goods are sold."

What could Maxim say? That he thought this girl was foolish? And overgenerous? She was not the first, though she was the last, but that was good—generosity commanded loyalty, though she already had his. He liked her, yes, he liked her.

A certain restless urgency warmed his blood. It was a gamble but yes, he would go!

"Mistress, allow me to consider the best route for your goods as you write your letters of commission. I accept the terms you have offered—and will be honored to do you this service provided my master agrees."

He bowed himself out of the parlor. Both women could hear the soft slither of his house slippers as he hurried away, back to the counting floor, to consult Meinheer Boter about this mad undertaking . . .

"That was gracefully done, Anne." It was Deborah's turn now. She only rarely called Anne by her name—most often at moments of great importance, when they were alone.

Restlessly Anne got up and strode over to the windows. The snow was falling again and the expensive leaded glass was very cold as she leaned her head against it. She smiled ruefully. No horn lights for Mathew Cuttifer—everything of the best! To be successful one must look successful: a good lesson to absorb. But if she lost, if this gamble failed, the promise of real independence— her own home, her own future, success on her own terms, making her own money—would disappear like mist in the morning.

There was silence for a moment between the two women. Finally Deborah spoke.

"Lady Margaret, our princess. Did William Caxton say when the wedding would be?"

"Summer. Sometime near to Lammas Day, he understands. When the vernal gales are long gone." She couldn't help herself— Anne grimaced at the word "gales." God knew, she was committing them all to great risk.

"And the king? Will he come here, to Brugge?"

Anne responded—her voice far away, as were her eyes. "Nothing is certain."

"I'll pray that your venture is a safe one." Poor Deborah—the anguish in her voice was plain.

Safe? Anne shivered. Was anything ever really safe in this world?

Perhaps if her cargoes were safely landed, and if the king did come to Brugge, she might meet Edward again—on her own terms.

Perhaps. Only perhaps—on both counts.

# Chapter Eight

There was discussion about the Lady Margaret's wedding in London, too, after a morning's hunting, for Edward was now deep in the planning to transport members of the Court of Westminster to Brugge, that is, if the king was finally able to convince his sister of her duty to marry Duke Charles.

Margaret was headstrong. Hers was the power of acknowledged beauty coupled with much of the king's own force of character. She was accustomed to being indulged. However, she was in her early twenties, old for a royal bride, and Edward was entirely determined to make her see reason before she lost the currency of youth on the international royal bridal market.

This alliance with Burgundy was most necessary if Edward was to win the ever-expanding battle for influence on the continent and head off French ambitions for European dominance. In a way his sister was making the marriage he might himself have made—to a member of the Burgundian Ducal House—if he hadn't met Elizabeth Wydeville first, sheltering from a storm under the oak trees at Greenwich.

Yet, also, Edward was neither stupid nor heartless. As a brother he understood his little sister might be repulsed at the thought of marrying a widower some years older than she was, especially when there were so many gallants at home literally panting to be her husband—but Margaret could have no choice if he so instructed her. To oppose his will in the matter of her marriage was, after all, treason. What did royal children exist for if not to help the future of their houses by intermarriage with allies?

Excellent in theory, of course, but difficult in practice. Margaret was his sister and painfully direct at times, just as he was. Only this morning, she'd flung into his face in the most strident terms his own hasty marriage to Elizabeth Wydeville. That had hardly been for the good of the country, had it? Edward hadn't brought a useful alliance of any kind to the House of York with that marriage, had he? And he'd defied Warwick's plans for a French alliance in marrying his base-born *old* queen—look at the trouble he'd caused doing that!

That same "old" queen, entering the room unexpectedly in the middle of this very frank confrontation, heard Margaret's viciously energetic remarks with unflattering clarity. Alas.

The queen knew well the king's family resented her marriage to Edward, and she was therefore implacable in her determination that they acknowledge her in every possible way as God's chosen, anointed queen. She was also more than sensitive to being five years older than her husband at a court filled to bursting with ambitious, well-born girls all enthusiastically determined to provide the king with any kind of sexual favor he might require.

Margaret's heated remarks, therefore, were fat on the fire when Elizabeth heard them. Outraged, the queen demanded from Edward that the Lady Margaret and her mother, Duchess Cicely, suffer for their scorn of her—and in a public way before the court!

Her dangerous mood was partly caused by the fact that she'd become certain at last, this morning, that she was in the very earliest stages of breeding again—no bloodied rags with her moon this month—which was something miraculous in itself, considering she and the king had had so little to do with each other recently.

So far, of course, Elizabeth had borne Edward only girls, and she was very sensitive about it. Each pregnancy raised the stakes; surely God would grant her a son this time? And her fragile emotional state was not helped by apparently "well-meaning" advice from her mother-in-law after the confrontation with Margaret.

Cicely, the mother of multiple sons herself, dared to offer advice to her, the Queen of England, about how she could ensure that the child in her belly was a son. She would not be patronized by either of the York women!

It was more than unfortunate, therefore, that the queen then happened to glance at a small letter scroll, partly unrolled on her husband's work desk. Neatly lettered at its foot was the signature Anne de Bohun—and, of course, it all came back: the searing humiliation of the tournament on the Feast of Saint Valentine last year when she'd been made such a fool of by that doxy! And that very letter, the letter he still kept so close, was evidence of her betrayal by her husband! Anne de Bohun had not gone far enough—nowhere would ever be far enough away, if the king still thought about her after all this time.

Elizabeth burst into tears, heedless of appearances. The king did not love her, had never loved her, no matter how much she tried to please him, to give him children.

Edward winced as he described the scene later for William Hastings's benefit. He'd done his best to settle matters, to reassure Elizabeth of his devotion, and thought he'd succeeded although he ignored a request to burn the scroll, since it was all he had left that Anne had actually touched. But then there had been a further confrontation between his wife and the other royal women as they'd begun to walk back from Mass in his own private chapel.

As usual in earliest pregnancy, Elizabeth Wydeville had had her gown laced especially tight, and only managed to get all the way through the Mass without running back to the garderobe in her chambers to vomit by the exercise of her formidable will.

However, imagining once more that her husband's mother and sister were condescending to her in her present vulnerable condition, she'd manufactured a further dispute about precedence at the end of the Mass.

The king, as a special mark of favor to the duchess, had wanted to lead his mother out of the Mass first instead of Elizabeth, but the queen had taken that very much amiss, for she would have had to walk down the aisle of the chapel alone, following Edward and the duchess.

This she had tearfully refused to do—had insisted, in fact, that the duchess and the Lady Margaret hold up the corners of her own train and that she walk beside the king. In terms of strict precedence it was her right as the consort of the king and a crowned queen; she was the premier lady of England and no one was permitted to walk in front of her except for designated (male) magnates on certain formal occasions. However, since Duchess Cicely visited them so rarely, it was not gracefully done to insist on full protocol, especially in their own private chapel where so few members of the court were ever invited.

Still, to keep the peace with Elizabeth, Edward had persuaded his mother and his mutinous sister of their duty with some difficulty, however, Cicely and Margaret were not appeased and made very little effort to hide their true feelings when the queen insisted on her rights. And so it was done, though there was much malicious delight among the few courtiers who saw the duchess and her daughter march behind Elizabeth with rigid faces, holding up the train of the the queen's robes as if they smelled of six-day-old fish. Altogether, a most entertaining contest to observe, and fuel for gossip for days and days.

And so, to escape the domestic storms raging around him, Edward had taken refuge with William Hastings again in his own private closet as soon as he decently could, desperate for advice. How should he handle the warfare among the women in his family and, even more important, how could he reconcile his sister to the fate God, and he, had chosen for her?

He himself was not planning to go to Brugge with the wedding party. The kingdom was too restless, and now, with news of the queen's pregnancy, there was another reason to stay; to go to Brugge just because he liked the place, liked Duke Charles, would be gross self-indulgence. Edward sighed. Truly one gave up much to be a king. Especially personal freedom. And women! The women in his family, now, they drove him to distraction—where was the pleasure in that?

William did all he could to suppress the disloyal laughter that burbled up from the depths of his stomach as the king continued his description of the disastrous scene after the Mass. It had been worse than a bad dream, because just after he'd personally—personally!—dealt with the precedence issue, the queen had been overtaken by the need to vomit as they'd all crossed into the great hall for the breakfast feast.

Try as she might to hold her wayward stomach in check, Elizabeth Wydeville had begun to turn an unattractive pale green—a notably displeasing contrast to the pallid lilac of her velvet dress. Suddenly the king's mother and his sister had been forced to an ungainly canter as the queen hurried into a side court, luckily finding a row of handsome potted bay trees to be sick into, out of sight of the gimlet-eyed courtiers.

Naturally, although Elizabeth's women had rushed to help their mistress, standing around her and holding their skirts wide to conceal her predicament from the inquisitive, the damage could not be hidden when the queen had finally emerged. Some of the vomit had stained the front of Elisabeth's gown, and she would need to change before joining the court for its morning meal.

It was at this point, when his wife had departed, head held high, for her own quarters—not too ill to insist that the other royal women continue to carry her train all the way there—that Edward had made a bolt for his own tiny office and William's company.

William set himself to cheer the king and it was the perfect moment, for tonight's feast in honor of Saint Valentine and the busy Saint Cupid would certainly serve the king's needs for distraction from his domestic problems excellently well. A man needed recreational sex if he was to keep a level head. It was relaxing and good for the body, and therefore the kingdom, for if a man, a man such as this king, lived in a state of perpetual sexual tension, how could he concentrate on the more important things demanded of him?

The person of the king was sacred. And it was his sacred duty, as the king's own high chamberlain, to see that nothing impinged on the well-being of that body. He was the guardian of the king's health, as he and Edward had "discussed" this morning.

So, yes. A woman. Perhaps more than one: even the queen

might understand at this time, for breeding women tended not to like sex greatly, if his own experience was a guide.

Therefore, it was his duty to think carefully on the topic of the king's bodily health and harmony, consider who might be complaisant—and he would start before tonight's feast. Yes, he would interview a number of interesting prospects—discreetly—before this evening.

"William, have you heard recently of Anne de Bohun? Is she well?" William's heart sank. After the girl had left the court in such astonishing circumstances, William had thought of her only in passing. Good-looking enough, of course, and clearly close to the king's heart. But then, many another had been so as well. Surely Edward was not still thinking of her?

"Your Grace, I have heard nothing for some time. Shall I enquire where she is living now?"

The king frowned and strode over to his casements, looking down onto the river sweeping past the palace with its freight of broken, dirty ice. "No. There's no need; she'd have told me if she wanted to be found."

Relieved, William hurried on, seeking to distract the king. "Sire, I think you're overtired with the affairs of this kingdom. As we were speaking of your health earlier today, I find I have an idea for a comprehensive tonic, one that you'll find so easy to swallow."

William's tone was so hopeful, so cheeky, the king was forced to laugh. His friend was right—a man could not be a monk for all his life, married or not, and it was ridiculous to be mooning after a girl he could not have. She had chosen her path—so be it!

# Chapter Nine

Hans Memlinc was annoyed. Anne was late. The midday bell had long tolled and he was ready to begin their "final" session—and yet she'd kept him waiting.

He was used to the caprices of women clients, but he'd thought Anne was different. She hadn't seemed flighty or stupid in their sittings together—the opposite, in fact. Now she'd disappointed him because she'd not even bothered to send a note from her household. He was a busy man, she knew that.

"Meinheer, I'm so sorry." He'd been so deep in disgruntled introspection, he hadn't heard her soft leather shoes on his stair. Now she stood in his open doorway—but she was in a blue housedress and her headdress was a plain gauze veil!

She saw him frown as he scanned her plain kirtle. "Something else to forgive me for, Meinheer. My red dress needs repair. And I've been so busy all today that there's been no time to reconstruct my headdress as you last saw it. Can you still finish the painting?"

Hans Memlinc grunted. If he was prepared to be even a little honest, he could make this the last sitting. All that remained to be finished were some elements of her eyes—the light had not been right to catch them truly, yesterday—and the expression of her mouth. Her dress and her hair—he realized with a start he could finally see the deep, blood-russet chestnut of her hair under her veil—didn't really matter for what he wanted to do.

"Well, mistress, I shall try. You can speak while I finish your eyes. After that, I shall need your silence. There are final touches to your mouth that I must make."

His phrasing was clumsy—he was speaking to her in French, in which she was fluent, rather than Flemish. She'd done well in attempting to master the language of the Lowlands since her arrival in Brugge but was always more comfortable expressing her lightning-fast thoughts in French. Somehow the language of the troubadours suited her better and he sensed that. It was part of the reason he was such a good painter.

So once again the afternoon fled past, but this time Anne was impatient to be finished. Finally, by the shadows lengthening on the floor in front of her, she could see the sun beginning the last part of its westerly journey. She didn't want to be out walking again after dark.

"Meinheer, surely you must be finished now?" The painter sighed, very deliberately. Well, perhaps she was right. He was happy with the eyes now, but there was something about the mouth, perhaps because her face was so mobile, perhaps that was it. No—just one more little touch with the carmine and a hint of the black—there in the center, where there was the shadow of the upper lip on the lower.

Anne had had enough. "Meinheer!" She spoke sharply and was immediately sorry for it. It was a result of the fear—and something else, the exultation—of this last day.

"Meinheer Memlinc. I'm sorry to be so impatient, but I want to be home before dark, especially tonight."

"Oh yes, the little incident last evening. Eva told me about it." Anne was astonished. She'd been careful not to bring the subject up—she didn't want to discuss how those men and the threat they represented made her feel—but she'd presumed he didn't know of it either. That he did, and didn't think it was important enough to talk about, said volumes about his absorption in his work. Nothing else mattered.

He threw her the ghost of a smile. "I'm not completely heartless, lady. But I didn't want you to talk about it with me—we would both have become upset." He was sincere and that surprised her very much. For Anne, the thought of this stolid man being emotionally affected by her feelings was difficult to understand. He seemed so self-contained.

"But there. You may see it now. It is finished." Solemnly he sketched a cross over his work, and over Anne, too, as she approached.

Anne gasped when she looked over his shoulder to see the canvas. For the first time, she saw herself as others must see her and it was a very strange experience. It was not like looking in her mirror—when she dressed in the morning, for instance—no, somehow the painter had captured something else, something naked in her eyes, and instinctively she looked away from her own face for a moment. Let the shock subside—see what else the picture held for her.

It was a very rich painting, with much detail in the lustrous, precisely depicted fabric of the clothes and the sensuously painted jewels, and now she saw why he'd taken so much time with her mouth and eyes. These were living faces he was dealing with, real people—he wanted them all to feel like that—alive forever, modeled as strongly as statues, yet somehow captured on the flat surface of his work.

So much of the painting touched her, touched her deeply. There was her shield, prominent on one of the walls of the room the painter had conjured up. On it was her grant of arms from Edward: the Angevin leopards and beneath them, two drops of blood—heart's blood he'd called them. And there, too, on the middle finger of the left of her praying hands, the square-cut ruby that had been his last gift to her in Dover. She was overwhelmed by the memories.

The painter frowned; his client was upset—she was crying! This was disastrous!

"Mistress? Are you unhappy with the painting?" Blunt. That was his way, but he could not disguise the anxiety.

"Not unhappy, maestro. Moved, so moved. Forgive me, there's so much to absorb; my silence is awe, not judgment."

She was sincere, and the painter slowly lowered his shoulders, flexed his neck. Viewings were always tricky, one way or another. He would try to relax.

He need not have worried. Anne was lost in what she saw, and the more she looked, the more there was to see. Some elements of the painting, for instance, almost seemed to overflow the flat surface. One of her own feet was about to slip down and out toward the viewer as if she herself would get up and move out of the frame!

As Anne had requested, there were four figures in the painting and together they formed a pleasing triangular composition. At the apex of the pyramid sat the "Holy Virgin" in a beautifully detailed, carved cathedra. The thronelike chair was itself on a dais with two steps, down which Mary's blue robe flowed and folded as cleanly as running water. Behind her head was an open window through which could be seen a view of the town walls and fields outside Brugge—the sun just beginning to set, throwing mellow light onto the limpid waters of the canals curving around the feet of battlements and walls.

The beauty of the countryside, just glimpsed in the painted distance, brought wistfulness. Anne had so little time to give to that part of herself now: those empty fields, the dark forest, and the glorious sky spoke of freedom, spoke of her childhood. How rare it was to be alone in this noisy city, how rare to touch natural things, smell the earth, listen to what the wind told her of the past, and the future.

Tears were near the surface again. Too many complex and contradictory feelings filled her now—she needed time to sort them privately.

It was a bold work she'd commissioned, herself at the center of it, not out of vanity but out of certainty, out of hope. She'd made herself Mary's companion and they looked like friends, because this Mother of God was young and blond like Jenna, with hair carefully arranged loose over her shoulders—the symbol of virginity. Anne recognized the model; she was a seamstress Deborah hired from time to time to help make up clothes for the household. That made her smile—how astonishing yet how apt to give the Virgin a servant's face.

The "Christ Child" sat on his mother's lap, one tiny hand raised in blessing as his charmingly benevolent gaze took in both the viewer and the supplicant, and commissioner, of the painting—Anne at his mother's feet.

Anne was delighted with the likeness of the boy—she'd persuaded Memlinc to use little Edward. The painter chuckled as he saw her look carefully at Edward's face. "He only squirmed a little, lady. I've had worse. Your sister's son is a fine child. She would have been proud of him—if I may say that."

Anne hardly heard what the painter said. She was lost in the face of the little boy in front of her. The baby looked amused; his mouth was open in a happy smile—she almost expected to hear the warm, milky gurgle of his laughter. He was the delightful, almost carnal center of the picture, his flesh painted with a pearl-like glimmer. Surely, this eternally giggling child was an affirmation that life could be good and that God loved each one of his creatures. And how odd that viewers of this painting, in years to come, would not know that it was truly a picture of a mother and her son—though Anne was not the woman with the halo.

There was a fourth figure in the painting. The image of a knight wearing jousting armor, his plumed helm open so that face and eyes could be seen in the shadow of the visor, and in his hand, a shortened jousting lance. He also had a shield with the red cross of Saint George upon it, plain and unadorned.

This knight had one foot firmly upon a vigorously writhing, quarter-size dragon, which, like Anne's own foot, seemed almost to fall out of the picture into the lap of the viewer.

And then Anne saw the color of the knight's armor. It was black; and the knight's eyes were a most intense blue. Breath deserted her; this Saint George had Edward Plantagenet's eyes—and his jousting armor. Ice touched her, fire also. Unwilling to believe what she saw, Anne felt her voice shake slightly as she spoke.

"Where did you find the model for Saint George, Meinheer?" Even to her own ears, she sounded strained.

"Well now, Sir Knight is an oddity; he's got a bit from here, a bit from there. I use ordinary people for saints' faces—as you know. I don't want to use well-known people; if you've met them, it breaks the illusion and it's too distracting. But this Saint George was hard to paint—he just wouldn't come, wouldn't form properly, even though I worked with two different men from the markets. They cost me to pay off, I can tell you that, though I kept something of each of them: the hands, there, they come from one man; the neck, the set of the shoulders from the other."

It seemed to Anne that he was holding something back. She breathed her question, "But his eyes?"

The painter shuffled his feet, embarrassed. "Well, they came from an English boy I saw once: a young nobleman. There were family connections to the court here and he spent one summer with the old duke and his family. Our current duke taught this boy to joust when he was young—the boy had black practice armor, and I used to watch them sometimes, at the quintain. I just imagined what he might look like now. It was a strong face even then, of course, and I've never forgotten his eyes, but that's my trade."

It was an omen, a sign. They were still connected; why else would his face find its way into this painting?

"Edward—the King of England? As a young man?"

He mistook her tone for dislike. "I can paint the face out if you like, mistress. I was guessing what he'd look like now, building on memory." He shrugged. "It's a small skill I have, to remember people's faces. But if you don't like it . . ."

Anne shook her head and she could not keep the joy out of her voice. "No. It is a wonderful painting. Extraordinary. You are not to change it, any of it."

That was enough for Meinheer Memlinc. If she was happy, so was he. He was reasonably unsentimental about his work generally. Perhaps, like a wet nurse, he knew that his "children"—the paintings he made—never truly belonged to him, even though he gave them life. Sometimes, after all the sweat and anguish of making a picture work, he was even glad to see it swaddled in wrappings, ready to leave his studio. But this one was different, perhaps because Anne had been such an intriguing subject.

He'd badly wanted to capture that combination of vulnerability, purpose, and sensuality he felt in her. She was capable of a direct innocence that generally deserted children quite early, but it was allied to an edge like a sword, when that was needed. And he wanted to paint her again, badly. A portrait this time—just of her. Perhaps as the Magdalene, if she would permit that.

He'd have to find a way to broach the subject tactfully when she was used to living with this work she'd commissioned. After all, now, as she aged, she would always have the reminder of what she'd once been. That might be disturbing, as beauty fled.

Yes, his picture might come to be a mixed blessing, in time.

# Chapter Ten

Anne was anxious as Phillip, the strongest man in Mathew's stable, tried his best to hang the picture of her unexpectedly real family group—Anne, her Saint George, and their son—in the parlor.

The painting had been brought home to Mathew's house with some ceremony, arriving at almost the same time as Anne's guardian and his wife tied up in their barge at their own water gate. Now the press of people in this small room, all giving poor Phillip contradictory advice, was actively getting in the way of what Anne wanted.

Mathew Cuttifer was the worst—he fancied himself a judge of artwork, having commissioned so much for Blessing House in London.

"No, no, Phillip. Look man, that's not nearly high enough. You want it to hang higher, where it's out of the afternoon sun. We don't want the colors fading!"

"Mathew, I can't agree. It needs the light to be seen properly—all those wonderful colors. It should come down a little and be farther toward the window. The light is not direct in any case—it will not harm the pigments. Meinheer Memlinc said so."

Lady Margaret, Mathew Cuttifer's sensible wife, was brisk. She knew a thing or two about painting as well. Deborah discreetly rolled her eyes at Anne—at this rate they'd still all be going by evening prayers. The girl did her best not to laugh.

"Sir Mathew, I think I agree with Lady Margaret. The painting needs the light. Each detail is so exquisite—they all deserve to be seen clearly. I will watch to see that the colors do not fade—perhaps we can have a cover made for summer days."

Sir Mathew was not convinced, but he saw he was outvoted. There were times when this formidable merchant found the look in his wife's eyes more frightening than facing the king. This was one of those times.

"Well then, I suppose we should live with it on the wall for a time. See if you like it in the place you have chosen. I find that things change—season to season, for instance, the light is different. You may not always want it on that wall. Or as low as that . . ." He caught Margaret's eye. Oh, very well. He would not say any more.

Deborah left the room quietly to see about something pleasing to drink—they must celebrate. Today, now the painting had come home, was an extraordinary day, and it was somehow a symbol of changed times and strange possibilities.

Anne, Lady Margaret, Sir Mathew, and Deborah. These four people alone—along with the formidable figure of "Saint George" in the painting—knew the secret of Anne's past.

Sir Mathew stood thoughtfully in front of the canvas of this unexpected family group. He knew it was a remarkable painting—finer than anything he had—and very bold, if one knew the true history of the figures within it.

It made him shiver that Edward's eyes, an impression of his adult face, had found their way inside that jousting helm. Like Anne, he felt it to to be an omen—something profoundly significant—but whom did the dragon represent? There was a snake in the garden of Eden—dragons and snakes were both symbols of evil and destruction, surely.

Mathew was at war with himself and he knew it. Hours before, when he and Margaret had landed in Sluis, he'd been presented with the news of the wedding-to-be, and of Anne's bold plans for beating the merchants of Brugge at their own game.

Mathew Cuttifer had not made his money from being timorous. He understood risk, but prudent risk was always best: risk when one broadly knew that the odds were running in one's favor. What Anne had proposed to him was something that ran against almost every trading instinct he possessed—almost, but not quite. A small flicker of excitement lay beneath the caution. He remembered the instinctive boldness of his youth, the boldness that had begun his fortune.

And so, with little time to assess all that Anne was proposing, he'd unexpectedly agreed: he would coinvest in the cargoes to come from Italy. Devilry lay deep in his soul it seemed; God grant that he would not live to regret backing his "ward," his ex-servant, the illegitimate daughter of his own "old king" . . .

Deborah brought Mathew back to the present, offering a blue-green Waldglas beaker filled with hot wine. He took it and turned back to the women who surrounded him. "To Saint George. The Protector of England, the protector of women."

So much was unsaid as they repeated his words "To Saint George," but Anne was deeply warmed. Once more, against his own good judgment, it seemed, Mathew Cuttifer had committed himself and his house to stand beside her when the risk was at its greatest. If he had truly been her father, she would have kissed him now; and somehow he knew, she was sure of that, for when he raised his own glass, he smiled and winked!

A discreet knock at the open door of the parlor broke the moment. Friar Giorgio stood there uncertainly. This was very much a family gathering.

"Father Giorgio, come in. See now, here is the Lady Anne's fine new painting. You know much of such matters, as I'm told."

Sir Mathew, like his friend William Caxton, was uneasy in the friar's presence but he hid it better.

Anne smiled at Giorgio and slipped an arm through his as they stood in front of the canvas together. "There. I cannot judge my own face, though others tell me that the likeness is good of the child."

Ordinarily the friar was scathing about the so-called arts of the Low Countries—he saw them as primitive, old-fashioned, and undeveloped. To him, real culture began and ended within the city states of his own divided homeland—and, just possibly, within the walls of Paris—but here, today, in front of this canvas, he was silenced. It was a great painting. Somehow the painter had caught the essence, the truth of each of his sitters.

The peasant seamstress who portrayed the Mother of God truly shone down on her audience, her own simple humanity as great a crown as that worn by the Empress of Heaven. Never had Christ's mother seemed more accessible, more compassionate, more comforting, and more real.

And the baby, the happy Christ Child, still gave hints of strength, even majesty, in the blessing of that raised hand, confidently signing the cross over Anne as she knelt at his feet.

But it was in Anne's face and Saint George's face that the greatness of the work was most strikingly displayed. The sheer technical accomplishment—the luminance of the flesh, the solidity of the figures, the pleasing balance of the shapes, the remarkable depth of the world they inhabited—was far outweighed by the natural power of these two painted faces. It was as if Hans Memlinc had dipped his brush in truth and laid it out on his canvas—and the personal qualities he'd found in each subject's face sent Father Giorgio's scalp into a prickle of strangeness.

Hans Memlinc had painted strength and purpose into Anne's eyes, and charm also. It was not a look he saw often from the girl herself; like many women she was careful to keep her eyes down in public so that she would not cause offense by glancing directly into a man's eyes—but in unguarded moments he had seen it. Sometimes those green-blue eyes were a sword in her service—a glance that said, "Be careful of what I could be if you cross me."

Yet her mouth contradicted the eyes. It was certainly sensual—deeply, softly clear red, the same red as her scarlet dress—and yet so yielding; slightly open with a hint of the white teeth beneath as the short upper lip lifted in an awed, tender smile for the baby Christ. The pure mouth of a child who was not yet a woman. An innocent mouth.

Giorgio was not a man to linger over the qualities of a woman's mouth, but he understood the vulnerable sensuality of it in this painting.

And Saint George—now there was a face. The nose was long

and fine, the planes of the face clear and well modeled within the shadow of the helm. But again, the eyes—peering out of the shadow, flecked with light as if they burned—were blue stars, glittering with the edge of a honed and wicked knife. There was no quarter in that face, no pity, but there was a powerful sense that the knight was there to protect the kneeling woman, and the child, as if this were the only task God had ever given him. And the blood pouring in ruddy, graceful coils from the dragon's neck was witness to that fact. Also the two faces, his and hers, were oddly alike. They might almost have been male and female versions of the same person.

Sir Mathew interrupted the friar's reverie. "And so, Father Giorgio, tell us. Is this not as fine as any work you might see in Florence or Rome?"

Gracefully, the priest bowed. "Indeed, sir, I am delighted and surprised to say that it is. I have never been a scholar of your northern painters, but this Meinheer Memlinc could have a most promising career if he chose to work at any of the courts in Italy."

Anne laughed. "But, Father, he's so busy here in Brugge that he has no need to go elsewhere. He already has a great career." The friar blushed a little—sensitive that he had unwittingly patronized these people, which was not clever of him. "Ah, lady, I did not wish to give offense. I merely observe that all the great masters working today can find ready commissions from the noble families of my country—and the Vatican—after all. So much building, so much adornment in all forms, so many extraordinary men at work. We can all learn from the greatness of others."

"Amen to that, Father. Amen to that. And now, it is our pleasure to learn from you. Since we have the attention of Sir Mathew and Lady Margaret, perhaps you and I should tell them of some of the wonderful things you have brought to us from your travels. What the ladies are currently wearing in Florence, for instance; this new fashion for flowers embroidered in precious stones on gauze overdresses for the warmer months? That will translate here. I believe we should have some made up to sell for the wedding of our new duchess-to-be."

Mathew looked at Anne speculatively. There was a new, confident tone in her voice; she was nervous, but she spoke as he would have, like a merchant who saw an opening in the market.

Friar Giorgio clapped his hands for Jenna—the girl had been waiting outside the parlor in case she should be needed—and sent her to bring the saddlebags from his room. He had many things to show his new business partners, things that could be made and sold in the next few months as excitement mounted in the town of Brugge ahead of the royal wedding; things that would deliver a great deal of money to the new joint venture between Mathew Cuttifer and Anne de Bohun—if the cargoes from Venice and Florence were landed in time; if they survived the spring gales; if the guilds allowed them to be sold.

And if none of these things happened, Anne would be ruined.

# PART TWO

# The Merchant

# Chapter Eleven

Anne woke with a start in the dead middle of the night—before even cockerels called out dawn to the sleeping city. She sat up in bed, hugging her knees, shivering, feeling sick. Bad dreams had pursued her after Edward's birth, but she'd thought that time was past.

Perhaps it was the imminence of the marriage—the marriage of Edward's sister—that was stirring up the emotional mud in her life once more. She still felt guilty about Elizabeth Wydeville—that she'd allowed the king, the man Elizabeth had married, to seduce her. Guilty, yes, but not regretful. If she was honest.

Thoughts of Edward always made Anne's heart lurch, even now; therefore, how could she go back to sleep? Quickly she pulled the fur coverlet from the bed around her shoulders and slipped out of her warm sheets, over to the window that looked down to the canal.

The winter ice was long gone and the canal was placid in the light of the setting moon. It was the still time of night—the hush before the world woke and stretched. The air felt different and suddenly Anne realized why—she wasn't cold.

Anne pushed one of the heavy, leaded casements open and leaned out into the soft air as far as she could. Spring! The air smelled of earth and green leaves after rain. The year had turned away from winter at last and summer was truly close.

What would the Lady Margaret be feeling in London now? Was she happy about this marriage?

And when she came to Brugge, would Duke Charles be patient with his new bride? He'd had three previous wives so he must be well experienced with the handling of highly bred young women. The Lady Margaret would also become stepmother to Mary of Burgundy, sole heir of her father, the duke. How would that be, to find yourself a bride and a mother in the same moment?

The sky was lightening in the east now—the air flushed with pink and a pearl-like glimmer deepening to incandescent silver as the sun began to rise. Slowly, color traveled through the world beneath her window—the bricks of the house turned rose and madder, and the new leaves showed brilliant green with the light behind them. Green and silver! That is what she would wear today, to salute the change of season!

Suddenly Anne was happy, happier than she'd been for months.

There was so much to look forward to, for she'd heard yesterday that the impossible was nearly accomplished—the goods that had been bought for her in Italy would be safely landed at Sluis this morning. Hurriedly she crossed herself at the thought. It was pride to believe something before the reality existed—please let her not be punished for it! But it was true—the *Lady Margaret* and another ship that Maxim had found in Venice had been sighted down the coast last evening and messages had been brought to her on horseback. They would dock this morning—God willing—ahead of any that the more timid merchants of Brugge had sent once they'd heard Mathew had committed the house of Cuttifer and its resources to Anne's venture.

Their boldness had made enemies for them, no doubt about it, and Mathew had been very worried indeed. He'd tried his best, and so had Lady Margaret, to persuade Anne to accompany them home to London—he was certain Anne's formal exile from the court could be bribed away—but his ward had refused. For her own good reasons; she wanted to meet Edward again, if meet him she did, on her own terms.

In the end, with many cautions and yet more security added to his house in Brugge, Mathew had been talked around and agreed to let her stay. Secretly he was proud of Anne, proud of her courage and her spirit, as was Lady Margaret. Mathew's wife had far fewer fears for Anne than her husband did and, in the end, her support and endorsement of the girl's practical good sense had won Mathew over. He'd agreed to go just as he'd planned.

Stretching by the window, Anne laughed grimly when she thought of the drama of the months since Mathew's departure as the English trading community faced up, reluctantly, to the unexpected competition offered by the house of Cuttifer. After scrambling to send joint orders for trade goods to the Italian city states, the so-called Merchant Adventurers had waited until they'd collected a sizable fleet and escort in Venice against the sea pirates before they trusted what they'd bought to the spring gales.

Normally, of course, they would all have preferred to import their Italian goods much later in the season. Each year, the regular June fleet left the ports of Italy and the Levant in the early summer to bring luxury goods to Europe; thus they worried deeply before hazarding expensive goods on the seas so early, but, finally, Anne's bold example had shamed them into trying. But now she'd beaten them home!

In a sudden ferment to begin the day, Anne hurried over to the door of the little chamber that adjoined her own: Edward's nursery, which Deborah shared with him.

Very quietly she pushed the door open to find her son regarding her steadily, wide awake—and sitting up! Her heart lurched; suddenly he looked much more like a little boy than a baby. Of course, as all fond young mothers, Anne had always been convinced that Edward was an unusually strong baby, and very advanced for his age; not much past six months. Let scoffers say what they liked, here was proof!

And the little boy was as delighted with his achievement as she was, for with a huge smile he held out his arms to be cuddled. One fluid movement and she had him clasped tight against her chest, his face nestled against her own as he nuzzled her with a delighted sloppy gurgle of baby laughter.

Then she plumped herself down beside his cradle and kissed

his soft, sweet neck, making him squeal with delight. She loved the smell of him, the softness of his skin, the purity of his mouth and eyes.

"You'll spoil that child, Anne." Deborah was trying to be severe, but Anne knew that tone. Deborah loved this little boy just as much as she did and played with him as happily when she thought no one saw them.

It was most unusual for Deborah to wake after Anne, but she'd been superintending the cleaning of the house for some days so that it was fit to receive whoever Anne's guests would be as the royal marriage approached, and every one of her muscles ached.

She'd driven the staff and herself hard, so that every corner of Mathew Cuttifer's handsome house was properly scoured with hot water, finely ground cold ash from the fires, and good fat soap she'd made herself. The windows had been polished with vinegar and three-day-old urine until they winked and flashed in the pale spring sunlight, and the expensive collection of silver chargers in the hall, and the pewter vessels in the kitchen, had been carefully buffed with a paste of the finest river sand, pounded hard in a pestle to make it finer still, before it was mixed with alum and more vinegar.

All the room hangings had been beaten outside in the heber, the linen in the bedrooms boiled and blanched and hung out over the budding hedges in the kitchen garden—just coming into leaf—to dry in the last of the blustery weather; and the fine Turkish carpets scattered with dampened sawdust before being vigorously shaken and beaten in their turn and hung back up on the walls.

Now the whole house smelled sweetly of beeswax polish and the fresh spring flowers placed in all the public rooms, and Deborah had gone to bed the previous night with a satisfied feeling that much had been accomplished. This house, their home until Anne could afford another, was ready to face whatever chance might send their way.

Deborah struggled up out of her truckle bed—her bed was beside Edward's little carved oak cradle—but Anne pressed her back against the bolster. "No, Deborah—I'll find Jenna. She can help me. You rest, I know you're tired. Come, Edward, let's find your breakfast."

Scooping the little boy up against her body, she wrapped them both more securely in the fur wrap and, talking quietly to Edward about all the excitements the day held for them both, walked quickly to the door of her room.

"Ivan?"

"Yes, lady, I am here."

There'd been no more attempts to kidnap her, but perhaps that had been because of the added security Sir Mathew and Ivan had insisted upon. Now, when she went out in public, she was accompanied not just by Ivan but by two other men he'd selected as well, veterans of the ongoing conflicts between the city states in Italy. Besides, it did no harm to the credit and importance of the house that Anne now had her own men-at-arms. All three, dressed in Mathew's livery and walking calmly beside her litter when she went out in public, signaled that the prosperity Mathew enjoyed was growing apace. But what none knew, outside a chosen few, was how much Anne's circumstances were likely to change if the cargoes landed safely.

And, like a jewel that was enhanced by its setting, Anne's beauty and desirability shone more brightly for the fact it was fenced around by good Spanish steel.

Ivan scrambled up from his palliasse and pushed it away from the door of Anne's room as his mistress asked him to find Jenna. As he pulled up his hose and laced them to the points of his jerkin while hauling on his boots, he could hear Anne singing to the little boy, a low, breathy song that told how the wind, in spring, liked to chase the birds across the sky because they were both free and enjoyed the game. There was a haunting, wistful sweetness to the words, and Ivan could understand, none better, how dear the thought of freedom must be to Anne on such a day as this. He could help her be free, would help her, if she needed him to. That was his job, but he liked her; it was his pleasure too . . .

Soon the household was in a bustling stir as Jenna dressed Anne to go to the Mass. Today, as she'd promised herself, Anne was wearing a new dress bought with almost her last stock of silver. Figured leaf-green brocade with a veil of silver silk tissue flowing from a low crowned cap of purple velvet—the colors sat well with her russet hair and matte white skin.

Anne was very grandly dressed for a working day, and there was a reason for that, for after the Mass, she would see Duke Charles at the Prinsenhof, the Burgundian ducal palace; that is, if her trade goods made it ashore to Sluis and could be brought to her in time.

But now, as her stomach contracted with a fizzy mix of pride, excitement, and terror, she clasped her hands together tightly, praying silently for strength and courage: the duke was the key to her future now.

# Chapter Twelve

Duke Charles was restless as he strolled out of his chapel in the Prinsenhof on his way to the breakfast. Magnificently dressed in a tight jacket of green velvet, in honor of the season and because green, as all the world knew, was the color of young love, he, too, was impatient this morning.

He was fretting to be away to the hunt because very soon the season would be over. Winter's ending always made him unaccountably sad, because he lived for the chase—of many kinds.

The chase. That made him think of Anne de Bohun. He had promised to meet her after the court finished its meal this morning and he was looking forward to that—she was intriguing—though it would cost him a little time outside the walls of Brugge in his hunting preserve. For someone so young, Anne seemed very self-possessed and so well connected it was a puzzle, and a scandal, that she lived alone, except for servants, in her guardian's house.

The duke frowned as he thought more. He did not like his merchants, even the foreign ones, to be unhappy because that was bad for trade and therefore bad for his peace of mind. Perhaps the time had come to listen to William Caxton and use his influence to intervene in the matter of this girl's marriage. Caxton, it seemed, had been rebuffed. He'd heard, too, of the attempted kidnapping earlier in the year—perhaps her very presence was bad for public order, then.

No. The timing was not quite correct. At this moment, he was not expecting Edward Plantagenet to bring his sister to Brugge for their marriage, but that might change; and if it did, he would seek advice from his new brother-in-law. Perhaps there was someone among the many English courtiers accompanying the bride who might be suitable for Anne, especially if it pleased King Edward to arrange matters. Anne could hardly object if her own king willed it so, and that would solve the problem. In the meanwhile, he would enjoy his breakfast and then await, with interest, what Anne had to say . . .

Anne had one nervous habit that would have been clear to those who knew her as she waited for the duke in a small anteroom to the Presence chamber in the Prinsenhof, the town house in Brugge of the Dukes of Burgundy. Mechanically, without being conscious she was doing it, she smoothed the precious brocade of her dress first one way, then the other. She knew that her green dress was something of an affront as it was the fashion at court for ladies to dress in scarlet and black—the red coming from the expensive imported dye, grana. Anne did have one red dress, it was true; she'd worn it for the portrait because red always caught the eye, but her tastes ran to more subtle colors generally, like the lustrous, changing green of today.

"It seems we think alike, Lady de Bohun." Her thoughts had been away, far away, so she'd not heard the duke enter the room, but as she looked up at him, startled, she was struck, as always, by his charisma. And the great good luck of his also wearing green today.

Duke Charles was not very tall, it was true, but his energy, the vigor of his movements, and the quick flash of his still-sound teeth in an alive, brown face were very attractive.

Anne dropped her head respectfully as she curtsied, thinking how lucky Princess Margaret would be to have such a husband. She sighed as she rose and the duke picked up her hand to kiss, in the French fashion.

"You sigh, lady? Come now. How can there be secret sadness on such a wonderful day as this?" He was leading her into the Presence chamber, followed by several of the courtiers he would share the morning meal with. All of them pressed as close as they dared, discreetly intent on gleaning all they could from the duke's conversation with this unusual English girl.

"Ah, Your Grace, I am not unhappy, but spring is a strange season, is it not? It makes the blood restless. I feel certain you understand that. But how fortunate we are both wearing green. I thought to honor your bride-to-be—and I see that was your thought as well." The duke laughed delightedly. It was said the English were governed by a phlegmatic humor, but this girl was warm and sparkling. She made him laugh and that was a charming quality. Charming!

Ceremoniously he conducted his guest to a small X-shaped gilded Italian stool, which was placed for her in front of his own cathedra under its Cloth of Estate. Having handed her into it, he waved away his few attendants and sat as well, allowing himself to look at Anne frankly. As always with this girl, he liked what he saw. After a moment Anne grew uncomfortable, a warm flush mounting up her neck and into her cheeks as he examined her face feature by feature.

"Tell me why you are not married yet, Lady de Bohun?" His directness shocked her, but she gathered her wits quickly for there was an opening here.

"Because, sire, that is my choice. I have no family to dictate where I should marry and I am minded to independence, which luckily my guardian, Sir Mathew Cuttifer, is happy to allow."

The duke smiled. He liked Sir Mathew. "Ah yes, your guardian. I believe he has returned to London?"

Anne nodded quickly. "He has, sir, and Lady Margaret, his wife."

"But please continue, Lady Anne. Why do you not wish to marry? Many of your compatriots worry for you, and that makes *me* concerned."

Anne blushed but somehow kept her voice steady. "Sir, it is my observation that ladies when they marry become absorbed into the lives of their husbands and their children. That is not my wish at this time."

"But perhaps you have not yet met the man who could

change your mind, Lady Anne." He was interested to see a strange expression chase over her face briefly—a yearning? "That was not well said. Forgive me. And sufficient answer to my impertinent curiosity. But I *am* curious, Lady Anne; why did you ask for this audience today?"

"To wish you joy of your marriage, sir, and, if you will permit me?" Anne rose and clapped her hands and the doors of the duke's Presence chamber were opened once more to admit a small procession. At its head was Ivan, magnificently dressed in a sweeping coat of many-colored furs, a pointed fur-trimmed felt hat on his head, and soft baggy breeches over red leather boots. They were the clothes of his country, which was still inhabited by fierce tribes of roaming horsemen, tribesmen, of which he'd once been part.

Ivan was carrying a large curved sword across his open palms sheathed in a scabbard of embossed gilded leather. Behind him marched Maxim, ceremoniously carrying a tiny silver box nestled on a velvet cushion, while beside him strode Leif Molnar, Sir Mathew Cuttifer's own Norse sea captain, the tallest man in the room by several hands' breadths. Leif, too, had a box, but his was made from black wood, ebony, patterned with a white inlay of African ivory.

And behind them both walked Deborah, proud and straight, bearing a bolt of peacock-blue silk and another of tissue of gold.

At a signal from Anne, her servants bowed low to the duke and then, one by one, brought forward the gifts they carried to lay at his feet.

"Duke Charles, these poor gifts are for you and your bride. Allow me to show you."

Anne lifted the scimitar and carried it to the duke. "This is from the Holy Land. It is reputed to be the very sword that one of my country's kings, Richard, the first of that name, used in the battle of Acre, even though it was a weapon of his enemies." Carefully, she slipped off the embossed, gilded leather scabbard to expose the beautifully chased, gleaming blade of white-blue steel. "It was forged in Damascus, and my people tell me it has a name. It is called Smiter of the Faithless, and the legend of its making says,

"He who bears this blade into battle will always be invincible." It is reputed to contain a bone from Elijah's hand in the pommel, under the great turquoise. King Richard had it put there."

She curtsied low and carefully placed the magnificent weapon across the duke's knees, beckoning Maxim forward.

As the steward advanced, the duke gently fingered the edge of the blade. It was marked like certain kinds of silk: a gift more than fit for princes.

"And here, Lord, some poor stones from the Levant with which to adorn your bride." Maxim knelt before the duke as Anne opened the tiny silver box in front of him. Nestled inside, gleaming with their own bloody light, were two square-cut rubies.

" 'A price above rubies,' I believe that is the quotation? You surely have surpassed even what the Bible might expect with these stones, Lady Anne. I am overwhelmed."

"To hear your gracious words for such trifles fills me with happiness, sire. Rubies, Your Grace, are a symbol to me of heart's blood: one drop for you and one for your bride."

As Maxim rose and backed away, Leif took a step forward and placed the black-and-white wooden box within reach of the duke's hand. Carefully, Charles lifted the lid of the little coffer and immediately the room was filled with the scent of roses and the heady smell of jasmine.

Inside there was a nest of tiny, stoppered bottles made from dark blue glass, and as Anne opened each one in turn, scent drifted like smoke. "Here, Your Grace, is ambergris from the Euxine sea. And this, attar of roses from the Lebanon. Jasmine from Palestine, gilly flower essence from France, myrrh from the Holy Land, and finally, this: the scent of violets, distilled from flowers that grow in our own heber."

When this last stopper was removed, the cool, green aroma of violets wove through the air like music as Anne scattered drops of the intense perfume around the Presence chamber.

"It is hard to tell which scent a woman may prefer, so here there are a number for the princess to choose from. I can always find more, or make more, if nothing here is to her taste."

A sensualist, the duke picked up the vial containing ambergris. "Come here, Lady Anne." The girl moved closer, curtsied to him, and he lifted one hand, gently rubbing a tiny golden bead of scent inside her wrist.

"There. This would suit you. You should always wear it—it has an intense, subtle beauty . . ." For a moment it seemed he would complete the sentence, but then he paused, contented himself with kissing the wrist that bore the ambergris, as Anne beckoned Deborah forward.

"Finally, Your Grace, we have something else, something to adorn your bride."

Deborah unfurled the bolt of peacock-blue silk, allowing it to spill, to ripple through her fingers. In that dim, quiet room, the luster of the cloth was a piece of sky trapped within darkness. And then she shook out the gold tissue. It floated on the air, insubstantial as a golden web.

"From the lands beyond India, my Lord, the land of the Khans. The gold tissue, if I may make so bold, will serve your bride as a veil or perhaps a light cloak when the weather is warmer. I am so delighted that our ships were able to arrive this morning, in time for me to proffer what I have on behalf of Sir Mathew Cuttifer, and myself."

"Lady, your kindness will not be forgotten. I have a portrait of the Princess Margaret, and I believe your choice of color will suit her marvelous well. Such an intense and brilliant blue; I have never seen its like, ever before."

"There are only two bolts like it in the world, so far as I am aware?" She looked questioningly at Maxim, who nodded discreetly, kneeling at the duke's feet.

"Maxim, our steward, was under personal instructions to find this silk in Florence, or not come home! I had heard tell of it, this shot, peacock blue, but never seen it before."

The duke was silent. These gifts would not have shamed a fellow prince, and for this girl to be the donor almost beggared belief. When his courtiers spread the word of this most remarkable extravagance the world would talk of nothing else.

"Lady Anne, your generosity, and that of your guardian, is

princely. My brother-in-law-to-be and my bride will also be most grateful. Perhaps you can advise me—I should like to present the Lady Margaret of England with a gown made from this most wondrous blue silk."

The duke had taken the bait! Now all Brugge would know of her goods and the frenzy of new trade would begin.

"Ah, sir, I should like to do that, but there is one small hurdle I must overcome."

The duke smiled. "Yes, Lady de Bohun?"

"Simply put, Duke Charles, I cannot trade as I would like to—as part of a joint venture with Sir Mathew, my guardian. The English merchants oppose us in this."

The duke looked sharply at the girl in front of him who was now modestly, steadfastly, gazing at his feet, as was proper.

"But, sire, they could not stop me trading, on behalf of my guardian." She was careful to speak humbly. "If I had your permission to sell our goods, the cargo just landed."

He laughed. She was breathtakingly frank; he found he liked her for it. "But would I not upset your trading community very much, Lady Anne, if I agreed?"

Anne, the blood booming in her head, became a little reckless. "It has happened before, has it not, Your Grace?"

The duke raised his eyebrows; she must have heard of the disputes between his father and the English. "And, honestly, sire, I feel these merchants are more than old-fashioned. Sir Mathew and I, we saw an opportunity they were too frightened to take up for themselves and we have landed our cargo first."

"And so you feel it is fair if I allow you to trade it?"

Anne nodded and, greatly daring, looked square into his eyes. He held that direct glance, until, after a moment she dropped hers.

"Hmmm. I do not like my merchants to be unhappy. Any of them. However, I like courage more." He laughed mischievously. "Very well, Lady Anne. You may trade this cargo, with my blessing. And assistance—if your English brothers become, how shall we say, a little agitated?"

Anne was so happy she could have kissed him, would have,

yet some tiny element of restraint just held her. Better to curtsy and leave. She had won.

And as she backed out from his presence, the duke agreed with the unspoken thought. Anne had beaten the English merchants with an excellent, a magnificent, throw of the dice.

He smiled naughtily. That would set the cat, a very attractive cat, into the dovecote. After all, the English were extremely troublesome, always had been, and just because he was marrying the sister of their king was no reason for them to become complaisant, especially considering their recent arrogance toward his city. He still bristled when he thought of some of the terms that had been forced on him when he'd asked them to return to Brugge.

Yes. Let the girl trade, let her see it through. She deserved it for courage alone. Then, later, he would see about her marriage. Such spirit was admirable, but perhaps, after a little experience of freedom, it would best serve to enliven the domestic sphere of some strong but lucky man.

He chuckled. That would be best, certainly. Anne de Bohun's competitive spirit, allowed free range for too long a time, might decimate the entire English trading community, and that would not be good for his city—in the long term.

But great fun to watch over the next few months!

# Chapter Thirteen

William Caxton was anxious. And very annoyed. His problem concerned clothing—women's clothing; specifically, Anne de Bohun's clever stratagem of offering free making of their dresses to every lady who bought material from her for the duke's wedding.

It had guaranteed customers, of course, far too many of them, especially since she'd also bought up the time, in advance, of every seamstress she could find between Brugge, Damme, Sluis, and even as far as Antwerp. In effect she'd treated the sewing women as if they were guild tradesmen with guaranteed rates—common sewing women!—and offered them all the same needlessly generous terms.

A scandalous idea, though he had to admit, very creative. No other merchant had thought so far ahead, of course—why would they? Now the result was that the cargoes of the rest of the English merchants, due to land at Sluis very soon, would most likely be ignored, and his companions would have risked their money, in the short term, for little or no reward.

Naturally, the English merchants had been furious when they'd heard, and William shared their anger. Whatever secret admiration he felt for Anne, he must persuade her to abandon this current game. She'd made her point, but undermining the long-term trading stability of her countrymen would earn their deepest enmity. She had to be careful. Desperate men goaded by outraged wives who could not persuade formerly loyal sewing women to work for them at any price were probably capable of anything.

Therefore, it had to be faced. She must be made to see the value of more conciliatory behavior to her unwilling colleagues, and he had been deputized to tell her so.

Truthfully, though, he wished he were anywhere else but here, about to knock on the door of Mathew Cuttifer's fine house on this dazzling spring morning. It was a day for pleasure, not for confrontation. He hated confrontation, especially with a pretty woman (Maud didn't count in that regard).

Therefore, he hesitated; he was quite hot and blamed his wife for laying out a particularly thick jacket, though, in truth, he'd not noticed when he'd dressed this morning. Damn the woman, she must have known he'd sweat. Perhaps she'd done it purposefully when he'd told her he had to visit Anne. There was no help for it, however. He couldn't take it off for this was a formal visit by the Governor of the English Merchant Adventurers to an illegal trader. He could not afford to look anything less than formidable.

Impatient with himself, he raised his hand and knocked sharply. It was only a moment before Maxim opened the door, but somehow it seemed an uncomfortably long time.

Anne was warm, too, going through Meinheer Boter's accounts. It had been an excellent month since the two ships had returned. And there was more to come because today she had arranged an especial viewing of a part of her cargo of silks, damasks, and the lighter "summer" furs, which had not been released yet: a viewing for the closest, most influential members of the duke's court.

Meinheer Boter was delighted, too, that Anne had been lucky with her ships—delighted and relieved to the point of actual physical weakness. As his ledgers spelled out the figures from this remarkable month's trading, his heart beat faster and faster, though he'd soberly, carefully, and diligently enumerated the goods sold, line by line, to his employer's ward.

Phlegmatic as he was, even he was amazed at the river of

good silver, gold, and copper coin flowing through the doors of
the trading house of Cuttifer and de Bohun; amazed, too, at the
nerve and composure of this young woman as she just as carefully,
item by item, checked the tallies with him.

Anne was more than content. "Enough, Meinheer. We have
more than enough. For that I am proud and happy—and grateful." They smiled at each other, relieved and grateful colleagues—
and conspirators!

Deborah knocked softly at the door of the workroom. "Mistress, Master Caxton has arrived and asks to see you." Her tone
was carefully neutral, but a fugitive little grin could not be suppressed.

Anne smiled broadly at her foster mother in return. "Master
Caxton? How very pleasant. Please ask him to join me, Deborah."

The chief clerk hurriedly closed up the ledgers that surrounded them both and bundled the sheaves of parchment back
between their wooden covers. Then, as Deborah showed William
Caxton through the door of the workroom, Meinheer Boter
bowed deeply, first to Anne and then to William, before hurrying
away, back to his own domain in the warehouse next door.

"Master Caxton, can we offer you elderflower wine?"

"Lady, I should be delighted. The perfect thing for a day such
as this." The man and the woman exchanged polite smiles as he
settled himself into one of Mathew's elegant chairs.

"The year has turned toward the sun at last, Master Caxton."

"Indeed. Gentle warmth enlivens all, although I have never
been fond of the great heats of high summer. I prefer the climate
of our native land."

He was reminding her of where her allegiance lay. Anne's
face did not change from the gentle, welcoming smile. "Do you
know, I think I agree with you, Master Caxton; though many
might see us as strange." For a moment the talk died between
them. They were both fencing to find the first advantage, but
Anne could wait for her visitor to speak—this meeting was at his
request, not hers.

Deborah stepped into the tiny silence with a silver salver on
which was a crystal flask, stoppered with a tiny, exquisitely made

dragon. There were two goblets as well, also of crystal, but of a deep rose. Caxton had seldom seen things so lovely, or so rare. It made him uneasy—they were symbols of Anne's success and the failure of his guild to match her in this battle for the wallets of the burgesses' wives of Brugge.

"A dragon for a stopper? Pretty. Why a dragon, mistress?"

"Oh, because I've never seen one, yet perhaps may, one day." William Caxton thought that a strange remark but said nothing. "And here you see the result. Do you find it pleasing?"

"The work is very fine—perhaps the best I've seen. Of its kind." They both smiled politely at each other, but Anne found it hard to suppress a giggle. *"Of its kind"* indeed! They both knew he'd never seen such a thing before in his life.

Involuntarily Caxton's eyes strayed to the painting on the wall. He'd heard about it; all Brugge knew about it in intimate detail, but it was the first time he'd actually seen the work itself.

"And this is very fine too. A charming likeness of you and your nephew."

And such a symbol of her growing self-confidence, he thought—the self-confidence that offended so many in William Caxton's trading community by its manlike unnaturalness. The merchant found himself sighing angrily at his own cowardice. Hard words must be said to this girl and it was his duty to deliver them, however much he might wish to avoid the task because he liked her.

Distantly a child could be heard crying from above stairs.

"Edward must have woken, Deborah. Would you see to him, please?" There was a brief pause as the woman left, then, "You seem troubled, Master Caxton?"

Very well. Fencing over now.

"Mistress, do you remember the conversation we had when I first told you of the duke's wedding?"

It was mesmerizing. Her hands gently stroking and stroking again the glimmering surface of the dress. He shook his head to clear the distraction.

Anne nodded, smiled faintly, but said nothing. He was forced to speak into the silence.

"The members of my guild, they are . . ." he cleared his throat. The choice of his next words was critical. "They are anxious. And puzzled."

Now she couldn't help herself. She had to laugh. Quite cheerfully, which unnerved William further. "Why, sir, are they puzzled?"

"By your behavior, Lady Anne. The steps you have taken to, er, control access to the milliners, the seamstresses."

"Trade, Master Caxton. Trade. That is what I am engaged in, with permission from the duke. I find that the offer of attractive terms to women who are accustomed to being treated very badly gives me a certain advantage. Forgive me for speaking plainly, but I do not believe any of our city's statutes prohibit me from the actions I have taken."

She was right, of course. She was in the stronger position, and had been as soon as the *Lady Margaret* and her companion vessel had docked at Sluis. Why should she give quarter to his companions in the guild when they'd given her none?

Idiots. They'd all of them, himself included, been idiots where this woman was concerned, but who could have known that then? He'd underestimated her and that hurt most.

She saw his confusion, though he tried to hide it, and took a little pity.

"May I give you more wine, Master Caxton?"

Perhaps the wine was stronger than it had seemed, for there was a buzz in his head; yet it might help this awkward conversation.

"A perfect drink for spring, your elderflower wine—pure and very bright."

The pale, brilliant liquid flowed like fine oil into the rose beakers, and involuntarily he was captured by the beauty of the moment—the crystal goblets, the radiance of the wine as it caught the slanting light from the window, the ivory hand gently returning the dragon to the neck of the flagon.

"So now, Master Caxton, let us leave this unpleasant matter and speak of other things. Things of advantage to us both."

There was the very slightest edge to her words. He could

sense power writhing like unseen smoke in this room. Very well.

"But there is something I can offer to you, and I have come to strike a price, Lady Anne."

The laughter was still light. "That may be so, but what could you have that I might need, Master Caxton?"

"Your life. If you cease to trade ahead of the duke's wedding." Reckless, badly said—he had never intended to be so unsubtle.

Around them the house was very quiet, though they could hear the cries of boatmen on the canal outside, calling for the bridge to be lifted up.

Anne was completely still; silent, considering.

Anxiety propelled Caxton over to the casement. It was open to the heber, and the scent of spring flowers came through into the room. He found he was breathing very quickly; he had to pause before he spoke next, frightened the words would dry in his throat.

"You see, mistress, I have been given knowledge. Knowledge shared by a very few members of my guild. You have enemies . . ."

Anne shrugged. He admired her for that. "This is not new, Master Caxton. I am protected. You know that." A flat statement of fact as her eyes fixed on his, unmoving. He could feel the blood rising to his face.

"Yes. However, we are not speaking of a forced marriage. This is very different. Powerful, very powerful people now know you live among us. They are not your friends."

Her eyes sharpened on his, but she refused to ask the question. He sighed again. "Lady, unless I win some accommodation for my brothers, they will not permit me to tell you what we . . . what is known."

Anne looked at him, through him, and he was suddenly shamed. He valued her good opinion, something he'd not realized until this moment.

"Well, Master Caxton, I am surprised. And dismayed. I have never expected that the merchants of your guild, and the others, would be friends of mine, especially now since they have shown themselves to be so chickenhearted and, yes, incompetent in the way they conduct their affairs. But I hadn't thought they'd be pleased to see me die over the issue of pretty clothes for their wives at a wedding."

Anne picked up a small silver bell that was beside her hand and rang it sharply. The door was opened by Ivan, his face impassive, even as the clean, shivering sound died in the air between them.

"Ivan, Master Caxton is leaving us. Please escort him to our door."

She rose and stood immobile, hands clasped gently at her waist as William Caxton turned away from the window.

He was upset, very upset, and it burned greatly, unjustly, that he had come here today against his own judgment—but still he had come and said what he'd said.

He could feel that his face was a burning red as he bowed to Anne and was embarrassed to see that her own was smooth, expressionless, not even flushed. Outside in the spring sunshine he actually felt he would vomit into the canal from the searing guilt he felt. And then there was anger. Mighty anger. Not for her, but for the fools he was tied to in the guild.

They were all cowards, and she was right. Chickenhearted she'd called them all, him included, and incompetent. How could he have thought she'd agree to the shabby terms he'd tried to offer? For a moment he actually contemplated knocking on the closed door, but then, fury propelling his steps to a march, he stalked away. He would go to the Markt, he would find the others and then . . . well, then they would have to think again.

After William Caxton left, Anne paced up and down. She was furious—outraged!—but also badly frightened by the malice and stupidity of the commercial rivals she and Mathew had taken on. Hurt worked like poison. It was sad and very lonely to be the eternal outsider, and a fearful darkness beckoned when she tried to imagine what it would be like to fight her rivals.

On the other hand, she had what she and her son needed to survive now. If she gave in to the guild, ceased to trade, it would be impossible to stay in Brugge, but she could start again. Somewhere else, she and Deborah and little Edward.

That made her shiver. There was risk to her child, either way.

The attack on the canal last winter had frightened her badly at the time, though Anne had never acknowledged it to herself, or anyone else. But with this new threat, could she really face the certainty of living with drawn blades her entire life? Shadows lurked in her past and now her present: beckoning shadows, greedy ghosts.

Like a phantom, like a wraith, a face took form from darkness. Elizabeth Wydeville. Edward's queen.

Was the wheel of fate turning again so that, like Anne's own mother before her, another Queen of England wished her to die because of the king, her husband?

Or was it now safer for Edward, for his throne, if she ceased to exist? Did he know about his son?

Brugge was the hub of northern Europe and news flowed through the Markt. Anne had often heard, in the last year, how the Kingdom of England continued unsettled, and how the rivalry between Edward and Warwick grew more poisonous; and also how the king had been a faithful husband to the queen for more than a miraculous year.

But Edward sat uneasy on the throne, so they said, his tenure challenged by rumors that the former French Queen of England, Margaret of Anjou, was planning to retake the kingdom with help from the French and reinstall the fugitive Henry VI, Anne's own father, the father she had never met, on the throne. And in this climate, Anne herself, and her son, Edward's son—his existence so far a secret—could, if she so chose, become a potent threat to Edward's reign.

Perhaps Warwick knew she was in Brugge. Was it he who had tried to kidnap her that night? As Henry VI's natural daughter, Anne knew that she and her son, the son of a king, could become the nexus of a new royal house. Just a quick forced marriage to one of Warwick's supporters—George of Clarence, for instance, the disaffected and jealous younger brother of the king himself—and it would be done. Perhaps Edward knew where she was and sought to kill her first. Perhaps that was easier: the pragmatics of politics and kingdoms winning over waning affection, dimmed by time.

Anne was queasy with the florid possibilities; these were formidable potential enemies, each one of them—and her life was worth a candle flame on a windy night if she was forced into play on the chessboard of England.

# Chapter Fourteen

 In London, Elizabeth Wydeville, the queen, was inspecting the contents of the jewel coffers that would travel with Margaret of England as part of her marriage dower. She was there at the invitation of Margaret's mother, Cicely, Duchess of York, and she was very annoyed.

Seemingly oblivious of her daughter-in-law's mood, Duchess Cicely was listing jewels from a long roll of finest calf-skin vellum, reading the description of each piece dispassionately, yet there was just the faintest glimmer of triumph in her tone, triumph that was causing England's queen to dig her nails into the palms of her very soft hands.

Elizabeth attempted to think cooling thoughts—ice in winter, hoar frost in trees, snow drifting to the ground—but it was not enough; she could have screamed from irritation, though she would not give the duchess such satisfaction. As usual Edward's foolish, blindly foolish, indulgence of his sister meant that her wishes, Elizabeth's wishes—the wishes of the Queen of England—were being disregarded yet again.

"Item: one collar of pearls—all pink—dependent rose-colored diamonds. Item: gold cloak pin, head thereof worked with diamonds to the shape of a sun, fully rayed about. Item . . ."

The list went on and on, many of the jewels items that Edward had promised to Elizabeth for her exclusive use from the treasury of England.

The queen simmered. Edward was weak—and blind! He

had not thought of her feelings, or, if he had, he'd thought it more important to placate his mother and sister! Seeing the queen compress her soft, pretty mouth into a thin line, the duchess read even more slowly, taking care to pronounce the name and kind of each jewel lovingly and clearly.

Edward strolled into this poisonous atmosphere unwittingly and was charmed by the graceful tableau he saw. Elizabeth was dressed in fashionable scarlet and black and was sitting in a gilded chair of state, the sun a halo for her yellow head.

The queen looked up as the women around her dropped into deep curtsies for the king. Edward smiled warmly, charmingly, and, reaching down, helped Duchess Cicely to her feet before bowing gracefully to his queen.

Elizabeth clenched her jaw violently to stop the scream.

Why even now did his eyes drop below her waist whenever he saw her! She'd been pregnant before—would looking at that small bump do anything to hasten the birth of a son? She was just an object—a pitcher to contain his precious seed. A pint pot! Not a woman—no, not that anymore; not the lover he had so lusted for—was it only so few years ago?

However, a warm and loving smile greeted the king when he looked up from his bow—so warm, he was astonished. "Dearest husband, your noble mother has been showing me the Lady Margaret's dower, from the treasury. But Edward, I am so worried."

"Worried, mine own heart?" The king grew nervous, there was something in the queen's voice.

The queen frowned charmingly and looked up into Edward's face, a picture of concerned duty and innocence.

"Yes, Edward—we shall look so shabby to the duke." Duchess Cicely looked up sharply, but before the king could reply, the queen swept on.

"Shabby—yes! The Lady Margaret is the sister of a king, the king of this great country, England, and yet we think fit to send her off to Burgundy with such shoddy trinkets in her dower! You know that Duke Charles has the most exquisite taste. He will think us poor and second rate if this is all we can send for her to wear at his court. And, besides, they will all laugh at her. Every one of these jewels is so old-fashioned—so badly made, even if some of the stones are passable—that they will think our rich and prosperous kingdom is but the fief of some petty little princeling who does not know how to look after his own family!"

The Duchess Cicely saw what was happening and hurried to intervene.

"Ah, but Your Majesty is too harsh; far, far too severe. These are fine jewels, very fine, it seems to me."

"Not fine enough, Duchess—not for our dearest sister-in-law and your daughter; you're just putting a brave face on it," the queen smiled charmingly at the duchess, implacable. "No, Edward—your mother's bravery must be rewarded. To have such a mother is a noble thing." Here the queen arose and curtsied to her mother-in-law, who, gritting her teeth, had to curtsy back more deeply.

"No, indeed, better must be found. Perhaps we can look at the treasure of some of the nobles at court. And yes—Duchess, I would not ordinarily express an opinion, as you know—because the Lady Margaret has no diamonds of her own worth speaking of, perhaps the York crown and collar of state might suffice? They are both very fine, and we none of us would feel ashamed for her to be seen in jewels such as these."

The duchess choked into a coughing fit, and as her attendants rushed to aid her, the king saw the trap he'd been led to.

"The York diamonds are part of the patrimony of my house, our house, Elizabeth. As a daughter of England, it is fitting my sister receive her dower from the treasure of England—not that of York."

Graciously the queen smiled. "But of course, my love. I quite understand your attachment to the jewels of your own house. Still, a mother is often sentimental about her daughter, as your dear mother most certainly is. It is understandable, is it not, if the duchess wishes to honor her child in this way . . . after all, we have seen the Lady Margaret wear the York jewels many times; indeed, I have often thought how well they do become her. As for the York coronet, I thought she looked touchingly sweet in it at my coronation. Oh please, Edward, make your sister happy, for the sake of this country."

"The only way I'd be happy is if I didn't have to go!"

Margaret had entered the Presence chamber, unheard by all of them because of her velvet house shoes.

Now the king was really angry. He had had enough from all of them, particularly from his sister. Sharply he clapped his hands and the breathless throng of courtiers and servants reluctantly trailed out of the room, desperate to know what was being said as the pikemen closed the doors of the Presence chamber behind the last of them.

"Margaret, this is nonsense. You are going because it's your duty to go. And, if there's any more fuss, I'll send you naked without one jewel to your name. The duke will like that!"

The three women heard the steel in the king's tone as Edward stamped over to his own chair of state and dropped into it. Would none of this end? Perhaps there would be some sort of peace when his sister was finally gone from court.

Then it came to him—the solution. He'd have some fun and do some good at the same time—he'd always liked Brugge!

"Very well, I have decided. To stop this nonsense from continuing, I shall take Margaret to her marriage. You will not disobey me when I hand you to your husband personally, sister."

The queen gasped; so did the duchess; his sister burst into tears.

"And before you all berate me with it—yes, I've changed my mind. This alliance is too important to be left to chance. I'm going, I shall personally give Margaret away and you, my dear wife, will remain in London as my regent—we must not risk the health of this child. And you, mother most dear, should return to York. Frail health is to be expected in one of your advanced years."

That made the duchess really, really angry—she was barely forty-five.

"For you are too precious to our kingdom for me to selfishly send you as my lone emissary on a long and dangerous sea voyage to Flanders. There. My final word."

And he got himself out of the room with great dispatch and as much dignity as he could muster, before any of the troublesome women in his life could gather themselves to reply.

There was a seething silence in his wake. Stiffly, after a moment, the duchess got to her feet and made a rigid curtsy to the queen, her daughter-in-law. Then, back straight, she left the chamber without even one more word, as did the Lady Margaret, gulping hard to swallow tears.

Elizabeth Wydeville watched them leave, white-faced. She had rarely felt such anger or indeed, such fear.

"Lacey! Lacey—I need you!"

The queen's chief body servant, a colorless woman who was heartily frightened of her mistress, slipped through the opened door and scuttled to the queen, bowing nervously. Elizabeth rarely raised her voice, but this was one of those times, the times they all dreaded.

"I want parchment and ink. And a quill. Now!"

Panicked by the queen's freezing eyes, her suddenly harsh voice, the woman bobbed a curtsy and rushed to obey.

"And a messenger! I want a king's man ready to ride for Dover as soon as I have done. You will bring him to me here and you will tell no one. No one at all."

Foolishly the woman dared to ask a question—she was only trying to be helpful.

"But must not the man tell the Sergeant of the Watch?"

"No!" The concentrated venom in the queen's glance made poor Lacey gasp with fear and she fled the room as quickly as thought.

Elizabeth Wydeville, Queen of England, twisted the seal ring on her left hand as the savage red rage ebbed only slightly. Fear took its place, lapping high in her chest.

This was a message she alone would write, she alone would send. It would be a cog in the great mechanism that turned the wheel of fate; she had set that engine running some little time ago. It was a powerful image, the wheel of destiny. The queen closed her eyes. Against all the odds, she had successfully ridden high and higher on the rim; surely she was rising on it still.

She relaxed. Even smiled. Destiny was her friend because she had the courage to shape her own fate. And that of others.

She'd done it before, and now, she'd do it again.

# Chapter Fifteen

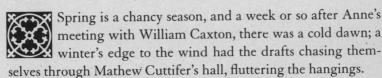 Spring is a chancy season, and a week or so after Anne's meeting with William Caxton, there was a cold dawn; a winter's edge to the wind had the drafts chasing themselves through Mathew Cuttifer's hall, fluttering the hangings.

Anne slept late and Deborah made sure that none of the household disturbed her. Ivan had been banished to the stables and Edward taken downstairs while still asleep, to find himself waking in the kitchen—hungry already as a fine piece of bacon broiled for his breakfast.

So it was very quiet as Anne began to wake, and for one eerie moment she did not recognize her room, did not know where she was.

And in that half-dreaming world it seemed she heard someone, something calling her name. Something so big, so dark, so frightening that she jerked awake and forced her eyes open. As if to stay asleep would cost her life, and more. .

Heart hammering, she sat up and before rational thought, ran over to the window seat and flung up the lid. There, inside, folded neatly under a pile of fresh linen shifts, was a faded but serviceable cloak. Impulsively Anne burrowed out the old worsted garment and buried her face in it, sudden tears blurring her vision as she inhaled the scent of lavender and wormwood in the folds.

"Anne?" Quick steps behind her and now Deborah was there, cradling and soothing.

"Now, sweeting, what's this, what's this? It's not so bad, not so bad now."

But it was, there was terror and it was coming for her—Anne was certain of that, waking or dreaming.

When life seemed impossible, as the bad dreams sometimes made her feel, Anne sought solace in the one thing left behind that her mother had worn. The cloak.

Alyce de Bohun, her mother, had been wearing it the night that Anne was born, the same night she had died. Deborah had kept the cloak during Anne's childhood at her cottage in the forest, and though it had been carefully washed, it was still faintly stained from her own birth blood, her mother's life blood. In exile, Deborah had given it back to her foster daughter—only the two of them knew of its existence.

If only she could wrap herself in its folds and become invisible, or, as some witches were said to do, put it on and fly away. Fly away to some foreign land where she was not known and could begin again, in safety and peace.

"Since you've missed Mass today, child, would you like me to bring you food?"

Deborah was frightened by Anne's wild sadness. Instinctively she tried to wind the rituals of a normal day around her foster daughter. Doing what you knew, what was expected, helped sometimes.

But Anne covered her face with her two hands and for a moment did not speak. Then, as calmly as she could, "I should like water to rinse my mouth, please, Deborah, and I will need to dress for the day. We have much to accomplish this morning."

But then it was too much, all of it, and she found herself clinging to Deborah, rocking in her arms, sobbing like a brokenhearted child.

The bells were tolling for None by the time Anne was settled in the working chamber.

"Maxim, have we received any replies?"

Maxim shook his head; he admired Anne's composure. To have heard her ask the question, so apparently casual, so unconcerned, was an act of courage. He knew how high the stakes had become recently between Anne and the English merchants, for Anne had decided to commission a special Mass in celebration of the future marriage of the Duke of Burgundy to the Lady Margaret, sister to the King of England. It would be held in the Speelmanskapel—the Minstrels' Chapel—in two days' time, and Anne had humbly asked that her countrymen, the merchants of the English Merchant Adventurers, join her and share in this joint celebration.

Anne nodded calmly. "No doubt we'll hear by tomorrow. Pass me the ledger for cloth sales, please, Maxim."

Quietly and resolutely, she and Maxim pursued their tasks together, each noting Meinheer Boter's very satisfying tallies of all their commercial activity this month, which continued unabated, and comparing them with the same figures of a month ago.

Anne exercised rigid discipline to keep her mind on the task, but unconsciously, her despair clamored for expression. For weeks and weeks she'd been building the hope that she and Edward would meet again at the wedding. Duke Charles had invited her to all the major festivities, and she, too, had had the seamstresses working day and night to make her new clothes, clothes with which to dazzle not only all of Brugge, but the King of England also, the man she loved.

But if William Caxton's warning was true, if she were to be murdered . . .

"It's not true, you know."

She was jolted out of introspection by a warm laugh and turned to find the friar, Father Giorgio, laughing at her from the doorway of the parlor. "Whatever you are thinking, it's not so bad as you think. It may never happen. In my experience God is good. Most things we care about, really care about, turn out well."

Anne did not comment as she carefully finished the last of the notes she was making in the margin of a ledger.

"There, Maxim—this is the last. Please return them all to Meinheer Boter, if you please."

Quickly and efficiently Maxim gathered up the great, wooden-bound books and, bowing respectfully to the friar—whom he did not particularly like; he was far too polished for a priest—hurried out. He'd have a word with Deborah shortly, though. He didn't like to see Anne so down, so worried, even if she thought she was hiding her low spirits from them all.

The priest strolled over to Anne's worktable and sat, elegantly disposing his robes to form pleasing folds.

"Now, dearest girl—so much work, so little joy. This is not our Lord's intention, no matter what some of my brethren might say. He gave us life that we might live. Not to hide away and frown and frown over figures and dry parchment!"

Anne forced herself to laugh, but it hurt her throat and chest. Suppressed tears burned like hayseeds in her eyes.

"Perhaps you have an easier time with Him than I do, Father. You have faith. Sometimes mine is not strong enough."

The friar looked sharply at the girl sitting in front of him, outwardly so composed, but pale, too pale for spring, the season when the blood should rise like sap.

"Perhaps I can help you, dear Lady Anne. As your guest, I can also be your confessor—if that would help you carry this burden. I am your friend, am I not?"

Anne had been pretending to busy herself tidying up the surface of her worktable, but now she stopped and her eyes strayed to the painting on her wall. Edward's blue eyes peered into her own; she shivered. What was the message, what was he trying to say to her?

"Yes, Father, you are my friend. And very precious to me."

"And so, therefore, if I am your friend, tell me, so that I may help your soul find peace."

Anne shook her head.

"You English! So stubborn! Very well. It is a man, of course."

Such an innocent request and so slyly dropped into the conversation that it took Anne's breath away—she choked and the friar laughed delightedly.

"And so! There! I was right. Now, we shall speak of this, you and I, when you are ready. Shall we say, perhaps, after the midday bell has sounded? Or shall we say now?"

Anne laughed out loud—he was outrageous. And then, of course, she felt better and the tears receded deeper into her body.

"Well then, Father, this is not a confession; it cannot be, because I do not want penance for what I am about to tell you."

The friar crossed to the door and gently closed it, signaling to Ivan that no one should be allowed entrance.

"I am listening, my friend—but I shall treat this as the confessional, believe me. There shall be silence on this to all but us."

Anne was looking out into the walled heber, unconsciously seeing, but not seeing, the nodding mass of spring flowers. There were tulips, clematis, the first rosebuds, and the last daffodils—the bulbs brought from England. She saw them all, but in each flower there were faces—Edward's face, Elizabeth Wydeville's face, Mathew Cuttifer's, and even William Hastings's. The illusion was so real that when the flowers suddenly moved in a passing breeze, it was as if each person she saw were turning to look at her accusingly.

"Ah, Father—how shall I begin? There is so much—and so little."

"Begin with the largest of all, the thing you are most frightened of, my child."

"Death, Father Giorgio. I am frightened of death."

"So are we all, lady. Even if we believe we are not. But you are young—and will live long."

He was solemn now, this sleek friar, and his eyes were black in his smooth, white face. Uncanny to see this laughing, worldly man—this funny, witty priest addicted to fine fashion and gossip—so serious.

"I am not as you see me, Father. And because my past is not what anyone could ever believe or understand, I am a threat to many people. Some would like to kill me, it seems—I have been warned—and yet I do not know who that person is."

"Well, then, it will be a simple enough matter to find out, will it not? Money works its way, and I who travel so very widely have many, many contacts. Tell me, give me the word, and we shall have the knowledge you seek. Perhaps very soon, if I can send enough of my friends out and about this world of ours."

Was it really so simple? Anne shook her head. How could she have been so slow? Of course, the friar was right—that was what was needed—information! And, yes, now she did have the means to buy it.

Did not the Bible say God would help those who were prepared to help themselves?

# Chapter Sixteen

It was the day of the service that Anne had commissioned to celebrate the royal wedding, and she waited nervously for her guests to arrive. Would any actually come?

The Minstrels' chapel itself, her chosen venue, was a small, charming building and quite modern—barely forty years old—and the great prosperity of the guild was clear in the beauty and quality of its adornments. Painted and gilded glass windows, most notably Christ, a smiling guest at the wedding feast of Cana—a choir of unmistakably Flemish minstrels providing the entertainment—plus the substantial plate and silver furnishings on the altar, were all designed to impress even the most worldly observer.

Anne, courtesy of her own recent prosperity, had dressed soberly in rich, dark blue broadcloth—good English cloth of the best quality. Her sleeves were lined in scarlet velvet, one discreet note of color that would only be seen when she moved her hands to join them in prayer during the mass.

As she stood at the door of the chapel, Anne's face was calm, but her heart hammered painfully behind the bones of her chest. None of the English traders had arrived and time was passing, but just as it seemed they would have to begin the Mass without its invited guests, William Caxton hurried toward her, accompanied by a number of the principal English merchants of Brugge. Not all of them, but enough.

Anne composed her face into a bland, calm smile and was

careful to curtsy to each one of the men who reluctantly filed past her into the body of the little church.

The Mass itself was gloriously sung, not only by the Minstrels' own priest, Father Jochen, but also by a choir of guild minstrels especially commissioned by Anne. However, at the time when the homily would normally have been given, Master Caxton himself advanced to the altar and, bowing to the priest, turned to face the congregation. Anne was surprised and affronted—this was not what she had planned.

"Dear friends and fellow countrymen, on behalf of Lady Anne de Bohun"—Anne raised her eyebrows; so did most of the congregation—"I bid you welcome to this special service. Soon the Lady Margaret of England, sister to our king, will become the most noble Duchess of Burgundy, and by this marriage, England will be united in ever stronger bonds to the great fiefdom of Burgundy. After all our recent troubles with this great house, we are now on the crest of a remarkable time in our lives, a time that can benefit us all, or, perhaps, destroy us if we do not change our ways."

His colleagues were shocked, and an angry mutter began, mouth to mouth, but William raised his voice. "Lady Anne de Bohun has asked us all to be present today at this Mass to celebrate a wedding, a new beginning. That is what we need, for surely if we do not accept this gift of peace, it may be that Duke Charles turns his face away from us, as his father did, and that would be a tragedy. His support of the lady who has commissioned this service should give us pause; and she is our compatriot."

Anne was astonished. William Caxton had decided to support her in this most public of ways, but he had no easy time of it. There was a rising hubbub, to the scandal of the priest and the choristers, which William had trouble talking over. "In token of this day, on behalf of the entire English merchant community, all of us, Father Jochen will read this special blessing."

The congregation of merchants was now thoroughly enraged. They'd all agreed with the offer Caxton had made to Anne on their behalf, but many had been uncomfortable with it, just as he was, and now they felt humiliated, shamed. And shame can be close to fury.

Father Jochen cleared his throat. He was, in all honesty, quite frightened. He began in a quavering voice, "Dearest Father, we ask that you look with favor upon the marriage of thy servants, Margaret, Lady of England, and Charles, Duke of the noble house of Burgundy. May their union be long, happy, and fruitful. May they be supported in all that they attempt by loyal and loving subjects and friends. And to this end we, the fortunate band of English merchants in Brugge, pledge that every year upon the anniversary of the date of the said marriage, will come together for a Mass of thanksgiving. And, at each Mass we shall give and bequeath a certain sum for the welfare of the sick, the widowed, the orphaned, and the poor of this noble city—in the name of the Duchess Margaret to be.

"And, Holy Father, we ask that you keep this noble company in harmony, each one with another, and to that end if among us there be dissension, double dealing, or treachery, we ask that thy wrath be visited on all those who foment this wrongdoing, or who stray from the path laid down by you, in their work. Otherwise, if the work of the English merchants in Brugge is pleasing to you, we ask that you continue to bless your faithful servants with prosperity, the better to serve you. May we be friends to the friendless, fathers to the fatherless, protectors to the helpless and to all women; and in token of which we swear these oaths, in thy name, on the relics of your saints and martyrs. Amen."

The priest bowed to the altar and then to the congregation, as Master Caxton spoke once more.

"Friends, I bid you all to a reception at my house to mark this most auspicious occasion. You will find litters at your disposal outside the chapel."

More than one English merchant looked mutinous. It was one thing to agree to come to a church service but another to be forced to socialize with Anne. It placed each one of them at a grave tactical disadvantage in the war that was being waged for their share of the river of gold that now flowed through this packed city.

However, Anne had already taken her position at the door of the chapel, where William joined her, and both nodded courteously to each man who passed.

Ten or so beautifully adorned litters were waiting outside the chapel, patient teams of men dressed in the Caxton livery standing beside the poles. It was an impressive sight.

Embarrassed and angry as they were, the English merchants found it hard to avoid Caxton's penetrating gaze and so, eventually, in ones and twos, they were carried away—not one of them with a happy face. Caxton relaxed fractionally and breathed a deep sigh as he handed Anne into the last of the litters, intending to walk beside it. She'd purposefully dispensed with her guards today as a visible symbol of her trust in reconciliation with the English merchants.

"Mistress, you cause me great trouble."

Anne laughed shakily. "Ah yes, but our colleagues cause you more. No doubt this little exercise has put you to considerable expense and pain."

"Warranted though. To stop a war in the making—if I can."

"If you can—that remains the question. There were things that I wished Father Jochen to say at the end of that service— about my desire for coexistence among us all; though he was also to say that I thought their behavior toward the House of Cuttifer was shameful in God's eyes. But he chose your words. I wonder why that was?"

She was not looking at him as she talked, graciously smiling and waving at those she knew in the street as the litter men found their way through the city's market-day crowds.

"A desire for lasting peace, perhaps. And the fact that the Minstrels' Guild wishes to add a new bell to their carillon. I told them the English merchants would be happy to contribute to the cost in return for the blessing I gave him to say. Don't blame Father Jochen. I said I had your approval. Now I just have to tell our colleagues they're contributing to the bell—as well as the orphans and widows of this city."

That made her laugh out loud.

"Have you forgiven us?" He was impetuous, looking down into her eyes.

Embarrassed, Anne flicked her glance from his. "Yes, I've forgiven you. Them?" She shrugged. "I'm trying. I know I have to. I will, if they will." There was the flicker of a tight smile between them. Caxton sighed.

"They're not bad men, but change is difficult for them. They're bewildered by you." As he was also, yet he still felt shame for the actions of his colleagues and he wanted her to know that. "The first steps have been taken toward reconciliation, but there is still danger. For us all."

Then Anne saw him. The man with the crossbow. Standing in an upstairs window of one of the inns that lined the Markt Square. She watched him in one frozen moment aim and then release his quarrel.

She saw the feathered bolt as it came at her; saw the small, dark blur against the light; watched him turn back into the darkness of the room behind, so sure he'd aimed true.

Anne threw herself back to the edge of the litter, but the jolt was like a fist, and then fire, as the steel head of the quarrel sliced into her flesh, nicking bone in its passage into her side.

It was the padding in her sleeves that saved her, plus the missal she'd been holding. The ivory covers of her prayer book were bound with gold wire and set with cabochon jewels; the quarrel was deflected by a small ruby. It gouged into her side beneath her arm, but it did not find her heart, though blood sprang from between her ribs like a fountain.

They were screaming, but Anne heard little. The world was slipping, slipping away into darkness, sliding into a dream. The soft breeze was on her face, then—nothing.

# Chapter Seventeen

It hurt badly, jagged and deep, and she screamed herself into the light. Like a child being born.

"Hush, hush. Over now. Sleep little one . . ." They were the words you said to a child, of course, and perhaps that fitted. She was, after all, very young. Perhaps they would feed her the nice warm milk and she would sleep again. She opened her eyes although she didn't want to. Pain was bad, and stupid. No mind behind pain, it just was.

There they all were, clustered around this vast black bed. It wasn't her bed, but she knew the people there. Maud Caxton, for one, didn't like her.

Maud? Anne sat up quickly when William's wife's face sharpened focus, but the pain surged up her side again, filling her mouth with blood and hot bile. Vomit burned her throat, but pride closed her teeth. There was no way that Maud would see her retch.

"Dame Caxton. And Master Caxton," yes, he was there too. "My thanks for your help." The words came out of her own mouth, from between her own teeth, she was certain of that, but where they came from was impossible to say. With great relief she saw that Deborah was beside her. Her foster mother looked very worried, which was foolish, for Anne could see the crossbow bolt now, lying in a bowl filled with blood. Probably her own blood. Still, better the thing was out of her. She could sleep now.

"Yes, we should let her sleep, that will be best. We shall know very soon if the wound is to suppurate. Then she can be bled to remove the evil humors." William Caxton sounded quite calm—he surprised himself.

"No. There will be no more bleeding. Strength is what she needs, healing!"

Anne did not open her eyes, but she smiled. She knew that tone—Deborah rarely raised her voice, but this was one of those rare times.

There was an astonished intake of breath. That would be Maud, thought Anne contentedly, as her husband hurried to intervene.

"Maud, we have guests. Guests who are very worried about this dreadful event."

"No, they're not." Anne was very matter of fact, but for the people in that room, the private bedchamber of Maud and William Caxton, it was as eerie as if a corpse had spoken.

"And we should return to them, allowing our Lady Anne to sleep, and recover."

Anne heard the agitated rustle as Maud snatched up her skirts and left the room with William, barely closing the door before berating him in an angry hiss as their footsteps receded. Only then did Anne open her eyes and find Deborah. Very gently her foster mother stroked one of the girl's hands, trying very hard not to cry.

"There now—not so bad. It's happened, the thing we feared . . ."

Anne was surprised at the pain of talking, but if she did not breathe very deeply, perhaps it would be easier.

"We know it's real now, the threat. Wasn't just kidnap, before. Stop crying, Deborah. Makes me sad."

Deborah smiled a watery smile, but dense, black despair was very close. The iron head of the quarrel was rusty and had burrowed deep; the doctor who'd been summoned had poked Anne's side with filthy fingers, searching for it, and Deborah would have to work fast to undo the infection that would surely follow this "treatment." She might be too late if Jenna did not arrive with her salves very soon.

Downstairs among his fellows, William Caxton was deeply, deeply ashamed. Upstairs in his bedchamber, Anne lay dying—he was convinced of that—and here in his fine hall there was a group of men, his colleagues, God help him, who could not meet his eyes.

They were all superstitious. The admonition and blessing at the chapel of the minstrels had been made in their name. They were all indirectly responsible for the attack on Anne—they had kept vital knowledge from her—and now, perhaps, God would punish them where it would tell the most: their businesses.

"We must make amends. If she dies, we deserve to be hanged and damned. All of us." William was blunt, but none of them spoke in response. He was right and they didn't know what to say.

Maud Caxton, however, was furious. Once she had seen that her unwilling guests had been given refreshment, her husband had hurried her out of the hall, their hall, insisting she must stay in the anteroom behind closed doors until he called her again.

She knew what was happening. He was about to do something really foolish, out of guilt. Something that would undoubtedly compromise them and their house just because that wretched Anne de Bohun had nearly got herself killed.

She didn't like Anne—it was outrageous that she had no sense at all of what was appropriate. All she did was upset the men and enrage the women, and justly so. There was a story here, undoubtedly. People didn't get shot at in broad daylight traveling home from church unless they had done something to merit it.

And now this wretched girl was under her own roof, bleeding all over her good sheets, and likely to stay for some days. Her lily-hearted husband had refused to have Anne removed to her own perfectly good house, such a short distance away, and so they'd have to sleep in the children's dorter tonight. And if the girl died under their roof, they'd never hear the end of it. Truly life was unfair.

"Life is unfair, my friends, and cruel, but we must face the consequences of our own actions. The girl who is dying in my house outtraded us all. Our greed has caused this calamity for we could, perhaps, have prevented it. If, by great good fortune, she lives, I feel I am released from my obligation to our guild. She must know what we know, and we must protect her from future harm."

That made them all sit up straighter. Hitherto they'd been lolling on long forms drawn up to trestles loaded with food intended to be a celebratory reconciliation feast after the service in the Minstrels' Chapel.

"William, we all respect you. And what has happened today is a crime, a sin against God." Hurriedly the merchants crossed themselves as John Fuller, well known for his choler, spoke up for them all. "But perhaps it is His own will in action we have seen today. It is unnatural for this woman to trade. She has been struck down, perhaps by His own hand. Did anyone actually see the archer?"

There was a murmur of "I didn't," "No, indeed," "Not me . . ."

"God's will?" William Caxton's voice took on a freezing quality. "God's will! So, John, you believe God himself punished Lady Anne de Bohun for making you personally, and each one of us here, look like a fool? Is that what you think?"

John Fuller looked embarrassed, but he was truculent.

"The Bible tells us that God moves in strange ways. What that girl does is condemned in the Bible, and well you know it. A woman should be subject to her father or her husband, even her brother, if she is not married, and be directed by them."

William held up the bolt from the crossbow, bloody at its iron head, and in two swift strides had shoved it under John's nose.

"So this is the instrument of God's will, is it? Do you smell that, John? Blood. The blood of an innocent girl. You know and I know that she is blameless. And we also know who is likely to have done this. If she survives, we will tell her so. Perhaps you believe you are a servant of God, but by his bones I smell sulphur when I stand next to you."

John Fuller was a bully but not a courageous man, and he was the first to drop his eyes from those of his furious host, but he felt bitterly resentful at being singled out. *Let William Caxton beware,* he thought; *he is alone in his support of the Devil's siren who lies upstairs in his own bed.*

Fuller was wrong.

Of the twenty or so men who were uncomfortably clustered

together in William Caxton's hall, more than half felt as their host did, and as information about the attack in their own town square flew around Brugge, William was touched to find much support for Anne as he left his house later in the day.

Anne, it seemed, was liked by the Bruggers, more than could be said for many of his own colleagues. As he left his door, two sewers, women who'd worked for Anne, hurried up to him with a basket of spring produce from their own gardens plus precious comb honey and new eggs. They had heard the news and their urgent, genuine concern touched William's heart. He promised to let Anne know of the special prayers her friends the seamstresses would say, day and night, until she recovered.

Other women, too, from all parts of the town, ran out of their houses, from behind their market stalls, from their gardens, as he walked past; Meinheer Memlinc's housekeeper, fish women, spinners, weavers, lace makers, even the Sisters from the house of the Beguines on the Minnewater—all desperate for news, all pressing little gifts into his hands to give to Anne.

William Caxton reflected soberly as he walked with his new burdens: would he inspire the same compassion, the same concern when he lay dying?

Mathew Cuttifer's house was orderly and quiet when Master Caxton knocked at the great door. It was opened by Maxim, still pale from shock, but the very silence inside—no sound from little Edward, no sight of any of the staff—made William very sad. "Is all well with the affairs of this house, Maxim?"

"Of course, sir." William sensed the dread that stalked the words.

"The doctor is optimistic, Maxim. He removed the head of the bolt, and your mistress was asleep peacefully when I left. Deborah and Jenna are both with her. We can only wait now; she is young. And strong, as you know."

"Yes, sir." Maxim's response was colorless. He knew, just as William did, how likely it was for a wound to turn poisonous, whatever the age of the victim.

"Very well. I have been sent by my wife to ask for some of Lady Anne's things. I have a list. I wanted to come myself."

Maxim nodded and escorted William into Anne's workroom, bowing him to a chair beside the small, sputtering fire.

"And the little boy, Maxim?"

"He is well cared for, sir. And blessedly, too young to understand the sorrow of this house. I shall have refreshments brought to you, sir."

He was gone before William could refuse the offer of food; he could not eat. After today, it felt as if he would never be hungry again, especially when he looked at Meinheer Memlinc's masterwork, and the face of the girl who lay dying in his bed.

# Chapter Eighteen

There was an odd smell and a high voice chanting words she thought she knew but could not form as the whole side of her body burned. Fear ran like acid as the cold hands held her down, for she could hear a wild sea rising through the sound of the fire; the smell of wet wood burning was like pain.

There was a man's face in the smoke, eyes closed. Then they were open: empty black yet bright, like frost on a whetstone, like night sky; but when she saw his open mouth she whimpered, for his teeth were sharp and bloodstained.

He danced toward her smiling, the black knife in his hand to cut her heart out, the rope to hang her with.

She struggled, but being tied, could not move. She screamed; screamed and screamed. He was closer, blood-rank breath in her face.

No! She would not be the sacrifice, would not be pressed down into the coldwater bog at the crossroads, mud and stones in her mouth. Travelers would never step on her bones, never grind her down into the unforgiving dark. Let them try, she could call on friends, powerful friends, she would fight! She struck at his face when he leaned over her, made talons of her fingers to slash at his eyes, his wicked eyes.

Deborah was desperate. Anne was delirious, raging and arching her body against the fever, the aching goad of infection. Rosemary and banewort burned in the heart of the fire as Deborah prayed to the Goddess Aine, the Mother, the nurturer—since entreating the Lady Mary, holy patroness of Brugge, had done no good thus far.

"Blessed Mother, let this girl live. My life for you, freely given. Life for life: the old way. Life for life, Mother."

The old way, and the new. Perhaps there was power in both; the thought wove its way through Deborah's tears, her terror. Did not the pale Christ, himself a victim of powerful men just as her daughter was, give his life for others? A small coal of hope flickered to life in her heart, taking energy from the prayer.

But Anne screamed and reared up against the bolster, alone in a blood-red world. Deborah, despairing, lay down beside the girl and held her, held her, rocking, soothing, chanting, crying out for help, for guidance.

She'd tried every treatment she knew: she'd stopped the bleeding with a strong simple boiled down from salt, old wine, and acorn cups and then packed a paste of ground elder leaves, comfrey, and dried powdered rosemary into the wound, and stopped it up with garlic and honey smeared on together. Then she'd bound sphagnum moss soaked in a garlic tea over the wound and held it in place with all the cobwebs she could find under clean linen strips. But still the blood and foul pus seeped, and the fever burned—hot and dry.

Desperate, Deborah filled a silver bowl with clean water. She saw nothing until, at last, light dazzled her. Light that came from inside the water.

The humming radiance filled her like a beaker as she'd asked the question, "Who? Who has done this thing?" but there were no pictures, nothing to see, only a sense that much danger lay outside the light and around the girl, a wraith on the black, shadowed bed.

Now they were alone, these two, alone. The fire in William Caxton's room burned low as wind hunted the sharp casements of the house on that first night.

Three more nights and days wore away. Then, on the morning of the fourth, Deborah woke, stiff, as cold light seeped past the shutters. Her first sense was pain—cramped muscles from holding Anne's body close for hours and hours; then horror gripped her. The girl was very cold and a dry, twittering whisper filled the corners of the still-dark room.

Panicked, Deborah sat up, pulling Anne's rigid body against her chest. There was no breath. Nothing. No pulse. The girl lay like marble in her arms.

Deborah understood the whispering: spirits were waiting. She'd heard them before in a stone-barrow tomb of the oldest people: cold, dry voices, breath like snow on the wind.

"No!" Deborah pressed her mouth over Anne's, holding the girl closer than a baby to her chest. "Anne, Anne come back. Anne! Hear me!"

It was a command, sent with all the skill Deborah knew, but Anne was a long, long way away.

She was happy. It was warm where she was, and the fear and pain were gone. The place was beautiful: a green, soft field graced with red poppies. There was a silver river with great trees on its banks, greater even than the forest of her childhood where the trees had been giants. She was waiting, love in her heart, for her mother. Alyce was coming; she would see her very soon and she was so excited. Then she frowned. Someone was calling her.

"Anne, Anne, by all the powers that were and are, I call you . . ."

The voice was so sorrowful that Anne frowned, though the sound was only a whisper on this drowsy, beautiful day. Soon she would not hear it, soon her mother would be with her and nothing would ever separate them again . . .

"Anne, come back to me." The voice was a sigh, a breeze through sweet grasses, nodding the flowers as Anne saw the faces. There was her mother, her much-loved though never seen mother—a girl, younger than she was now—and another woman. Deborah. Both were gazing at her with infinite love, infinite sadness, but then her mother's face and Deborah's were the same and the meadow disappeared.

The scream was so despairing that William Caxton was jerked from his sleep beside Maud in the children's dorter, and when he hurried through the door of his erstwhile bedchamber, his worst fears were given flesh. There was Deborah, weeping and keening over Anne's corpse in his fine carved bed; but then the girl sobbed a deep breath, her chest rose and fell. And she screamed, like a lost soul, as she opened her eyes at last.

"No, ah no."

Deborah's agony was over but Anne's was fresh—another wound.

"She lives . . ." William Caxton hardly dared breathe the words, the relief was so immense. Anne turned her head toward the sound, still disoriented and made desolate by loss. A few moments more and she would have touched her mother, held her hand. All she felt now was searing, breathless, helpless pain.

Gently Deborah slipped an arm around the girl's frail body to help her as Anne looked up into her eyes, oblivious again of the man at the door.

"You have my mother's eyes." Her voice was a breath . . .

Quiet tears slid down Deborah's face as Anne's expression transformed into a faint smile—pale lips in a white face, but the pain cleared for the first time since she'd been shot. "I can sleep now."

And deep, dark sleep took her into a place mercifully free from dreams.

Leaving Deborah to care for Anne, William Caxton dressed thoughtfully as Maud woke to scold their noisy children and complain to her husband yet again about the permanent guest in their own quarters. William's servant Mathias was diligently scraping his master's face with a well-whetted knife, removing the hot oil that was supposed to make taking the bristles easier, and doing his best not to look interested as his mistress, in a lengthy tirade, was breathtakingly frank about the character and ambitions of the girl in the room beside the children's dorter.

" . . . and it's not as if we haven't been good to her, William. No one could ask more, but if she's recovered, surely we should get her people to remove her to her own bed. She'll do better there—after all, it's said whores only flourish in their own stew."

William was very annoyed, yet he should have been accustomed to Maud's jealous lack of charity. After all these years together, he knew to his cost that it was a waste of time to expect his wife to see the world as he did. He controlled himself with considerable effort.

"Maud, we shall speak on this matter after Mass. For now, we must be grateful that the Lady Anne, our guest, has survived. Enough, Mathias. You've flayed me!"

Mathias rapidly bowed and backed himself out of the room, scurrying down to the kitchen to spread the fresh gossip about Anne. Yet another source of annoyance to William Caxton: Mathias, while he had many qualities, was a chronic gossip.

William Caxton turned on his wife. "When you come to meet Saint Peter you will remember and rue this day, wife! For now, I expect you to recall your wedding vows. You will obey me, as you promised to do. I want the sheets on our bed changed and nourishing food prepared for Lady de Bohun—and I want it done now. Or, by God, you will feel my wrath."

Maud for once was silenced. She'd never been beaten by William—normally he was a patient, courteous man, but today was different and she felt an almost pleasant thrill of anticipation at his unexpected response. In a long, boring marriage, anything new and different was to be welcomed. Normally there was an unspoken agreement between husband and wife that she had permission to goad William with her requests—she nagged and cajoled and nagged again—and it was his role eventually to accept and agree, though out of pride he rarely gave her everything she wanted.

Today, though, was different. When he thought about it later, he saw this was the action of guilt. For days now it had been easier to focus on his wife's callous behavior than address what had to be done, for that was proving very difficult to face.

Soon Anne must leave his house and he could not protect her anymore. Therefore, he must seek an audience with Duke Charles and ask his advice, for Anne's shooting was a fearful matter. William Caxton did not want, past a certain point, to betray his English trading partners in their underhand dealings, but a much greater wheel was turning now, and if he and his family, and Anne, were to avoid being crushed under that iron rim, he must speak to Duke Charles.

God grant that he, the messenger of bad tidings, not be shot also.

# Chapter Nineteen

 On this warm spring day with more than a feel of summer, Duke Charles felt smiled upon by all the gods at last.

When he had much to think about, hard exercise made him cheerful, and this morning after Mass, he and some of his affinity had taken turns at the quintain, running course after course, watched by a small group of friends and companions from the court. And while many of his young companions had been belted out of the saddle by the returning arm of the wooden warrior, Duke Charles himself had escaped. Thirty-five might be getting on in some people's eyes, but his own timing, his vigor, had never been better—of that he was certain.

And now, too, he had the pleasure of watching that troublesome English merchant, William Caxton, squirm as he asked for help.

Not so long ago, their exchanges had been anything but cordial. William Caxton had been a longtime resident of Brugge and had been the governor of the English merchants for some years, during which time the court and the English traders had frequently clashed over taxes and terms of trade imposed on their community by Duke Philip. The English merchants had even recently decamped en masse to Ghent when Philip had refused to renew the Wool Treaty on terms favorable to the English.

However, following his father's death last year, Charles had seen how ruinous his father's "victory" over the English merchants had been for Brugge, and Burgundy, and had come to a commercial agreement with Caxton for an entirely new arrangement: one that brought the English merchants back to Brugge and set the golden river flowing through his city again.

Duke Charles was, at his very heart, a man who believed he should be a king. Everything he did, everything he dreamed of was focused on elevating his dukedom, both by commercial transcendence and then by alliance, to a kingdom. This English marriage was very, very important as part of that plan. As were continuing good relations between him, his court, and the English merchants.

"What cheering news this is, Master William. I, for one, would have been deeply sorrowful if Lady Anne had died. Is there any more knowledge of the assailant? When last I asked they said he'd escaped."

"Your Grace is kind. But no, we have no further news of the man."

Carefully composing his face to show polite concern and nothing more, the duke observed William swing in the wind of his own fears. He liked Lady Anne and was delighted she would live, but undoubtedly there was a mystery here. One that was intriguing.

"Sire, it may be that my colleagues and I had prior information regarding the Lady Anne—and who might wish her dead."

The duke laughed. "What, Master William, you mean it was not your own that shot her?"

Momentarily, the gloves were off and William winced—and was immediately furious with himself. Had he been so unmanned by events of the last days that he could not control his responses, even when the stakes were as high as these?

"Lord Duke, it is true that some of my colleagues have had some concern with what they see as Lady Anne's unfair success in trading."

The duke smiled gently. "Unfair? It seems to me you tried to shut her out, and she still made you look like fools. She has a lot of friends at my court. I count myself among them. Though, naturally, I would wish this . . . mystery to be successfully addressed so that good relations among *all* your community can be speedily restored."

The slight stress on "all" was a warning note, and William swallowed a sigh. He hated this, every bit of it.

"That is my hope also, Your Grace. But there are others, it seems, who had stronger feelings, more dangerous feelings, about the Lady Anne than any of my colleagues. And we were told who they might be. I tried to warn her myself." He guttered to a halt; he could not avoid the knowledge that by his running with the many against his own judgment, the girl had nearly died.

"In fact, my guild asked me to warn her, but . . ."

Now was the time, there was no help for it. "We"—yes, it was true, it had been "we"—"attached certain . . . conditions to giving Lady Anne the information we'd been given. Under those circumstances she refused our help. And you are aware of the result."

Confession vented, William waited for the duke to speak. But Charles was silent. His practice armor having been removed, along with sweaty felt jerkin beneath, he was now being rubbed down, naked, with oil and salt on a specially constructed high table by a Moor—a giant man with very black skin and very pink palms—who was a deaf mute; useful during confidential conversations.

William allowed his last sentences to drift off into the silence. He could hear the shouts of those who were still practicing at the quintain, but the noise was dreamlike, distant. All his attention was concentrated on this one small moment, this unpretentious little room that smelled of new sweat and sweet oil.

The silent Moor massaged his master's glistening shoulders. Duke Charles sighed with pleasure.

"Ah, this is good; so good for the body. I'm never stiff, even after the quintain. You should try it yourself, Master William."

"I do not joust, sire."

The duke chuckled at the irony. "Why do I get the impression of fear from you, Master Caxton?"

The mercer was shocked. And embarrassed. Things had

come to a dreadful pass indeed if his very emotions were now on public display!

One, two, three—a silent count to calm his ragged breath . . .

"Duke Charles, those who wish to kill Lady Anne de Bohun have a vested interest in destroying the alliance of your house and the English Crown."

The duke became very still under the masseur's hands. Then he turned his head so that the Moor could see his eyes, and his mouth.

"Enough, Aseef. You will be called." The gigantic Moor, understood. Bowing to his master and then the merchant, Aseef left the room.

The duke sat up. "Think extremely carefully about what you want to say to me, Master Caxton."

"Sire, I have come to ask your advice, for truly I am grieved beyond measure by all that has passed in the last days. And now, so close to your wedding, I truly fear that events are moving almost too fast to control."

"Who do you think tried to kill her?"

William swallowed.

"My information is that Queen Elizabeth Wydeville wants the girl dead. And she wants you implicated in this murder."

The duke was puzzled.

"But how could the death of this pretty lady, even though she is English, affect me?"

"My information has it that King Edward once had a profound tendresse for the Lady Anne. He does not know she is in Brugge, but sources at court say he loves her still. Now there are many powerful forces in Britain who do not approve of a union between your two houses, not least the French. If the queen made the king believe you had killed his former love out of jealous passion perhaps—there have been rumors, forgive me, Your Grace."

Again the duke snorted. "Spread by the very jealous wives of your merchants? Because it is known that I have rarely favored English women—until now."

The merchant nodded. "Perhaps, but if the queen succeeds and makes King Edward believe her, then this alliance between

Burgundy and England will be mortally weakened before it has begun; and she can use the fury of the king to increase her own power and the power base of her family. He will have no one else to turn to. Besides, she would have preferred the princess to marry a man of her choosing, not the king's."

The duke frowned.

"But the archer disappeared. What proof is there that he worked for the queen?"

Caxton nodded. "He did escape. There must have been . . . friends. But we have this."

William Caxton pulled a small parchment scroll from within his sleeve.

"One of our merchants was given this on his last journey to trade for wool in the Cotswolds. Slipped to him at dinner one night. We think it is the copy of a dispatch, in cipher, from Queen Elizabeth herself to an unnamed accomplice."

The text of the letter, which began with an admonition to thank God and ask for His blessing each day by repeating the Paternoster, was in a mixture of French, Latin, Flemish, and a few English words.

It seemed a perfectly innocuous request for confirmation of prices quoted for raw wool, worked wool, and various types of cloth available in certain towns in England and Europe at the date of writing. It was the kind of utilitarian communication, penned in the universal argot of European trade, that merchants routinely sent to their partners in other countries.

The duke frowned. "Prove to me this is a cipher, Master William."

William could feel sweat slip down his sides as he unrolled the document onto the massage bench and weighted it at each corner with flasks of oil and a strigil left by the Moor.

"The key, sire, is in the numbers. As the great Greek sage Pythagoras tells us, seen correctly, numbers decipher the universe."

The duke frowned. "Careful, Master William. This smacks of heresy, or even sorcery."

"No, sire, just practical common sense. See, here is mention of the price of, say, greasy wool per pound in various villages of the Cotswolds, including Upper Slaughter. Now here is the same item in Venice, here in Ghent, here in Brugge, and here in Florence. And farther down, we have other separate prices quoted for washed and carded wool, in the same places. Not only is each sum very different for greasy wool, washed and carded wool, as you see . . . they also vary wildly from town to town."

The duke nodded. Looked at closely, the prices made no sense.

"I can assure you that these values are nothing like the real prices paid during this current season, nor the last, nor the one before that. They are false. Therefore, to find the cipher, ignoring the fact that each number is supposed to be a price, you group each of the numbers/prices as they are mentioned for separate items like this . . . greasy wool across ten named towns, then carded wool in each place, then spun wool, and so on."

The merchant now offered another piece of parchment.

"Each of these groups of numbers can be used to find a letter, which in turn will spell out words. The Paternoster is the key. It is mentioned at the start of the letter—the unnamed recipient is instructed to say the prayer at the commencement of each working day—so the prayer itself is the source of letters that will make up the eventual message. And now, if we look at the groups of numbers we have created with this in mind . . ."

William had brought a missal with him, and as he and the duke pored over the words of the ancient prayer, while consulting the numbers—the first number in any group locating a line of the prayer, the second number pointing to a word in the chosen line, and the third number indicating a letter within the word—slowly, a message emerged.

"Kill A de B at Brugge before king arrives for wedding. Use weapon of Christ. See separate token as evidence of good faith. Payment as agreed. Woman of oak tree."

The duke said nothing until William rolled up the scroll. "I have many questions. But this is the first. Why did you not come to me before this?"

William swallowed. He was walking on very, very delicate ground.

"This letter was given to a colleague of mine. He told me of it, but also he told others who hold office in our guild. None of us wanted to believe it—after all, it seems preposterous—but there have been many among the English merchants who are opposed to Lady de Bohun, as you know, and so first we searched among ourselves to see if, if . . ."

"You or yours was responsible for a hoax?"

William was grateful. "Yes, sire. That had been our first thought."

The duke felt cold. Perhaps he was just cooling down after the massage, since he was only draped in a linen bath sheet, toga-like, but perhaps it was something more. He shivered and held out a hand, interrupting William.

"Pass me my clothes, Master William."

William hurried to obey. Quickly scooping a cobweb-fine linen shirt, britches of woven scarlet wool, soft calf-length blue boots, and a peacock-bright jacket of blue and yellow, he helped the duke dress, noting ruefully the magnificent body of the man he did not serve but had come to respect and, yes, even like.

When the duke was dressed, the conversation continued.

"Woman of the oak tree. What is this nonsense? It sounds pagan."

"Your Grace is perceptive. Oak trees in England have much significance. The common people associate them with the old ways. The old religions. And magic."

Both men crossed themselves quickly. Magic was definitely heresy. And heresy could mean death even in such an enlightened city as Brugge. "It is said that the current queen first met our King Edward under an oak tree while he was fleeing from a storm out hunting. The English believe Elizabeth Wydeville's mother is a witch and that she engineered this meeting. And it is said Elizabeth further enchanted the king with spells. They say she keeps him at her side through magic to this day. It is certain that she is powerful, for her beauty remains unnaturally perfect and her influence at court grows daily."

"But how can anyone be sure the queen is the author of this message—if message it is? What proof do you have?"

"None. Except for this letter. And the fact that Anne was shot by a crossbow here in this city, ahead of your wedding; perhaps the name means it could be seen as the weapon of Christ. The shaft of the quarrel was oak, by the way. That is unusual. Ash is more commonly used."

The duke looked consideringly at the merchant.

"Anne de Bohun will live?"

William nodded and sighed. "Yes, praise God."

"Does King Edward know of this incident—the shooting, I mean, not the strange theory that you have advanced today?"

William shook his head

"No, sire, it was felt by my colleagues that we should speak to you first. We need your advice."

"And I yours, merchant, I yours. This is most perplexing."

There was silence for a moment.

"Have you told Anne your suspicions?"

Williams eyes were bleak as he shook his head. "I have not, Your Grace. And until we have more proof I will not disturb her convalescence. I pray that all I have told you is untrue."

"And so do I, merchant. I need allies and Burgundy, therefore, needs this marriage with England. I must frighten off the French, who nibble at my borders even now, and for that I need friends."

He looked piercingly at the merchant.

"We will not speak further of this, William Caxton, until you know more. But guard that girl well. If she is important to the king, then she is doubly important to me. To Brugge."

# Chapter Twenty

Seven more days had passed and the first really hot day encouraged the people of Brugge to abandon the wool, velvet, and furs of winter in favor of lighter clothes. Bright new linens and Egyptian cottons printed in block, bold colors were seen everywhere on the streets as the housewives of Brugge tried to keep the dust down by sprinkling water on the unpaved streets before their doors.

Anne was healing well now and was impatient to go home. But strange things were happening: nothing was the same as it had been before the shooting.

In her other life in England, before her arrival in Brugge, there had been times when Anne had seen strange things.—daytime dreams she had called them in her own mind, and mostly she'd rationalized them away in the bright, unclouded light of reality. Now, sometimes, since the shooting, when she looked into a person's eyes, she received strange images, sounds, even smells. Frightening at first, she'd begun to accept they were impressions of what might come for that person: the good things and the bad.

Mostly she remained detached, as if seeing figures in a landscape from high up in a castle wall, yet today Anne was very troubled. For as she said good-bye to William and Maud, there was a moment, a flash, when she glimpsed William's wife lying on a black-draped bier surrounded by candles. Dead. William, head bowed, was accepting condolences from mourners as he stood beside the wax-white corpse.

Shocked by what she saw, Anne instinctively, out of pity, reached out to embrace the other woman, but Maud drew back slightly; she did not like this girl and only duty to her husband's position kept her standing there while William embraced Anne and wished her well.

"Mistress Caxton, and you, Master Caxton, I thank you most humbly. Your kindness will never be forgotten."

No, she would not forget what William had done—she valued his kind heart. He would go on living well, and, yes, accomplish great things—things she half saw, in London, near the Abbey Church of Saint Peter. But Maud, poor cold, jealous Maud, would end her days in Brugge and be buried here, so far from family, so far from the land of her birth. Her children would be brought up by another woman and would barely remember what she'd looked like.

Anne's eyes filled with tears.

"Good-bye, Mistress Caxton. May you be kept well in God's love." It was only a whisper and it could not have carried to the proud woman standing before the door of her handsome town house, yet Maud felt something touch her; she shook her head at the strange feeling of loss as Anne was carried away. Good riddance! Time to get on with their own lives again—and the wedding to look forward to! Now, if only she could get her grumpy husband to concentrate on the future, not the past . . .

"Deborah, did I die?" Both women had been avoiding the question while Anne recovered, day by day, in William Caxton's great bed. Now as they rode in the litter together, back to Mathew Cuttifer's great house, the time had come. Deborah sighed.

"Yes. I called you back."

Profound anguish wrapped Anne in a suffocating cloak; she could hardly speak.

"I could have stayed. I should have stayed."

Deborah reached for Anne's hand. "There is your son. And his father."

The king and little Edward: the baby she'd not seen for days and days. She ached to hold him, kiss him; this was the real world, the prison of the flesh with all its attachments. Its joy and its pain. Slowly, very slowly, Anne was reentering this life of the body from somewhere else, somewhere that she could half see in dreams. Somewhere that resonated with the sound of her mother's voice.

But her confused and confusing thoughts were swallowed in joyful shouts as the litter stopped in front of the house where Maxim was holding little Edward, waving fat arms and crowing joyfully as soon as he saw her.

Anne refused to be carried in—the days of weakness were past—but as she kissed the little boy for the first time in so many days, the feeling grew and grew on her. It was time this child met his father, no matter what the consequences.

And it was time for her to meet Edward the King again.

# Chapter Twenty-one

It was the greatest English fleet that had been assembled since the late French wars and they were all impatient to leave Dover, if only the wind would set fair.

The queen had journeyed with the court and her husband as far as Battle Abbey, where a great feast was held on the night before they sailed to farewell the Lady Margaret. And it was there that Edward had formally announced that Elizabeth, his queen, would be regent of England, with a council headed by his brother Richard of Gloucester, even now riding to London from York, in the absence of Edward at his sister's wedding.

Elizabeth smiled and nodded, graciously acknowledging the honor, but those at the high board, where she and Edward sat beneath twin Cloths of Estate, saw her twist her rings round and around, round and around. And saw, too, the dangerous frost in those famous blue eyes.

The queen was not happy. Not happy at all, and her servants knew they would pay later. It did not help that the Duchess Cicely, her mother-in-law, was also now journeying to Brugge with Edward—a regular family gathering—while she and her own mother, the Duchess Jacquetta, were left behind.

Of course, Edward had used the excuse of her pregnancy again, saying it was unsafe for the queen to travel at such a time, and that her mother should keep her company.

Such concern for Elizabeth's health was rubbish. Had she not hunted almost until the birth of their second child, the Princess Mary, last year? Besides, she was not so pregnant yet that her condition need bother him, or her. The early to middle part of breeding always suited her well. It was only the very beginning and the very end that had caused her problems in the past.

But she had won no arguments with the king. Very well. If that were so, she had her own means of influencing events.

The queen was seen to smile, which pleased the king; he was always nervous when Elizabeth put on her most majestic persona. She still had the capacity to charm him, of course, but he was relieved she seemed to have finally accepted that she should stay safe in England while he and his blood family were at Margaret's wedding.

It had been chancy, of course; Edward acknowledged that to himself. At first Elizabeth had absolutely refused to hear him when he'd said she must stay home for the good of the baby. She'd been only partially mollified when Edward had sacrificed Hastings's company so that he could entertain the queen in his master's absence.

What he found hard to disguise, if Edward were truthful, was that the prospect of a month with his immediate family in one of his favorite cities—Brugge—was intensely exciting. Elizabeth was his wife, he honored her as queen, and she was attractive to him still, but she was increasingly hard work and it would be a relief to be out of the humid court atmosphere for a time, an atmosphere that caused him to weigh every word in her presence.

He'd feared, too, that when he made the announcement of her regency at tonight's feast, as a way of keeping her anchored in England, she'd find a way to oppose his will, some subtle thing he'd not thought of. She was clever and sometimes, he had to confess, he actually relished the mental games of dominance they played.

It was a relief, though, to see her mood change after he'd made his pretty little speech honoring her good sense and his hopes for her careful stewardship of his kingdom. She seemed to relax a little; she even leaned toward him as she selected particularly choice gobbets of dolphin and langouste to place delicately on his tongue. And times like these, when she was so agreeable, so biddable, reminded the king all over again why he had been content to wed her, to the scandal of all of Europe.

He smiled at her. Yes. Those times were worth remembering, especially when he had had her first; very fast, immediately after they'd been secretly married at her mother's house. Hastings and the men had stood patiently outside beside their saddled horses, and he'd enjoyed the taming of her, if that was what he'd actually accomplished.

Elizabeth smiled back meltingly. She knew that look on Edward's face and it pleased her. It meant she still had power over his body, as she had over his life, did he but know that. Tonight, after the feast, she would work at that power. Let Richard be regent—what did she care?

Brugge was a very fashionable destination—the clothes and the jewels were renowned all over Europe, and attendance at this wedding would be the chance she craved, the chance to play at politics in a wider, deeper game: the allegiances of great states, and the building of great houses. Her own in this case.

Delighted at the thought, she clapped her hands to the master of the music—louder! Faster! Soon it would be time to dance, and after that, bed!

Anne was deeply asleep, exhausted, when the face swam up, laughing, from some cloudy, deep place inhabited by fear. She was jerked awake as terror hooked her heart.

Deborah woke too. Since they'd come home she'd slept on a palliasse in Anne's bedroom. Her foster daughter was physically recovered, her spirit another matter.

"Deborah?" The voice of a child—too proud to confess to night fears.

"Yes, I'm here."

"It was him. The man who shot me. Why does he come to me?"

Deborah had no answer as she scrambled onto Anne's bed and took the shivering, naked girl into her arms, unconsciously rocking her, soothing her with little pats. Anne was whispering, trying not to wake Edward and Jenna, asleep in the annex to her solar. Anne would not be separated from her son again, waking or sleeping.

For a few minutes Anne was content to be rocked. "Deborah, will I see the king again?"

Deborah said nothing. Anne freed herself from the other woman's embrace and leaned over to find the flint and candle beside her bed. The flint made a small grating click in the dark and struck white sparks. A second later, the candle flame wavered into being and Anne's fingers glowed red as she cupped them around the light.

"Deborah, please. Look into the flame for me. I must know. Something's coming and I'm so afraid."

Deborah shook her head.

"You've got the sight. As yours had grown clearer, mine has faded." It was a lie, of course, but a kind one. She was too frightened to look into Anne's future.

"Mother, if it is your wish, let me live to see the boy grown—but you must protect this girl for I'm not strong enough."

It was a constant prayer, and she prayed it now, for Deborah had not forgotten offering her own life as a sacrifice for Anne's in that terrible moment when the girl had died. Yet, though Deborah prayed each night for guidance, and offered cock's blood at full moon, she could not tell the auguries. Anne had been allowed to live—for now—but for how long?

"Please help me?" Anne was as frightened as she was, all defenses stripped away. She sighed, a great gusting breath, almost a sob. Poor Deborah. What choice did she have?

"Yes. I will help in the name of the Mother."

Hastily, Deborah drew the heavy curtains around the bed. That would keep the light contained so that Jenna, sleeping beside Edward in the annex, would not be woken. But they would have to whisper the invocations . . .

The two women were now within a red tent, for the brocaded bed curtains had a blood-colored ground, a pattern of vine leaves picked out in gold, writhing over the surface.

Silently Anne held out the Jupiter finger of her right hand as Deborah searched for a brooch in the jewel coffer kept beneath Anne's bed. Quickly she pricked the girl's finger with the pin and held it over the flame so the blood dripped into its transparent heart.

The flame wavered and nearly died, then hissed up smoking, blue, green, then white again. "Will you say it?" Deborah nodded and began the invocation as Anne held the candle dish between both hands, eyes fixed on the shifting, trembling flame.

"Mother of all. Mother of all. The sacrifice has been made. Hear us."

Deborah's voice was barely a rustle, a breath of wind through standing corn. "By the four winds, and the seven seas, hear us. By the sun, by the moon, by the stars, hear us." The night had been still and hot. Now, suddenly, there was a thread of cold air and the curtains nearest to Anne rippled and stirred, very gently.

"Mother of all. Mother of all. We are your children and we cannot see in the dark." The flame of the candle flared and dipped. A dancer's shape, nearly human.

"Mother of all. Mother of all. Come to us. Help your children." Now Anne had joined her voice to Deborah's in a husky whisper, and the older woman saw the girl's pupils were immense—black wells drowning the topaz.

The candle snuffed out so suddenly Deborah jumped in fright. But not Anne. She sat rock still, breathing more and more deeply. Her eyes closed into the silence. And then she began to speak.

"You ask for help. I will give it. Wings of darkness—you are right to feel afraid. Wings of darkness. But the power is stronger. Trust that. See what is needful, but beware the message, and the messenger. Fate twists in your hands. Sacrifice. Storms. Death in your service."

It was colder now, much colder. The goddess was most often a benign force, but tonight there was something older, fiercer, wrapping them around. There was a grating noise, barely human, as Anne cleared her throat, then, "You asked for help. I answered. I am who I am. I guard. I guard."

The voice trailed away as Deborah touched Anne's arm.

"Anne. Anne! Can you hear me? Anne!" The girl was unresponsive as Deborah searched for the candle and the flint. Seconds later the warm flame showed her that Anne was staring out into the red darkness, eyes wide and fixed. Deborah made the sign of the goddess in front of Anne's impassive face.

"Do not be frightened, I am here. I won't leave you." Deborah tried to offer comfort, but the waver in her voice told the truth.

"I know that. I am grateful." It was Anne's own voice, and Deborah swallowed the acid of relief. Just at that moment, a warm wind stirred the curtains of the bed and the candlelight winked on the gold thread of the woven vines. It was as if they were alive, twining around them, making a bower to keep them safe from harm.

"It wasn't the goddess, though, was it?"

Anne tried to keep the fear out of her voice. She'd heard what had been said, but from a great distance; now all she felt was empty and cold.

"No. It was not. But it was real."

On the other side of the curtain, in the annex, Jenna lay awake. She had not heard everything, but she had heard enough. She shivered. Demons. Her mistress raised demons. Fearfully, the girl crossed herself. What should she do and say in confession? Would she be damned for all eternity if she did not tell the priest what she knew?

The little boy stirred and turned restlessly in his sleep beside her. His sweet breath was on her cheek, and Jenna felt the tears slip down her face. She loved her mistress, she loved Edward—but she could not face hellfire.

# Chapter Twenty-two

At last the news arrived. The English ships! They'd been sighted as dawn rose out of the sea. The whole, huge wedding fleet was off the coast near Sluis and would be docked in the before-noon. The mayor of Sluis had journeyed out in his official lighter to meet the flagship of the fleet and conduct the party to shore while his town erupted in long-planned celebration: wine running in the public fountains, and choirs gathering at every street corner to welcome the bride, her brother the king, and Duchess Cicely, the king's mother, as they set foot on the land.

In Brugge, sudden noise and energy convulsed the Prinsenhof as an exhausted courier nearly killed his horse riding from the coast in foam-splattered record time to bring the news; but he was well rewarded for his loyalty by Duke Charles, receiving twenty-one gold angels—one for each year of the bride's age—to ease his quivering muscles.

And, of course, the news could not be contained. Like fire it burned outward from the duke's palace into the town, carried from mouth to mouth, leaving, at its passing, a rising babble of sound and running feet. The Bruggers shut their shops, abandoned their Markt stalls, and scattered, as one, to dress and join the wedding procession. It was common knowledge that once Margaret reached Damme, the little town on the river Zwijn that linked Brugge to the seaport at Sluis, she would be married to their Duke Charles in a private ceremony before a small number of invited guests, followed by a Mass in the cathedral there. Later, the bride's party would journey by barge along the river to the city before a ceremonial entrance and progress through its streets. It would be the first, and the biggest, of an expected ten days of semi-riot and extravagance designed to celebrate the wedding.

Before she heard the news, Anne was with Hans Boter in Mathew Cuttifer's warehouse as she dictated a letter seeking extra bales of the newest, jewel-bright velvets from Florence ahead of the winter to come.

Truce might have been declared between her and the English Merchant Adventurers, but she had not forgiven or forgotten. Or retired. After her near murder, Anne had decided that advance rather than retreat was the only way to show the world that she was alive and intended to stay that way.

Now, in the cool of the counting floor, where it was dark—the shutters having been drawn early against the morning heat—she finished the text of her letter and signed it calmly, fixing her signet into the wax carefully so that her device, the arms given to her personally by King Edward, would not smear or distort.

"Yes, Maxim?" The steward arrived flushed and agitated, though hoping he'd disguised the excitement he felt.

"Lady, the English have been sighted."

At last! Legs suddenly weak, breath short in her throat, somehow Anne sounded calm. "Enough for today, Meinheer Boter. Now it is holiday! Maxim, tell them all, we must make ready. Quickly!"

This wedding had been the focus of their thoughts for months and now it was finally here. The house was spotless, the kitchen, the pantry, and buttery stocked with food—fresh and preserved—and their own beer, newly brewed, with which to keep open house. All that remained was to dress in the holiday livery Mathew and Anne had jointly provided and decorate the outside of the hall with ropes of flowers, ribbons, and hangings entwining the initials C & M, in honor of the bride and groom. Margaret's barge would pass directly beneath their windows on its way into the city before the bridal party progressed through the

streets to the Prinsenhof—their house must outshine all its neighbors.

Outwardly Anne remained quite calm, though she could feel
her heart thud unevenly as the blood boomed in her head. As
Deborah and Jenna dressed her—in shimmering jewel-green
satin, the color of new love and new beginnings—stable boys took
invitations to a select few friends and, yes, even some of the English merchants, since the house, right on the canal, had an excellent view and many large windows.

Never had Brugge sounded and seemed more like a beehive
than today. As Deborah wound ropes of pearls and emeralds
around her throat, Anne stood in the open casements, sunshine
flooding down as laughter and happy shouting from the town
filled the air outside and inside the room.

This marriage was welcome, this princess most welcome. The
trade worries of the last ten years were melting away—the future
of Brugge was assured by this strong alliance. Let others worry
about the rumors that the river was silting up—the Zwijn, which
was the conduit of all the city's wealth—today the times were
pregnant with promise. New opportunities would flow from this
marriage and Brugge would once more eclipse her rivals; good
English crowns and angels passing from hand to hand would see
to that.

There was a booming crash on the front door downstairs, so
loud it was heard even here, upstairs in her own solar—guests! It
had begun!

Within an hour, closer and closer to the midday bell—around
which time the bride and her new husband were expected to arrive—Mathew Cuttifer's fine hall was filled with brilliantly
dressed, happily anxious guests; there were even some of the English merchants, including the Caxtons. The household servants
passed to and fro among Anne's friends, her rivals, and some of
her enemies in the perfumed hall conveying food and wine and
beer as Anne herself held court.

William Caxton caught Anne's eye and bowed, sweeping off
his flat velvet bonnet. Maud caught the movement from the other
side of the room where she was standing with friends, other mer-

chants' wives, in rigid disapproval and envy of the opulent display all around them. She frowned; her husband was fond, much too fond, of this trollop. She'd have to rescue him from his own partiality.

Too late! William had sauntered over to Anne, and though Maud could not hear what they were saying, it was flagrantly clear he was enjoying her company.

Angry, Maud went to swallow some of the admittedly truly excellent wine offered by this pestilential house and choking, had to be thumped on the back, which most unfortunately broke the string of her necklace—her best necklace!—so that gold beads, coral, and garnets were scattered all over the waxed floor tiles and skittered everywhere.

During the ensuing fuss, Maud was distracted and so she did not see, though others did, William raise Anne's hand to his lips.

"Lady, your beauty confuses me. I do not know how to describe it. But I am so thankful, praise God, that you are restored to us, so that I may at least go on trying to find the words!"

"A long speech for such a little subject, Master Caxton."

Anne was warm and direct when she spoke to men she liked—another plus in William's eyes—another outrage to those who were jealous.

"You are better?"

Anne nodded. "Yes. I am healed. And because of Deborah, there is only the very smallest scar—which none but those closest to me will ever see."

She laughed. And so did he, giddily. Thinking about that part of Anne's body added distraction to his words.

"It is surely a miracle that the wound closed at all. I thought you would die."

It was a dark thing to say on such a sunny day—not the bright, meaningless party chatter expected from a guest—and the shadow of the truth he had spoken was nearly tangible. "Some say I did, Master William."

A strange and dangerous remark, and William only just stopped himself from sketching a cross in the air—that made her smile.

"It's mentioned in the Bible, you know. A glimpse of paradise and then, return to life. And there's Lazarus too, isn't there?"

This was a worrying conversation. William didn't think of himself as a bigot, but surely this was close to blasphemy.

Maxim appeared at Anne's side, visibly swelling with the news he contained. Anne listened as he mouthed something in her ear, then, face radiant, clapped her hands for silence.

"My friends, Maxim says that the barges have been sighted! Come, join me upstairs so that we can cheer them on their way to the Prinsenhof!"

The stair was wide to the upper quarters, but the rush of her guests, while it was decorous, was determined, so some were in danger of being pushed over the carved balustrade by the press of people.

Anne led them herself, and as they entered her own private quarters, many were astonished. For the occasion her bed had been moved against one wall, but the space around it was still great, great enough to accommodate forty or so people—and all the servants—with ease.

As they crowded to the casements, thrown open to let in the air and the view, Anne did her best to arrange matters so that each one of her guests could see—tallest at the back, youngest and smallest seated on the window seats—while she managed to reserve a place for herself in the far corner of one of the windows. She also made sure that Maxim, Deborah, and the other household people had one casement all to themselves—to the continuing scandal of Maud and her friends.

Looking down, Anne could see the banks of the canal, curving away toward the Kruispoort, and each window of every house filled to suffocation with the people of Brugge—colorful as the heber in high summer.

Everywhere there were banners, embroidered or painted with the red bear, the symbol of the city, and images of the Virgin, special patroness of Brugge, many personally designed by Hans Memlinc. And, too, freshly gilded busts and bas-reliefs of the Holy Mother and Child were everywhere in niches at street corners, while polychromed life-size statues of Mary were set up on plinths at each raised bridge over the canal, garlanded with white roses, as an honor to the Lady Margaret of York, princess of England and now their duchess.

And, then, at last, yes, preceded and enveloped by wave after wave of the deep roar of many voices, there came the procession of barges drawn along the canal by huge and patient horses—braided, polished, hung with precious trappings of silver and gold—led by young men, each more handsome than the next, in white tabards emblazoned with the red bear of Brugge.

The first three barges were filled with minstrels, puce-faced with the effort of making themselves heard above the din. Then came three more filled with very young girls, selected for their beauty, all dressed in white and green, long hair crowned with wreaths of white roses and ivy--singing a continuous, plangent epithalamion to marriage and scattering white petals on the water. Immediately behind them came a barge of state, the largest, brightest of all; the carved arms of England linked with those of Brugge, and everywhere, on all its surfaces, C & M linked together as a device.

There was a raised dais in the stern of this barge and there, dressed in red and gold, was the new bride, the new duchess, the Lady Margaret of England, smiling, waving, throwing flowers to her delighted new subjects as she sat beside her husband, the duke. A glowingly handsome couple, and it was well noted by the crowd how pleased with each other they seemed.

Anne smiled ruefully when she saw the new Duchess of Burgundy. Today there was very little left of the handsome, difficult girl she remembered who'd fought so often with Elizabeth Wydeville, the queen. This was an assured, beautiful young woman, conscious, in her splendid scarlet-and-gold dress, that she'd come to fulfil a destiny that now seemed much less onerous than it had before.

Then there followed another great barge with the king's mother, Cicely, Dowager Duchess of York, mother of the bride, seated beside a tall man with broad shoulders who was laughing, and waving to the citizens of Brugge as they screamed and threw flowers in a blizzard of white and red, green and gold and blue.

And when Anne looked down, pealing bells clamored in her mind and the world slowed. The man who had filled her dark nights, her dark dreams for so long, Edward, was turning his head slowly, slowly, white teeth glinting, red mouth smiling. Edward. The father of her son. Edward, the King of England.

He, too, was dressed in cloth of gold, but green sleeves and a green flat cap surmounted by a light crown honored the day and the new love he hoped would grow between his sister and her new husband. Green—there had always been green between them.

Anne fingered the emeralds among the pearls lying around her own neck and, before she had time to think, time to curb instinct in any way, unwound the jewels and watched herself throw them, seeing the priceless rope of gems land in that golden lap.

And watched as Edward the King looked up for the source of this unexpected, precious bounty.

"From the merchants of Brugge to the King of England."

It was her voice, she heard herself say it, saw that it cut through, knew that he had heard.

She would remember that look all her life—when his eyes locked to hers as he stood up in the barge, searching for the owner of the voice. From shock, she said nothing more. From shock, too, he was mute, but he saw her, saw her face.

And as the barge swept by beneath her windows, he stood and watched her until nearly the last moment; then he bowed. To her. And she bowed back. There was a buzz all around her, she heard it, but it made no difference to Anne de Bohun. It had begun again.

# Chapter Twenty-three

The city was in ferment. After the first ecstatic welcome to the Duchess Margaret and her triumphal, painfully slow progress through the streets so that as many of her new subjects could see her as possible, all the Bruggers were avid for gossip—how had the first meeting been between their duke and duchess, and how had the wedding service gone?

There was good reason for all the giddy pride and interest. The bride herself was much approved of, and not only by the people. Duke Charles himself was in barely contained fever now to have the wedding banquet out of the way, for when he had first seen Margaret, first looked into her eyes, something hot had flicked from him to her. He could feel it in her hands as he reached down to help her from the deepest of curtsies. They'd been shaking. He'd pressed them secretly for reassurance. And she'd smiled up at him.

The long Mass before both court parties in the packed cathedral at Damme had made the new duchess dizzy and exhausted, but the noise of the city and its citizens, their clamorous demonstration that they were determined to love her, was restorative. As was the warmth of this man she had never met before.

Well might Duke Charles be warm to her. From what he could see of her body, she was well made, better than well made. Nearly as tall as he was, but with such a face—not just glowing youth, real beauty—and such a strong spirit that her schoolgirl

French and complete lack of Flemish would not matter once they were in bed together. It would please him greatly to match his body to hers, breast, belly, and thigh. He sighed luxuriously at that thought, felt the blood begin to itch.

And for her part she'd seen a man whose strongly made body—excellent shoulders, flat belly, long, strong thighs—affected her more than she understood.

During the rich tedium of the Mass, he'd smiled at her, looked deep into her eyes, and winked! And then, breath had deserted her when her hand was first placed into his by her brother, the king, in front of the archbishop of her new city. And he'd certainly made her blush when he looked happily, and not very discreetly, at her breast as he swept down into a deep bow at the conclusion of the service while whispering compliments, in slightly awkward English, about her peerless eyes, her charming teeth, her lovely hair. He was comical and he knew it. She could not help smiling, quite broadly. And he smiled back at her. That delighted everyone from his court. And hers.

Her ladies in the cathedral had seen the exchange also, and even her mother, Duchess Cicely, had not rebuked their ribald sallies as they dressed the new duchess Margaret for the wedding banquet that evening. The duke would plainly be a demanding husband, they giggled, and this warm and brilliant wedding night would surely be guaranteed to exhaust both groom and bride. Their young lady must be well supplied with strengthening drink at the wedding feast in anticipation of such a handsome, well set-up husband!

Only Edward was silent as he, too, was dressed in his suite of opulently furnished rooms, his mind working on many levels simultaneously: the politics of this visit, the pleasures of old friendships to be renewed—and Anne.

He closed his eyes as they dropped the clean linen over his lightly sweating skin and he replayed the images of the day. As King of England, intent on cementing an alliance between his kingdom and Burgundy, he knew it was his task to prepare himself mentally for the evening but he was still shocked by that moment on the canal when the skein of pearls and emeralds had landed in his lap. Still shocked. Then, to look up and see her face. It must have been her, Anne.

He was haunted now, so eager to see her, to touch her, so afraid he was wrong. Had he hallucinated her face onto another woman's because the magic of this wedding day cast glamor over reality? He shook his head, almost groaned.

Edward forced himself to concentrate as he reviewed the day, to prepare himself for the politics of the night. After the final, triumphant entry of the English court party into the Prinsenhof— he ceremonially advancing with his mother on his arm, step by step in time to the music of tabors, pipes, flutes, and drums, to where the new bride and groom were waiting on a dais outside Duke Charles's palace surrounded by the Burgundian court—Edward had been conducted by the duke himself to this opulent suite, so familiar from his boyhood, to prepare for this evening's wedding feast.

Elaborate and warm courtesies had been exchanged by both the duke and the king—presents given and received. Every mark of honor from each side to the other and compliments: on the beauty of his sister, the dignity of Duchess Cicely, the magnificence of their welcome.

Meeting Charles again, Edward remembered the time he'd spent at the Burgundian court in Liège and in Brugge; he the younger, Charles the elder getting them both, very willingly, into endless games and scrapes. Charles had been a good teacher in the tilt yard, too, finding ways to give Edward confidence to trust his natural timing and hone his focus so that, when he fought, Edward thought of nothing else but the next blow, the next feint. It was to Charles that he owed the steadiness he still had in the lists. Edward the King smiled; he would enjoy the play contest that was to come in the next ten days of celebration—perhaps he could show his erstwhile tutor a few new tricks.

His belly contracted. It was not the thought of jousting that caused it. He could not deny or suppress the image of Anne's face looking down at him from the casement above.

It must have been her. She looked barely older than the last time, though a year and a half had passed. So many questions to ask—what was she doing here? What did she feel for him now? No matter what his duty, no matter how late the feast, he would find her tonight.

Impatient to be done with the dressing, Edward strode over to the casement and flung the windows back, trailing body servants desperate to smooth his hair and finish buttoning the tight black velvet jacket he must wear for tonight's wedding feast under a full robe of scarlet cloth of gold lined with ermine.

God knew, the weight of all that material was a trial, for though Edward's dress of state was artfully made, velvet on such a warm night was tiresome, not to mention cloth of gold! Edward closed his eyes again, dreaming of the pleasure he would feel later, when he could strip the heavy cloth from his body, feel the warm air on his naked skin.

He stretched luxuriously, disrupting the hair brushing, the primping once more. "Where's Dickon? I've had enough of this!" His valet had hurried to fetch his light crown; it was the last thing required; then Edward would be fully arrayed.

The sounds of Brugge celebrating were everywhere on this still, hot night—happy shouts, hurrying feet, and laughter. Edward smiled briefly. Heat. There were many kinds of heat. He looked down the canal toward the bend he could just see in the distance. That was where it had happened: that great house set back from the curve—there. He'd seen her in the upstairs room—she'd thrown him the rope of emeralds and pearls.

"The jewels that were thrown to me today. Where are they?"

Just then, Dickon, his chief body servant, hurried back with the light ceremonial crown of England for his master. "Sire, I have them safe."

"I'll wear them."

There was complete silence in the room. Looking out at the dark water, Edward knew what they'd be thinking. The queen would be furious when she heard that Edward had chosen to wear jewels thrown to him by an unknown lady on his first night in Brugge. But the queen was in London, without him. He'd won the contest at Battle Abbey.

That made him smile again. For once, he'd outwitted Elizabeth, though she'd sought to please him in every physical way she knew the night before they'd left. He'd enjoyed himself immoderately, and left his refusal to change his mind until the very last moment—so she'd been icy when he'd embarked.

Thinking of that moment, in the biting wind of the dock when the queen had turned him a very cool cheek, the king swung back, away from the window and saw their faces. He laughed out loud and those who heard him were astonished. He sounded so free, so young. They hadn't heard him laugh like that for, well—Dickon said it later—the king laughed like that only when he was in love.


Anne stood perfectly still in the middle of the solar as Jenna and Deborah laced her tighter and tighter into the dress. Her body felt insubstantial, light-filled. And her mind. Perhaps her fiercely elevated pulse was to blame for the strange way the world appeared tonight.

Time was fleeting, though, and downstairs her barge waited by the water gate, but Anne was clear—she would arrive as late as she decently could at the Prinsenhof for the wedding feast tonight. It was time to make an entrance, time that she shed some of the anonymity and mystery that she'd so carefully wrapped around herself and her life in these last months.

And even though she tried to banish the thought—fearful of presuming too much—tonight she knew she would meet Edward again. It would be his doing, not hers. She was certain of that.

Therefore she was calm, patient, and attentive to the last rituals of preparing. It was lucky that at dawn, when none of them had known what today held, Deborah and Jenna between them had washed Anne's hair with sweet rosemary water to enhance the deep lustrous bronze, drying it first with bleached linen in the sun of her heber, before polishing it with silk cloths.

Now it was braided high on her head in a thick, glossy crown—a foundation upon which to fasten her elegant hennin embroidered with gold thread and pearls. Veiling as fine and light as sea mist floated from the peak of the headdress almost to the

hem of her gown, the most insubstantial of cloaks swirling gracefully with every movement, every slight flutter in the air surrounding her body.

Anne herself had designed this dress, and they had carefully
dropped it over her naked body a moment or two ago; tonight's
heat meant she would not wear an undershift. Deborah held her
tongue—it was not fear of Anne's catching cold that concerned
her.

The dress was very simple, cut from a volume of the finest of
gossamer silk, and like Anne's headdress it was deep topaz green-
blue, the color of her own eyes. And unlike the heavy dresses most
often worn at court, which moved so stiffly, it was cut to flow with
every movement, the material falling like water from a belt jeweled with emeralds caught up high beneath her breasts. The
sleeves were simple, too—scandalously so—tight, unadorned, except for buttons made from pearls, which closed them from wrist
to elbow.

As Anne moved, light caught the precious, strange material
and it seemed to change color: peacock hues, gold, even rose pink,
flushed through the folds of the fabric.

Jenna, astonished at the mysterious, changeable beauty of the
garment, crossed herself, hoping no one saw; to her it was a garment fashioned by magic, a dress that only a witch might wear.

Anne, standing quietly as Deborah made the last, careful ad-
justments to her veil, felt breath catch in her throat. Unconsciously, she turned her head and caught the last movement of
Jenna's hand. Something icy touched her as the girl looked up,
and then glanced quickly away, guilty, as she hurried into the
shadows of the room, stooping to pick up discarded garments, setting the room to rights.

"Shall I tell Maxim that Mistress Anne will be ready for the
barge soon?" Jenna addressed the question to Deborah, but she
sounded breathless, panicky.

Deborah, preoccupied, waved an absent yes, but Anne fixed
concerned eyes on the girl as she scurried from the room; then she,
too, was distracted—a sudden gust of sound swept down the
canal, the high whinny of trumpets, cheering, shouting, laughter.

The guests were arriving at the Prinsenhof—the wedding night was beginning.

"Something wrong?" Deborah had felt Anne stiffen under her touch. "Nothing," but there was—Anne was reluctant to give it words, this uncertainty.

"You're finished. Or rather—I'm finished." Deborah stepped back and looked critically at her handiwork. Strange and rueful thoughts flowed through her.

Anne smiled at her. "There, dear friend. Don't be concerned. You've spoken about the fates to me often enough. Do you think the spinning women are weaving me happiness tonight?"

Deborah gently touched the veil one last time, one last tiny adjustment that only she could see. "I cannot tell, so I will not lie to you. But I will pray."

Anne walked quietly to her door, the trailing silk whispering over the tiles. "Which gods will you pray to, Deborah?"

The last words floated on the air as Jenna returned to open the door for her mistress. Perhaps she heard, perhaps she did not. Perhaps it was all too late, and at some very deep level, all three women in that room, that night, knew it.

# Chapter Twenty-four

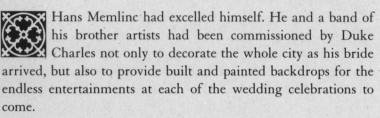 Hans Memlinc had excelled himself. He and a band of his brother artists had been commissioned by Duke Charles not only to decorate the whole city as his bride arrived, but also to provide built and painted backdrops for the endless entertainments at each of the wedding celebrations to come.

Their greatest triumph was in the creation of a sumptuous tentlike hall to house the wedding feast, a structure made by roofing the duke's new tennis court—a novel imported sport to which he was recently, most expensively, addicted—with a vast piece of painted gold silk. The walls of this extravagant structure, a noble chamber almost as high as it was wide—and it was very wide— had been draped in deep blue silk and swagged and gathered between enormous displays of white roses for the white rose of York, Princess Margaret, the bride.

Fat wax candles burned in bunched sconces and flickered from brass candelabra, dangerously close to the tented ceiling—so many brilliant little suns it seemed like day.

The tent hall itself sat proudly on a terrace above the canal, the same canal on which Anne was now being rowed toward the landing. A broad, noble flight of steps led upward from the water toward a wide bank of glassed doors, flung open along the entire front where the hall faced the canal. She could see the people processing to and fro behind them; the doors themselves were a fashion imported from Venice and had caused much controversy because they were more expensive than cannon to make. Constructed from surprisingly large pieces of pale pink glass, they came into their own tonight, thrown open to the warm evening air; now the Bruggers were proud of how much they had cost, the faces of their English guests said it all—who had ever seen that much glass in one place ever before? Truly this was a wealthy city.

Anne's was one of the very last barges to arrive at the water stairs and yet it took some time for the press of people ahead of her to step onto the landing beside the canal. Patiently Anne waited—anxiety mounting, until at last her men were able to dock.

Gathering her skirts in one hand, Anne breathed deeply and, having steadied herself, began to ascend the shallow stone steps in front of her.

At the top, a broad path led straight to the hall, well lit by lines of liveried servants, each side holding flambeaux. It was only at the last step that Anne saw the path was empty in front of her; all the other guests were either already inside the hall or still climbing the water steps behind her.

She would enter the hall alone. That would cause scandal, she knew, as she'd been asked by several other guests to join their parties—and had refused. Now, however, as the moment could not be denied, her courage almost failed for there was no escaping the attention such an act would bring.

The light in the hall was dazzling, and in one sense her entry was badly timed because as she stepped through the rose-glass doors, trumpets sounded so loudly, so suddenly, she stumbled from surprise.

Around her, fellow guests turned toward the high dais set at the far end of the great tented space. They breathed as one—a quick inhale, followed by a long, long sigh, for the duke and his new duchess had arrived. With the collective whisper of expensive material being gathered up in jeweled hands, the entire company knelt.

The trumpets sounded once, twice, three times more, and Edward of England and his mother processed into the hall, to be greeted by their host and his duchess, sister and daughter no more, but coruler of her own domain.

For a moment, Anne, dazzled by the sight, stood alone in the doorway, in clear sight of the dais toward which the royal party was moving.

Edward, as the chief and most honored guest at the feast, bowed graciously to left and right as he escorted his mother to her own ducal throne behind the high table, but then he paused, his eyes fixed on the open doorway where Anne found herself trapped: Anne, standing alone in her dress of mutable silk.

Gracefully, unhurriedly, she, too, sank to her knees on the painted tiles joining the other guests. But her heart was hammering—he was wearing the jewels she'd thrown him.

The court, the hall, was a frozen tableau; then Edward bowed expressly to her, Anne graciously inclined her head, and the king moved on with Duchess Cicely.

A great feast is a hive of gossip—elaborate manners and courtly gestures are merely the pretty garments on top of the flesh and bone of expectation and speculation. So it was here. Many eyes had noted Edward's expression when he saw Anne de Bohun, among them Duke Charles. And many had seen, too, that the skein of pearls and emeralds thrown to him by this same English lady was slung around his shoulders, in place of the more usual gold collar of state. Where was William Caxton? Had he seen what had come to pass?

But now the bride was seated beneath her own Cloth of Estate, with the duke at her right hand, and Edward on his sister's left. The guests all rose quickly from their knees as the silver trumpets brayed once more, and hurried to their allocated places while servers hurried the first spectacular dishes to each long board.

Whole baked peacocks redressed in their plumage, gilded raised pies in the shapes of mythical animals, fricassees and ragouts of spiced porpoise, and venison, crane, widgeon, teal, tench, and pike.

Duke Charles, as aware of Anne's spectacular entrance as any man in the room, flicked a glance at Edward. How much did his guest know of what Caxton had told him?

The king had chosen to honor Anne by wearing her jewels. Yes, Charles had heard the gossip, too, though he'd not seen her throw them. So perhaps there was truth in Caxton's story about this pair of remarkably handsome people—but then his bride smiled at him, charmingly and shyly, and the duke abandoned his uneasy thoughts and concentrated on his new duchess. Time enough for politics later.

After the busy chaos of being seated, Anne, with consummate good manners, applied herself to conversation with her neighbors, apparently unconscious of the interest that one glance from Edward had engendered among the other wedding guests.

Fierce joy burned her; Edward was glorious still.

And they were Edward's thoughts, too, when he gazed down into the hall, elaborately casual. Yes, it *was* Anne; flesh and blood, and beautiful, more beautiful; remote but real.

But she would not look at him. Well then, he would have to change that calm detachment. The dangerous heat in his blood, the churning elation in the pit of his belly conveyed utter certainty; there was much to be said and done between them again, whether she was prepared to acknowledge him or not.

William Caxton, however, on the other side of the hall at a board filled with fellow members of the English Merchant Adventurers, was deeply uneasy. He had nearly choked when Anne entered the hall and Edward bowed to her. In her simply cut peacock-silk dress she was impossible to miss among the sea of red velvet, black velvet, and cloth of gold. His own wife was trussed into a gown of heavy burgundy figured damask, in complement to the duke, and was nearly scarlet with the heat, sweat dripping from her chin into ample cleavage as she tried to sustain the weight of her monstrously padded jeweled headdress.

And it did not please Maud when she saw her husband gaze at Anne: God damn that whore for her cool poise. She wasn't even slightly flushed, though she must have known that nearly every male eye in that great hall was pulled to her as if by a lodestone by the unvirtue of that flimsy dress!

Anne must have felt the heat of Maud's wrath, for at that moment she glanced up and saw the Caxtons. Gravely she bowed to them, then laughingly answered her left-hand neighbor, a Flemish knight of excellent birth who had only just lost a wife and was looking to replace her. "No, Sir Piotr, I do not think of marriage. My trading interests are husband enough for me."

Sir Piotr snorted. "Ah, lady, that can only mean you do not understand. The right husband, now, he could cause you to think differently." Greatly daring, he allowed one of his hands to touch hers, touch and linger, as he reached across to a dish of green-baked larks with gilded sandalwood powder scattered across their surface. They were sharing a trencher, Anne and he, but theirs was no slab of bread—it was a massive silver tray, a most fashionable and extravagant addition to the table for each pair of guests.

Without fuss, Anne slid her hand from beneath the knight's as she contrived to signal to one of the servitors. "Sir Piotr, let me assist you with these larks before they can fly from you."

"Lady, songbirds need freedom, we all know that. But they can live happily in a cage—if it is of the right sort. It is said they reserve their sweetest music for their owners."

Anne smiled graciously. "How fortunate you are, Sir Knight. Your knowledge of birds is remarkable. However, I think it a shame—caged birds make me sad. I love to see them fly and prize their captive songs less than you."

She turned politely in response to a sally from her other neighbor, leaving the knight only a little dashed. Sitting next to Anne was plainly the work of destiny, he was convinced of it. He would not let such a chance go to waste!

Unseen by all but the duke himself, Edward, at the high table, narrowed his eyes. That clumsy oaf who sat by Anne was ogling the girl, even daring to touch her hand! She was a jewel, a glinting, supremely precious jewel in a setting of base metal. He was still getting used to her presence, so close he could almost hear what she was saying to the idiots who sat beside her at the board below the high table. He would have to work hard tonight to be properly attentive to the festival, to play his part, for if he allowed himself, it would be noticed he had eyes for nothing and no one but the girl dressed in peacock silk.

With an effort, he tore his gaze away from Anne to see, with pleasure, that his erstwhile so rebellious little sister was nearly speechless and slightly dazed sitting next to Duke Charles.

Her manners were exemplary, of course, but Edward knew Margaret well. Color glowed high on her cheeks, and when Duke Charles turned to address her, Edward could see his sister making every effort to be graceful and pleasing to her new husband. Duke Charles's physical presence was formidable; Edward had seen its effect on women before, many times.

Yet it was a strange sight watching Margaret flirting with the man she'd been determined to despise. She looked up and caught Edward's glance, even threw him a slightly defiant smile as if to say, well, so, perhaps you were right . . .

He smiled in return and shook his head. *Silly girl—trust your brother*. She understood and shrugged, making a little moue. And then turned back and smiled brilliantly at her duke, who raised her hand and kissed it lingeringly. Paralyzed, she left it within his grasp, drowning in his dark, brilliant eyes.

Below the high table, Anne picked up the byplay between the new bride and groom and her gut contracted. To see the dawning of passion so clearly reflected on both faces was to remind her of the past. Images of the time she had spent in Edward's arms flashed behind her eyes unbidden. His mouth, the hardness of his arms, his strength. The beauty of his body.

Edward's face swam into focus. He was gazing down at her, eyes boring into her own as he loosened the first few buttons of his jacket, just as if he were feeling the heat. Quickly Anne dropped her eyes, her blood fizzing like the Moorish sherbet even now foaming in the precious white glass beaker she was holding. Duke Charles rose gracefully to his feet, breaking the moment as horns, viols, and tabors struck up to signal the end of the first part of the feast.

Bowing firstly to his bride, and then, more deeply still, to his honored guest the King of England, and the king's mother, Duchess Cicely, the duke cleared his throat to speak.

"Dear friends, I have waited for this day!" The new husband was beaming as he looked out over his magnificently dressed subjects. "I am a lucky man, for God has seen fit to bestow on me the sister of my dearest friend," he bowed again to Edward, "the most noble, the most gracious, the most beautiful Margaret of England, to be my duchess."

Now it was to his bride that he turned. "Dearest lady, you are the living symbol of the precious unity that has always bound Burgundy and England. We welcome you to your city with love, and from this day I am your joyful and faithful servant in heart and in body; and as a loving champion and husband should, I will worship you all the days of my life, which I attest before this noble company here gathered. England and Burgundy are now joined forever. Or will be, as soon as that can be arranged."

There was a little gasp of shocked laughter at the boldness of his last words. Their duke was certainly well pleased with the choice of this, his new duchess; and plainly he meant to worship his new bride very thoroughly on their wedding night. Margaret herself looked down quickly out of suitable embarrassment, but many remarked on the pleasure that flashed from her eyes at her husband's words. This was to be a warm night in more ways than one.

Anne smiled, even laughed, as did her neighbors at the bride's blushes, but it was hard not to feel wistful sorrow mixed with the pleasure of this celebration. The princess did not understand how lucky she was: she was adored by her new subjects and, it seemed, by her new husband. And he had acknowledged his feelings for her, and his delight in her person, in this most public way. Yet she, Anne, would never, could never, receive such an honorable declaration from the man she had not ceased to love.

Edward, too, had been stirred by the Duke's speech with its frank reference to the physical pleasure he was impatient to enjoy. The duke and he shared a common, urgent desire to be done with the public part of the night so that the private might begin.

It took all of Edward's will not to look down at Anne again as he rose to his feet to respond to the duke's graceful little speech on behalf of his sister, the bride.

"Duke Charles, it is hot tonight, plainly. I am warm, I swear; and from your looks it seems that you are also; why, even my sister, the duchess—seems right fevered. Perhaps prayers can cool that heat for she is most devout, your new duchess—she will not fail to match you in piety, prayer for worshipful prayer, of that I am certain." This time Margaret couldn't help but giggle, and even her dignified mother was seen to smile.

Edward held up one hand to quell the delighted, rising babble. "I, too, see this marriage as a symbol of the joining between your state, Duke Charles, and our own. A joining that is very precious to us." As the king bowed gracefully to his host he allowed his eyes to sweep the room, deliberately catching Anne's glance in his own like a fowler netting a bird.

"In this toast," Edward had raised his goblet filled with the richest wine from Duke Charles's best vineyards, "we seek blessing on your marriage from God and his most Holy Mother, the patroness of this fair city. May the children of Burgundy multiply, may this noble state prosper, and may the ties between us be ever deepened. We drink to you!"

"We drink to you," was echoed around the great hall, and as the sweet wine slid down Anne's throat she found herself looking up and, in that moment, the king raised his goblet to her, and very deliberately drank it to the lees.

The intensity of his look made Anne choke with shock on her own wine. Piotr, taking advantage of the moment, banged her delightedly on her back, briefly allowing his hand free range of her shoulders and spine. "Careful, lady, burgundy can be very strong if you're not used to it." He thought he was being gallant, but his grinning obviousness of purpose had the most unexpected effect on Anne. She laughed giddily. "Sir Piotr, it's plainly not the wine I should be concerned about. The men of Burgundy are stronger. You nearly broke my back!"

# Chapter Twenty-five

It was time to put the bride to bed.

The feast, despite the best efforts of Duke Charles to hurry the ceremonial pace along, had wound its way well past midnight, but now at last the final course had been finished, with one last extravagant "subtlety"—this time a gilded marchpane model of Brugge with the bride and groom standing in the Markt square, waving to the assembled people of Brugge, complete with canals and all the principal buildings of the city—and Duke Charles rose to his feet.

"My friends, since it is my wedding night, and the duchess's, I'm sure you will understand if I thank you all for your attendance and wish you all a fair good night!"

"And you, Your Grace! And you, Duchess." Delighted shouts and good-natured laughter rippled around the hall at the Duke's impatience to be alone with his bride, as an energetic measure struck up from the musicians. Quickly the guests sprang up from the boards as servants hurried to clear the trestles so that the hall was readied in a trice for the bride and groom to progress to their bridal suite together.

Some few lucky guests, as a special mark of favor from the duke, had been invited to witness the official bedding, and Anne was one of those. She could feel her heartbeat ramp higher as she accepted Sir Piotr's help to stand from the long backless bench they had both been sitting on. Thinking this would guarantee him a moment's more conversation with his charming dinner companion, the knight attempted to become her champion.

"Lady Anne, since you have no member of your family to escort you, perhaps when the bridal party has departed I can be permitted to accompany you to your home. For safety only, dear lady; the town will be rowdy tonight."

Anne smiled at him and shook her head gently.

"How kind you are, Sir Piotr. But I shall be here a little longer in the palace. And I have my own barge waiting, with my servants. They will see me safely home when the time comes."

That dashed the knight's confidence. He himself was not invited to witness the bedding. Lady Anne must be in high favor, yet another evidence of her potential value to his house. He decided to take the rebuff gracefully.

"Ah, lady, you devastate me. But perhaps I may call upon you tomorrow so that I can personally assure myself that you are safe."

It would have been grossly impolite to reject the knight further, so with grave good manners Anne curtsied to him and he bowed deeply in return.

As she rose, Anne was astonished to see a much older man in front of her, Sir Piotr, but much, much older: fatter, red-faced, and beaming, and beside him a woman of about his own age who was laughing happily. Sir Piotr patted the woman's hand affectionately as she gazed up at him and then . . . the image was gone.

Sir Piotr, the young Sir Piotr, was smiling at Anne eagerly, unwilling to let her slip away. "Did you say something, mistress? I thought perhaps . . ."

Anne shook her head. "No, Sir Piotr. I wish you a good evening." And before he could speak further, she moved away, smiling, toward the back of the crowd, which was arranging itself with the help of the palace chamberlain and his people so that a wide central corridor of space permitted the exit of the court party.

The duke and his new duchess processed through the crowd, bowing jubilantly right and left, followed by Edward, who had Duchess Cicely on his arm once more. Nearer and nearer they came to where Anne was standing as chosen members of the assembly fell in behind the duke and duchess on their way to the bedding. Soon Anne would join them and face the moment when she must meet not only Edward but his mother and his sister. And other members of the English court.

It had been two years since she had been one of Queen Elizabeth's body servants, but Anne knew, though she was dressed in fine clothes, that she would be recognized. Her life, one way or another, would change from tonight. What she had once been would throw her back, for good or ill, into the world of the English court. And the English king.

Ribald shouting and lewd jokes preceded the slow passage of Duke Charles and his bride, sound so boomingly loud it had the percussive force of the sea hitting a gravel beach.

Anne, in the shadows beside the silk-draped walls of the banqueting hall, was lapped and caught up in it so strongly it shook her body, and suddenly she was not in the hall but standing on a high cliff—and when she turned back she saw Saint Hilda's great Abbey, crouching above the cold gray sea far, far below.

Whitby, she was in Whitby again, but this time she was alone, cold, and very frightened. She'd lost someone, someone dear to her. And when she looked down at herself and saw the blackened wood crucifix clutched in her hand, saw what she was wearing, she choked down a scream for she was dressed in the rough-spun robes of a postulant—a novice nun.

The shock brought her back to the present and the heat—and the joy. The court party was passing by where she was standing, and like a magnet she found she was drawn toward them through the crowd. Around her, the guests squeezed aside to let her through, allowing her to join with the members of the combined courts of England and Burgundy as they trailed out of the hall, singing lewd versions of popular songs and shouting, to accompany the bride and groom to their bedchamber.

Many covert glances slid toward Anne as she made her way, smiling and nodding to friends and acquaintances, but detached, so detached, out of the hall, oblivious. She had a focus now: blank out what she had just seen, blank out the feeling of trapped desolation, the certainty of truth the vision had given her. To see forward was to be armed. To see the future merely conveyed possibilities, nothing more.

She would never be a nun, willingly or unwillingly. And she would never return to England again. How could she?

And, of course, the feeling ebbed as she found herself so solidly in the present again, pressed up against her fellow guests as they crowded onto a staircase that wound up to a great gallery off which was the duke's own private suite of rooms.

Up ahead she could see that the bride was being taken into the nuptial chamber by her mother and a crowd of court ladies from both England and Burgundy. Behind the closed door, they would undress Margaret and clothe her in virginal white before placing her in the marriage bed. The duke, impatient to take his place beside his new wife, hurried with his suite, including Edward, into his own rooms where he, too, would be arrayed for the long night to come.

Anne waited patiently with the remainder of the excited, chattering court outside the bridal chamber; soon there would be the invitation to view the bride in her bed, before the ceremonial entry of the duke into his new wife's room.

William Caxton was waiting too, with Maud, as he spied Anne.

"Excuse me, wife. I'll return in a moment," and before Maud could stop him, William plunged into the press of people, quickly navigating a path through the crowd to Anne's side.

"Lady Anne. We have not spoken, but I did not want the night to finish without saying how pleased I am to see you looking so well, so very well."

He meant more, of course. He wanted to say how beautiful she was in her fine silk dress, how worried he'd been for her, how grateful he was that she had recovered.

Anne understood something of the turmoil of his feelings and smiled so sweetly and, yes, so intimately at him that he found himself speechless. It had been such a long time since he'd experienced such intensity of feeling. For one mad moment he felt himself leaning down, felt himself moving closer and closer, felt as if he would . . .

But Anne was no longer looking at him. She was staring over his shoulder. Involuntarily he turned to find himself looking directly into the eyes of the King of England. And the king was glacially furious. Furious with him. Somehow, Edward had noticed the moment between him and Anne. As had Maud—her face also swam into focus behind Edward's shoulder.

In the horror of that second, poor bemused William felt immensely guilty—and confused. Surely he'd dealt with his own body demons and women long years before, yet here, incongruously, he heard words booming in his mind: *Render unto Caesar, that which is Caesar's* . . . Did that mean the powerful effect Anne had on him, wearing that dress, was treason? The look in Edward's eyes said as much. William gulped as the king advanced toward him, toward Anne.

Fortunately, the moment was masked by the rowdy bunch of young men surrounding the duke as they were swept up along the gallery to the door of the bridal chamber, catching and herding the guests ahead of them toward the bride's sanctum.

Loudly, at his young suite's urging, the groom himself knocked at the bronze-bound doors.

"I am Duke Charles! Where is my bride?"

The crowd laughed heartily. The urgency in the duke's tone sounded very real, joke or no joke.

There was flustered giggling from behind the great door until, at last, "We need a few moments more, Your Grace. Just a few moments."

That was not good enough for the duke.

"I am waiting! Who dares keep me from my bride!" He was mock angry but looked enough like a lion to inject a certain nervousness in his courtiers and honored guests. They added their voices to his.

"Come on now, you've had long enough."

"Open for the duke!"

"We're all dying of heat out here!"

It was a confused, rising babble of sound, but it must have had some effect for at last the door opened and a most appealing sight was there to be seen.

The new duchess, Margaret, was clothed in a modest but semi-diaphanous white bed gown, sitting in the very center of a vast bed covered in a green velvet counterpane thickly strewn with white petals. The bed's size was so great, Margaret looked like a girl in a flower-quilted meadow.

Quickly the duke's young men pushed the groom ahead of them to the side of the bed, only just in front of the surging mass of guests, all trying to crowd through the doorway together. Protocol seemed suddenly abandoned and Anne, hanging back as much as she could, felt for the poor bride, who was looking rather alarmed by this shouting mass of red-faced, drunken people surging toward her.

Vainly the duke called for quiet, but the crowd, which had been looking forward to this moment all night, were having none of it. Suddenly a great cacophony struck up; many of the wedding guests had purloined silver plates and other vessels from the feast and were banging on them with gusto as they shouted for the duke to join his wife in bed.

A certain madness seemed to infect the stifling heat of the bedchamber. Though it was vast, it was jammed with sweating bodies and the candles, on their great stands, caught the brilliance in many a girl's eye and added to the heat. The young men were moving through the pack of courtiers around the bed, surging closer to any good-looking woman, taking advantage of the crush to press themselves against equally willing bodies. Lust was in the air. Weddings always did that.

Anne, doing her best to wriggle away from impertinent hands and over-bold glances, had worked her way toward the back of the crowd. It would be soon enough for Duchess Cicely, or someone she had once known at the Palace of Westminster, to catch sight of her. Besides, she wanted the chance to watch Edward from a little distance, unobserved if she could. It took a few moments, as the duke and his chamberlain continued to ask for quiet, but soon she found her back against the wall, standing in front of one of the precious tapestries that lined the chamber.

Anne found that there was a low chest beside her and it took only a moment to clamber up so that now she could see clear over the crowd to the center of the room where the bed stood.

Then she frowned as she scanned the room—where was Edward?

"And so, dear friends, the time has come, and I claim your indulgence."

"No indulgence, no indulgence"—it was a chant. No one wanted to leave; they wanted to play this game out for as long as possible.

Then, reluctantly, a hush settled at last as the crowd allowed the duke to be heard.

"But yes! I am your duke and I command it. It is time for my bride and I to . . ."

Anne did not hear the last words that the duke said, for suddenly a powerful hand was over her mouth and she was pulled backward through a gap between tapestries and into darkness.

It was so quick she had no time to feel fear. That came a moment later, for suddenly a fine scarf was pulled tight over her eyes and she was picked up bodily by what felt like two men—two strong men.

Her instinct was to fight but her hands were securely held and another scarf was tied around her mouth to give her no chance to scream. Abruptly the noise and the heat of the bridal chamber disappeared into muffled silence and she felt herself being quickly carried, squirming and kicking at her captors, through some sort of stone-lined space. She could tell it was stone; she knew the sound of boot leather on flags well enough.

The men were silent as they hurried on their way, but they were careful how they carried her, and though her heart hammered, she found some slight reassurance in their treatment, though it was a fleeting thought for equally suddenly she heard a door open, then close, and she was placed on her feet again.

And then she was alone, for before she could pull the scarves from her eyes and mouth, she heard the men leave, closing the door gently behind them. And a key scraped as it turned in the lock.

Angry she was, certainly, and fearful. But very soon something much more complex ran through her.

She was in an exquisite room hung with rose-colored damask.

And what she least expected, there were doors opening out to a spacious balcony. There was food and drink, too, and in Moorish fashion, in one wall of the room was an alcove in which was a sumptuous ivory and ebony wood couch draped with lustrous green silk.

This was not a prison, and yet . . .

Anne forced herself to breathe more slowly and as if unconcerned, sauntered out to the balcony. She could see the canals two or more floors beneath her feet. She could even make out the bend in her own part of the canal above which stood the Cuttifer house. And when she looked directly down, there was her barge, waiting patiently in line with those of the other guests. Such irony; none of her servants was to be seen, and they would not hear her even if she called out. And there was no way down of course, unless she tried to jump.

"A pretty view, is it not? Especially on such a mild night."

She hadn't heard the key turn in the lock again, but she knew that voice.

"I apologize for the fright you must have felt. There was no other way to remove you without comment."

Suddenly he was real again, and close, so close.

"I was not frightened."

She turned to see him standing in the open doorway. Edward.

Never had he looked so magnificent. Or more grim. Unblinking they stared at each other.

Sometimes it is hard to see, to really see. Anne wanted to remember this moment, to remember each of his features, his clothes, his hands. To hold time from moving forward because as soon as they spoke, as soon as they moved . . .

Deliberately he walked toward her, oblivious to all else but her face, her eyes, her mouth.

"Anne, where have you been?"

It was a whisper, a husky whisper, but it contained more longing, more yearning than she had ever heard in her short life. She shivered, her throat so tight it hurt to try to speak.

He was beside her now—how could she have forgotten he was so tall?

"I have been here, in Brugge."

"All this time?"

"Yes."

What they said was irrelevant, mere words. The speed of her heart, the lack of breath, made Anne's head swim. Unconsciously she took a step toward him.

"Hello." She whispered the word. It seemed such a childlike thing to say. But it broke the dam for both of them.

In a breath he was kissing her, so hot and so hard that her knees buckled. She molded herself to him, heart beating against his chest, nearly sobbing as she tried to speak, trying to hold some semblance of where she was, and what she was doing in the midst of the dark, hot tide that engulfed them both.

Quickly he pulled her back into the room and, in his haste to kiss and hold her at the same time, picked her up to carry her to the couch in the alcove.

"Wait, Edward. Wait. Please."

"I don't want to wait. Trust me, please trust me." He'd ripped off his magnificent jerkin, careless of buttons and frogging, and in a moment his fine linen undershirt had followed as he tore at the lacing of her dress.

Sandalwood and ambergris. She closed her eyes fleetingly; that had always been his smell; and his sweat—musky, warm, so male it bypassed her skin on its way to her bones. But they had to talk. Had to. Before this went any farther.

"Stop." Could she stop him? Further words were wasted by his urgent mouth on hers.

"No!" Somehow she slipped out of his arms, although the bodice of her dress was half-unlaced.

"Why!" There was such agony, such longing from the king that she swayed on her feet as she tried to contain his roaming hands. "Don't deny me. Please don't deny me, Anne."

She saw the love in his eyes, and the heat and the power. She knew he saw the same in hers. His presence was so formidable that her mind almost surrendered to the clamor of her body. She said, "I have a child. A boy. And I've made a life. Without you."

There was stillness, and silence, except for their breathing: two athletes after a long, long race.

"A child? Whose child?" He was deeply wounded, tears in his eyes.

She took a step back from him, careless of her seminakedness, and lifted her head fearlessly. He felt a great surge of love for her, for her magnificence and her courage.

"What is his father's name?"

She paused before she spoke. "Edward. That is my son's name also.

"Your child—and mine?"

There was such a surge of jubilant hope, of joy in his voice, that tears sprang from her eyes and she could not speak.

Now she let him hold her, now she let him kiss the tears away as he rocked her tenderly.

"Ah, sweetest, dearest Anne; how hard it must have been for you. And I did not know. Why did you not tell me?" For a moment he was angry, and then proud. Of course she would not have told him.

He sighed. "How much I love you. Do not cry . . . there, I am here now, we are together. Nothing shall harm you, nothing."

Sweetly now, gently now, he held her closely, soothed her as she cried as if she would never stop. All the pain, all the loss, all the agony of their parting was in those tears.

Then he turned her face to his as she sobbed and he kissed the tears, kissed her soft mouth; kissed and kissed her. Deeply and sweetly and more deeply still. And the tears stopped, although Anne was profoundly shaken to feel the depth of the fear and sadness she had suppressed for so long.

"We have time. We have time. And we must never be parted again. You, and my son—we are all connected now, by blood."

He murmured the words, breathing them into her. Willingly, she tasted his mouth on hers, her breath quickening, closing her eyes, losing thought, losing sense.

He kissed her ears, the column of her throat, the division between her breasts as he detached the pins from her hennin.

"Your hair, unpin your hair."

It was so easy to do, and soon her hair was a warm bright cloak falling to her waist. Slowly, agonizingly slowly, Edward undid each of the pearl buttons on her sleeves, and a moment later the topaz dress slithered to the floor. Anne stood naked in the king's arms.

Edward's body was against hers, his hard torso, his belly pressed with hers, skin to skin.

"Will you stay with me, Anne? Let this be our wedding night too." He whispered it, his voice shaking slightly. She sighed tremulously and opened her eyes.

"Sire, there can never be marriage between us."

She spoke without thinking and in no sense was she bitter: it was the honest statement of a fact.

Mutely he pulled her to him. "Perhaps fate has meant to torment us in this way. I do not know why. I only know I love you and I cannot bear to have you leave me again."

Now it was Anne who rocked the king gently to and fro, holding him for comfort—hers and his.

"I have told them all that he is Aveline's son. My sister's son. I'm called his aunt."

She found it difficult to tell the king—as if the deception had betrayed both of them.

Edward stepped back from her, holding her from him at arm's length as he looked into her eyes.

He smiled as one fingertip gently traced its way down the planes of her face to find her mouth.

"We do what we must to survive. And you've survived right well, it seems to me. You are very rare. A prize of great worth, not merely a prince of the blood."

He tried not to drop his gaze, but he lost that battle. His voice grew husky as his eyes roamed over her body though his hands stayed still on her shoulders.

"Stay with me, Anne. I've dreamed of you."

Perhaps a sensible woman would have had the strength to walk away, but Anne was fiercely hungry and she wanted this man with the same passion he wanted her.

Thus, for answer she kissed him lingeringly on the mouth, as she began, slowly and deliberately, to unlace the king's close-fitting hose that was all that separated her naked body from his.

It took all the physical discipline he had to stand there, shivering voluptuously, as with tantalizing delicacy she slid her hands down his body, easing the hose down over his buttocks, down his thighs, and yet farther down so that he could step out of them.

For one incandescent moment they stood apart, completely naked, before Edward pulled her, unresisting, into his arms and down onto the couch.

At first she found that she was lying on his chest, conscious that her legs had parted. Then, suddenly and deftly, he had her underneath him, sliding deep inside her body in the same moment. They both gasped as, mouth to mouth, he began to move so gently, so sinuously that she began to moan; she could not help herself, wanting him deeper, ever deeper.

His hand was between them and he was stroking her as he moved a little faster, a good deal harder.

"Ah, Jesu . . . you're so wet;" he was panting, trying to control the pleasure as she writhed beneath him, eyes wide, mouth open and hungry for his.

"Let me kiss you." She could barely speak as he took her buttocks in each of his hands so that he could pull her closer, more closely onto his body as he moved more and more powerfully in and out of hers. He plunged his mouth down as the heat built in his belly and he felt himself grind against her hips as she moved beneath him, opening herself, allowing him higher and higher.

The rhythm between them was so perfect that as he thrust she rose to meet him. They were helpless in the moment as he drove into her again and again, and she began to moan louder and louder, almost singing as the sense of their separate beings was dissolved and they were connected in a brilliant, fierce, incandescent wave that built and built between them until it crashed and took them both down, down so deeply, into resonant peace. They lay together, silent now, slick with sweat as sweetness flooded their bodies and the sounds of the night gradually returned.

It would have been easy to glide into sleep, and blessed also, but Edward lay with his eyes open, one hand gently caressing

Anne's rounded hip, as the candles guttered in their sconces.

She, too, was silent, content, and determined to hold thought at bay for a brief period more as she savored his smell and her heart ceased hammering in her chest.

"I am here for ten days. Then we return to England. I want you to come back with me."

Anne sat up and looked down on her lover. It was a reflex action to cover herself with the green coverlet. She smiled a little sadly.

"Edward, you exiled me."

"That can be revoked! If I choose."

"But listen to me, my love. You know nothing of my life. I have commercial interests here, a business."

"And you have our son." He said it gently but with purpose. "He must meet his father. And if I have no other son . . ."

There, it was said. An acknowledgment that their child figured in the succession of England; if he had no other son. Yet Anne knew the queen was pregnant; it had been freely gossiped about as the wedding barges made their way up the canal. Had that only been this morning?

"Let me see you. We have nothing to hide from one another now, and you are very beautiful." Was it strange that she felt no shame? Perhaps she was a child of the Devil after all—the priests would certainly tell her so. Anne shrugged to herself; she did not care for priests' opinions now. Did she?

The king smiled tenderly at her, unaware her thoughts were so far away, but then he frowned as he traced the white line of scar beside her breast, which was all that remained of the attack.

"What is this?"

"I was attacked. A crossbow. Someone paid to have me killed, and they nearly got their money's worth."

There was a moment's shocked silence and then Edward was furious. It was terrifying. Anne, for the first time, was frightened of what Edward might truly do, might truly be capable of. God, never let them be enemies!

"Who? Who has done this thing?"

Anne said nothing. There was so much to absorb now, so

much to take in and consider; it was not the time for impetuous unburdening.

"I have made enemies, commercial enemies." She was reluctant to say even this; touched his arm to calm him.

"Anne, do you know who tried to murder you?"

A sudden, discreet knock at the door shocked them both. Edward shouted out, raging, "Go away! I am not to be disturbed."

A timorous voice answered.

"Sire, a thousand apologies, but it is reported ships have been sighted off Sluis, bearing the queen, your wife's, standard. The Duchess Cicely instructed you should be told."

Edward's face hardened as he absorbed this news. He pulled Anne protectively closer, slipping an arm around her waist as he shouted.

"Does the duke know?" There was a momentary silence, during which whispers and shuffling could be heard on the other side of the door.

"We sought to tell Your Majesty first." The inference was plain. No one was brave enough, or foolhardy enough, to disturb the duke on his wedding night.

Edward cursed roundly under his breath. "God's very bones . . ." then shouted out, "I shall let you know my pleasure shortly. Go away!"

Anne couldn't help it; at this moment of greatest tension she giggled—and the almost tangible cloud of black fury around Edward began to dissipate. "Your pleasure, Lord King? I doubt that's for discussion or publication."

Edward smiled down at her, kissed her softly, then sighing, held her unspeaking. Elizabeth Wydeville was close and it was a shattering blow to them both. Anne took the initiative.

"I will leave, Edward. But you know where I—where we live."

Edward was angry now, with a deep, controlled sense of purpose. The queen never did anything without a plan, and following him to Burgundy, after he had left her as regent, was not only strange, it was dangerous. He would look a fool in the eyes of the European leaders assembled for this wedding. If the King of England could not rely on his wife to support him in his decisions, what could he expect from his subjects?

Anne put one finger to Edward's lips. "No doubt there is a most important reason she is here. We have ten days . . ."

"We have a lifetime, Anne. Yours and mine."

She said nothing. He had married the queen in haste, that was fate. But Edward and Elizabeth were married; they would stay married—a king did not put aside his queen for love.

And Anne would never become his leman, his official mistress—she was too proud for that.

Nothing had changed.

# Chapter Twenty-six

Elizabeth Wydeville had surprised them all. For a woman halfway through her latest pregnancy, she had proved a good sailor, and even though the crossing from England had been unseasonably wild and others of her court had been gutted by seasickness, she had not succumbed.

Much more important, she'd got her way and, as she waited in the cathedral at Damme the day after the wedding to receive her husband, her mother-in-law, and the Duke and Duchess of Burgundy, she had reasons to feel well pleased with herself.

She was nervous about meeting Edward, of course, but that was only to be expected. Soon he would understand and praise her for the action she had taken. Yes, Elizabeth was sure he would be pleased by her presence when he came to understand.

Why then, if she was so certain of her actions, did she change her dress three times ahead of the audience with Edward; rising from her unfamiliar quarters in the bishop's best bedroom well before dawn, to drive her servants and her ladies to near insanity with her constantly changing demands?

Simplicity had seemed best to her, in the end, since she was to play the part of penitent but frightened wife and queen, rushing to her husband's side with news no one else knew or could be burdened with.

Dressed in white almost as plainly as a nun, she was on her knees before the rood screen in front of the high altar of the cathedral, still decked with the flowers and banners of yesterday's wedding, when Edward was announced to her.

Only iron control continued to keep the smile on her face when she turned toward him as he stalked up the aisle, face clenched and fierce.

Impulsively Elizabeth, Queen of England, bowed her head and knelt most humbly as he approached.

"Dearest husband—Lord and King—I have dreadful information. Information that only you can hear, and that only I can give."

She'd voiced the words in a low but urgent whisper, and with eyes still respectfully cast to the floor, hurried on.

"I would never have dared to disobey your order and desert my post as regent—you know that—but the safety of your kingdom is at risk. And the alliance with Burgundy—there is more, much more than you know at stake here." That brought the king up short. Burgundy? "I've been so frightened since I heard, Edward, you must believe me!"

That gave Edward pause. Especially as the queen looked up at him, beautiful eyes filled with frightened tears.

Unwillingly he asked the question. "Therefore, tell me what you fear."

Elizabeth looked around as if expecting assailants to jump out of the shadows of the side chapels. Edward ground his teeth—if he had not known her well, this would have been a dazzling display of sincere terror. But he did know her, intimately.

"Well?" The tone was freezing.

Elizabeth Wydeville straightened her back and raised her head proudly. If he was a king, well, she was a queen.

"Your brother, sire. And Duke Charles. Treachery."

A slow prickle made its way down Edward's back.

"George?"

The queen nodded her head and whispered.

"Yes. He has brazenly joined with Warwick and this time there is no hiding the fact. And there is a plot against you here, in this dukedom. Duke Charles is not your friend."

It was a blow to the heart, but the king was conscious of passing time. Outside, in the Cathedral Square, the duke and his new duchess were waiting to welcome Elizabeth to Burgundy. Edward's mother, Duchess Cicely, had remained at the Prinsenhof, pleading gut-sickness after the feast of the night before. Perhaps it was an insult to the queen, perhaps not.

Automatically the king bowed to his wife and bent down to raise her up, noting in a detached way that she had chosen a dress that hid her pregnancy. He could not deny she looked very beautiful, almost ethereal, washed by a great shaft of rosy light from a window of the cathedral.

"Come, Duke Charles waits with my sister the duchess. He is delighted you have joined the wedding party, of course. We will speak of this later . . ."

Elizabeth suppressed a smile. How like the king it was to buy time to think. But she had unsettled him, she could tell.

Charles, however, was wary rather than delighted, though he was intrigued to know why the Queen of England had suddenly elected to join her husband in celebration of his marriage. If this woman truly was a witch, would she have the power to see he knew her secret, knew about Lady Anne?

His new duchess was hard-pressed to look welcoming also; and for a moment Charles was alarmed by the mulish frown that transformed that flowerlike face so briefly. There was a sudden glimpse of a formidable woman beneath the skin of the girl-bride. But then he shook the concern away in welcoming his sister-in-law. He had wanted a wife of spirit; all would be well if she consented to learn from his teaching.

And as he bowed to Elizabeth Wydeville, he could not avoid the thought: what a very handsome family they were—and this queen particularly so. If he had not been so well pleased with Margaret, and so suspicious of Elizabeth's motives, Edward's wife might have proved an interesting target for pursuit; but then he patted Margaret's hand fondly. It was far too early in this marriage to be thinking of another woman, a friend's wife, too, when she was the partner of his partner in a most important alliance.

And his new wife was undeniably delectable, as he had

found, for they sorted very well together, he and she, last night. It was not often as easy with a virgin.

Briefly, he cast Margaret a warm glance as she sat waiting for him in their great carriage, a glance that distracted her from sulking and made her smile through blushes. The duke's belly shifted with the memory of how pleasant it had been overcoming his new wife's natural modesty when the wedding guests had finally been chased from the bridal chamber. And there was another night to come very soon, and another . . . Yes, he would enjoy teaching this one to lose all vestige of shyness, very slowly and very, very thoroughly. It would be pleasant relief from this new anxiety he could not quite suppress.

Yet Charles was the perfect host as he kissed Elizabeth's hand. Curtsying deeply in reply, the Queen of England rose to find a handsome man, a foxlike man, who somehow managed to make each compliment both graceful, funny, and knowing.

Transferring her hand from her husband's arm to the duke's, she let him conduct her proudly to where his bride was seated in her own throne on a great wheeled chariot. It gave Elizabeth considerable pleasure to see that Margaret, because of precedence—a reigning queen would always outrank a duchess—was forced to stand and curtsey to her unexpected guest.

Elizabeth sighed happily. It would be a difficult interview with the king later, but incontestably there was disturbing evidence from the north, evidence gathered by men she paid—and she had been right to come. And now that she was here, well, she was determined to enjoy the rest of the wedding celebrations. In her rightful place at their center.

Not so Anne de Bohun. In twenty-four hours her world had been completely rearranged and it was spinning.

She had returned very late to her own bed, and though deeply weary, had slept little.

A hot, early summer dawn had not improved matters, for there were things to be faced that would not go away. At least it felt a little easier in the light of day.

She did not doubt the strength of her feelings for Edward, nor his for her, but as she sat in the kitchen feeding breakfast to little Edward as the house came awake, Anne, try as she might, could not see the way ahead, especially now that Elizabeth Wydeville was in Brugge.

Wearily she closed her eyes, fingers to throbbing temples. She had drunk very little last night and eaten less. Somehow the sight of Edward at the high table had robbed her of appetite . . . now it felt as if she would never hunger or thirst again.

Deborah watched her foster daughter with concern as, covertly, she stirred powdered wormwood and sanicle in a cup of honeyed sage tea that she was preparing for the girl. Perhaps the herbs would help her foster daughter in the days to come. Wormwood might moderate desire, the sanicle would help with the profound wound to Anne's heart—her love for Edward—and sage might bring wisdom where the king was concerned: only might; Deborah was a realist.

It would be little enough to stem the floodtide of emotion on which Anne was swimming.

Of course the celebration of the wedding and the first great banquet last night were only the beginning of ten days of hectic events that would be piled one on top of another, culminating in a tournament to commemorate the marriage.

This first day, however, Anne had previously arranged to sponsor the staging of an archery competition—a nice irony that, for the weapon of the contest was a longbow. It was to be shot this very afternoon in water meadows outside the town's gates, and even now word was circulating throughout the city as details of the competition began to be made public.

In Deborah's view Anne could not have thought of anything more likely to be popular among the people of Brugge—and more likely to enrage the merchants of the English trading community—since the duke himself had agreed, on behalf of Margaret, that his bride would present the major prize: an English angel for each year of her age.

And no doubt, no doubt at all, Anne would see Edward there again—and now his wife also, if rumor was true.

Deborah added extra honey to the tea she was brewing—something sweet was certainly needed, for today would be a difficult day, for all of them . . .

\* \* \*

Duke Charles remembered the contest belatedly, as his party rode back from Damme. The flurry of the queen's arrival had distracted him, and his new duchess, but now he formally invited Edward, Elizabeth, and all the members of the English court to the archery butts in the water meadow beside the Zwijn to witness the championship.

Edward, of course, swiftly agreed that he would be pleased to attend and suggested his people should participate in the competition as an honor to the duke, Duchess Margaret, and the people of Brugge. English prowess with the longbow was, after all, a matter of pride to him and his countrymen.

"But what merchant could have the resources to give such a handsome prize, Duke Charles? He must be truly a man of enormous wealth." It was the queen who spoke, astonished when she heard how great the purse was to be.

The duke smiled a slightly chilly smile.

"The 'he' is a 'she' ma'am. And remarkable for that fact. Perhaps you did not know, but we have a lady who trades as a merchant in this city with my permission: a very beautiful, unmarried English lady. Sadly, someone tried to assassinate her recently—commercial rivals, we believe. An ironic comment on her power and influence, it seems to me." The courtiers gasped—it was bold to joke about such things. And Edward, too, was shocked though rigid training kept his face impassive.

The queen had become very still as the duke continued. "Some think this lady's life a scandal, but I consider her to be a marvel of nature: a woman with the skills of a man. And the courage."

"You astonish me, Duke Charles. A manlike woman—how unusual." The queen's tone was detached, only faintly interested, but the observant duke had seen the queen's lightly clasped hands clench convulsively as he told his story. Duke Charles smiled at Elizabeth charmingly and shrugged.

"'Manlike' would not be used by many to describe this lady. She is very lovely to look upon, as I said."

Edward, his face a polite mask, turned to Duke Charles.

"Perhaps the duke will tell us the name of his unusual merchant."

"Lady Anne de Bohun. She has lived quietly among us for a time at the house of her guardian, Sir Mathew Cuttifer, a prominent English mercer here, but I believe she was originally from the west of your own country."

Edward smiled charmingly at his wife.

"Anne de Bohun. Elizabeth, you're so much better at this than I am. Do we know her? Has anyone of that name ever been at court?"

The queen smiled innocently in reply.

"No. But perhaps Your Majesty might have met the lady at another time and been unaware it was she."

The court party was fascinated. Clearly there was subtext to the king and queen's exchange, though their faces remained so politely disengaged they might have been discussing the weather.

"If Your Majesties will consent to accompanying the duchess and me this afternoon, you will see for yourselves. We will not need to stay so very long, just time enough to judge the winners and for my dearest wife to award the prize. It will greatly please my subjects and yours, I feel sure, for us all to be seen at the butts."

And so it had been arranged. A message was sent to Anne from Duke Charles that confirmed the presence of himself and the duchess at the prize-giving, to be accompanied by the English king and queen.

And Anne, once she had seen little Edward well fed and sent away with Jenna to dress especially well for the day ahead, asked Maxim and Ivan to join her for a final discussion of the events to come.

It was more than hard to concentrate now that she knew Edward, and also Elizabeth, would be present at the archery contest. Yet she had sought this, arranged it, and on one level, though it was foolhardy, a clear signal was being sent to her enemies: Anne de Bohun refused to go away. Anne de Bohun had very powerful friends. Anne de Bohun had survived and would prosper.

Proud and strong, that was the subtext of this message. And yet, today of all days, Anne did not feel brave. She would not have been human if fear had not colored the elation and exhaustion of last night.

Edward. She would see him again after their tumultuous night together. Gods grant she found the strength to appear unmoved by his presence at the contest.

But she had barely sat down to review the timetable for the contest when Deborah announced William Caxton. Anne, out of politeness, had no choice but to invite her guest into the workroom.

"Maxim, and you too, Ivan, I shall spend a little time with Master William, but that is all; please be ready to continue our discussion."

The words were barely out of her mouth as the two men left and William was admitted, but Anne could not suppress concern when she saw him.

"William, what is wrong?"

It was as if her capable, vigorous friend had aged a decade overnight.

"Anne, did you know?"

"Know what, William? You are agitated. Please sit here in the breeze from the window. Are you thirsty, or hun——"

He did not allow the words out of her mouth.

"Did you know that the queen has arrived?"

"Yes." Anne was astonished at William's intensity.

"The archery contest. When did you decide to stage it?"

"When the marriage was announced, Master William. This is for the duke, his bride, and the people of Brugge. It is my gift to each one of them."

Poor Caxton; this contest would create yet more trouble over the days ahead for it would place Anne at the center of the court's attention once more, and that had to be good for trade. However, the warring factions of the Merchant Adventurers—those who opposed, and those who supported Anne—were only a distraction here today.

Anne sensed William was hiding something, something important. "What is wrong, Master Caxton?"

Caxton suddenly lost his nerve, his certainty. What if he was wrong? The Queen of England plotting to murder this girl? What if it was all fevered imaginings, paranoia?

He got up abruptly and leaned out of the casement window,

snuffing up the rich scent of freshly scythed grass from her heber. Such a comforting smell, so real . . .

Then, making up his mind, he swung back to look at Anne.

"Have you ever met the king before? Or the queen?"

"I . . . William, I'm so sorry, but I have so much to do."

"Anne! You must listen to me. I think it was the queen who tried to kill you. There may be proof."

That was a shock. He hurried on, his words tumbling into Anne's stricken silence.

"Perhaps you know why, perhaps you do not. I believe it is true, however. And there is more."

"Mistress?" Deborah had knocked and pushed the door open in the same moment. She did not necessarily trust William Caxton, whatever debt her mistress felt she owed him.

Anne was distracted; she was also angry. But that was from fear.

"That was not well done, Deborah. Master Caxton and I were speaking privately."

It was unlike Anne to be cold; even less likely that she would stare her foster mother down with such command. Deborah was undaunted, however.

"Lady Anne, Baron Piotr Windhoven has called to see you are safe after the banquet last night. He says you asked him to call on you."

And behind Deborah, waiting in the hall, Anne could see the knight himself, well within hearing range, though pretending to gaze with great attention at the Saint George over the mantelpiece.

Anne had no choice.

"Master William, do we see you at the butts this afternoon? You would be most welcome and we could finish our conversation then."

The merchant picked up one of Anne's hands to kiss it.

"Nothing that I know on this earth would prevent my attendance. Such august company—the duke, the duchess, the king, and his queen."

He did not have to say more. Anne had seen fear in his eyes; she would not let him see it in hers.

William bowed himself through the door as Anne moved forward to welcome Baron Piotr. "Baron, you grace our house. Deborah, would you bring refreshments into the heber, if you please?" Her tone was neutral, but Deborah was dismayed and had the terrible feeling that she had interrupted something of vital importance, and she knew it now.

# Chapter Twenty-seven

In the perverse way of late summer, the perfect, still morning turned ominously heavy by early afternoon.

A fitful wind from the west was blustering from a darkening horizon, a bad omen for an archery contest. Old men who knew such things nodded to each other and said a storm was building, yet that did not dampen the enthusiasm of the crowd gathering at the contest ground, impatient for the archers' heats to begin.

Maxim had excelled himself. Anne had instructed him to spend whatever was required to make the day a success, much to Meinheer Boter's despair. How would the townsfolk of Brugge have ever known the difference if his mistress had just been sensible? Surely the stands erected for the audience needed only to be simple, unvarnished wood, yet he'd been made to use Anne's only recently acquired coin—the foundation of her future—for extravagantly gilded, painted galleries, decorated with bright felt banners.

And as to offering free food to the endless crowd! Had Maxim no idea what such a thing would cost?

Maxim had, of course, and it worried him greatly; he, too, had a responsibility. Not so, Anne—she was determined to provide for the entire town of Brugge, if that was what it took to make men remember this day. It would be an excellent investment—goodwill was a priceless commodity for a merchant!

She had just finished walking over the contest ground with Maxim, and she was excited and delighted with what she saw.

It was such a pretty sight. A line of tightly braided straw butts had been arrayed, back-on to the river Zwijn, while lining each side of the ground, the stands that had occasioned Meinheer Boter's heartburn were bravely painted in red and green, enhanced with lavish gilding in all the most prominent places.

Flags flew, snapping and flapping in the fitful air: the red bear of Brugge and the arms of England hung from alternate poles, arranged at intervals behind each of the galleries. And, too, because she had the duke's support, a special stand had been erected in which the expected royal party would sit.

It was most luxurious. Backless benches had been ranged in tiered rows, each supplied with part-colored red and green wool cushions tasseled in heavy gold, and four chairs of state were placed at the very front, in clear sight of the common people: one each for the duke and his duchess, the other two for the King and Queen of England.

These last two chairs had taxed even Maxim's ingenuity to the breaking point. Where, at the very last minute, did one find two extra chairs of estate fit for reigning monarchs? Find them he did, of course, but it had taken a truly indecent sum of money to bribe Duke Charles's own under chancellor to permit use of the very chairs that had been used at the wedding feast the night before.

A quick re-dress with new green velvet cushions and they looked, well, if not completely different, different enough to puzzle those who were about to sit in them.

And so it began.

Anne's seamstresses had made her a dress of her own imported forest-green damask, a tribute to the famous Lincoln green of England's archers, which had a number of whimsical additions.

Slung around her chest was a silver-gilt quiver containing gilded arrows plus a tiny hunting horn studded with emeralds. She also wore a jaunty green cap with a long curling pheasant feather, a feather that matched the deep russet of her hair caught back behind her head in a simple bone clasp.

Now Anne waited in front of the stands packed with happy townsfolk as distant trumpets announced the arrival of the court party from the direction of the Prinsenhof.

With a bright smile, she signaled Maxim to advance toward the duke and the bridal party.

Anne did not immediately see Edward, but when she did breath left her as their eyes met. She would not hold his glance, however, dropping into a curtsy, ducking her head for a moment; anything to regain poise in his physical presence. The images he evoked in her—the sense of having been with him, naked, only such a short time before—was confronting, exciting, strange; for now they must pretend to be strangers, even though he smiled so yearningly at her bent head as he dismounted.

Elizabeth missed the glance from Edward to their hostess, however, for at that moment—to contrive maximum focus for herself—she'd covertly spurred her horse as the court party advanced the last few paces toward the contest ground. Not unnaturally, her palfrey—a finely bred steel-gray Arab with a white mane and tail—had reared in outrage and leaped forward, unsettling other horses in the party and causing courtiers to jump out of the way.

The crowd in the stands was therefore treated to the sight of the handsome King of England personally calming his wife's horse. What they did not see was Edward's angry frown at the blood running down the Arab's belly, a wound that could only have been caused by Elizabeth Wydeville's vicious spurs.

But the queen had achieved what she set out to do—all eyes were on her, not the duchess, not the duke, not even the king her husband, as the court party was bowed forward by Maxim to where Anne waited, pale but resolute, in front of the crowded stands.

One, two, three more strides and the dazzling court party was within touching distance. One, two, three more breaths as the trumpets blew and Anne dropped into a perfect court curtsy from which she was raised, personally, by the duke.

There was a moment's breathless silence in the stands as those lucky enough to have seats leaned forward to hear their duke.

"Lady Anne, you have excelled yourself."

He gestured around the beautifully laid out ground, the lavish seating for the common people, and the exquisite stand created for the court party.

"Ah, Lord Duke, this is a trifle. And only to express the humble gratitude of my guardian, Sir Mathew Cuttifer—who is not with us today—and myself for your great kindness to us." Anne bowed to the duke, which he gracefully acknowledged with the merest hint of a smile, "and the joy we all feel today at the sight of your most lovely duchess." Another even deeper bow to Margaret, who, as she was now close enough to see Anne's face clearly, was looking puzzled.

"And we are also particularly grateful for the presence of our sovereign, King Edward," now Anne knelt, head humbly bowed, at Edward's feet, "and his most gracious queen." It was beautifully done, and though most who looked at the little pageant were merely dazzled by the beauty of the moment, there were others among the court party who found themselves perplexed.

Perplexed by the expression on Queen Elizabeth's face—a frozen smile that did not change, yet was strange indeed for its lifelessness—and that on Edward's face as well. For the king gazed down with unusual intensity upon the bent head of Anne de Bohun.

Nothing escaped the duke, of course.

Those who knew him well were confused, for he looked like a man enjoying a private joke as he, personally, insisted on raising Anne to her feet once more, much to Edward's barely concealed annoyance as he, too, had stepped forward, holding out his hand to Anne.

But all Anne's nerves vanished when she saw the mischievous glint in the duke's eyes. He was being profoundly naughty, she could see that, and the gambler in her heart stirred and stretched. There was a plan being hatched here but Duke Charles was on her side, or so said his sidelong wink as he helped her up. Now, if she could just work out what he wanted her to do.

Anne's guests were soon seated, as the crowd stamped and cheered, whistled and shouted. They wanted the contest to begin; that's what the men had really come for. For the women it was different, of course. They'd come to see the bride, and the clothes. They weren't disappointed. The noble guests in the royal stand were all lavishly attired, none more so than Anne de Bohun, the remarkable English girl who had made this happy day possible.

There was a sudden mutter of thunder and anxious eyes were cast to the western horizon again. The clouds were ominously darker and the wind had dropped. Livid sulfurous light cast a strange glimmer abroad; even a neighbor's face looked eerie, let alone those of strangers, in the odd greenish glow from the sky. People in the crowd hurriedly crossed themselves: let this not be a bad omen for the start of this marriage they'd all wanted so much.

A hunting horn rang loud as a golden arrow flew to the center butt, finding the black circle at its heart. There was a shocked gasp from the crowd and the court party. Anne had signaled the beginning of the heats by firing the first arrow herself. The crowd could not know, but Anne had been brought up as a child to shoot true with her own small bow; she and Deborah had lived in the forest alone and there was much wild food to be found, especially in hard winters. She might be rusty from lack of practice, but the instinct had never gone away.

To the delighted applause of the crowd and the court party—though not from the queen—Maxim announced the form of the contest in a loud voice, as he signaled the first contestants to step forward.

The archers had been selected on a first come, first served basis and as expected, there had been a frenzied rush of entrants from both the city and the court when the contest had been formally called out by criers, hired by Anne, on the streets this morning.

In the first round there would be twelve heats, each composed of twelve archers apiece. Then the three top-scoring archers from each heat would compete against each other in a further three rounds of twelve archers, but only the winning archer from each of these semifinals would go into the final round. The victor of the final three would take the entire money prize plus Anne's silver quiver with its uniquely valuable arrows.

As the first twelve men took their place before the line of targets among loud encouragement and jeers from the citizens in the stands, the members of the court party settled into their luxurious seating, determined to enjoy the day.

Not so, Queen Elizabeth. Only rigid will allowed a smile to stay in place, but her eyes, those famous blue eyes, were as cold as the deep North Sea as Anne returned to her place, a deliberately small though luxurious stool, to the right of the thrones in the court stand.

The duchess smiled at Anne and beckoned her forward, speaking quietly as the other girl curtsied.

"Lady Anne, it seems we must have met before today, but I cannot recall where that might have been. Was it at court in London?"

Duchess Margaret was a shrewd girl, and she had a good memory for faces. But for once she was questioning what she remembered. Surely it was not possible that a servant in Elizabeth's suite only a few years ago was now an ennobled merchant, in high favor with the duke in Brugge. She must be mistaken, surely. A case of two women looking remarkably alike?

The queen, pretending to be entranced at the sight of her subjects contesting with the Bruggers, did not appear to be listening, but Edward was, as was the duke.

"Duchess, you have never met Lady Anne de Bohun before. I have lands in the west country . . . and I have always preferred a simple life." It was curious wording—to speak about yourself in the third person was almost the conceit of a poet—but for Anne, it was the truth. She had not been Lady Anne de Bohun at Westminster; that came afterward when she told the king who she was, and he had ratified her right to the title given to her mother.

And she did, indeed, prefer a simple life. It was just that life had not worked out that way.

"A simple life, Lady Anne? How can the life of a merchant be simple? And such a successful one as yours seems." Now it was the queen who spoke, and she had never sounded more gentle, more sweet.

Anne answered the queen in a low voice. "Your Majesty, I strive to live quietly, giving offence to none. And some might call that simple."

The crowd suddenly roared into life. The victors of the first heat were announced to another crack of thunder.

"Simple to me means the life of a peasant—would you not agree, my liege? Servants, too, are often simple. But then, servants do not necessarily stay servants." The queen had turned with a glittering smile to Edward, determined to involve him. There was a moment of sweating silence—the crowd was stilled, waiting the first shot of the next heat, and the wind had dropped so that the queen's words were unnaturally loud.

Edward's eyes were fixed on Anne's as he answered.

" 'Peasant' is a much abused word, wife, as is 'servant.' We are servants of our people, are we not? And to be simple is a noble condition—it was our Lord's way. And some would have called Him a peasant, since He was the son of a carpenter."

"Ah yes, but he was of noble descent, was he not?"

The queen was pleasant, for all the world playing a courtly game of banter, engaging her knight the king in a contest of wit and allusion.

"We are none of us as we seem—Christ recognized that. He looked for the noble beneath the rags, it seems to me; fishermen were good enough for him. And lepers and tax collectors. Even women of ill repute."

Elizabeth allowed herself to become arch.

"Ah, women of ill repute? Yes, that was indeed gracious of Him. If legend is to be believed, many an earthly king consorts with whores, though for different reasons than salvation, I suppose." That got the attention of the courtiers; it was unlike the queen to be coarse or to allude to Edward's famous appetite for other women. She must be feeling very threatened to be so frank in public.

Edward was furious, though he would not react or show his hand, for that was plainly what the queen desired.

The duke caught his new wife's eye and raised an eyebrow. She dropped her eyes from his, but not before he saw a wicked smile to match his own enjoyment of the sport before them. And it was not the archery.

Below the glittering court, the contestants stood and fired, whistle and thud, whistle and thud . . . the heats were moving through quickly as the crowd groaned and cheered alternately, native Bruggers battling to best the motley assemblage of English who had entered the contest for glory, and gold.

Anne, meanwhile, sat humbly before her noble guests, apparently listening politely as debate passed to and fro between the king and queen.

But her heart beat faster and faster. She had to stand this ground, appear indifferent. If the queen had wished to unmask her, it would have happened by now, except that the king had come to her defense.

The queen was momentarily silenced by a mighty yell. The crowd was saluting the winner of the third heat—a young man, barely a teenager, it seemed, who had triumphed over his much more grizzled and experienced opponents. Anne clapped her hands delightedly too.

Duke Charles enjoyed Anne's spontaneity. "You know this boy, Lady Anne?"

"I do, Your Grace. He is a page in our household—Stephen. I had no idea he could shoot as well as this."

"But if he wins the contest, would it not pain you to lose such a valued servant, Lady Anne? The prize you offer is very great, enough to set the ambitious winner up for life, it seems to me." It was the queen again, silky smooth. She was walking on dangerous territory, and she knew it, but anger was making her incautious. She hated this girl who should be dead, hated her!

"Freedom is important to us, Your Majesty. I would welcome it if this serving boy won the contest. I would know that he gave of his best to do it; he would always be welcome in our house."

Anne looked Elizabeth directly in the eyes as she replied; yet suddenly, the sky split with white light and thunder burst directly overhead. The kettledrums of hell.

In that moment rain began to fall fiercely, and then hailstones the size of lemons, the size of oranges; they drummed on the roof of the royal stand like the beat of war drums, but at least the planks above their heads held, though the noise was so intense it was impossible to speak, much less be heard.

The common people in the open stands were not so lucky. The size and ferocity of the hail was so great that as the people shoved and jostled to climb down quickly and find shelter underneath the tiered seating, many were struck and wounded. Screams and blood were added to the confusion.

Elizabeth looked at Anne in triumph, and only the girl heard what she said.

"It seems the Lord has spoken, Lady Anne. Harlots who puff themselves up before their betters are invariably struck down."

The words were blows, but something strengthened Anne.

"Are harlots better or worse than murderers in Christ's eyes, do you think, Your Majesty?"

Anne murmured the words, but Elizabeth heard. Edward turned back at that moment from helping his sister avoid the hail bouncing into the royal stand.

"Are you well, Elizabeth?" The queen was so pale she was almost green, but the king's automatic concern for his wife was a scrap of timber to grasp in a whirling flood of emotion. Terror, fury, outraged pride.

"No, Edward, I am not. I must rest. It has been a taxing day."

Anne watched the ducal party depart in the last of the rain, the morass of emotions she had plunged into given outward expression by the carnage, the litter from the sudden squall.

The contest had been abandoned—too many people had been injured in the rush to avoid the hail, and the downpour that had followed it had washed out the contest ground. Perhaps Anne would be able to restage it before the end of the wedding celebrations, perhaps not. For now, she had to focus on what needed to be done. Heal the wounded, comfort the disappointed, pick up the pieces of life. Was it ever different?

Anne asked all her personal gods for the fortitude she would need to see the contest through to its end.

And she did not think of archery when she made her prayer.

# Chapter Twenty-eight

Mathew Cuttifer's house was a haven that evening.

There were to be court festivities later—another feast, this time to be given by Edward in honor of the bride and groom, with entertainment from a troupe of celebrated English mummers. But for now Anne, all alone by strict instruction, soaked in an oak tub of cool, lightly scented water before her open casements.

Perversely, of course, it was now a perfect evening with high brilliant stars. Once again the noise of distant revelry in the city wafted into her private solar on a warm and gentle wind.

Behind her, in the shadows of the room, a dress of delicate ivory silk was laid out on her bed. A present from Mathew Cuttifer as a thank offering for Anne's acumen—her bold spirit and natural ability as a trader had made him an even richer man. The dress was simple and unadorned except for diamond sleeve buttons. Anne would wear it with nothing but pearls.

Tonight there would be formal gift giving to the bride and groom at the Prinsenhof, and the dazzling gift from Anne and the Cuttifers had been brought up to the solar so that Anne could inspect it one last time. It was a wedding chest, a cassone, but one that had few equals.

Built from fruitwood to symbolize fertility, it was ornamented with ivory and lignum vitae and studded with exquisite little bas-reliefs worked in jasper and chalcedony. Mounted on each panel of the chest, these perfectly executed, tiny scenes displayed moments in the marriage of the duke and his duchess.

First, there was the journey of the bride over the water from England; then the arrival of the duke outside the cathedral at Damme; the marriage itself inside the cathedral—when the duke met his bride—was accompanied by the most fortunate omens: the roof of the church itself opening to show God the father among glorious clouds, surrounded by angels, himself blessing the duke and his bride. Then there was the celebration feast presided over by the Virgin Mary; next came the bedding of the bride with her groom (while suggestive, it was not salacious); and then, finally, the birth of a baby, the heir to the ducal throne.

This last was wishful thinking, but loyal wishful thinking, as the duke and his duchess would no doubt appreciate.

But it would all be for nought if Anne decided against attending tonight's celebrations at the Prinsenhof.

After the confrontation with the queen and the fiasco of the archery contest, did she have the strength to do what must be done—face the royal party again and bow and smile and pretend that nothing, nothing at all, was wrong between her and Elizabeth? And that she and Edward were strangers?

Caxton's information that Elizabeth might be behind Anne's near assassination was both confirmation, fear, and, yes, relief made manifest. Relief that she at last knew whom she had to fight. And oddly the guilt she still felt about Edward made it almost understandable that the queen had acted in such a way. The reach of royal power was very great it seemed—perhaps Elizabeth had been the agent of last winter's attempted kidnapping as well.

But why, why continue so implacable when Anne had left England, clearly choosing exile over a life near Edward as his leman?

Suddenly there was a loud offended squeal from the annex next to her solar—a declaration of will from little Edward in his nursery next door as Jenna tried to get him ready for bed. He was still excited by all the comings and goings of the day, and Jenna was having a difficult time persuading him into his tiny nightshirt.

There was a rising note of temper in his voice and Anne couldn't help smiling. Not for nothing was he Edward Plantagenet's son.

"Jenna? Let him come in. I've finished."

Anne clambered over the side of the big wooden tub as the little boy staggered into the room holding on to the edges of the furniture. Anne was very proud of her son and she marveled at how physically forward he was. He'd recently taken his first steps and now, wobbling forward, crowing happily, made an unexpected dive at her wet legs as she tried, in vain, to swaddle herself in the linen bath sheet as he clung to her knees.

Anne scooped him up to cuddle, delighting in the smell of him, his skin, his hair. Her son had no way of knowing how much she wanted to stay and have a very quiet night at home in the solar. Perhaps even read Edward a story from her beautifully lettered and illustrated copy of *The Parliament of Fowls* by Geoffrey Chaucer, or even one of the fables of Aesop, another precious, wonderfully decorated manuscript, bound between ivory plates, that she now owned.

Sometimes when she looked at her books she was awed. The transformation of her own fortune, her great good luck, meant her small recently acquired library of books was worth more than an actual house in the city of London itself! Soon, perhaps, she would find her own home, begin to live a truly independent life when the king had gone back to England.

Letting Jenna dry her, Anne stroked her son's head as he looked up at her.

"Well, sweet child, I think I must go tonight." He set up a howling and she almost laughed: he was too little to understand what she meant, surely. She placed one finger on his lips, "If you are very good, after Jenna has dressed you, we can have our story before bed."

Anne could see the disapproval in Jenna's eyes as she kissed the child and made him giggle again, but she ignored her. All the staff thought she indulged little Edward too much, but how could it be a sin to love a child too much? That was all anyone needed, wasn't it? Love, enough food and warmth, and security? Children, at heart, were simple beings; perhaps adults too, were simpler than they seemed.

She sighed, eyes far away, then, shaking her head, smiled.

She'd made up her mind. "Just one story, Edward. Then I must dress. Jenna, can you fetch Aesop for me please?" The girl said nothing as she went to the small locked cupboard where Anne's books were kept, but her mistress understood her reluctance. Aesop was a heathen, a pagan. In Jenna's terms, to read the little boy these beguiling fables was to invite the Devil to take possession of his small defenseless mind.

"Thank you, Jenna. Would you like to stay and listen?" It was kindly meant. If Jenna could only bring herself to hear what Aesop said, she would find there was no harm in his stories.

With a slight shake of the head, the girl curtsied quickly and made for the door, her arms full of the wet bath sheets—Anne was now decently covered in a silk dressing robe—and the child's dirty clothes.

Edward might not have the words to say it yet, but he saw that he'd won this battle, so he was a happy little boy as he settled himself beside Anne on her big bed to hear the story. The triumphant expression on his small, shiningly clean face made Anne laugh and turned her heart over.

Could she ever allow this child to figure in the succession of England? Should they go back together with the king, if he revoked her exile? The thought was a knife in her heart for so many reasons. None could have a greater right to the throne, ever, than her son—the son of a king, Edward, the grandson of two more through her—but thrones came at such a price. And Elizabeth would be there, the rightful queen, wife of the king. Elizabeth, who'd tried to kill her, possibly twice; what would she do when she found out about Anne's son—Edward's son—she who'd only had girls?

The little boy snuggled into her side and Anne gently smoothed his brow, feathering the soft, soft hair. "So which story tonight, Edward?"

One small fat finger hovered as she turned the pages of the precious manuscript carefully, until he pointed insistently at the picture of a sorrowful-looking lion holding up his paw.

"Very well—the lion with a thorn in his paw. Are you ready? We shall begin." The little boy was drowsy and content now as they cuddled together, just as a barrage of heavy knocks beat on the solar door.

Anne was annoyed—Edward was wide awake again with this interruption to their nighttime ritual.

"Yes? What is it?"

Suddenly the door was thrown back and a tall figure, muffled to the eyes in a long cloak, stood staring at her. Behind him she saw Ivan, face contorted by fury, ripping his sword from its scabbard.

"NO!" Anne screamed at the Magyar servant, and he faltered in his charge for one astonished moment as Anne sprang off the bed toward the unknown man. The little boy was so confused by the drama he forgot to scream, though his mouth fell open in surprise.

"Ivan, no! It's all right. Truly. At least, I think it's all right. You, sir, must be a messenger from the king. Deborah?"

How Anne found the presence of mind to concoct the story was impossible to tell, but her foster mother running in behind Ivan lent breathless, instant support.

"Ivan. Yes. The king has sent his messenger to Lady Anne. Maxim let him in. There is no danger, truly."

The last words were delivered heavily; Deborah thought the opposite, since Anne's face was transfigured with joy, staring at the stranger.

"Come. When we are needed, we will be called. Shall I take Edward, Lady Anne?"

"No!" The man spoke suddenly. "The king wishes to know certain things about this boy."

It was very unlike little Edward to remain silent. Usually he was irrepressible, even with strangers, but now, gazing solemnly up at this pillar of darkness, the stranger in his "aunt's" room, the little boy allowed his jeweled gaze to rest, detached and benign, on this interesting intrusion into his life.

"Deborah? Before you go, give me a shawl. Ivan, please remain outside my door and do not allow anyone, I mean anyone, entrance. Is that clear?"

Deborah wrapped Anne's shoulders in a swathe of embroidered silk. Then, as her foster mother left, quietly closing the door behind her, Anne swallowed the panic she felt as if it were a physical thing, and broke the silence.

"Come here, Edward." Heart pounding, she picked the little boy up and held him tightly. He wriggled in her grasp and suddenly held out his arms to the man.

The stranger laughed warmly and dropped the cloak back from his face. Reaching over, he plucked the child from Anne's arms.

"And are you good to your aunt, Edward? You have much to thank her for, you know."

The little boy giggled, almost as if he understood what the king, his father, was saying. Then his eyes chanced on the glittering jet buttons of the king's tunic: they were fascinating; he tried to bite one.

"Edward! No!"

Anne tried to detach the little boy from the king's chest but he set up an enormous howl and clung like a welk on a rock.

Suddenly both adults were laughing at the absurdity, and the baby stopped crying. Even gave them a watery giggle. That set all of them off, and soon all three were clinging together, helpless with happiness.

Then, after the laughter, Anne and Edward gazed at each other.

"I want to touch you, Anne."

He whispered it, almost a breath.

"And I you. But we cannot."

She was shaking.

"Will you come tonight?"

"Should I?"

One part of Anne's brain, what little caution was left, remembered Elizabeth's face when she'd spoken of murderers today at the butts. Had Edward seen?

"She knows, Edward. The queen knows about us."

Edward frowned and then sighed, instinctively rocking his son as they stood there together.

"Perhaps that is for the best."

Anne opened her mouth to speak the words that waited there, the words that would change things between them and make it harder, much harder for her to return to England: *your queen tried to kill me* . . . But the little boy yawned in their arms, close to sleep after all the excitement—and the moment was gone. Some instinct, buried deep, had spoken. *Not now, later. Think on this more. Get proof before you tell him.*

Gently the king cuddled the boy to his chest and carried him to Anne's bed. With the ease of a practiced father, he made a nest for his son from pillows and a bolster. Kissing the baby gently, he laid him down and pulled the coverlet up to cover him.

Anne's heart caught to see the two of them together: the tiny boy so trusting as this enormous stranger, the lover she craved beyond food, beyond salt, smoothed his son's brow until his eyelids fluttered and closed.

Standing, the king held out his arms and Anne, as trustingly as her son, walked into them.

"And so, will you come?" He whispered it into her hair, unbound from the bath. Soon he was nuzzling her neck, lower, lower. "Say you'll come."

Anne was breathless instantly. "Stop! Edward!"

He had his hands inside the silk wrap. "Say it."

"Yes! Yes, oh, please stop."

The warm hands on her body stilled. But he kissed her; she did not prevent that.

"Very well. I have your word."

Swathed around once more in the cloak, the king bowed himself from the solar, wrenching the door open so quickly that Ivan nearly fell into the room. Anne smiled dazedly at the embarrassed servant.

"Ivan, fetch Deborah for me, please, after you have seen the king's messenger from our door. I must dress."

So the die was cast, and she would go to the reception tonight. Last night when she had told the king of the plot to murder her, he'd been outraged, but today she'd seen the fear in Elizabeth Wydeville's eyes when the word was given voice. Somehow Anne had to find solid proof that the queen had tried to have her murdered.

And for that she had to be brave.

# Chapter Twenty-nine

Once she was dressed Anne made sure that tonight she would be among the first of the duke and duchess's guests to arrive.

Tonight, also, she would do her best to be inconspicuous; masks were to be worn—they would help her in the task. So, clothing herself with a confidence she did not feel, she was carried to the Prinsenhof in Mathew Cuttifer's own litter.

The tented wedding hall was crowded with many of the guests from the previous evening, but tonight the focus was on the wedding gifts burdening the press of liveried servants as they tried, in vain, to push through the milling, excited, overdressed throng.

It might have been Anne's intention to be inconspicuous this evening, but the cream silk dress was a lamp lit on a dark night. Its very simplicity brought a ripple of comment as Anne arrived to join a happy crowd of her own friends: merchants from the Italian community of Brugge, gold dealers and jewelers, principally, with their wives and sons and daughters. They might all be masked, but the brilliance of the group—flashing dark eyes behind the masks, white teeth, and the Florentine style of their opulent clothes—made them a center of attention.

Envy is a powerful underground river in human affairs and it was flowing strongly tonight; Maud Caxton was not the only woman to cast hostile looks at Anne. Intense, unacknowledged fear provoked and fed Dame Caxton's anger, and Anne caught an almost physical sense of it as she looked up to find Maud glaring at her across the throng of guests from behind an eerie white half-mask that gave an impression, disturbingly, of the bones of her skull surfacing through the skin.

Anne nodded graciously and then turned away, anxiety flooding her gut. Such concentrated spite was a wild force loose in her life. How many others felt as Maud did? And how could she bear their implacable opposition, year after year, if she continued to live in Brugge?

The king had said he wanted her to return to England with him; she and Deborah could go home maybe, to her mother's lands—her lands now—the place she'd never seen, and bring little Edward up decently in peace, in quiet obscurity; if the queen could be persuaded to let her be.

And if she could bear to part herself from the king.

She had no time to think further as the courts of Burgundy and England processed together into the great space of the banqueting hall, stepping gracefully and rhythmically to music from a gallery filled with the members of the Guild of Minstrels; they alone had license to play at public events of this kind.

Edward, his face impassive, walked forward ahead of the duke with his sister, the new duchess, on his arm; following them was Duke Charles, conducting Elizabeth, while Duchess Cicely brought up the rear escorted by the cardinal, the papal nuncio to the court of Burgundy, who had officiated at the marriage only yesterday.

The king was careful not to let his glance sweep too obviously over the guests tonight in search of Anne, yet he'd seen the cream dress laid out in her solar and his peripheral vision registered she was there because of it—a source of light among a sea of darkly glittering courtiers. His belly clenched. How would he see her alone again tonight?

That was Anne's thought, too, as the royal party sauntered past on their way to the line of chairs of state—yes, Maxim had managed to restore what he had hired just ahead of the setup for tonight's entertainment.

There'd been little time to think between the king's visit and arriving at the Prinsenhof, but now another aspect of the nightmare hit Anne with a hammer's force: Edward's wife had plotted her death just as the previous Queen of England, Margaret of Anjou, had tried to kill Anne's mother and, indirectly, succeeded.

The similarities between the lives of each generation were eerie: was she living out her mother's life? She'd not died with Edward, the king's child, as her mother had with her, but what if there should be another?

She closed her eyes for one brief moment: to think of children, conception, conjuring up the moment she and Edward had first touched each other again—was it only one day, one night ago?

"Are you well, Lady Anne?" Anselm Adorno touched her hand; he was twenty years old and the son of a famous family of Genoese merchants long settled in Brugge. Anne turned to look into his concerned face; she was grateful for his friendship.

"The heat, Anselm, it's just the heat."

And it was hot again for this second night of celebration of the marriage between the Duke Charles and the Lady Margaret of England. Sweat slid down between Elizabeth Wydeville's swollen breasts as she endured the ceremony of gift giving, a pageant that seemed endless.

Sitting in an exquisite but unforgivingly hard chair of state beside her stony-faced husband, she contrived, through iron will, to smile and smile until her face ached as overdressed merchants and their wives presented yet more opulent chess sets, glass from Venice, jewels, carpets, musical instruments, even horses and dogs to the ducal couple—all extraordinarily valuable and many in execrable taste.

It had been explained to Elizabeth that the tradition of masking at the gift giving was meant to save the blushes of those who could not afford to give lavish presents; yet the pretty conceit did little to disguise the identity of donors since the groom invariably greeted them, correctly, by name, which seemed part of the entertainment, and brought vulgar squeals of delight from the onlookers whether he got it right or intentionally wrong.

Elizabeth shifted in her seat. Would this tide of lumpen Low-landers never recede? She must speak to Edward, and soon, and alone. Anne de Bohun was alive; it was a terrible blow, but some-how she must deflect the king, get him to concentrate on the po-litical web she was trying to spin for her own defense and his. Yes, his safety too, she was convinced of that!

Beside her, Edward also was impatient but for different rea-sons. He wasn't certain if Elizabeth had recognized Anne yet this evening, but he knew the moment could not be far off.

"And now, Your Graces, an unknown lady wishes to ap-proach with her gift."

The herald had a penetrating voice, almost as loud as the brass whinny from the two trumpeters who signaled the arrival of yet another donor.

"Long life and may you have much joy of each other, Duke Charles and you, Duchess Margaret. For this, my poor token is symbol of all our prayers."

Edward felt rather than saw Elizabeth tense at his side as Anne, in her simple ivory-cream dress, bowed deeply while four palace servants placed the cassone at the feet of the bridal couple. There were gasps as the crowd surged closer, ogling the exquisite chest.

"Lady Anne—I believe I recognize you—unmask, so that we may thank you properly!" Smilingly, Anne removed her mask. "This marriage casket is most elegant, most sumptuous; it will be an adornment to our chamber. Do you not agree, Duchess?"

English princess though she was, Margaret had been stunned by the wealth of her husband's dukedom on display tonight, but this cassone was a most noble gift indeed.

"Lady Anne, I must thank you doubly for your magnificent generosity—and for your exquisite taste."

Anne, in her cloudlike dress, couldn't help smiling happily. She was still young enough, vulnerable enough, to be thrilled when others enjoyed her presents. Edward felt love and lust flush through him like hot butter—she was adorable.

"Also, my . . . husband, the duke," the hesitation was pretty and endearing, "has given me your betrothal gift—the perfumes, the most exquisite material I have ever seen, the rubies; and now this! I shall very much enjoy planning with you what good uses I can make of all your generous gifts to us."

Time slowed and though Anne saw the duchess speak, she heard not one word as the hall dissolved around the newly married couple and Anne glimpsed something, something unexpected: Caxton and the duchess happily poring over a large book together, the merchant pointing to the letters with ink-stained fingers; and there was a smear of ink on his expensive doublet too. Strange in such a fastidious man. And it was winter, for the duchess was wearing fingerless gloves and a fur-lined cloak.

" . . . when you visit us very soon." Anne was back in the hot hall of the present as she smiled uncertainly at the new duchess and then bowed to each of the royal family before gracefully backing away, leaving her cassone in pride of place at the duchess's feet.

Elizabeth had smiled gently, nodded approvingly at Margaret's speech—altogether the picture of courtly grace—but she'd observed her husband leaning forward, just slightly, to better see Lady de Bohun as she rejoined her friends, and a flash of rage, of intense heat, transformed her normally fair skin to hot rose.

The duchess smiled graciously, too, as was appropriate, but she found it hard not to grin in triumph at the queen's expression. She, too, had seen her brother watch Lady de Bohun with all the fixed purpose of a hawk out hunting.

Something of the duke's spirit of mischief had flicked Margaret into granting Anne extra recognition tonight, just because she knew it would make Elizabeth furious. Which it had.

The bride sighed happily. How wonderful that she had her own court now, well away from her scheming sister-in-law.

For a moment the queen and the duchess crossed glances. Each smiled sweetly at the other—and neither was fooled.

War had just been declared. Over Anne.

# Chapter Thirty

It was very late, well past midnight, but the celebrations at the palace continued.

Tonight there was no curfew bell, no chaining of the streets, and people were still gathering at corners and in the squares and courtyards all through the city in happy, roiling crowds. All the municipal fountains ran with excellent wine, day and night, so if they were drunk, they were mostly happy drunk and expecting to sleep very little for the next nine days.

Warm nights, much food, much excitement, even more sex: taverns and whores were bathing in a money shower, yet much of all a man could want was provided free throughout the city.

A wedding such as this pumped red gold through all the veins and arteries of Brugge and tonight, as they drank deep, the citizens hung on the stories of all the entertainments—the clothes, the gossip, and the scandal of last night's wedding feast—from those who'd been lucky enough to be there.

*Have you heard about the cunningly trained flock of goats? Yes, they sang, really—though some said, brayed—a specially composed motet to the wedding couple. What about the white whale?* At first, none could see how the leviathan had moved, swam rather; then a very drunk mechanist in the Markt gave the secret away to his enraptured audience. Massive wheels concealed in the fins and the tail, that was the secret; the great fish had entered the hall spouting water, which alarmed all the rich women in their sinfully expensive dresses—and then, when it opened its mouth, there were exposed fully forty men dressed as mer-people warbling an epi-thalamion to the duke and his duchess!

And as if that had not been enough, now, tonight, after the formal gift giving, a troupe of English mummers was still per-forming, even now. *Did you hear that the players had ridden into the hall on the backs of live lions and tigers?* Even an elephant, which had defecated and voided great rivers of piss, to the shame of the animal handlers, but everyone else's great merriment.

It was said, too, that as the guests sat down to eat, girls dressed as angels, wings and all, had flown down from the roof on invisible wires, startling some elderly guests so much that they cast them-selves down on to their knees and begged forgiveness for past sins!

There was much chortling and some envy. *What you wouldn't give, eh, to be there? Close enough to touch royalty, maybe goosing some of those rich bitches as they stuffed themselves near to bursting their laces?*

Their duke looked after his people—that was the general verdict. There'd be plenty of free entertainment in the days ahead—like the archery today, even if it had ended so badly. A shame for the pretty English girl who'd paid for their pleasure on behalf of the duke and his bride.

Lucky bastard, Duke Charles, when you thought on it. Three wives and each one more good-looking, and younger, than the last. And now this new one, very toothsome.

"But no better looker than her brother the king. What shoul-ders he has, and hair—just like gold, I say!" shouted one very drunk whore, boozing at the sign of the Golden Fleece, an inn much patronized by Genoese and Italian clerks.

"Reckon he's got a golden fleece too? Or maybe his sister has. Lucky old duke!" There was ribald laughter, heartiest from the whore. Everyone knew that the most prestigious chivalric Order of the Golden Fleece, founded by Duke Philip, this duke's father, and kept up with much pomp by Duke Charles, was not so much named for the mythical treasure that Jason sought, but more for the remarkable pelt that had adorned the former Duke Philip's mistress's delta of Venus.

Anne heard the drunken laughter as she was carried home

after the gift-giving feast. If she had arrived at the feast tired, she was going home with blood fizzing through her body from a combination of fear and unslaked longing for the king.

She'd been so careful all night, since Queen Elizabeth was a guest at the feast, never to look at Edward, but spending the evening talking cheerfully to Anselm Adorno.

He was a stocky, good-looking boy and she knew that he would marry her in a moment if she gave him the least encouragement—an arrangement that would have pleased his family, and the Cuttifers; probably even Deborah.

Anne liked the Adornos. They were sophisticated and clever but welcoming to her, seemingly without the prejudice of her own countrymen toward her flourishing commercial activities. Native Genovese, they'd been in the city of Brugge since the last century and were known for their piety, even having built their own church, the spectacular Jerusalem Chapel, so that they could worship privately as a family together.

And the gray skies of the north had not dimmed the passion and energy they'd brought with them more than eighty years ago. They were so wealthy that Anne was not a commercial threat to them—they'd even talked together of specific joint ventures for the buying and selling of jewels, pooling their resources so that under certain circumstances, they could buy together and get better prices all around.

But Edward had returned, and if there had ever been a moment when Anne had considered that Anselm might, one day, become a potential husband, that idle thought was blotted out yesterday—before, during, and after the wedding.

Edward was a man, not a boy. He was her match, and he was a king.

But that same king had become increasingly furious during the gift giving. That, Anne had not known. And he'd become even angrier when she'd left the feast, with special permission from the duke, pleading a headache so blinding it was hard to see.

The headache was real since she'd spent a tension-filled night trying to avoid Edward's glance and being scrupulous not to look in his direction, not even once, after presenting her gift.

After Anne left, Edward's anger was tempered by confusion and, yes, even hurt. As king he was completely unaccustomed to a woman who did not do what he wanted. It was taken for granted by him, and his court, that a girl or a woman would come to him should he merely beckon. But tonight Anne had placed herself beyond his reach. Deliberately.

Rationally, he knew it was the way this game must currently be played; he was on the high dais, in the public gaze, with Elizabeth beside him, watched avidly by two courts: his and the duke's. If he wanted to slake the fever that had returned to his blood—and the hunger to consume, to devour, Anne with the single-minded fervor of a starving man—he must continue to be discreet, continue to wear the bland, distant mask of a king.

He had profound fellow feeling for the lions that had been ridden into the banquet by the English mummers after Anne's departure; they'd roared hugely, shatteringly loud, to the fear and delight of the crowd. But it was empty sound, without real threat—they were too well controlled by their masters.

Were they, too, ravenous, as he was? Forced to perform—claws blunted, teeth filed to lessen the damage they might do—these poor emasculated animals were the very mirror of his own state. Elizabeth had him trussed and controlled. She believed she'd tamed him by her presence in Brugge. God! They would talk tonight, together, Elizabeth and he, and by God's bowels her story had better be good or . . .

Duke Charles signaled that his brother-in-law should be poured more wine. For some reason, Edward was angry and becoming angrier by the moment—they knew each other well and he could sense it.

The duke felt queasy suddenly. Should he speak with Edward, ventilate all that William Caxton had told him? Shaking his head to banish the uncomfortable thought, Charles softly caressed his bride's fingers and she squirmed in her seat. He smiled at her warmly, and privately let her see him slide his tongue over his lips lasciviously, which made her blush. He laughed. Yes, he would enjoy tonight with his bride first and then, perhaps, after Margaret's performance earlier this evening with Anne and Elizabeth, something useful might be encouraged. He sat straighter and smiled, relieved at the thought: his wife might be a most useful go-between for him and her brother.

The duke was certain of only one thing: Anne held Edward's heart, and other parts, within her keeping. Now, if what Caxton said was true, she could be an asset or a liability in the stratagem that the English queen had set in play between their two countries.

He used to be a rather good chess player—so, too, was Edward; perhaps tomorrow would put their joint skill to the test.

Meanwhile, Anne, in her bed, tossed and turned—hot then cold, cold then hot—and burned and froze; and in her dreams, she was once more the sacrifice.

She dared not look at the sorcerer's face in her dream, but he was moving closer, closer than he'd ever been.

With a jolt she woke, heart thumping painfully. Anything, anything was better than facing those empty eyes.

Sitting up against the bolster, she was glad of the light breeze from her open casement. It dried the sweat on her naked body, the sweat that came from terror.

She needed guidance if she was to walk unscathed through the dangerous maze her life had become—and find the way to the other side.

*Sword Mother? Sword Mother?* She did not voice the words but they cannoned around her mind. If only she could still her ragged breathing and sink deep to summon up the presence who'd spoken through her before. But nothing came, nothing, even though she lit the candle, made the blood sacrifice and the invocation. Finally, truly exhausted and with headache returning, Anne gave up.

"Oh, Sword Mother, Sword Mother. Why give me the visions if I see so little of my own fate?"

She whispered the words, despairing. And Jenna, despairing also, heard them as she lay, eyes open to the night in the breathless annex to the solar.

# Chapter Thirty-one

Dawn came reluctantly to Brugge as suddenly cold and violent air flowed into the city on a north wind.

The trees in the heber shivered as the light straggled up. It was only August—the world couldn't be turning from high summer to winter overnight, could it?

Deborah woke suddenly as the wind banged a shutter back against the walls of the house. She was anxious, breathing as if she'd been running, but from what? Darkness. It had had a form. And eyes.

Shuddering, the old woman groped under the straw-filled mattress of her box bed to find the little drawstring bag she kept there. It was still dark inside the annex to the solar, and Jenna and the boy were fast asleep, but she knew what she wanted by feeling for it. When she was frightened she needed the touch of her sacred things: carved rune stones given to her by her own mother during long apprenticeship into ancient knowledge. Stones that were frowned on in this world ruled by Christ. But still, they were things that had power; power to protect, power to speak when the people she lived among would do neither of these things for themselves.

Deborah had been worried for days now, dread her constant companion. Edward was the cause, and Elizabeth. And Anne. Tomorrow the English court would embark for home and that should have been a cause for rejoicing.

If only this house could pass unscathed through this last day, all might yet be well, but over this last week, every night, covertly, she'd read the rune stones and they'd said the same thing.

Seven times over seven days and nights, she'd thrown the stones and seven times Nauthiz, Isa, and Hagalaz had rolled apart from the others: the runes of cold that personified the three fateful sisters, weavers of all lives, great and small.

So it was again, today.

Nauthiz, "the teacher," brought hard lessons that must be learned, sometimes at bitter cost, yet the rune also offered some small hope that strength of character might bring luck in among adversity with the help of true friends.

Hagalaz said storm, fierce winds, bad weather: an uncontrollable blast of cold winter fury. Chaos inextricably connected with past events—gale-brought havoc that no power, no person, could avoid, coupled with great impending danger.

And Isa, the ice rune, the cold, iron rune against which there was no defense, for its power was the implacable strength of winter. Winter cannot be resisted, it must be endured; short days, long nights can bring patience—patience and hope, for the cold season can be tolerated knowing that light and warmth will return with the spring.

The message was always the same: bad times coming, lessons to be learned that could not be escaped from—and the need for courage.

But Anne could not hear Deborah, would not hear her; too caught up in the game of chance, the dance of flesh, Anne refused sight and hearing if it intruded too far into her rapture with the king. All the world contrived to keep them apart yet he and she found ways to savor each other in dangerous, snatched moments—moments that fed the ravenous fire between them.

Deborah shuddered.

The great storm was close, so close. She could feel it, even smell ice on the north wind this morning. Yet, remove the king, remove the queen and perhaps the danger might be averted.

Dawn light was seeping as the shadows of the night receded and the old woman sighed. Foolish to deny or avoid understanding when it was given. She, Deborah, had these tools for a purpose and it was her right and her duty to use them in the service of others. And Anne was the center of her duty and her care.

Very well, she was resolved. Today Anne would hear what had to be said because today she would be given no choice.

Anne had taken a long time to wake.

Finally sleeping last night, she'd descended very deep into a red world: a voluptuous place filled with sighs and heat where half-glimpsed naked bodies coupled together, endlessly twining and writhing. She'd been reluctant to leave it because Edward was there with her, and he had been the source of the sighs, the melting kisses. There was no night, no day, as sleeping and waking blended into one long, heated half-life filled with the most exquisite, unslaked, unslakable hunger. Hunger for him. And, in loving Edward, accepting him, the empty-eyed night demon had been banished from her dreams; passion had vanquished him. She was free!

Now, as the light rose, Anne opened her eyes and stretched, delighting in her senses as sight came, smell came, touch came. Every surface in her bed was sensuous: silk, velvet, fur, ah, fur.

How glad she was that finally she'd not withstood Edward's wooing. How foolish her fear seemed now. He was the king, he could protect her from everything, anything; for though she'd asked for help from the Sword Mother, nothing had come to her, nothing. Better then to turn to mortal power—the power this man had over her, and around her; binding her, protecting . . .

And when she'd faced it, how wonderful her capitulation to him had become. Each stolen night she drowned in surrender. She was exhausted, but still not sated with him, or he with her. Let others sleep, the darkness was a gift—and they'd made such good use of it.

And if she closed her eyes, she could see him as she'd seen him not even three hours before. Naked, lying with her and inside her on a great cape lined with black fur. He'd thrown it down so that she'd not feel the stone floor on her bare skin and be chilled.

Ah, but he'd chilled her: like ice, like fire, as, slowly and carefully, he'd undressed her, kissed her, running his hands so lightly over her skin that she had shivered as if freezing. Shaking so deeply that she could only center by sliding him hot and deep and hard into her body, by kissing him so that warmth flowed from mouth to mouth, tongue to tongue as he had rocked her, rocked her and she straddled him and the itch between them both became deeper and hotter and hotter and . . .

"Good morning, mistress."

Anne was annoyed; Deborah's voice had cut through the reverie and forced her into the present.

"I was not fully awake, Deborah."

"Will you wash, mistress?" Her foster mother's voice was brisk.

Anne knew that tone—it reached back into childhood when the winter dawn came late and she didn't want to get up in the dark. Duty. Obligation. Right now.

Anne closed her eyes defiantly. "Yes. I will wash. But when I call you." She knew she sounded sulky, but all the rest of her life revolved around work and duty to others. Could she not just enjoy, if only for this one last time, lying in her bed with the luxurious sense of other possibilities in life? Being with the man you loved, for one? Dreaming of a future with him?

"That is inconsiderate, Anne. Jenna has labored up the stairs to bring you this hot water and she has much to do."

That "Anne" was significant. Deborah was always entirely scrupulous to avoid personal address between them, especially in front of other members of the household.

Anne sighed and very reluctantly opened her eyes. It took a moment to register that she and Deborah were actually alone, though two large brass cans of hot water were gently steaming on the blue tiles in front of her fireplace.

"Where is the baby? And Jenna?"

"They're both in the kitchen, where I sent them." It was an unspoken accusation—Anne was failing in her duty to her son, too caught up by passion to notice. Deborah's face was implacable as she waited for Anne to get out of the bed.

Anne said nothing. She would not acknowledge she'd lost the

contest of wills, though she shivered as she slipped naked out of the warm bed.

Silently Deborah held out the robe and Anne, just as silently, wrapped it around her as Deborah poured hot water into a washing bowl for her.

"We will need to inspect the winter clothes for moth damage, I suspect, and make them ready for wearing. We're in for an early autumn."

"Perhaps you're right. Mathew would want us to check and see who needs last winter's livery replaced. There will be idle seamstresses in Brugge now and their rates will be lower, too, since the wedding is nearly done . . ."

Nearly done. The words echoed. Neither said anything for a moment as Anne wiped the soft curds of soap from her body with a linen cloth.

Taking the cloth, wringing it out, Deborah touched Anne on the cheek, looking deep into her eyes. "It has to be faced, Anne." The girl said nothing; she couldn't speak, wouldn't speak, so her foster mother hurried on.

"You have to let him go. You must. I've asked for guidance, but the messages do not change, try as I do to make them. There is very great danger. You must listen to me."

"Am I cursed, Deborah?"

Her foster mother was suddenly angry. "Cursed? How can you be so foolish, or so selfish? You, who have so much given to you?"

Anger. Guilt. Shame. Defiance. They ran together like acid in Anne's gut. "Ah, that is not fair. The queen tried to kill me."

"And you have stolen her husband—and deserted your child for an adulterous affair. Night after night he's cried himself to sleep without you."

It was like a slap with a cold, hard hand. And it was true; it was all true. Anne had sunk herself into sensuality to avoid reality—for reality carried the choice she had to make and would do anything to avoid. The blind and heedless passion she felt for Edward had been more powerful than love of her son, and her responsibility to his future.

The swaddling cloak of denial was ripped away and suddenly, so clearly, she saw that she'd surrendered her hard-won independence to the king like any other lovestruck witless ninny. And deep in lust, she'd compromised everything she believed in, everything she'd so painfully built. Her behavior proved the English merchants right. She was a foolish woman, totally unfitted to carry authority, a mere chattel ruled by her basest instincts. A plaything.

The shame was overwhelming as the rosy dream of the last days snuffed out.

Deborah took the girl's hand and led her to the window seat. Silently they both sat, so close together that whispers seemed natural.

"Have you told the Duchess of Burgundy about the king? Does she know?"

Dazed and humiliated, Anne shook her head as she thought about the conversations of the last few days. Margaret had invited her to the Prinsenhof to see the betrothal gift of peacock silk made into a magnificent dress, and, as they got on so well, other pleasant meetings had followed. It was natural, Anne told herself, they were both English; both spoke the same language.

"No, I haven't told her. But she suspects, of course she suspects."

Anne closed her eyes. Was it only yesterday that she and Duchess Margaret had been laughing as the final fitting for the peacock-blue dress was carried out, and Edward had found them together. And stayed, just the three of them, alone in a rare, warm moment of peace in the crowded palace.

"Anne, heart stakes are only part of this. Betrayal is all around you. The queen is playing politics on a very deep level. This is not just about love, it's about survival for you and the boy."

"What do you know?" Dread and uncertainty crept into Anne's heart on a gray tide.

"Edward and Elizabeth have been fighting and not just about you. It's said Duke George is vying for the throne again with Warwick's help, and for her part, the queen is trying to implicate Duke Richard also in the plot. It's why she came to Brugge;

Maxim was drinking with the king's valet two nights ago and he said she's trying to isolate Edward from his own brothers, make him more dependent on her own family."

Anne shook her head violently, unwilling to hear.

"But Duke Richard has always supported his brother, and he hates the queen." Anne had only seen the Duke of Gloucester from time to time when she was a servant at Westminster. Normally he stayed in the north at York, the stronghold of the king's northern affinity, though he'd also lived, when younger, at Middleham Castle, the Duke of Warwick's favorite dwelling. She'd liked him for his quiet straightforwardness, the sense one received of his pride in his elder brother, and his loyalty.

Impatiently Deborah shook her head. "Richard and Edward spend a lot of time in different places and distance breeds suspicion very easily. The queen's also trying to drive a wedge between Edward, the duke, and Duchess Margaret too. Estrangement between Burgundy and England could be very profitable if you knew about it in advance—if you had links with Italian bankers, for instance."

Anselm Adorno! Recently he'd tipped Anne off about a meeting he and his father had been summoned to at the Prinsenhof: just Elizabeth, and the two Italian merchants, in secret.

The queen had hinted that opportunities might open up in Britain; valuable monopolies could go to the right people with the right connections in return for financial support of the king in the current fluid situation in England. Monopolies that, if successfully farmed and managed, could make their owners wildly rich.

There was one requirement for potential partners, however, if they wished to be considered for such a valuable prize: relocation of their chief place of business to England, to London, out of Brugge.

Anselm had told her of other similar meetings held with other trading houses in Brugge, the principals of each having been sworn to silence as he and his father had been. If it was true, it was a remarkably brazen thing to do under the roof of her host.

Mathew Cuttifer and his ward, Anne, had not been consulted, of course.

Anne's face darkened. "Duke Charles and the king; surely they know what's happening?"

Deborah was grim. "Things are changing in Brugge. We both know that this marriage is about trade being the cement in a valuable strategic alliance. Our new duchess is a symbol of the faith the king places in Burgundy's power as his chief ally against France. But the duke's power and wealth is based on trade, is it not? What if the rumors about the Zwijn are true? The silt in the river gets worse each year, you've said so yourself."

Distractedly Anne nodded. The silt in the river always caused concern to the merchants in Brugge, though there were wildly varying reports of its level year to year. It was ironic that the city itself was at least part of the problem. All the extra building and digging of canals had dammed up and effectively lessened the river's natural flow; that and the slow creation of a delta at the Zwijn's mouth to the sea.

It was a frightening prospect, the permanent silting of the river.

An intermittently navigable river meant no reliable trade into the city: no trading wealth, no political power. Brugge would slowly die if trade dried up. Simple.

"I know it's only servants' gossip, but Edward's valet was adamant. The queen has told Edward that Duke Charles is hiding the truth about the Zwijn. She's trying to convince him he's been tricked into throwing his sister away into an alliance with a potentially waning power. And then, if she hears you are planning to go back to England with the king . . ."

Both women were silent. Servants' gossip? Anne shivered. Servants' gossip could be very powerful—true or not.

"He leaves tomorrow. There's no time—for anything." She sounded so forlorn, so young.

Silently Deborah put her arms around Anne. After a moment, the girl sighed deeply. "I need to think. Can you ask Jenna to bring me some more water? I'm sorry to ask, truly, but I can't abide washing in cold water when I'm chilled."

Anne was standing now, looking down on the busy canal beneath her windows. The sun had broken through the low clouds and was throwing diamonds into the water. Even so early the town was alive, busy, shouting, prosperous, determined to enjoy each moment of this last day of celebration.

The Zwijn in terminal decline? Surely that was nonsense. Anne turned away from her casements. What she needed were facts. It would be hard, but she needed to find a way to see the duke. If anyone knew the truth about the silting of the river, it would be Duke Charles—and she must ask him, she must know.

But today was also the day she'd promised to give Edward an answer. She'd so wanted to return to England with the king, to a home of her own, to a future of a kind with the man she loved, but that would happen only if she agreed to become his acknowledged mistress. And she saw it clearly now—that meant placing her fate into his hands at a time when the kingdom was increasingly unstable.

And once back in England, the truth about her own and her son's birth would be harder and harder to hide. What chance, too, would she and little Edward have with Elizabeth Wydeville their implacable enemy? How could she knowingly expose her son to such a life—and live with herself? All the money she'd made, all the battles she'd fought for recognition on her own terms —these were nothing.

Little Edward, tiny defenseless Edward, needed her to be strong, needed her to turn her back once more on the only man she'd ever loved. She would say good-bye to the king.

He would return to England without her.

# Chapter Thirty-two

"These are nothing but malicious rumors. The river is deeper and better dredged now than it was in my father's time. Some of the duchess's dowry will see it stays that way."

Duke Charles was angry and bewildered by Anne's question. She was talking to him for a few snatched moments in his tiny working office at the Prinsenhof just before the Mass that was to be celebrated on this, the last day, of his wedding celebration.

Bribery had got Anne there—that and calling in a long-owed favor from the duchess's newly appointed chief dresser, a former servant of the Cuttifer's whom she'd recommended to the duke as a trustworthy body servant for his new wife.

But something felt strange, Anne was sure of it. Most often Duke Charles was easy to approach, direct looks and mischievous laughter his normal style. Today he was distracted, even harried.

"Lady Anne, let me ask you something now." As he waved Anne to a padded stool, signaling she should sit, he nodded at his groom of the chamber. Silently the man withdrew, closing the bronze-bound doors behind him.

"May I be frank? We have little time and it's important that we be honest with each other."

Anne nodded politely, but her pulse quickened; dread floated around his words. "I should like that, Your Grace."

"Has there been progress in finding your would-be assassin?"

Anne shook her head, swallowing guilt. "No, Duke. We've found nothing, though friends still seek information on my behalf."

The duke nodded.

"Do you have any opinion on this matter, Lady Anne?"

She shook her head decisively. "No opinion, sire."

"No opinion? I am surprised by that."

Anne spoke the words before thought could stop her.

"Duke, I have no opinion because I am certain. The assassin was hired by the Queen of England—though I lack the means to prove it."

The duke narrowed his eyes but spoke very softly, almost a whisper.

"The queen? Think carefully, Lady Anne. Why the queen?"

"Because of her husband, the king. He and I share a . . . connection. One that will be severed very shortly." Try as she would, the pain still found a way into her voice.

"Because of the queen?"

Anne sighed, then shook her head.

"Not entirely, sire. Because of me. It's what must be done. The king and she are married and there is my nephew to consider, and my guardian. I would shame them by my behavior if I returned to England as the king's leman."

The duke was astonished by her frankness. Anne had trusted him with information that could destroy her reputation and her life in Brugge in an instant if knowledge of the affair became common.

"Does the king know?"

Anne shook her head.

"Shall I tell him your suspicions?" Anne sighed, shook her head once more. She had no proof of the queen's involvement, and without it, there was little point.

If she'd told Edward her fears ten days ago . . . but now he was about to leave—without her. In his certain anger and confusion, why should he believe her? And also, since the political situation between England and Burgundy was so delicate, the balance would tip even further if the king believed the duke had had knowledge of the assassination attempt against Anne—and hidden it from him; let alone that his wife was responsible!

The irony was rich. If she'd risked it, if Anne had told the king her suspicions ten days ago, his rage might have distracted the queen from her current strategic game, might have prevented the seeds of estrangement from being planted between Edward and Charles. Anne despaired. She'd helped the queen, with her silence, actually helped her!

"Why did you ask me about the river today, Lady Anne?"

This was neutral ground—safer for both of them.

"Long ago politics once nearly destroyed my life for I was caught up in a most unjust situation, even accused of treason by the man I loved." Anne faltered, fighting distress. "I felt I had to walk away, start again. Brugge took me in and I am grateful to this city, grateful for the life I've been able to make. And many people's living depends on what we do as merchants."

Anne looked up at the duke, tears starting in her eyes.

"If this is to be my permanent home, I need to plan for the future. We must all help you safeguard the trading alliance—and the political alliance—with England. That is why I asked about the river."

"And do you think you can help me, Anne?" The duke was pragmatic—real power often lay in the bedroom, after all.

"Perhaps. If I could speak to the king before he goes—for one last time. It might be he would believe me about the Zwijn, where he might not completely trust . . . other reports."

"You mean he would not believe me?" The duke was harsh. He had a right to be, for it was unexpectedly perilous becoming the brother-in-law to the King of England. Thanks to Elizabeth Wydeville and her "secret" meetings with the trading community, all that his father and his ancestors had fought for might be at risk if Edward believed the rumors about the river.

Anne said nothing, but the swirling misery she felt rose high: Edward would leave tomorrow. Most likely she would never see him again. For a moment, darkness descended like a curtain and with it, the fury of a distant, howling wind, the voice of her own unvoiced despair.

There was a discreet knock on the cabinet door. A signal that Mass would begin very shortly.

"It will be possible. I will make it so—tonight. Please be ready when you are summoned."

The duke bowed and then hurried away through the now open door, leaving Anne all alone. She took a deep breath. Somehow she would get through this day, and the days after that, because she had to.

Misery, guilt, and shame. They made uncomfortable companions, but she had invited them in.


Deborah was perplexed. Jenna was missing. She had not been in the kitchen for the breakfast and now there was a strange report—her clothes had been removed from the female servants' dorter, beneath the roof.

But Deborah didn't tell Anne, for when the girl returned from the Prinsenhof she was clearly distressed, though doing her best to hide it.

Now that the die was finally cast, Anne called on depths of control she had not known existed. After playing with Edward in the heber, delighting the baby with her playful attention, she surrendered him to his nurse for a feed and a nap before stolidly working on, ignoring the last of the festivities she'd been invited to.

This final entertainment—an allegorical pageant in which Neptune, a man who bore a remarkable likeness to the duke, took Venus, a simulacra of Margaret, for his bride—was stunningly created on a series of great barges, which slowly toured the entire canal system of Brugge, passing the crowded banks, the bridges stacked high with exhausted, drunk, but ecstatic townsfolk all desperate to wring the last drops of joy out of the remaining holiday. From every source, flowers rained down and music played in happy cacophony, saluting the barges as they passed. The noise outside the house made it very hard to concentrate and Anne was suddenly smitten with guilt—if she was unhappy, that was no reason for the servants to miss the last pleasures of the wedding. Hurriedly she summoned Maxim to the parlor.

"Maxim, you may tell everyone that they have all worked well this morning. Now they are free to enjoy the last day. There, go. And tell Deborah as well. Edward will enjoy watching the procession."

"Will you come also, mistress?"

Anne, working on a pile of ledgers under the eyes of the great Memlinc portrait, shook her head.

"No. I'm better here for the moment. I've neglected matters for the last few days—there's much to catch up on."

Maxim bowed and left. At the last moment, Anne called after him.

"Can you ask Jenna to bring me something light to eat before she goes, please?"

Her steward returned briefly, frowning. "But mistress, we cannot find the girl—I thought you'd been told."

Anne shook her head, but once started on the topic of the missing servant, Maxim was eager to inform his mistress, if only in an effort to sift through the strange facts again for himself.

"It is very odd, mistress. No one saw her leave or knows where she is. But we will pursue this matter, never fear. I shall ask among the crowd if anyone's seen her."

Anne was briefly confused, as he was, but the miserable ache created by impending loss, fear, self-discipline, and longing dulled her curiosity. Dismissively, she waved the incident away, out of her life. "Never mind. Tell me when you find her. I'm not very hungry anyway."

Maxim nodded and left. Anne returned to her work, but the lines of neat black figures in front of her, Meinheer Boter's meticulous work, suddenly blurred into the shape of spiders, spiders that began to crawl all over the page in front of her.

Anne suppressed a scream and leaped up. It was true! The numbers, the words, were crawling about as if they had life, as if they were creatures. She blinked, and then sighed with relief.

She'd been mistaken. The ledger was the ledger, the words were the words. And the numbers had not changed their form. She was tired and very strained. Unwillingly she looked up and found the eyes within Saint George's helm. He would protect and guard her, wouldn't he?

"Witch"—the word was a breath on the slight breeze from her window. "Witch." She heard it again and whirled around, searching for the source of the sound, her heart beating as if she'd run and run and run.

Darkness filled her mind and briefly there was a vision of one frail leaf being blown before a storm; something, a powerful force, was loose in her life. She might not be strong enough to control it.

A sudden soft thump and Anne looked up.

Too late.

Black-masked men were jumping off the heber wall, running toward her, the leader boosted through her casement by a man behind him.

Such was the noise from the rowdy crowds lining the canal and the street outside that no one heard Anne scream. And scream again; then, nothing.


Maxim, Deborah, and little Edward had had a happy afternoon, as had the whole household. And when at last they returned after the water pageant finished, nothing seemed wrong. The parlor was empty, but Deborah presumed in despair that Anne must have changed her mind and slipped away to see the king.

But night came down and though lights burned in every window of the big house near the Kruispoort, Anne did not return. Then, in the morning, the truth was clear.

Anne was missing.

PART THREE

# The
# Triple Death

# Chapter Thirty-three

Edward, King of England, stood in the parlor of Mathew Cuttifer's house under Hans Memlinc's great devotional work and despaired.

There was nothing to see in this house. No blood, no disorder, and nothing had been taken. Anne had vanished. All that was left now was this, an image of her face. He gazed at the picture, focused on it as if this painted panel could give him the living girl.

Within the frame Anne seemed so real, as if at any moment she might turn her head and see him, and smile. Unconsciously he held his breath, waiting, hoping for the moment but of course the figure did not move. Tears pricked Edward's eyes. Foolish; this was rank foolishness. Anguish had turned his brain. Gently he touched the surface, touched her sweet mouth with one finger. And unwittingly followed Anne's eye line to the face of the Christ child—and suddenly understood that the baby was his own son.

A slow shiver began at the nape of his neck and traveled like a worm down his spine, for then he focused on another detail in the painting—the face of Saint George. His face—he was Saint George! But how could that be so? Was this sorcery?

"Liege, we found her."

Wild hope ran like hot lead as Edward swung around to Maxim, joyous, dizzy with relief.

"Anne?" Please, God, anything, an Abbey, a chantry for each year of her age, anything.

"No, sire," Maxim shook his head. "I meant Jenna. The girl who . . . ran away."

It fled, his happiness, snuffed out. Ashes and fear, that was all that was left. Ashes—and fury!

The look on Edward's face terrified Maxim.

"I do not believe in coincidences. Therefore, she must tell us what she knows." The king was rigid, remote as an icon, standing beneath the portrait.

Maxim, mute, fear nesting in his bowels, hurried to the door and called out in a shaken voice, "Bring her."

Jenna, too, was terrified, but only for her body and its fate. For her soul, she was certain she had done the right thing—her priest, and then the bishop, had told her so. Even as Ivan propelled her through the door of the study, she remained clear about that; until she saw the king's pitiless face and resolve fled like water from a cracked bowl.

"They tell me you left this house, girl, on the very day your mistress disappeared. Perhaps you can explain why."

How to tell the king that Anne's very love of this man before her, against all the dictates of the scripture, had made her path finally clear.

"I had no choice, Lord King."

She could not help it, she heard the plea in her voice.

"Lady Anne is a witch. I've heard her work spells. She bewitched you into betraying your wife."

The king looked hard at Maxim; the steward, agog, understood and hastily bowed himself from the room, closing the door behind him.

"Be clear, Jenna, be very clear. You could burn for this accusation."

The king skewered Jenna with such fierce eyes, the girl blanched and her knees turned to noodles; she sagged to the floor, a heap at his feet. Edward unbent a little; this stupid girl believed what she said, that was clear.

"Witchcraft? Nonsense. Superstition!" He said it loudly, clearly, turning his back on Memlinc's painting. He did not address the adultery.

"Ah, sire, I love my mistress, but it was wrong what she did. The priest said it—so did the Lord Bishop."

A hard hand gripped Edward's bowels: priests! This stupid, sincere girl had called up a tempest with her moralizing.

He kept his voice low now; he would not frighten her further. He needed to know what she could tell him.

"The bishop?"

She nodded less hesitantly but was blinded by sudden tears of relief. The king didn't sound so angry now; perhaps all would be set to rights.

"My priest, he took me to the bishop when I confessed what I had seen and heard," she pressed on bravely. "My mistress called up spirits, spoke to them—I heard her several times; and then, to see her dress and leave this house for adultery . . ." A horrified whisper; she would not look at him.

"Enough!" Sudden, violent thunder as his voice filled the room. Deborah and Maxim, together in the hall outside, were horrified by the fury.

"But the bishop said . . ." Somehow she had to make him hear that he was in grave danger, his immortal soul at risk. She was God's instrument in saving a Christian marriage from the snares of the Devil, for the evil one had possessed her mistress: a fitting punishment for challenging the role of men in the world, as she had done. The bishop had told her that and reassured her then that she'd be safe in his care. He'd lied about that for they'd found her anyway: a king was more powerful than a bishop, in the end.

"What have you done?"

The king looked at her, his eyes bleak, dark pools. She felt so sorry, so sorry for his pain.

"Ah, sire, if there had been another way to . . ."

"Yes!" The king strode to the door and hurled it open. Someone had knocked.

The Italian priest, Father Giorgio, stood there, hand still raised.

"What!" Anger was a clean response to dread; it was all that kept terror at bay.

The priest bowed as his eyes took in the frightened girl, the outraged man in front of him.

"Sire, the Lady Anne commissioned me, some time ago, to obtain information. I have a little and now I am at your service, for I think she would want me to share it with you."

# Chapter Thirty-four

The smell was foul and she was wet, covered in vomit, and shivering violently. It was mole dark. And cold. And she could hear groaning. Hers, it was her own voice she heard, and the timbers of a ship. She knew it was a ship because she could feel the sea rush beneath the keel stem.

Panicked, Anne struggled to stand, but the movement of the ship threw her violently against the bulkhead . . .

Time passed, a night, most of a day, and then the rats woke her. They were running all over her body and she woke screaming. Let this be a dream. A nightmare. But it wasn't. And there was no one to hear her.

Then, blessedly, a wavering light shone down as a hatch cover was removed: there was a lantern above. She couldn't see the man who was holding it because light blinded her, but she heard him, heard his voice.

"Behave or it'll get worse." The man sounded wary and that was good—that gave Anne the beginnings of courage; more came when she saw deep scratches on his face. She remembered now: she'd clawed him as he'd bundled her down into this disgusting hole and it gave her fierce pleasure to know that it was his dried blood under her nails. And she was alive, even though she hurt all over her body. She would survive, had survived worse than this.

"Then give me no cause to hurt you." She said the words bravely and was greeted by a loud laugh. "Hear me, oaf, or you will live to fear me more." She sounded detached but quite certain.

That silenced the man. For a moment. Then he grunted. "Stand aside."

The rope ladder thumped down beside her; it was greasy but unfrayed, which was something. It would bear her weight.

Normally, since she was young and fit, climbing out of her filthy prison would have been easy, but Anne was weak, dizzyingly weak, and she could feel the muscles of her arms and legs denying the effort as she tried to haul herself upward. Her head swam, too, and as the ship lurched around her, she felt like a spider swinging wildly on the end of a silk line after her web had been suddenly destroyed.

*But a spider perseveres, never forget that. A spider perseveres and rebuilds its web. It's no bad thing to be a spider.*

It was Deborah's voice Anne heard, and the confidence in the words made her smile; a smile that greatly disconcerted Wulf of Bremen as Anne slowly emerged from the dark of the noisome hold she'd been kept in as they cleared port. He wasn't used to this. Generally they cried a lot, the women his captain dealt in. They didn't fight back very often. Certainly didn't smile very much—it wasn't natural in their condition.

"I promise I will not harm you, if you do not harm me further."

She said it looking him full in the eyes and that shook him again. She had very strange eyes—an odd green-blue. Unnatural.

Quickly, Wulf crossed himself and hurried her, all stinking and wet as she was, up through the under storage and the crew's quarters, then over the heaving deck toward the captain's cabin under the fighting castle. He couldn't get her there fast enough. Anne, angry at his rough treatment, played the only card she had.

"You should be careful, very careful. If I choose, I can see into your soul, though it is foul and very black."

That did it for Wulf. He didn't care if she was worth money or not; when he heaved the door of the cabin open without even being asked to enter, he threw Anne through as if she'd been plague goods. It hurt when she hit the deck, hurt her knees and her elbows, but she made no sound.

Annoyed though he was at Wulf's treatment of valuable merchandise, the captain of the galley—*Maid of Bremen,* out of Kiel—was impressed by Anne's stoicism.

Gaspar Neidermeyer saw himself as a specialist, a well-respected one, and this woman and those like her were the reasons for the pride he took in his trade.

He made an excellent living carrying human flesh, women principally, up and down the shores of Portugal, Spain, France, even the Barbary Coast and through the Mediterranean; he'd also traded north as far as Denmark on occasion.

He delivered on his contracts promptly, delivered what was expected, on time and alive, if at all possible, and kept his mouth shut. Discipline and self-control—those were his watchwords, the key to any successful business—and he expected the same from those who worked for him.

Therefore, yes, he was angry at Wulf's poor handling of valuable goods—that would be dealt with a little later—but he looked with professional interest at the girl on the floor of his cabin.

Filthy and bruised as she was, she represented a pleasing turning point in his life. She was very important to someone because he was making so many solid gold angels out of her safe delivery: ten on taking the contract up when she'd been brought to his ship, with ten on arrival at the other end. Because of this one girl, he had real hopes of acquiring another neat little galley, *Star of the Sea,* currently being refitted in Kiel harbor, much sooner than he'd thought possible.

Then Gaspar wrinkled his nose disgustedly at Anne's stench as she tried to stand. He'd have to do something about that if he was to spend any time with her. Her captors, those he'd contracted with, had not said anything about delivering her intact so presumably her virginity, or otherwise, wasn't an issue for them. Still, he was a fastidious man and didn't like to bed dirty women: she would have to be washed.

"Take your clothes off. They're ruined and I have others."

"Have we been introduced?" She responded in French, and the tone was dry as a bone. That made Gaspar laugh. Was it good the girl still had spirit? He found it tedious when women wanted to talk. She spoke good French, though, better than his.

"Gaspar Neidermeyer. I am the captain of this ship."

"Lady Anne de Bohun."

Gaspar frowned again. She said it as if she believed it. He shrugged. Perhaps it was true, perhaps she was a noble lady. That was no concern of his and it wouldn't help her now; he owed loyalty to the people who were paying him.

"Captain, I'm cold and wet and hungry. And yes, I would dearly like dry clothes. I'd be very grateful if you could give me water to wash with—and leave me to this cabin. I can pay you for it."

She made him laugh, but he shook his head at the futility. She must be stupid also. What did she think she was doing here?

"Girl, you could be Mary, Queen of Heaven, for all I know, but I still wouldn't give you my cabin."

As he guffawed at his own joke, Gaspar looked Anne over a little more carefully and saw an attractive body under the filthy clothes. Perhaps she was pretty, too, though her face was too swollen from bruising to tell—that was to be expected.

"Captain, I can see you are a very clever man—this is a fine ship. I know about ships. I have a number of my own. I'm a merchant."

Something tugged at the captain's mind. A female merchant. He'd heard of one, in Brugge, was it?

"Yes. I trade out of Brugge. I trade with my guardian, Sir Mathew Cuttifer. He's very wealthy and I, too, have resources. Treat me well and it will be to your advantage."

The mind-reading trick didn't faze him, he'd seen it at too many fairs, but if she was who she said she was, that changed things. Perhaps, just to buy a little time to think this novel situation through, he'd arrange for hot water from the galley.

Judging the roll of the ship nicely, he stood. Anne looked at him measuringly. Not particularly tall, somewhere in his twenties and compact, with a hard-fleshed face and unnaturally broad shoulders for a short man; and he had quite delicate hands. A scholar would be proud of such hands, so white and fine.

Then desolation swallowed her. What did it matter what this man looked like? She was his captive. Would she ever see any of them again? Her son? The king? And Deborah?

A sudden dark void threatened, so bottomless, so powerful, Anne nearly fell. Perhaps it was the ship rolling.

Gaspar put out a hand to save the girl against his better judgment. He'd seen the anguish, but he did not allow himself emotional involvement with cargo. Ever. Trade was trade. They all went the same way in the end—to their buyers.

"There are clothes in the coffer. I'll get water."

Then he was gone in three quick strides, a dancer partnered with the lurch of the sea. And even though she heard the key turn in the lock, Anne was grateful in some small part of her being. Odd how the mind worked in so many layers: one part of her was a storm of misery and fear; another was calmly calculating how she could use this man. The question was, in the violent, silent hurry of her capture, what had she been left with?

Anne's fingers stole to her throat. The little filigree cross of pearls and garnets, the gift from Mathew Cuttifer and Lady Margaret a long time ago, was still there on its fine gold chain. The filth on her body, even caked between her breasts, had effectively hidden it. That was something.

But she had another, secret resource, one she hardly dared search for in case her captors had found it. She'd been taught the trick by Sir Mathew Cuttifer, and since the attack last winter, he'd insisted she adopt it for her own security.

Security. That brought a bleak smile to Anne's face as she ripped off the rags of her dress. Once it had been pale gray-blue silk with a fichu of web-fine embroidered gauze at the breast and throat; now it was slimy green-black with the filth she'd been lying in for who knew how long. But, yes! They were still there, nestled in carefully constructed little pockets sewn high up into the seams under the pit of each arm: two flat-cut diamonds on one side, a ruby and a brilliant star sapphire on the other. Much smaller than coin money, but far, far more valuable. God bless Mathew Cuttifer for his foresight.

Where to hide the four stones now?

Naked, shivering, and streaked with filth, Anne padded over to a coffer under the thick-paned cabin window. Heaving up the lid, she found a number of dresses, many made from expensive fabrics and well cut, though several still smelled of the bodies and the long-contained sweat of the previous owners. There were even the robes of a postulant nun: all that remained of some poor unfortunate scooped up from her convent and now lost forever. Anne shivered as she handled the robes of the novice, dropping them quickly as if they hurt her hands. Consciously she blocked the image as it came—herself in nun's clothing.

Determined not to be caught unclothed, Anne riffled through the rest of the clothes at speed, at last finding something she could bear to put on: an old but clean linen shift for underclothing and a kirtle of dark green wool—good quality, very soft—laced at the front with a crimson silk cord. The previous owner had been quite fastidious in her person since the dress did not smell of anything, not even old perfume.

Looking around, Anne also found a large pewter water jug held by its own bracket above the captain's bunk; she could begin to clean herself.

Gaspar Neidermeyer was unused to performing domestic tasks; normally his cabin boy kept his clothes in order, brought his food, and organized such washing as he allowed himself. Yet today, the bemused captain found himself back at the door of his cabin with two leather buckets full of hot, fresh water, no less—part of the ship's precious store of collected drinking water.

And as he stood outside his cabin, he found himself tempted to knock. Stupid. Shaking his head at such folly, he pushed open the low door.

"Hot water to wash with . . ." The words stopped of their own accord. The cabin was empty.

"Thank you, captain. You are kind."

The girl was behind him, pushing the door she'd hidden behind closed with one fluid moment as she whipped the captain's dagger from its place on his belt. An observant girl, she'd seen it earlier—and the captain had no hands to stop her.

"This is not intelligent, girl." He was annoyed, regretting his gesture. There was never gratitude from cargo, no matter how well they were treated.

"Strangely, captain, I do not agree. Sit on the bed." He paused for a moment, then, watching her eyes, grudgingly agreed, depositing the buckets on the deck first.

Mentally he shrugged. This would end soon enough, and if she wanted to make a dangerous little game out of their inevitable physical relationship—well, that was a change at least from the ninnies who wept and wailed.

"Such a shame we'll never ever know each other better in any sense, captain." Now she'd moved toward him, quite close, but anger at her presumption was close to the surface and he shook his head from growing irritation; the sudden movement accidentally slid the tip of his own very sharp knife across his face. He could feel blood!

"Enough. This is dangerous." Abruptly, he tried to rise from the bed, but there, for once, his ship caught him. The cabin tilted and Gaspar was thrown back against the wall above his cot, cracking his head painfully on the shelf set above it. He collapsed onto his bed, groaning.

Anne, however, stayed on her feet and that moment was enough for her to reclaim the initiative—she had prepared well in the few minutes he'd been out of the cabin.

Knife between her teeth, she bound the captain's hands behind his back with the lacing cords of one of the dresses in the coffer: silk was strong, it would not break easily; then his feet, and lastly a length of ripped linen for a gag.

The captain lay groaning as consciousness returned—and with it the dawning knowledge he'd been outsmarted. That made him furious and he convulsed his body, violently trying to sit up.

"Lie still or . . . oh, very well. I don't want to do this."

Anne picked up a sturdy joint stool and brought it down sharply on the captain's skull. She flinched—there was a nasty, muffled *wock* and he slumped back onto the cot, out cold.

She'd never done that before, actively hurt someone, and it shocked her; it had seemed the natural thing to do, and so easy.

Then, as she stood in awed, shaky contemplation of the uncon-scious man on the bed, her mind worked: *get out of here—quickly! They'll come to find him very soon!*

Then Anne laughed, relieved. Of course, the men of this ship would think the captain was pleasuring himself. They'd wait to be summoned. That would buy her priceless time.

The captain's own waxed-skin bag was hanging behind the door. It was cunningly made with a flap attached to the neck, which could be stuffed like a lid over the contents, and the sides laced tight over the top to keep out water. In went a rough blan-ket, a pair of women's soft leather slippers, another kirtle . . . but meanwhile, a plan was forming, a terrifying, reckless plan, the only thing she had on her side. But she needed different clothes to make it work, men's clothes. Instantly she stripped off the green dress, throwing it, too, into the bag, hastily knotting all but one of the jewels into the hem with unsteady fingers.

The captain's own clothes were in a brass-bound sea chest: a spare pair of light leather breeches, a woolen jerkin, and a heavily waxed sea cloak. There were even sea boots, which, when Anne tried one on, came almost up to her hips, they were so huge. She discarded them, they'd be too heavy, and if she fell into the sea, they'd drown her.

Hastily she tied her still filthy hair high on her head and then, shivering at the sweat smell, pulled Gaspar's spare jerkin around her, tying it into a neat shape with a broad leather belt: his knife made short work of an extra hole for the buckle.

The breeches were another matter; they dragged on the floor and were more the width of her hips than her waist. Quickly she unfastened the belt, and pulling the breeches high under her arms, hauled everything tight with the captain's belt again.

The clothing, swaddled around her body, added bulk, espe-cially when she pulled the sea cloak round her. Finally, folding up the bottoms of the breeches, she left her feet bare, the better to grip the deck. For that was her intention: get out onto the deck, now that night was falling and . . .

Then what? Quickly she grabbed a heel of black bread and a large piece of cheese from a pewter plate on the chart table—a late supper for the captain, no doubt—and drank all she could from one of the buckets.

It was a fine evening, but Wulf was annoyed. He'd been left alone at the tiller while the current watch went to the galley to eat. Ordinarily he wouldn't have minded, but he'd been ribbed all day about being bested by the cargo they were carrying, for others had seen and heard the exchange with Anne. Wulf was offended and embarrassed but it was best to ignore them all, pretend he was above their jibes. It would be forgotten by tomorrow if he added no fuel to the fire.

But he wouldn't forget the cause of his humiliation. He'd really appreciate teaching the girl to mind her manners when the captain had finished with her and she was back in the hold.

"Don't turn around." It was a whisper. A woman's voice. Her! Then he felt the brief cold peck of a blade through his clothes, prinking the flesh of his back.

"Don't you listen?" He'd tried to turn, so Anne allowed the knife to just pierce the skin above his kidneys. He swallowed as his own warm blood trickled down his arse—he could feel it.

"I said I wouldn't hurt you but that depends. Lash the tiller. Go on. Lash it!"

Now the dagger was at the base of his throat, unwavering, as was the tone of her voice. Hard. Unwomanly.

"Hurry, we have much to do."

Fumblingly, Wulf, who was at bottom a coward, especially when confronted with things he did not expect, did as he was told.

"Better. Much better. Now, where are the boats?"

He was confused. What was she talking about?

"Mistress, we're on the only boat I know."

Her voice was sharp from fear. "A rowing boat. There must be one on board. A lighter?"

There had to be one; every galley had to be able to row crew into harbor if the ship itself had to stand off the port, out into the roads.

Wulf's mind was beginning to work. He had to stall her; she

was only a woman. The blade was real enough but she was a tiny thing . . . he'd be a real laughing stock if she bested him now.

"No lighter, mistress. Had to leave it behind for repairs. Ow!" Anne deliberately slashed the soft flesh of his throat, not deep enough to do much damage but enough to make blood cascade down onto his jerkin. It was a very sharp knife.

"I don't believe you. Where is it? Quickly!"

Unwillingly his eyes strayed to the canvas-covered shape lashed below them on the deck. She picked up the slight movement of his head.

"I see it. Come."

Anne had no pity because there was no time, and as she hurried the bleeding seaman in front of her, prodding him down the stairs as the ship lurched and rolled beneath them, her mind was working fast.

It was a small coracle that Wulf showed her when he peeled the canvas back. Perhaps he was right, perhaps there was no lighter and this was all they had. She had no time to find out. It had one outstanding advantage, though, for it was light, light enough for just one man and a girl to heave over the side, if she could just persuade him to do it.

"I've been unfair. And you've been kind to me. What is your name?"

The words stuck in her throat, but still she said them. The man, wounded as he was, looked at her warily. "Wulf."

"If you help me now, of your own free will, Wulf, there will be a reward for you. If you do not, I shall curse you, waking and sleeping. Which is it to be?"

Anne looked at him, unwavering, as she hissed the last words, and Wulf dropped his eyes first. He was scared. He'd been scared of her ever since he'd hauled her up on deck earlier today.

"It's an easy choice, Wulf. But you'd better think quickly."

Now she used the soft, soothing voice that Deborah had taught her to use with wild or maimed animals. He reminded her of a dog that had been badly treated; perhaps she could reach him, but the moon was rising and the cold light caught the edge of the blade in her hand.

Wulf swallowed. The girl might sound calm, but she was holding it against him, poised over his heart in such a way that suggested she could strike quickly.

He found himself nodding "What have you got?"

"This." Anne opened her other hand and held it close to his eyes. The small, flat diamond lay in her palm like a cold star. Involuntarily he moved to take it from her, but the knife touched the skin above his heart.

"Be careful, Wulf. You and all your family will wither away if I curse you."

Ice touched his spine—he believed her.

"Throw it down into the water." She was nodding toward the coracle. "Quickly." The seaman made up his mind; he'd think of an excuse later, somehow. That diamond would buy him out of this ship and take him home, get him a farm, even, if he could just . . .

"Do it!" It was a command as, from the direction of the captain's cabin, loud, insistent thumps began; the coracle was heaved out of its bonds and thrown into the sea.

Wulf yelled, "Give it to me!"

Anne hurled the diamond to the far side of the deck, and in that same moment she jumped after the coracle, bag clutched in one hand, knife in the other, invoking all the gods that one panicked thought allowed her.

Even though it was early autumn after a warm summer, the water was very cold this far out to sea, and shock nearly made Anne lose hold of the bag when she hit the surface. She dropped the knife as she struggled, trying to keep herself afloat, trying desperately to locate the coracle, but Gaspar's clothes filled with water and their weight was dragging her down. Shed them now or drown.

She did it. Unclasping the sea cloak—which spread out like a giant lily pad—somehow she kicked her way out of the britches; now she was naked but for the captain's jerkin. There was commotion on the ship behind her as she struggled in the water. Men shouted, waving torches, and Gaspar yelled, "Port, port side! She's over there, over there!"

A sudden whine: an arrow plowed the water, perilously near. Her face, they could see her white face!

The seacloak was her salvation. She dragged the heavy leading edge over her head, and holding it in place with her teeth as the cloak fanned out behind her, she struck out with her free arm toward the bowl of the coracle, just glimpsed in the dark, resting lightly on the sea. So close, so agonizingly close.

*Weeeesh.* Another arrow. Then another. Desperately, Anne kicked and thrashed, trying for rhythm: trying to picture how her childhood friends, the village boys, had swum in the millpond in summer. She remembered they'd made their arms and legs work together, why couldn't she?

*Wheesh-shaaaah.* That was farther away! They couldn't see her in the dark, and suddenly Anne was moving her free arm and legs rhythmically, no longer floudering—much better, learning fast. That or die—no other choice.

The cries from the boat were fainter as Anne realized she was being carried by something: a sea current was moving her on quite strongly, carrying her away from the boat but no sooner had she formed the thought than she found herself within arm's length of the coracle. One last desperate flounder and she caught hold of it; now she just had to get in without swamping the strange little craft.

Her body was close to the end of its resources, but the feel of the rough hide covering the wickerwork frame of the dishlike boat, if boat it could be called, summoned her last shreds of resilience. Somehow Anne managed to heave the achingly heavy sea cloak over the side—she knew she would need some sort of covering in the open sea—followed by the skin bag that had been her salvation. Then with both arms free, she tried to roll herself over the lip of the coracle.

But the thing was very light and as she tipped it down toward her, to clamber aboard, the sea rushed in, threatening to drown both her and the little craft.

Then she knew despair, nearly gave up. She was cold and weak; it would be easy, so easy, to drift away, to sleep.

"Anne," the voice was a breath, "Anne . . . you will not die here."

Dreams and visions are a comfort as death beckons; Deborah had told her that—often she'd been the last to attend a dying villager, at home in the forest of Anne's childhood. She'd told Anne many of the strange things people saw and heard as the body sank toward its last long home. Was this a sweet phantom voice, one that would ease her own passing into the realm she had glimpsed before?

"Anne!" the voice had changed. It was urgent, commanding, harsh. The Sword Mother's voice. Obediently the girl opened her eyes to find the coracle had righted itself and she was still holding on with one hand. This time when she tried to roll over the side as slowly and carefully as she could, the little craft rolled with her on the swell and then Anne was lying in its center beside the skin bag and the sodden sea cloak. There was water in the bottom of the boat as well—that had been the extra weight that kept the coracle from tipping this time.

Thus for a time, as the current carried the little craft along, Anne lay in the lathed bottom of the coracle and watched the stars pass by overhead. She had no means of directing her boat: no oars, no paddles, and no strength left in her arms. She wasn't uncomfortable any more—though she knew she was wet—for the water she was lying in became as warm as her body.

After a time, as the moon dipped below the western horizon, she slept . . .

# Chapter Thirty-five

The embarkation of the English court was slow, but to the watching crowd in Sluis, packed in behind the red silk ropes that cordoned off the wharf, it was as good as an Easter pageant. Slow was good therefore, slow was satisfying: it gave you more time to look at the clothes properly—and compare the English court women against the Burgundian ladies, when they finally deigned to arrive.

First, after the early dawn, came the animals, helped on board with much swearing and yawning from the ostlers—the sumpter mules of the prelates, the palfreys of the ladies, and the very expensive destriers of the great English nobles; then an endless, sweating mass of liveried men servants loaded boxes, chests, rolls of carpet, hangings, trappings, pictures, even furniture, aboard the King of England's fleet.

It was a hot day—one of the last of this autumn, said sage heads—and as the morning wore away, the crowd's patience diminished. The women were especially restless—they'd come to see the wedding clothes on the backs of the court parties, most particularly their new duchess and the fabled Queen of England. Where were they all? They'd miss the tide soon . . .

In Brugge, Edward, haunted, was pacing—up and down, up and down—waiting, desperately hoping to hear more from Father Giorgio before the iron machine of protocol forced him to leave the city, to return to England.

Even now, more than three days since Anne's disappearance, an endless, nauseating cycle of certainty, uncertainty, certainty, uncertainty distorted every thought, every action: each moment, each emotion raised the stakes and brought terrifying specters in its wake. Trust was gone, belief was gone, hope was fading—and suspicion filled the yawning void.

Could they be true—how could they be true?—the rumors that Father Giorgio had brought him? Elizabeth, his queen, behind the attempt on Anne's life? Edward squeezed his eyes closed, tried to focus on the pain in his head as a means of clarity, but images of the recent heated interview he'd conducted with William Caxton, governor of the English Merchant Adventurers in Brugge, kept intruding.

Giorgio had led Edward to William—tipped off by Maxim, who'd heard more than he should have of conversations between Anne and the merchant. Poor grieving Caxton—he was distraught about Anne also—had shown Edward the note, the supposed proof of his wife's involvement in the attack on Anne. But ciphers—even if this one was real, which Edward doubted, had to doubt—could be made to say anything. Anything!

Elizabeth was his queen, anointed by God, and she was his wife. He could accept a wife's jealousy of a husband's affair, but to plot his lover's murder? And for him to believe it on the basis of such flimsy "evidence" as he'd been shown? No! Not possible.

And even supposing Caxton was right, where was the link from the attempted assassination to Anne's disappearance?

Nothing made sense!

And, of course, when he'd questioned his wife—as he'd had to—he'd been met with outraged, furious denial and tears—gales, storms of tears. He'd felt like a fool and worse because he could prove nothing.

He blamed himself, of course. In the delirium of his affair with Anne the need to find her enemies had taken a distant second place to living in the moment. He had her, she had him; she was safe with him in Brugge—and they'd find the culprit later. He was the king; if it was his wish, it would be done!

Too late, too late now.

Thus, exhausted, Edward paced up and down, up and down, trying to think his way through the tangle. By order, he was alone in Duke Charles's working closet at the Prinsenhof as he waited for Giorgio, yet he heard the scuffles, the whispers, outside the door. They were all there: his valet, his body servants, courtiers—even his wife's servants—all waiting for his order that the court should join the barges and journey down the Zwijn to the ships waiting at Sluis.

Distantly he heard noon ring out from the Markt belfry. Time was his enemy and the bells were pleased to tell him so. The tide, remember the tide, that's what the bells said.

He heard the door behind him swing open and barked.

"Leave me! How many times must I . . ."

Charles of Burgundy cleared his throat.

"Come, brother-in-law, the fleet will not sail today if you delay further."

Edward shrugged, desperation and exhaustion burning his eyes. He'd not slept since Anne's disappearance.

"Another day, just one more day, Charles. We may hear more. I'm waiting for news even now."

The duke was troubled—he had some sympathy for the king's tortured state over Anne de Bohun because he liked and admired her too. Perhaps a light touch would help.

"But, brother, there is not food enough to feed you all—no, not even for one more day!" Charles laughed, of course, intending the words should be ironic, but there was truth in them. The cost of entertaining the English court for the ten days of the wedding had been enormous, added to by the unexpected extra days they'd since spent in Brugge. All because Anne de Bohun had disappeared.

"Come, sire, your people are impatient to be away home." Charles spoke plainly, bracingly. It was not for a duke to tell a king his duty, but he was older than Edward and a soldier. And if the English delayed any longer, it would be most unfortunate for he, Charles, had many problems to address, not least the wily Valois king Louis XI once more circling Burgundy's territory. He could not afford the distraction of pleasure any longer. Unconsciously he sighed. Soon he would have to leave his young bride to go on campaign; yes, he understood how hard it was to leave a woman behind.

"Edward? Shall I give them the order?" He was sad to see his friend in such a tortured state. And they were friends still, just, though both knew, without acknowledgment on either side, that their relationship had been much compromised by the mischief manufactured by Elizabeth Wydeville—and the disappearance of this girl.

Edward was silent, staring out of the window as if he'd heard nothing. Charles grimaced—and then brightened as the idea came to him. When the English court had left he would compose a most careful and confidential letter to Edward setting out clearly, once and for all, assurances as to the health of the Zwijn and the strength of the Burgundian economy. And he would also redouble his already considerable efforts to find Anne. "Come brother, leave us to find Lady de Bohun—we seek her diligently and so shall continue."

Edward swung round to stare at this brother-in-law. Strange thoughts surfaced from some dark place. Was this man still an ally? Should he trust him still? Perhaps he was in league with Anne's abductors—even the queen, if indeed she was responsible—for his own good reasons.

Charles returned the king's suspicious gaze for a moment saying softly, "You must trust me in this. I am your friend, Edward, and Lady Anne's friend. I always will be." Then he strode over to the door, where he turned, saying formally, "What is Your Majesty's pleasure?"

Fingering the rope of pearls and emeralds slung around his shoulders—Anne's prodigal gift flung to him so few days ago—Edward sighed, deeply, consciously willing away the black demons that haunted him. He nodded. "Very well, tell them we embark."

Relieved, Duke Charles opened the door and called out to the waiting courtiers, "Load the barges, it is the king's pleasure to depart!" Turning back to Edward, the duke made a deep bow.

"Your Majesty?"

Edward stood, as wearily as an old man. One by one, he touched the pearls, touched the emeralds, as if they were so many rosary beads. The duke was right—more days would make no difference. It was not a matter of time, it was a matter of fate.

Very well, he would journey back to his kingdom and pick up the pieces of his life in London, with Elizabeth. And trust to providence, and to Charles, and to Father Giorgio that he would hear news of Anne. That they would find her. That she would find him.

For if she did not, how could he live?

# Chapter Thirty-six

There was much interest and speculation in the district behind the mouth of the Humber when news of the near-naked girl cast up on the strand near Spurn Point spread through the surrounding countryside.

Cod fishermen returning home from the autumn fisheries sighted the body lying near the rip at the mouth of the river, yet the girl was still alive, though barely, when she was gathered up and taken to the Nunnery of Our Lady of the Sands, a small convent set back from the shores of the estuarine mouth of the river.

The nunnery was a sadly shabby little place, for it was many years since they'd had even one well-dowered novice, and the Mother Superior, Elinor, was neither a confident nor efficient manager of her seventeen unruly sisters in Christ, so its fortunes continued to decline. However, the day the unconscious girl arrived in the back of Beck's wagon was to begin change at Our Lady of the Sands—change that Elinor would, in the end, welcome.

The feathered cacophony of geese warned of visitors before the cart was even sighted, and though Mother Elinor was on her knees praying for the continued good health of the convent's only patron, the irascible Baron Stephen Hardwell, she was curious to see what had set the sisters running past the chapel, calling out.

Therefore, Mother Elinor rose to her feet. With strict attention she crossed herself, genuflecting to the altar table, and then calmly stepped out from the choir, walked past the bench for the few remaining lay sisters, and out of the chapel door to see what the noise portended.

The sisters, all of them, both lay and choir, were clustered at the back of Beck's wagon blocking her view.

"Sisters!" Elinor was cross and they all fell quiet for once, which pleased her.

"What is so important you must disturb my prayers?"

Better and better, she could hear the authority in her voice today.

"But Reverend Mother, look, she's dead!" It was an obvious pronouncement, but Sister Bertha enjoyed the drama of voicing everyone's opinion; then the girl's chest rose and fell microscopically. She was alive after all.

Elinor, never decisive, was nonplussed for a moment, then inspiration struck.

"It is our duty to be charitable. Warmth, I think, then food."

"What are you all standing there for! Listen to our mother—get the girl into the dorter. She can have your bed, Bertha, since you'll be on your knees thanking God tonight for this miracle." It was Sister Aelwin who spoke, suddenly obsequious. Elinor kept the surprise off her face—Sister Aelwin, the prioress, was her nemesis at the convent: she thought she deserved Elinor's position. Nodding graciously, Elinor crossed herself with decision.

"Let it be done in Christ's name, sisters. I shall finish my prayers; Sister Aelwin, see I am not further disturbed. And meanwhile send the infirmaress to attend our unexpected guest."

She made a stately turn upon the worn-down heels of her outside clogs and left an abashed but busy silence behind her as her sisters in Christ hurried to obey.

The little cracked bell, all the sisters could afford, was tolling Compline as Anne opened her eyes. She was confused. Around her there was pale, windy darkness, and somewhere far away, an unmusical bell was calling her insistently to prayer.

Tears came: a bell had rung the night her son was born. Her son. She had lost her son, and Deborah.

And Edward.

"Hush. There, there. Save your strength, child." A cool hand wiped away the tears and a surprisingly strong arm helped her to half-sit.

Now she could see it, a wavering flame from a cheap tallow candle. Anne hated the smell of burning animal fat, hated the greasy black smoke, but now she was grateful for the pungent reek. She was on land, that's what the stench meant, even though everything around her rocked and swam.

Slowly the milky darkness receded, translating into a narrow room filled with shadows and the sound of the sea. A rising wind rattled the shutters, closed for the night, but if she forced her eyes to remain open though the lids were so heavy, she saw rough, lime-washed walls and a line of primitive bedsteads. She was lying between coarse sheets and she felt light as air, less than air. Like a cloud must feel, like mist.

Anne heard the soft rustle as someone else sat beside her and she felt another warm hand on her forehead.

"Can you hear me, Sister?"

For a moment, the words meant nothing. She was so used to speaking French or Flemish that the English made no sense. But they had an accent, a familiar one. How could that be?

"Yes, I hear you." The words were a breath, and when Anne struggled to see the woman who was speaking to her, the world blurred again. There were shapes; perhaps the pale oval leaning down over her was a face—it was hard to tell, hard to tell.

"Thanks be to Mary! Here, help me, Sister Joan; we must get some food into her or I think she will truly die."

"That would be a sorrowful shame, Sister, after all that this poor girl has endured."

The words floated above her head as Anne felt herself lifted higher into a sitting position. She winced as she smelled foul breath from rotting teeth.

"There! Look, she's back with us again. You hold her up, I'll try getting the broth into her."

Focus was abruptly sharpened. The wavering shapes were two smiling women, both dressed in gray hand-loomed habits. Anne dearly wished that her feeder, Sister Bertha, did not breathe quite so earnestly or so often—the smell from her teeth was truly shocking.

The mutton broth, however, was delicious—Anne was sick, thus could legitimately be given animal flesh—and the glistening little lake of pearly, silver fat floating on the top was the most beautiful sight Anne had ever seen. She was ravenous, ravenous! Very soon she had taken the bowl to herself, spooning the liquid into her mouth as quickly as she could.

"Does the heart good, doesn't it, Sister Bertha? Poor thing must have been perishing hungry."

Sister Joan, the infirmaress, had a kind heart and a sweet smile. "Yes, indeed, Sister. She's just like a starving child." Sister Bertha was the infirmaress's longtime particular friend—even though the rules of their convent forbade such close relationships between sisters—and because of this, Joan had never had the heart to tell her companion about the halitosis, though she grew a lot of mint in her garden; it served well to sweeten the breath—temporarily.

"She shouldn't have too much at first. She'll be sick."

Behind them as she arrived, Sister Aelwin was chilly with disapproval. Bertha scrambled guiltily off the bed, sure she'd be made to do penance later for unnecessary propinquity; that was the prioress's way.

"Did you ask her where she comes from?"

Sister Joan resented Aelwin's tone. "No, Sister. It seemed best to let her eat something before we talked further." But Anne had finished the soup and started on the good bread supplied with it. As she chewed, she considered what to say in response to Aelwin's enquiry, just now impatiently repeated directly to her.

"Where do you come from, girl?"

Anne bowed her head and her voice shook. "I don't know, Sister. I'm a lost soul." This last part was the truth.

Aelwin, nonplussed by the girl's grief, did not question further—a rare moment of sensitivity.

"I shall speak to Reverend Mother Elinor after prayers. She will instruct us in what will be best."

The prioress soundlessly left the dorter in her felt house slippers, clearly expecting the other two nuns to follow.

Joan delayed for one moment, brushing the crumbs from Anne's bed—this one instant expressing most clearly, for those who understood the politics of Our Lady of the Sands, that obedience was a continuing problem for this bride of Christ, especially obedience to the prioress.

"I'll leave you the candle." Joan sketched the sign of the cross over Anne; then she and Bertha hurried away.

The reek of singed, rancid animal fat—the candle's main constituent—was a severe trial to Anne, but for the first time in many, many days she was not wet, hungry, thirsty, or cold. And she was grateful, very grateful.

There was so much to remember, so much to forget. But though she would have welcomed darkness, oblivion, she was granted neither. Instead, like a pustulant wound, the memory of all that had happened, all those she had lost, ached and burned: her belly griped as if it had been punched.

The sound of the distant sea wash brought pain: she hated it, hated to hear the waves break and shuffle back on the sand; hated to hear the wind's cry over the mudflats—the almost human keening as sand whipped and shifted uneasily in the dunes near the nunnery.

Somewhere, far away, nuns sang the evening prayers, the sound drifting, changing with the wind from the sea.

Anne could not stop the images, the sounds as, dreamlike, she remembered . . .

The stars had voices, surely? She'd begun to think they did as she lay in the coracle, going wherever the winds took her, for the days and nights had blurred in a fog of thirst: sun, stars, and the sea, the sea, but she had heard the stars sing, hadn't she?

She knew there had been a storm once and after it had gone, the rainwater saved her life. She'd lapped it up, sucking and licking the fresh water from the bottom of the coracle. Then it had become cold, much colder, and she'd wrapped herself in the sea cloak, cold and damp as it was, shivering, hallucinating as the winds blew her north, ever north.

She remembered talking, too, holding long conversations with her son and Edward and Deborah. She'd had dreams about them: they were all safe; they were all dead; the house in Brugge had burned to the ground; often she woke with tears running down her face, tears that, one freezing dawn, had turned to ice.

And then another, bigger storm had come.

Calmly she'd closed the mouth of the captain's skin bag, lashing it to her wrist, and then huddled in the bottom of the coracle. If she was going to drown, she didn't want to see the wave coming . . .

But if Anne had looked she might have seen—through lumped-up mounds of black water, through veils of rain—that there was land ahead and the mouth of a wide estuary. But she didn't, so her wish was granted: the wave that finally swamped her little boat was an unseen monster and so the violent sea took her, tumbled her, skinning her of clothes as a hunter takes a rabbit's fur.

Swallowing so much water nearly killed her, should have killed her, but just before Anne's lungs stopped functioning, she was thrown up on the shingled strand at the mouth of the river, still clutching the skin bag. There she lay, so close to death that she looked like part of the beach until Beck found her and carted her off to Our Lady of the Sands.

But she heard the singing stars again. They joined with her, in the back of Beck's cart, joined in high clear voices as she tried to sing her baby a lullaby from far, far away as the cart jolted on toward the nunnery, and life.

Now, days later, lying in the dorter, all Anne could hear was the sea. The hungry sea. It wouldn't get her now, wouldn't get him, little Edward.

Anne rolled over and in the moment before she slept, she prayed they were all safe, reciting their names like a novena, "Keep them and bless them: Edward, Edward, and Deborah. Keep them and bless them: Edward, Edward, and Deborah."

All she had were their names and they were her comfort, her only comfort.

# Chapter Thirty-seven

 Edward shivered violently and wrapped the fur-lined red cloak tighter as he strode into his own Presence chamber with Hastings, his chamberlain.

Why did the Palace of Westminster always feel so much colder than his other houses? Shene, for example, or even York? And it had been so warm in Brugge, so ripe in its last, late, radiant summer. London never felt ripe, especially now, deep in the dank mists of autumn.

"More braziers! Quickly, it's like a tomb in here."

It was unlike Edward to be petulant or demanding, but there was a dangerous edge to the king's tone today and at a discreet signal from Hastings, two men at arms hurried out of the Presence chamber to obey.

The king mounted the three shallow steps to the Chair of Presence under his Cloth of Estate. This morning would be tedious as he must address a series of petitions from the merchants of London asking for tax relief.

Tax relief! Anger burned his gullet at even the thought of the words. As king he was a pragmatist, a good one. He'd understood there would be resentment about the extra monies he'd asked for from the country, via the parliament, to make the necessary brave show at his sister's wedding in Burgundy, but it angered him, undoubtedly it angered him.

Did none of the idiot merchants waiting outside this room

understand that the magnificent clothing, the largesse to his host the duke, the lavish entertainments he'd paid for during the wedding, had all been for the future of this country? For the future of trade?

Margaret was marrying into one of the most powerful, and arguably, the most wealthy families in Europe. This was an outstanding strategic alliance for the country against France. It was good for England that the money was spent. Could these knaves, these fools, not see that?

"Sir Mathew Cuttifer."

To hear the man announced opened the wound. Anne! For a moment he had to close his eyes and blink back hot tears.

Hastings was astonished. And worried now, deeply worried. Since Edward and Elizabeth had returned to London from Dover, only a day or so ago, the king had been deeply distracted. And it was very clear there was trouble between husband and wife.

Hastings felt for the king; the queen had defied his express orders making her regent while he was absent from the kingdom; no wonder things were difficult between them. And though Edward was punctilious as always in his observances of Elizabeth's dignity as queen, he barely spoke to her, never looked at her, and had kept to his own suite of rooms as much as possible since they'd returned to London. The court was puzzled at first, but now fizzed with rumor and joyful innuendo about the imminent fall of the Wydevilles. There was even gossip that the king meant to repudiate the queen, pregnant as she was, and insist she enter a convent. There were even some who said the child was not the king's—and that was why she was to be put away.

William, never an ardent supporter of Elizabeth Wydeville's, automatically discounted the more dramatic whispers flooding Westminster, and found he even admired the queen's iron discipline, since she appeared untroubled and serene in public despite the king's odd behavior; although there were rages, tears, and tyranny in her private rooms, as the chamberlain well knew.

There must be fire behind the smoke for the king to behave as he was doing; yes, something had gone wrong, badly wrong between the royal couple in Brugge; yet, so far, William had been unable to get the king to speak to him about the breach.

A flash of gold caught William's eye: Mathew Cuttifer was bowing, deeply, ever more deeply, as he approached the king's dais, sweeping off his flat velvet cap lavishly piped with gold cord and hung with ornate gold tassels. Dangerous to wear such an opulent hat in front of the king. Perhaps it would remind Edward that his merchants were prospering a little too much—at the king's expense.

"Sir Mathew. You are well?"

The king's tone was neutral, detached, but William saw Mathew Cuttifer's nervousness. He had a certain fellow feeling for the man; he'd not have wanted to be the first to talk to Edward on this delicate matter of tax relief, especially since the king, after Anne had tried to escape him the first time more than a year ago, rightly blamed Mathew's interference for the difficulties that resulted. Relations between the king and the merchant had never been the same: it was the chief reason Mathew had not ventured to Brugge for the wedding.

"I am, Your Majesty. Very well." Mathew Cuttifer spoke confidently, though he hid shaking hands in his wide sleeves; there was a moment's silence, which the king allowed to hang. Mathew, though his breath smoked in the cold air of the frigid Presence chamber, felt sweat slip down his sides and he had a terrible urge to cough; his throat was dry as sand from nerves.

Yet now the king was gazing out of the windows, seemingly oblivious to the fact he was conducting an audience. The merchant glanced beseechingly at the chamberlain.

Hastings coughed loudly and the king, startled, looked around confused. Now it was William's turn to sweat; was the king becoming distracted? Dread squeezed his heart. Suppose this king should begin to suffer the same strangeness that had gripped the previous king, Henry VI? They were cousins, not so different in blood. *Let it not be so, please God, let it not be so, for all their sakes.*

"Very well, William. Where is this petition you wish to present, Sir Mathew?" Mathew Cuttifer bowed soundlessly to Edward and from within the capacious sleeve of his houppelande, the standard court dress of a generation older than the king, withdrew a scroll.

Bowing as he advanced, he stepped up the three shallow treads of the dais and placed the scroll across Edward's knees. Then, with anxious care, he slowly backed down the steps again, dreading that he would trip in the long skirts of his heavy velvet gown.

There was no disaster, although his breath was ragged as he found his place once more before the dais—a fact observed by William Hastings. Yes, he had some sympathy for Mathew Cuttifer. In the king's current state, anything was possible.

The king frowned. "You are the first of many to present documents such as these, I understand?" Mathew was uncertain how to reply, so he said nothing, merely nodding his head respectfully.

The king's hand shook as he unfurled the scroll; it would have been good to scream, to bellow abuse at the hapless merchant just to relieve the tension he felt, but Edward restrained himself, although his eyes glittered strangely. This was frightening enough for everyone in the room to shift uneasily in his place. Suddenly the air felt charged, thunderous.

"Why do none of you understand what I was trying to do?" The king was dangerously quiet, almost whispering. Mathew flinched as if from a blow when the next words were addressed to him directly.

"How can you not see that money makes money, you of all people? Trade!" Finally the king did bellow, "Trade, you fool. You helped vote me the aid to defray the wedding costs. Now we have stronger links with Burgundy; that will bring more trade so you all become richer! But what thanks is there in this for me? Only demands!"

Plantagenet rage had been famous for three hundred years and Edward, once truly roused, lost nothing in comparison with the legends.

Brave man that he was, William Hastings found himself trembling at the sight of Edward IV as berserk as he'd ever been in battle. Mathew Cuttifer, no warrior, felt as if he was going to faint or wet himself.

"I will not do this! Never! Do you hear me! And I shall have the needle monopoly back if you persist! Tell them that, Master Cuttifer, your greedy city compatriots. Tell them that. What I gave I can take back."

The noise chased itself around the vast room and dissolved into ringing silence.

Abruptly the king waved his hand. The audience was over, but not before Edward took the petition and in one swooping movement, ripped it from top to bottom, throwing the two halves with their dangling, dependent wax seals onto the flags in front of the now kneeling merchant. Many of them shattered into little jagged red shards.

Trying to hide the trembling of his hands, Mathew Cuttifer shuffled the pieces of the petition together, leaving the bits of wax where they lay, and backed away from the king toward the now open door of the Presence chamber more rapidly than he would have thought possible.

"No. You!" The merchant froze and surreptitiously looked around for William. Whom did the king mean?

"Yes, Sir Mathew, I meant you. Lady Anne de Bohun—have you heard anything?"

There it was again, something like a tear in the corner of the king's eye. Mathew's mouth closed with a snap; it was either that or let it drop open in astonishment, for he'd not seen what William had earlier. Quickly, the merchant found his wits, but he shook his head heavily.

"Sire, all my interests in Brugge and farther afield are working to find information, any information at all. So far . . ."

He didn't have to finish the sentence. The king nodded, went on in a dull voice.

"Father Giorgio, your Father Giorgio"—Mathew was uncertain if he liked the king calling the man "his" priest—"sent me news from Sluis. Around the time the Lady Anne disappeared, a ship left port before she was due to; the captain is a notable flesh peddler. There was some suggestion that a woman had been de-livered, bound, the night before. No port we trade with has re-ported seeing the ship, the *Maid of Bremen,* in the last month, so until we have the captain in our hands, there's no way of knowing if it was the Lady Anne."

Flesh peddlers. Mathew shivered, said nothing. If it was true, they would never see Anne again.

Hastings cleared his throat and the king waved his dismissal.

Mathew bowed deeply, spoke bravely. "We will find her, Liege. She's a strong girl. Very capable. And I will redouble my efforts. We must find the ship. We will find it!"

William hurried the merchant out of the chamber as fast as he decently could. He was even more worried than Mathew, if that was possible, since the king said nothing more, anger shading into grief all too visibly before their eyes.

There were other petitioners outside in the anteroom, but they'd all heard the king's rage earlier and were only too happy to be dismissed, as was Mathew.

William waited until the subdued little knot of men had been sent from the anteroom and then, clearing the Presence chamber of guards and functionaries, he rejoined the king, alone.

"You know, I wanted to bring her back here; revoke the exile, have her near me. But she never arrived, that last night, when we were supposed to meet. I spoke to that fool of a bishop in Brugge." William heard the king's teeth grind together. "Witchcraft! The witterings of a servant, that was all! But she vanished. And I still don't know the connection, if there's a connection. No one can tell me what happened. No one!"

William was relieved by the anger, if confused. Witchcraft? Bishops? Connections to what? At least the king was talking at last—that was something—but what, by the bones of God, had happened? They must resolve this mess for the good of the king-dom, but for a boil to be lanced it had to come to a head. He needed facts, just as the king did.

"Your Majesty, we have the means to find her. I promise you. I will scour Europe if you need me to, but you must trust me with the truth, all of it."

There was some pain in William's voice. He was truly close to Edward, or so he thought. Why had the king not told him earlier? And why had he not heard of this fiasco earlier? His normally reliable network of intelligence had let him down badly this time, and someone would pay for that lapse.

Edward shrugged wearily. "I was relying on the duke. Brugge is his city. He set himself to find her, any trace of her, but he's distracted by the French, it seems. Father Giorgio, now, at least he's found something definite, and continues to work on my behalf."

Sometimes William forgot that Edward was a young man still, with a young man's passions. William envied the king. He'd never felt as deeply for a woman as Edward so plainly did for Anne. He and Edward had been so alike once, both sexual predators, but something had changed for Edward, something that filled his chamberlain with deep unease.

Not for nothing did the Greeks call love a curse—a curse that destroyed reason. Yet Edward had a country to think of, not just a girl. A woman could not be allowed to disturb the peace of the kingdom and disable its king.

Yes, she must be found, and, if necessary, she might need to be destroyed before the king was informed. For the good of them all.

# Chapter Thirty-eight

Stephen Hardwell thought of himself as a kind man. In his little world of the Holderness, the world in which he was still the most important man for many miles, he was used to being agreed with, used to being flattered. The ghost of family money—mostly long gone—and traditional position guaranteed him automatic deference, though he'd forgotten the truth of that long ago.

But recently Stephen Hardwell was more and more troubled by the knowledge that in his long life he'd sinned against God's holy ordinances many, many times, and especially with women. Thus, heavy with increasing guilt for the past, he'd thought to smooth his soul's eventual entry to heaven by good works. He began to set his own house in order by meddling with those of other people, for their own good and his. If he was fearful of purgatory, others were too, for it was what he visited upon them.

Our Lady of the Sands, for example; it had become a special project for Sir Stephen to save the sisters from themselves, from their own financial ineptitude. With the permission and support of George Neville, the Archbishop of York, the illustrious brother of the Earl of Warwick, Stephen Hardwell had recently become patron of the nunnery. And for that he gave himself the right, no, the duty, of interfering in everything that was done under that holy roof: from what the good sisters ate, to the quality of the sheets they slept within, to the number of prayers that were said for his continuing good health and that of his family.

Creating order where there had been none before had became a passion he could offer up to God as evidence of his dedication here on earth. Therefore he'd felt certain, when news was brought of the girl cast up on the shores of the Humber and now lodging at the convent, that he must counsel Lady Elinor in what was best to be done. He would meet this girl and assess her personally, sending his report posthaste to his friend the archbishop in York, who would no doubt pass it directly to Duke Richard, their young duke, the king's brother.

Strangers should be received as Christ, the unknown guest at the table. However, happenings such as this should also be investigated thoroughly. God had chosen to send the girl to the sisters, therefore work must be done to divine His purpose, for the good of them all, for the shriving of their souls.

On the day he chose to visit Our Lady of the Sands, however, the weather turned bleak with the first big slashing autumn gale; weather that drove small pebbles, hail, and veils of sleet against him and his annoyed party of attendants as they rode into the teeth of the unforgiving easterly wind. And after a tiresome journey, it felt like the drear edge of the world when they arrived at the comfortless huddle of convent buildings near Spurn Point, where the land hooked back into the river as if to defend itself from the battering sea.

But Stephen Hardwell looked around the nunnery with real satisfaction. His son, Henry Hardwell, mocked him for what he'd accomplished in this place and had even dared to question his father's motives for visiting the convent today; yet Stephen had ridden out nonetheless. He knew his duty as an honorable knight, a humble servant of Christ in His work on earth; Baron Hardwell was proud of the service he rendered to the Lord—a pride his reeve, Simon of Wallingdon, did not share.

The sour expression on Simon's face said it was good money chasing bad that his employer chose to throw away here on this poxy little convent: money that he, the reeve, must nonetheless squeeze from the villagers of Upper and Lower Hardwell. Their tears, for instance, had paid for the new roof on the convent's chapel—a slate roof, ruinously expensive—when thatch of river reeds would have done just as well.

Simon knew, too, that the baron's only son was deeply impatient with the good coin his father was wasting on the convent: the sisters of the Sands had better watch out when the old man died. There would not be a penny more from Henry; the old man had run the manor into the ground for years with his extravagant and foolish schemes, and it would take a strong man to wrench it out of debt and the moneylenders' hands, but Henry Hardwell was likely to be such a one. Simon was cheered at that thought, as he plodded along in the wake of the impetuous baron, as he was at the conviction that this dangerous, lung-baiting cold would quite likely knock the old man off, if nothing else did; the baron had always had a weak chest in winter.

But Stephen Hardwell had other thoughts beside mortality when the castaway was brought into the parlor to speak to him in the presence of Mother Elinor and Sister Aelwin. The latter, her eyes unwaveringly fixed on their patron, saw an unusual expression pass over the old man's face as Anne was presented—lust. A remarkable emotion in a convent, but one the prioress recognized—this particular sin had haunted her youth.

Aelwin hid a smirk. Men, especially old men, were so usefully weak sometimes; perhaps the baron's obvious susceptibility could be used to advantage in the never-ending battle for authority inside these ramshackle walls.

Elinor, oblivious to the sudden change in emotional temperature, nervously cleared her throat, signaling that Anne should get up from her knees.

"Baron, this girl has no memory of the time before we found her cast up on the strand. She could not say where she comes from nor how she came to be at sea."

"Hmmm. A mystery then. Most interesting. I shall speak to the archbishop about this. Between us, he and I shall decide what is best for this poor child."

Elinor bit back an unusually hot response—this was her convent! "Alas, Baron, I fear no decisions can be made until we know more of her history, her family."

The baron huffed a little—he was unused to opposition from the milk-and-water mother superior.

"You can see for yourself, Mother. Plainly, this girl is gently bred and in her survival I detect the hand of God." Hastily the little group crossed itself. The baron had never been known as a religious man until recently, but perhaps he was right. God moved in strange ways to fulfil his purposes, after all.

"Yes, this girl has been saved for some purpose." In concert, they all crossed themselves again. "Her presence here in this convent is a remarkable occurrence, almost miraculous, in fact. Perhaps, before I speak to the archbishop in York, we should pray, each of us, to see if Our Lord will speak to us of your guest."

Anne was careful not to raise her eyes from the floor, but the mention of York sent a shiver down her spine. Richard of Gloucester, Edward's brother, held that city for the king. She'd seen him often at Westminster before everything in her life had changed, before the birth of her son. Vividly, suddenly, she saw little Edward, saw him reach out his arms, heard him call her— and her eyes filled with instant tears.

"What? What did you say?" They were all looking at Anne now, the baron suddenly tender when he saw her tears drip onto the slate flags. "She's crying, Abbess. Why would that be?" He was generally impatient with crying women, but this one touched his heart.

And once started, Anne could not stop. She collapsed to the floor, sobbing as though her ribs would break open and expose her heart. Uproar resulted and the baron, completely heedless, knelt down with some trouble and clasped Anne's frail hands in his rough palms. "There, child, there. Can you tell me why you cry?"

Elinor turned on Aelwin and sharply gave her a direct order. "Fetch Sister Joan. Now!" She too knelt hurriedly beside the girl, snatching Anne's fingers away from the baron: it was entirely unseemly that a man should lay hands on their guest, even if she was not professed—and in the convent's parlor! "Baron, let me . . . please. There, child, there, there."

Sister Joan hurried into the parlor and joined Elinor in patting and soothing, but none of the women could stop Anne from crying. Finally, Elinor decided that the girl should be taken to the infirmary and given valerian tea, as strong as possible, to prevent her from falling into fits.

As he watched the girl leave, held up between Sister Aelwin and Sister Joan, two things came to Stephen Hardwell: one, he was being ridiculous, and two, he had to have this girl, crazed though she might be; the feelings she evoked in him made him feel young and potent again.

With new resolve, he strode out of the parlor, the twittering mother superior hurrying obsequiously at his side, full of obscure apologies for the girl's odd behavior, and also full of anxiety that their only patron had lost his wits just as fully as the girl had. None of this boded well for the little foundation of Our Lady of the Sands.

Simon, of course, had seen it all before , and as the little party rode away from the convent, he rather thought that Henry Hardwell, the baron's son, would be interested in what he had to report of this morning's fiasco.

The baron was a widower. It would grieve Henry mightily, not to say make him very annoyed indeed, if his father were to take an interest in women again, as opposed to settling his account with God and making a pious death, preferably soon while there was still something of the manor left to save.

# Chapter Thirty-nine

"What are you doing, father?" The baron jumped and slewed around to see his son watching him from the doorway of the muniment room in that alert, impatient way he had.

"Nothing, Henry. Just mulling plans, this and that . . ."

Henry reminded his father, uncomfortably, of his second wife, the boy's mother, dead now these ten years past. She'd been a formidable woman, an adequate manager of his household, but she'd never been fragile. Or delicate. Not like the girl from the sea.

Henry strolled into the room. "I hear the girl at the convent is crazed?" The baron did not dignify the question with a response; instead he scratched figures busily into the margin of a tenant roll, ignoring his son.

"Is that all?" Henry persisted into his father's silence.

"What do you mean, all?" The baron was angry; he disliked the insolence of his son's tone, it was presumption! He would not be treated as if he, Stephen Hardwell, knight, were the child, not the father. "You chose not to accompany me this morning, therefore I do not see how the girl's state can be of interest to you." That was well said: stern, lofty, just as a dignified father should speak to an errant child.

"But surely there is more to tell about her?" Henry was smiling slightly now, though it did not reach his eyes. Stephen chose to interpret his son's tone as contrite, therefore shook his head, a little mollified. "Nothing. They know nothing. She will be questioned later when she has recovered. Meanwhile, we should pray for guidance."

"You're taking a personal interest then, Father?"

Stephen Hardwell was suddenly furious—Simon! He would not be undermined in his own house by gossip!

"No more than you should, Henry. We are Christian knights and have sworn to protect all women. I am merely assisting the nuns in their duty to this girl. Now, there is much work to be done here." And huffily he turned away, frowning heavily at the tenant rolls.

Henry left the muniment room, but he was uneasy. What Simon had told him seemed true—his father's dotage was coming on rapidly, it seemed. Old men were vulnerable to the wiles of young women, especially this old man, and that could cause havoc in an orderly household. He would not allow such a pass to occur here. The sooner he had the running of the manor, the sooner they'd be out of the hands of the foul money-lending Jews. Age had not made his father less prodigal—women had frequently been the shameful cause of needless extravagance in the baron's youth and middle age—but this latest budding foolishness could be stopped, would be stopped. He, Henry Hardwell would see to it.

Anne, meanwhile, the subject of such ire and suspicion, was in the infirmary at Our Lady of the Sands with an aching head, a constricted chest, and eyes near swollen shut from crying.

Sister Joan was perched beside her holding one of the girl's hands and praying quietly. From time to time she made the sign of the cross, sweeping from the crown of Anne's head right down to her feet and then from one side of her body to the other at the level of her heart.

"Thank you, Sister, I am better now." Anne spoke in a reedy whisper but was careful to affect an aristocratic intonation: the nasal timbre that distinguished women from the English court. If the nuns in this convent thought she was well born they might not turn her out into the world immediately. Could she offer

Mother Elinor a reward for her safekeeping? How best to reach her?

Anne allowed her eyes to flutter open. "I remember something," she murmured. "Pirates."

Joan's eyes bulged. Pirates? It was long indeed since the Viking had raged up and down this coast, even into the very river on whose banks the convent squatted, but the mention of sea wolves was a frightening thing to a nun, even in these quieter days.

"What happened, dear sister?" Sister Joan was agog with a pleasurable sense of horror.

"I was kidnapped and found myself a captive on a vessel captained by a German devil. Flesh peddlers. I was destined for the slave markets of the Barbary Coast. Blue or green eyes command a fine price, I was told." It made a good story and therefore would reach the Mother Superior that much quicker.

"But how did you escape?" Anne breathed deeply as she began her story, but the telling exhausted her, and as she described swimming up into consciousness only so few days ago, the nearly physical pain of loss hit her once more.

Joan was sensitive to Anne's tears; she helped the girl sit up and pressed a cup of sweet-smelling, warm liquid against her lips. "I've made you a strong tissane: valerian with chamomile and honey. It will help you sleep dreamlessly, I promise you."

Perhaps sleep would heal, would bring strength in time—along with the good food of the convent, the eggs, the new bread, the goat cheese, and the fresh butter. But Anne's heart was still a stone in her breast, a burning stone.

It was blustery and cold again the next dawn, and the infirmary was the warmest place in the convent.

Once awake, Anne had thought through her situation most carefully, and when Mother Elinor, accompanied by Aelwin and Sister Joan, visited her shortly after Sext had been sung, she was ready for them.

The mother superior settled herself on a joint stool and fixed her gaze upon the girl in the bed.

"Are you better today, my child?"

Anne nodded. "Yes, Mother, I am well. Much stronger, thanks be to God."

"Therefore, recite your history for us so that we may help you."

Anne could not have had a more attentive audience. Nothing much had happened at Our Lady of the Sands for many years, certainly nothing dramatic. The quiet changing of seasons, the breeding of animals, the crops being set and cut and stored, these the sisters understood and were at ease with. The story that Anne began was wilder and stranger even than events in the Bible, told to them by their visiting priest in his sermons.

"Someone certainly wants me dead, Mother, and that is how I came to be kidnapped. Now I am friendless and alone where before I have been a wealthy woman; and I have nowhere to hide, no protection, except here at Our Lady of the Sands."

The nuns' eyes became wider and wider with all that she told them, though Anne was careful not to say which city she had been kidnapped from, her past as a merchant, or any of her history in England.

"Though I need your help, I can prove to you that I am not a pauper." Anne unlaced Gaspar's bag and emptied its contents onto her bed, searching for the green dress she'd found in his coffer. Quickly she felt along its hem looking for the knot she'd tied. Her jewels—the ruby, the sapphire, and the remaining diamond—were still there in a lump. Each of them was worth more than all the plate, the livestock, and possibly even all the buildings of the convent put together.

If the nuns had been entranced by Anne's story before, they were astonished beyond words now. Such beautiful jewels—how strange it was to see them in this poor, comfortless little place.

"Reverend Mother, if you help me on my way to Whitby, this is for your convent. I can take sea passage from there and go home." Anne held the sapphire high so that the long morning light was caught in its depths and something like a star glimmered at its blue heart.

For the first time in many years, some long-buried worldly instinct stirred in Elinor's heart. She saw herself in pure white robes, and around her neck, a gold chain from which hung a cross adorned with pearls, misshapen pearls—pearls that formed the precious body of the Savior.

And her chapel, the convent's chapel, was warm and beautiful. New glass windows shone glorious colors down on snowy altar linen. And as she looked out from her richly carved choir stall toward her sisters, fully one hundred of them, she sank to her knees singing as the Archbishop of York himself processed up her aisle, preceded, as was proper, by a brother censing him from a golden censer . . .

Elinor shook her head vigorously. The vision, sweet as it was, could be a satanic temptation to worldly pride. How could she be sure that this improbably mysterious young woman was not, in fact, a tool of the bestial one?

"I must pray on this. Put your gems away, child. No, wait. Would you like them stored in the plate chest in the chapel with our other treasures?"

Anne understood the delicacy of the moment instantly. It would insult the Reverend Mother if she seemed not to trust her, but these stones were her only means of going home to her son. To her life.

Anne knelt beside her bed and kissed the hem of Elinor's robe. Speaking humbly from her place on the floor, she looked up imploringly. "I am so grateful for your kindness and understanding: truly God is good to those who are lost, as I am. I believe that He wishes me to give the convent this sapphire and I am sure the Reverend Mother's prayers will tell her so also. I, too, will pray and wait on her summons."

It was an unsatisfactory answer to the question, but the convent geese suddenly honked an alarm. They all heard the uncompromising jangle of the outside bell as the door ward pulled the slide open behind the grating in the outer door. Henry Hardwell was outside—they heard him bellow for admittance.

Mother Elinor tried to compose herself with a quick Ave. Confronting their patron's son was always an ordeal; his glowering physicality and arrogant manner frightened her and he took every opportunity to frustrate the baron's plans for Our Lady of the Sands.

Elinor shivered. Why had God sent this man to her house? Was it a trial of her purpose, her commitment to doing his will? And now she had a secret to hide from him, a secret that, though it might free the convent from financial obligation to his family, was also a terrible burden.

She'd never been any good at keeping secrets and indeed, looked so positively shifty as she greeted Henry Hardwell that he snorted laughter as he seated himself, without invitation, in the convent's damp little parlor.

"Come, Mother, no point lying to me!" The nun went wimple white at his words. "You have a guest?"

He was menacing, but though jagged little splinters of fear lodged in her throat, Elinor felt sudden defiance like a physical thing, deep in her stomach. She crossed herself to ward off the Devil, real and imagined.

"Merely a poor creature who needs our compassion and our aid, Sir Henry. As Christ himself tells us in the fable of the Good Samaritan—"

He would not permit her to finish the pious story. "Yes, yes, I am familiar with the parable. Who is she?"

Unlikely dignity stiffened Elinor. "Sir, we do not know who this girl is for she is very frail and confused. And she nearly died, should have died, it must be said, except for the will of our Lord who reached out his hand and—"

This time a loud and cynical snort stopped her.

"Come, Mother, this is all too convenient. I have told my father that I will escort the girl to York. We will allow the duke to decide her fate."

The abbess shook her head firmly. "I cannot permit such action. She is in my care, and the care of this, God's house. Good day to you, sir."

Elinor moved rapidly to the door of the parlor and pulled it open with vigor. Too vigorously for Aelwin, who'd been "guarding" the door on the other side and nearly fell through it into Henry Hardwell's arms.

As she stumbled to her feet, Aelwin was fascinated by the thunderous look Henry cast at Elinor, who stood with her hands correctly hidden within the sleeves of her habit, her face composed into lofty calm. Together, the two nuns watched Stephen Hardwell's son stride toward the convent portal.

As the porteress struggled to pull the warped little door open within the larger, iron-bound great door, the man turned back to look at them.

"I shall return, Reverend Mother, and when I do, I shall have the duke's warrant. Make sure your 'guest' is ready to accompany me."

Elinor and Aelwin watched Henry Hardwell step out of their world, his exit somewhat impeded by the malice of the convent geese who surrounded his party, honking, hissing, and flapping.

The two women giggled. Geese always knew; they were better than dogs. It did them both good to laugh, helping Elinor swallow the fear.

"Sister Aelwin, I must pray. I need our Lord's guidance."

Sister Aelwin watched Mother Elinor walk toward the little chapel. It would take a day for one of Henry's men to ride to York and back. If the duke's warrant was obtained quickly, however, Henry and his men could be back before nightfall tomorrow.

Yes, the convent needed good advice, fast. This cast-up girl and her sapphire spelled trouble—or advantage—to Our Lady of the Sands.

The question was, which would it be?

Aelwin turned away. She, too, would pray, but she would ask advice for different things, very different things.

# Chapter Forty

Truly the mind of a baby can be difficult to fathom, yet Deborah understood perfectly that little Edward was very annoyed with her today. Normally an easy child, he'd howled with rage when passed up into her arms this morning to ride on the pommel of her handsome mule. He wanted to ride with the men on their great horses as he had done yesterday—they went so much faster!

Deborah sympathized with Edward's frustrations, even if he didn't have the words to tell her his feelings, but she was terrified of trusting him again to the mercies of the soldiers of the king's guard escorting them north to York. She'd allowed it yesterday for a little while, when she'd become exhausted from holding the boy, but the men were just a little too casual for her liking, though kind, of course. Like all children, Edward wriggled when he got bored—and what if one of the men should lose hold of him? It was the stuff of bad dreams!

It never did any good, however, with a spirit as strong as this little boy's, to oppose him directly, so now Deborah was telling him stories as they rode of when his mother was young, just as he was now. He was too little to know what the words meant, but her singsong tone was pleasant to listen to and he allowed himself to be distracted.

The past came back so vividly as Deborah remembered. She told Edward how Anne had loved to amble about while riding their old donkey in the forest, for to travel slowly gave her more time to admire the plants and animals they passed, rather than charging ahead and missing things.

"See, Edward, look at the robin over there; he's flying beside us. He likes us because our nice mule is walking very quietly in his wood." Edward settled into the crook of her arm and before she could stop herself, she squeezed him lovingly and kissed the top of his small, perfectly round head. He squawked in surprise. Even in one so young the outrage was very real and it made her smile wistfully. This was King Edward's son, even if the child did not know it yet; he was proud, not to be cuddled now unless he himself wished it.

Deborah grimaced. She was weary, so weary: she was getting too old for long, cold journeys in foul weather and they'd already been riding for some days now. It was at least five days' ride to York from London: thanks be the weather had held so far.

London, York; London, York——the names matched themselves to the rhythmn of the mule's neat little hooves, and Deborah's mind ranged freely as the boy dozed in her arms; she allowed the animal to pick its path as it trotted, sure-footed, behind their guards.

How sad and strange their lives had become since Anne's disappearance. The fates had swept them up and though Deborah had repeatedly asked for guidance, none had been given. Thus when King Edward insisted that she and the boy travel covertly to London a day or so after the court removed from Brugge, she'd agreed they should do as he asked. Deborah, bereft after Anne's disappearance, could hardly disagree with the king's wishes in any case—she and little Edward were at Westminster since he'd commanded it and because, after all, the boy was his son. But weary as she and the child both were, the king had issued further instructions.

"You and Edward must go north to my brother at York. The child will be safer there." The king was holding the wriggling boy on his knee as he said it, looking down, bleak and tired, at the small, bright face turned up to his.

Deborah dared not ask why they would be safer away from the king's protection; if he said it, it must be so. But she was brave enough to ask, "Has there been any more news, sire?" She was suffering just as he was.

"We have heard nothing more. Nothing! And not for want of trying. And we must keep Edward safe, Deborah. For his mother. He's very important to us all; even more, now."

He'd fallen silent then, looking down at the little boy trying to extract a jeweled dagger from the scabbard on his belt.

"Here, Edward, let me show you something." The king took the knife from the little boy, who, surprisingly, let him have it without protest.

"See, sharp, very sharp." With great care, the king placed the tiny forefinger of his son on the edge of the blade.

"Soon you will be old enough to have a knife just like this; but feel this edge. Sharp things can cut deeply when you least expect them to."

"Sage advice, husband, sage advice." Deborah turned quickly to find Elizabeth Wydeville standing at the door of the king's closet, surrounded by her ladies. Deborah curtsied deeply, dropping her eyes to the floor.

"And whose is this charming child, my liege?" The queen smiled delightfully at little Edward, who smiled widely in return.

"He is the nephew of Lady Anne de Bohun, wife."

"How sweet that you should concern yourself with the welfare of even your smallest subjects, Edward. I was not aware that Lady de Bohun had a nephew. And have we heard aught of his aunt?"

King Edward stood up carefully, holding the child in his arms.

"The lady is still . . ."

"Lost? Is that a correct word, do you think, husband, to apply to her state?"

Perhaps it was the flash of white canines from the queen, perhaps because she peered so closely into his face, but something about the queen's expression frightened little Edward. The boy burst into tears and buried his head in the king's neck.

The king looked coldly at his wife. "It seems you've upset him, Elizabeth."

The queen looked abashed, the picture of penitence. "Ah, sire, then I am sorry. Will you not accompany me to the Mass, where I may pray for your forgiveness, and his?"

The queen looked tenderly at little Edward as he sobbed, and her ladies were touched by the concern she showed for the child; the king watched the queen gently pat the little boy's head. "And what is this charming child's name, my Lord?"

The boy raised his head and looked at the queen. Jewel-blue eyes drowned in tears. No one answered. Elisabeth Wydeville turned to Deborah. "Will you tell me his name, woman, since my lord the king seems dumbstruck?"

Deborah's blood boomed in her head, but she was trapped by the queen's eyes and could not look away. "His name is Edward, Your Majesty."

It was a frozen moment. Quietly the queen exhaled and turned to the king, smiling sweetly.

"How loyal his mother must be to Your Majesty."

Something in the queen's tone touched the child like a whip and he lifted a defiant, tear-streaked face towards Elizabeth. There was a collective intake of breath as the queen's attendants saw the man and the child together, head beside head.

The queen broke the silence, her voice shaking slightly.

"They wait on us, Edward, it would be rude to keep the abbot waiting, and the court."

There she stood, Edward's graceful queen, gently patting her belly. "Soon there will be another small boy. May his tears be as few as this little one's will be, forever more."

The strange little speech made Deborah shiver.

Silently Edward carried his son to Anne's foster mother; then he left with the queen to go to Mass, but when he reached the door, he looked back one last, long moment at the boy. There was fear in the king's eyes.

And the next morning, at dawn, Deborah and little Edward were on the road at the king's express order, riding for York accompanied by a troop of his own horse, with orders to travel as quickly as possible.

Now, at the end of the third day, they were all weary, and as the busy jolting of the mule on the rutted road worked deeper and deeper into her bones and muscles, Deborah found herself praying, unvoiced.

*Send me a sign, send me a sign. Does she live? Will we find her? Send me a sign, send me a sign.*

But there was no sign, nothing, just the wind cutting into her face and the ache in the arm that was clamped around Edward's small body as he nodded against her, fighting sleep.

# Chapter Forty-one

The prayers of the Reverend Mother had an answer and that answer was strangely clear.

For the first time, the very first time in all her long religious life, Mother Elinor heard the voice of God as clearly as she heard the voices of her nuns singing the morning office. The Lord even said her name, "Elinor," which startled her. And then he asked her to do His will, to help the girl cast up from the sea.

In her gratitude that God had finally sent her a clear signal that He existed, Elinor almost forgot the message, but then, as she hurried back to the infirmary with Sister Joan beside her, reality intruded.

It was very dangerous, what God was instructing her to do. She was the Reverend Mother Superior of an enclosed order of nuns and he was telling her to send one of her own sisters out into the world as a companion to help this castaway escape the Hardwells, father and son. The question remained, why did He want this perilous action? Why single out this unknown waif for His special protection?

Sister Joan, however, did not care whether God had spoken or not: she had not hesitated when Mother Elinor told her of the daring plan. If the girl, Anne—she had told them her name at last—accepted what the abbess offered, then the two of them would leave the convent today, companions on this great adventure.

"It will be safer if two of you take this 'pilgrimage' to Saint Hilda's Abbey in Whitby. But you must make your way up the coast, avoiding the towns. And you must leave now, immediately. God has told me of this."

Resolute as she was, Sister Joan gasped as these last words hit home: she was to leave the convent, leave the safe haven that had protected her for half her life, at the bidding of the Lord God. Anne didn't hesitate, however—she'd been given the means of going home and she embraced it. Some days of good feeding and rest had done a great deal to bring back her strength and her certainty.

"For you, Reverend Mother, for all your kindness to me, God wants you to take this." Anne pressed the star sapphire into Elinor's hands and refused to hear Elinor's pious objections as she hurried to dress in the clean postulant's habit she'd been given; nun's clothing might offer some protection, at least on their journey. Her hands shook as she pulled the scratchy wool over her head, but there was no time to waste; Elinor accepted the gift. Anne was even slightly amused when she remembered the vision she'd had at Duchess Margaret's wedding: this nun's habit was a means of escape, not entrapment. Surely fate wove its thread strangely, for nothing was as it seemed.

Once Anne was dressed and equipped with an old pair of rawhide boots with nailed soles, Elinor, Anne, and Joan hurried to the convent's lean-to stable, which huddled against the wall downwind from the chapel and the major convent buildings.

"Here, you must take Brendan." Elinor hauled the donkey away from his manger—he put up a mild protest since he lived to eat, but the abbess was implacable.

Since the gift of the sapphire, the offer to take the donkey was given with less regret than it might have been, for Brendan, named after the blessed saint, was a great favorite amongst the sisters.

"Are you sure, Reverend Mother?"

The abbess nodded nervously, though she wasn't at all certain. God had not mentioned the donkey to her; he was the convent's only beast of burden. Brendan's loan had been her idea, hers alone. She hoped God approved.

"You will travel faster. Now . . . you must hurry."

Quite why she felt such dread, such urgency, was not clear since God had not laid down a clear time frame for her to follow, but Anne knew why, even if Elinor didn't. Danger loomed over this little huddle of buildings like a darkening sky. It was tangible as the smell of fire, and the strength of the stench made her quiver, nauseated. It was the first prescience she'd experienced since her near-drowning and it hit her with an almost physical blow of certainty.

Urgently she turned to Elinor. "Reverend Mother, you must bar the great door very stoutly. Then put the wagon across the portal to block it after we've gone, and all the heavy furniture you can find to strengthen the barrier. They will come tomorrow. You must be ready."

Mother Elinor accepted Anne's words unquestioningly though she was puzzled; however, accept them she did, and for that, later, she was most grateful.

For now, leading Brendan, the two young women slipped away through the side gate in the wall that led out toward the marshes beside the river. Beyond, in the far, far distance, lay the sea, a misted, gray line between land and sky.

Mother Elinor thought she was the only one to see Anne and Joan leave. She was wrong—Aelwin, hidden out of sight behind the dung heap, heard what was said, saw them go.

She had valuable information now, tradable information. And she knew it.

# Chapter Forty-two

York had always been a good place from which to defend the north—a good staging place, and as such it had been inhabited for well over fifteen hundred years since the Romans and before.

Not too far from and not too near the broad river Humber, the city had become a natural crossing point from west to east and, more important, from south to north and back again.

The owner of vast properties all over England, Commissioner of Array for Nine Counties on behalf of the king (his older brother), and most often in residence at Westminster, Richard, the young Duke of Gloucester, held the north for Edward Plantagenet. Though still a youth and inexperienced, he was beginning to be well liked, well respected by his people as one of the few fair magnates in the lawless counties toward the Scots borders. Richard took his crushing responsibilities seriously and that made him seem much older, more careworn, than his years—a blessing since he was much depended on by Edward.

Today, as the evening drew down, there was more than an unseasonable chill in the air. The trees in the fields around the city were turning color rapidly as a cold wind from the east tore leaves from the branches, and Richard pulled the new marten-fur cloak tight up to the throat as he strode back from the stables. He was worried, and the weariness from days of riding was only just kept at bay by the knowledge of all he had to accomplish before he saw his bed this night.

After swift and bloody action in a recent sortie as far north as Durham—pitiless, some said he'd been—he was feeling a little better about the simmering rebellion toward the borders, but he was not pleased by the knowledge of who had stirred up the lowland Scots to come raiding while the king was away for their sister's wedding: Richard Neville, Earl of Warwick—the man who'd taken him into his own castle at Middleham and taught him to be a soldier and a courtier.

And his stupid brother George—once more the catspaw for Warwick's ambition—he was in on the plot, nothing more certain.

Unconsciously Richard sighed again more deeply as he strode on. The two of them, George and Warwick—what stark sadness that they'd become hornets with poisoned stings, attacking ever more fiercely however hard one tried to clean their buzzing, heaving nests.

He was near his lodgings now. He would eat; then he had urgent dispatches to write about the situation hereabouts, which must be encoded for the king's benefit before they were sent south.

"My Lord?" A figure stepped out of the shadows and Richard just managed not to break stride or jump in shock as reflex brought sword out of scabbard in one sliced-off second. Fear made him furious.

"Guard! Guard! To me, to me!"

The duke was ringed by men two heartbeats on, all with drawn swords, white boar badge clear in the torchlight, as Richard pressed his own blade against the man's unprotected throat.

Terrified, the child—guttering light from a guard's torch showed the duke that he was dealing with a boy barely into his teens—tried to fling himself to the ground to embrace the duke's legs.

"Mercy, mercy, please God."

In that small moment of chaos, the duke detachedly noted that his heart was hammering in his chest. As always. Battles he'd fought in, sorties he'd led—even so young as he was—and it all made no whit of difference because to relax was death. And there were many who wanted him and his brother the king dead.

"Enough." Richard resheathed his sword as he waved his men away. Fearfully the boy looked up from his position on the cobbles.

"What do you want?" The duke's face was impassive.

Terror had done two things to Michael of Holmpton: it had deprived him of speech and it had made him piss his breeches, and he dearly hoped the men would not see the wet he'd made. But one of them began to laugh and pointed: steam was rising from between his legs into the cold night air.

"Well?" The duke's hard tone choked life out of the laughter.

Shaming tears burned Michael's eyes, though he did not let them fall. "I have papers, Your Grace. From my lord, Henry Hardwell. Urgent papers."

The duke grunted and signaled one of his men to take the flat leather pouch the boy was offering as he stood, semi-crouched, trying to cover the dark stain spreading from his groin.

"Take him to the kitchen. Food; he'll have had a cold ride. And a bed."

The duke held out his hand for the pouch and was already turning away to more pressing business when the boy dared to speak again in a wavering voice.

"My master asked me to wait, Your Grace."

The duke turned back, perplexed. "Wait?"

"Yes, my Lord. Wait for an answer; then I'm to ride back tonight."

The duke just shook his head and nodding at one of his men, stalked on toward his own private quarters in one of the towers of the inner ward.

"Come on, lad. I'll take you to the kitchen. And find you some breeches." It wasn't unkindly meant—pikeman William Fuller wasn't much older than Michael himself, but Michael had had enough humiliation for one day and found a bit of truculence. He didn't work for Henry Hardwell for nothing.

"Take your hand away, oaf. I must have an answer and ride back tonight."

William Fuller sighed. Why was it that country lads were so above themselves these days? No manners at all. With a well-placed blow he swatted the side of Michael's head, not so hard as to knock him out but hard enough to lift him off his feet.

"Listen lunkhead, if the duke says you're to go to the kitchen, that's where you go. Now, are you coming or d'you want to freeze your balls off out here when the piss ices over?"

Sulkily the boy got to his feet and nursing his ringing head, stumbled after pikeman Fuller until they both disappeared into the bowels of the building under the great hall.

The duke himself was having his wet and muddy riding boots pulled off in the privacy of his own sleeping chamber. He was weary, bone weary, but his working table, lying in the shadows, had a visible pile of work on it and now this. Urgent, the boy had said. Everything was urgent and all he wanted to do was just close his eyes, even for a moment . . .

"Next foot, Your Grace." Snapping his eyes open, Richard raised his other boot to his valet as he ripped the wax sealing the back of the vellum document he'd been handed in the inner courtyard.

There was just enough light from the fire and one branch of candles to read the first few words, with difficulty, since the writing was crudely made. Richard grunted in surprise.

"A spy? What?" Unthinkingly he sat up, unbalancing the valet who sat down suddenly, taking the second boot with him to the floor.

Unconsciously, unpretentiously, the duke reached down a hand to help his startled servant up to his feet again.

"Warrington, I want that boy up here."

The valet de chambre was a man of some dignity, and normally he'd have taken a little time, silently, to allow the duke to register he'd been thoughtless, but Richard's tone put that thought from him. The duke was worried about something.

"Certainly, Your Grace. Immediately. If I may just inquire . . . ?"

"Yes?" The duke was sounding quite dangerous tonight, which made Warrington nervous.

"The boy, Your Grace? Which boy?"

# Chapter Forty-three

Anne and Joan spent their first night away from the convent in a barley rick, and as they burrowed down into the barley straw, they were both grateful for the beauty and peace of the evening, for the stars, for the rising moon.

It had been a good but tiring day.

After taking it in turns to ride Brendan, Anne and Joan had made considerable progress through a sullen afternoon, bearing east as far as they could and then north beside the coast.

Keeping to sheep roads rather than cart ways, they'd made sure to avoid all habitation, skirting homesteads and villages, yet trying to stay within sight and sound of the sea: the sea would be their guide. Follow the coast and they'd find their way to Whitby eventually.

Anne tired easily after all her privations, so toward evening, Joan had insisted Anne ride as she, Joan, walked. The nun, once she was over the strangeness, the height of the limitless sky, was enjoying herself greatly. She wasn't even afraid—and if that wasn't a miracle then she didn't understand the workings of God at all.

Now they both lay on the top of their chosen rick, having eaten a small meal and fed Brendan as much barley straw as he would take (Joan crossed herself and asked the Lord's permission first because this was stealing another's property) while they talked quietly and watched the moon rise out of the sea. It was close to full tonight. If they needed to walk at night over the next days, they'd have excellent light.

"Good night, Anne. I hope you sleep well."

"Good night, sweet Joan. I shall, knowing you're here."

Very soon, even, gentle breathing told the nun her companion was sleeping. Joan herself planned to say her prayers just as she would have at the convent, and, as quietly as she could, she sang vespers.

Very soon though she, too, was deeply asleep, wrapped in her cloak and covered deep in straw.

She'd never had a softer, warmer bed. *Perhaps this is heaven* was her last blasphemous thought before sleep claimed her.


Triumph was a good feeling, a warm feeling. Especially since this little triumph was a demonstration to his father, the baron, that old must finally give way to young.

Or so thought Henry Hardwell as he ripped open and read the dispatch from Duke Richard at dawn the next day.

Michael of Holmpton stood wet and shivering before his master, dripping onto the flags of the hall, so tired his legs would barely hold him up, yet filled with pride. Not everyone could say they'd ridden to York and back within an afternoon and a night, could they? Now, if he could have something to eat and just a little sleep.

"Michael, find Simon. Now!"

Michael's dreams of glory and reward from a generous master were gone like smoke on a windy day. The look in Henry's eye said a kick in the backside was all the reward he'd be having unless he did as he was bid.

Simon was at the manor's mill—berating the miller on the suspicion of doing private business on the side out of the Hardwell family's property—when the filthy boy found him.

Poor Michael, this time all he got was a clip around the ear for keeping his weary horse out of the stable, but at least Simon said he could get breakfast from the kitchen.

The reeve found his master's son in the manor's hall, pacing back and forth, back and forth, a fixed, frightening smile on his face—or rather his teeth, thought Simon. A nasty piece, Henry Hardwell, but an energetic man. Simon would go far with Henry, as opposed to his spendthrift father, who did not know the value of a good servant when he had one.

"Read this! Tell me I'm right!" Henry couldn't read very well, but he'd seen enough to get the sense of the duke's reply. Simon held the parchment up to the light of one of the east-facing windows in Stephen Hardwell's hall and rapidly scanned it. Finally, he nodded.

"You've won, Sir Henry. The duke wants the girl brought to York." He smiled. "I would say that the use of the word 'spy' was what did the trick."

Both men laughed. An unpleasant sound. In these uncertain times, paranoia spread easily. Implying the girl might be a spy for the French had worked: the duke wanted to question her as soon as possible.

"Got them, got them both!" His father and Mother Elinor could wriggle on the hook all they liked. Here, in his hands, Henry had the means to force the convent to give him the girl so she could be taken to York. And woe betide the convent for hiding a suspected spy, a threat to the realm!

Henry held his hands up to the fire to warm them. It was a cold day, but it was more and more promising. Influence with the duke, now that was a fine thing to have.

"Ah, sir?"

"Yes, Simon?"

"What will you tell the duke when he finds the girl is not actually a French spy?"

Once again that dreadful smile.

"Well, I just have to get her out of that convent and away from my father, don't I? How can I help it if she, the spy, tries to run away en route and so unfortunately dies an accidental death? So sad, but a dead spy is just as useful as a live one, wouldn't you say?"

They both laughed. Clever, very clever.

"Any word of Ewan?" Simon shook his head. "No, Sir

Henry, your father's man has been delayed in York, waiting for the archbishop to return. It seems His Grace is not expected back from a jaunt to Reivaulx Abbey until tomorrow at the earliest."

Simon was well informed—he was well paid to be. Henry relaxed and yawned expansively. "Then see to it that he's even further 'delayed.' Find me someone in York who'll get his hands dirty for money—Ewan will be no loss to anyone but my father."

Even Simon was surprised at the extent of Henry Hardwell's ruthlessness in pursuit of his own way—something to remember and consider when the time for choosing sides declared itself. However, while he was in high favor, all would be well and he'd be rewarded. He'd cast his lot with the son now, no point in holding back.

"As you wish, Sir Henry." Simon bowed to his master, his real master, and hurried away to rouse Michael from the kitchen.

Henry called after him, "I feel the need to pray, Simon. Return to me soon for we are both sinful men and it may be that the words of a certain holy abbess can be a comfort and a shriving for both our souls."

# Chapter Forty-four

It was evening of the following day and Duke Richard was furious. He'd just received word that the presumed spy had disappeared from the convent of Our Lady of the Sands. Angry, too, was the Archbishop of York, though his anger took a different form.

The two men stared at one another. One was just older than a boy, the other a well-fed man in his thirties, younger brother of Earl Warwick and therefore a covert enemy of the pup standing before his archbishop's cathedra daring to masquerade as a duke.

George Neville saw with unvoiced satisfaction that his summons to Richard had made this stripling very angry indeed.

"I am confused, Duke Richard. You instructed one of your vassal knights, Sir Henry Hardwell, to attempt armed entrance to one of my convents to abduct a girl in the care of the nuns?"

The archbishop's tone was freezing. Richard of Gloucester might be the youngest brother of the king, but church lands were sacrosanct, as were those who lived on them. In this incident, he would not deal with a boy, the issue was far too serious. Unfortunately his contempt for the young duke flashed over his face for a moment, one fatal moment.

The duke's impotent fury compressed sharply into something hard.

"Be careful, Archbishop. Be very careful. I am my brother's chief vassal in the north. If I am told that a spy for the French is hiding within my domain it is my duty and yours to hunt that spy down. To do else is treason to the king my brother."

He could be as wintery as the other man when he chose. Gaze locked on gaze and an onlooker might have heard each man breathing as if at the end of a long race.

The archbishop sucked in breath and spat his words back. "Treason, Duke Richard? I owe allegiance to a power greater than any king's."

Richard bared his teeth and in that moment the archbishop felt fear. He'd known the boy's father, the great Duke of York. This boy's eyes were suddenly formidable.

"Ah yes. You are Earl Warwick's brother after all."

This was a most direct insult to him personally and to his office, and for a moment the archbishop struggled to find suitable response. The ingratitude of this pup! As a boy he'd lived with Earl Warwick at Middleham!

"Viper! After all my family has done for . . ."

Richard raised his voice, shouting the prelate down.

"Henry Hardwell was doing his duty when I asked him to enter that convent. These are desperate times; as well you know. We've had alarms from the French all year. And now the girl has gone. Fled. What does that tell you!"

He roared out the last sentence—a bellow of rage and frustration distantly heard even by the monks in the cloister of the Minster's Garth. In some things, he was like his brother.

Fire with fire. The archbishop was only a man and he was sorely tempted. "This audience is over. Leave my palace! Your brother will hear of your insolence to the church."

"My brother, or your brother?"

Richard was normally moderate and careful in all he said, but he had rarely been so angry. This archbishop had been a burr under his saddle from the beginning and never more so than now. But Richard, as Duke of Gloucester, was second heir after his brother Clarence to the throne of England, and he would find that girl; and when he did, the archbishop would be made to eat his own insolence, slowly and painfully.

"This girl was in the care of the Church; if she fled it must have been in fear. From your thugs! Anathema, this is worthy of anathema!"

It was a powerful threat and most men would have been cowed by the thought of the ultimate power the archbishop held: excommunication. But these last menacing words were delivered to the duke's back as he stamped away from the archbishop's throne without one look behind him.

In a churning blur of rage, Richard rode away from George Neville's palace toward his own, where Henry Hardwell waited. Angry as he was, the duke knew that having botched what he'd been given to do, the knight would be more than keen to prove himself in the task he was about to be given.

Together they would catch that girl; his brother the king would expect nothing less.


The prioress of Our Lady of the Sands had finally overplayed her hand and the mischief she'd made came home to roost with a vengeance.

"What did you tell the Hardwells?" The Reverend Mother's voice was sharp as she inspected Aelwin, prostrate on the flags in front of the altar, facedown, weeping.

"I was only trying to help us, Lady Elinor, help the convent."

The bald lie incensed the mother superior. Kneeling down beside her sister in Christ, she hauled Aelwin's head up by the veil.

"I want the truth, Aelwin. He wants the truth." She flourished a crucifix in one hand so close to Aelwin's eyes that the suffering, bleeding body of Christ seemed like a weapon. "If you do not tell me, then blood will be on your head and I shall thrust you out from these walls naked. Tell me!"

Aelwin wailed with terror. "I thought it was my duty. They're our patrons."

"God is watching and judging, Aelwin. Be careful, very careful for your soul. Did you tell the Hardwells where Anne went?"

Elinor had Aelwin by the shoulders now, eyes burning like coals. Aelwin gave up with a gasp. "Yes." Her eyes filled with frightened tears.

Elinor was brutally direct. "For money?" The other nun said nothing. "Oh Aelwin, Aelwin, they paid you to betray that girl."

Aelwin thought about speaking the lie, but here in the chapel, in sight of the great rood—the nunnery's chief treasure—hanging in bloody, tortured majesty above them—she found she couldn't do it.

"Yes, Mother." Her voice rustled, wind through dead grass.

"You have accepted money; you have therefore put their souls, the immortal souls of both father and son—and your own—at risk, if they find that girl. It will be your fault if anything happens to Anne or your sister Joan—or to the Hardwells. Judas was paid to betray Our Lord also, and he was cursed for all eternity."

Aelwin, with shaking hands, attempted to set her veil to rights but did not dare get off her knees.

"But Mother, once Sir Henry forced it out of me, I had to tell his father also—I was so frightened for Anne. Then the baron said he would find her and protect her from his son. I was terrified, too, that Sir Henry would burn the convent if he wasn't told where Anne had gone. I saved this place, Mother—and I was going to give the money to our treasury."

Aelwin had nothing to lose and a certain resentful courage seeped back with the boldness of the lie.

Mother Elinor closed her eyes, crossed herself. When she spoke, her voice was bleak. "I do not believe you. God does not believe you. Go to your cell. You are to stay there and meditate on your sins without food until you are summoned. The archbishop must advise me in this matter."

Aelwin shuffled from the chapel, badly shaken, in the custody of the porteress. It was so unfair. She had been threatened by the baron's son when he'd tried to force his way into the convent looking for Anne, until later he'd found that money provided a more useful path to knowledge; money that Aelwin planned to use in buying herself the abbess's seat when the nuns next elected their superior.

That dream was now ashes and the prioress snuffled tearfully as she was locked, locked! into her cell by the porteress to wait on the pleasure of the abbess. Aelwin now knew with searing clarity that money *was* the root of all evil. She'd taken Sir Henry's coin and that had made her think of milking the baron as well, to add to her election hoard. But Sister Bertha, her enemy, had betrayed Aelwin to Elinor. She'd seen the prioress talking covertly to the baron outside the walls of the convent—the day after Anne and Joan had left the convent, the evening of the same day his son tried to storm the gate—and watched as Aelwin solicited the old man's bribe.

Aelwin was deeply, deeply resentful. It seemed the world had come undone; her career at Our Lady of the Sands was over; the mother superior would see to that when she spoke with the archbishop.

Elinor had won, the convent was hers now. God and Mammon—perhaps it was true? The evil one had tempted her and she had fallen; fallen for half an angel and one silver sixpence. Nowhere near thirty pieces of silver, nowhere near.

# Chapter Forty-five

The third day since Anne and Joan had left the convent was nearly ended, yet the women continued to push themselves and their little donkey as fast as they could heading north, always north, toward Whitby, driven by Anne's passion to go home to Brugge, to go home to her son.

The hare meat, the bannock, and sheep's cheese Mother Elinor had supplied them with were finished, and now they were chilled and hungry as the last light of day leached out of the western sky.

Behind them, the empty moor stretched away with no sign of shelter anywhere among the billows of heather.

Beside them, they could just make out the line of cliffs in the evening gloom. They'd have to stop soon, find what shelter they could, for walking tonight would be treacherous—too much cloud cover for the moon to light their way.

Anne shivered. Over the last days they'd been careful to avoid all roads and most tracks, reasoning that some few travelers would still be abroad while the ways were passable. But it was very lonely; this world of heather and sky was nearly silent, and walking close to the edge of the gorse-clad clifftop, Anne longed, really longed, for the sound of voices, for lights to break up the gloom.

Would the candles be lit in the big house in Brugge now? Would her son be in the kitchen, warm and snug, with Deborah? And where was the king? Did he think of her, as she did of him?

Sometimes Anne's courage failed as night came down, for it was then she felt most achingly alone in the world. Joan had become a friend, yes, but she wanted her son and she needed his father! If only they could hurry the journey to Whitby. Each day that passed brought them closer to winter, closer to the time when a passage sailing across the open sea could not be bought at any price.

Anne trembled convulsively. The wind from the east cut to the skin. *Be practical, be sensible—and first, find somewhere to sleep tonight.* They might find a way down to the shingled beach far below and perhaps there'd be a cave to shelter in. Anne was suddenly despondent. A cave, a dank cave? Had they become animals?

"Anne!" Joan's voice was unnaturally loud and jerked Anne out of her reverie. "Look!"

From her greater height on top of the donkey, the nun had seen another, broader track joining the path they were on. It was just beneath the brow of the little hill that Brendan was stolidly plodding over and it led toward the edge of the cliff.

There was a way down to the sea!

"Should we?" Joan was nervous, but unless they could face sleeping on the open moor without a fire—in this large, rolling empty place, flames would be seen for miles and miles at night—they had little choice.

"Yes. It will be fine on the beach, a good place, you'll see. Perhaps there'll be welks or even oysters to find." Anne was determined to keep Joan's spirits up.

Suddenly a woman's voice called to them from nowhere. "Hola! Hola, Sisters. Are you lost?"

A woman's head appeared over the lip of the cliff, immediately followed by the rest of her body, clothed in home-woven woolen cloth. Then they caught her reek. Fish! She smelled of fish and smoke in equal parts—pungently.

"Not lost, kind friend. That is, we're on pilgrimage and may be a little off our chosen path."

"Ah, aren't we all now, Sisters?" The stranger laughed heartily, kindly.

Anne took the initiative. "Do you know if there's somewhere we could pass the night nearby? A farmstead, perhaps?"

The woman shook her head. "There's nowt up here." Seeing their faces fall, she smiled broadly. "But, never despair, the bay's just below."

"The bay?" Joan was disheartened all over again. To sleep on the shingle strand on a night such as this was a more than miserable thought.

"Aye. Just let me get my Gwennie and I'll take you down."

Gwennie? Anne was puzzled, but a goat's bleat of welcome made her and Joan swing around to see their new friend stride up to a very handsome brown nanny goat, udders heavy with milk, who was hobbled in a dip beside the path.

"There, sweet Gwen, time for home and the byre." The woman uncoupled the hobble from her legs. "Come now, Sisters, a fire and food is what you need."

The girls were considerably cheered as Anne led Brendan, carrying the apprehensive Joan, over the lip of the cliff-top path and there saw, far below, a group of tiny gray houses huddled into the base of the tall cliff. There was a harbor, too, crowded with fishing smacks moored for the night. It was a fishers' village with well-lit windows and the sound of human voices washing up on the wind from within the natural amphitheater of the cliff.

Anne's prayer had been answered, and for a moment she closed her eyes in gratitude. She opened them quickly, as wind rising off the sea below fluttered her veil and the skirts of her habit. Below, seabirds flew beneath her feet in the air of the dizzying drop, for it was a narrow track they followed on the cliff face in the last of the light.

Gwennie, bleating, led them, anxious to be home. After her came Margery, for that was their new friend's name, and then the terrified Joan, who was perched, sweating with fear, on Brendan's back.

"Just trust to the donkey's feet, Sister, he'll not let you down." Margery was a kind woman, and a moment before she'd chanced to look back to see Joan's rigid face and terrified eyes. Others were frightened of heights, that she knew, but for one who came up and down this path twice each day, and had since she could toddle, it was a wonder to see that fear so freshly in another.

"Not far now, see, there's my cot. You'll stay with me and my good man."

Robin Hod's Bay had been part of the cliff a long time, a very long time, one of the few natural harbors on this wild part of the northeast coast. Fishermen had come and gone from here after the cod and the herring schools for times long past remembering.

"Come now, Gwen, milking for you." Anne and Joan no longer noticed Margery's smell, for the evening breeze off the sea brought them an even greater one—the pungent tang of beached and rotting kelp, fish guts, and coal smoke from the houses. It was a stink as sturdy as the solid stone of the houses they now walked among. Anne, breathing deeply of the cold, moving air, decided there were many worse things in the world than a stench she was unused to. This was a good place. And good people lived here. Friends.

Margery led them to the last house in the steep, twisting street. It sat huddled by itself directly next to the curve of the sea wall protecting the harbor.

Anne, who had never thought of herself as tall, had to stoop as she followed Joan into Margery's house through a narrow door barely wider than her own hips.

As the door shut behind the women, it took a moment to adjust to the gloom and the noise, for the communal downstairs room where Margery's family ate and lived was filled with the sound of the sea, wash and slump, wash and slump. That, and the clamor of small, busy children.

It was low-raftered and small, the room they'd entered. And hung from numberless hooks on the ceiling—just to be glimpsed in the light from the fire, the only source of illumination now that last light had gone from the sky—was row after row of drying cod, stock to last the family through the winter. The eye-watering fish miasma, coupled with smoke from the kelp and sea-coal fire with its salt-blue flames, set Joan choking until Anne banged her vigorously on the back.

Margery, who hurried in just after the two women, made rushed introductions as she found her milking pails.

"Bernard, here, is my husband, Sisters. Big Bernard, he's

called, because he's the da of my babies. And this is little Bernard, and Alice, and Mary and . . . there you are, Jennet. Seat yourselves, I'll just milk Gwen and put Brendan in the byre with her. Then we can eat."

He wasn't especially big, the man who stood to greet his guests, a wriggling, giggling two-year-old clasped in his arms. He'd been sitting by his fire on a settle, bare feet companionably toward the flames as all around him and under his legs played three other children of ascending ages, scrabbling as they threw "jacks" made from knucklebones on the beaten earth floor.

"Welcome to my house, Sisters. Welcome." A surprisingly deep, very slow voice rumbled up from inside Bernard's chest as he pressed the women to sit where he'd been roosting in the warmest part of the room beside the fire. For Joan and Anne, his slow, gentle ways, his calm, were comforting after days spent facing the uncertainty of the world outside the convent.

Bernard, seeing how exhausted both women were, took horn beakers and filled them with hot, steaming broth from a three-legged pot stationed at the front of the banked fire.

"Drink!" The man held out a beaker to each of the women in turn as Anne, shaky with gratitude, tried to thank Margery's husband for his welcome.

"Sir, you and your wife are most kind. It was dark on the moor and we had nowhere to sleep."

"Well, Sister, sleep you shall here." Margery appeared through the door, a bleached wooden pail in each hand filled with milk that was plaster-white in the gloom. A gust of sea wind came with her, skirling through the little room, sparking up the fire and causing the cod overhead to sway and nod. Almost like a field of flowers, thought Anne absurdly.

Flowers. And the smell of flowers. Edward had given her flowers, a bunch of roses, white ones, the last time they'd made love in late summer on his fur-lined cloak on the floor in the Prinsenhof. To dream so sweetly, eyes open, was to remember what came next. What the runes had said. Storm, sacrifice. Hard, hard lessons and loss.

Anne's eyes filled with unwilling tears and Margery was

kind, for the light of the fire caught the welling glint in Anne's eyes. "Ah, you're tired. We will eat and then you can sleep, both of you. Tomorrow will be better."

It was quickly done, the children scattered from under their mother's feet as she and Big Bernard quickly assembled a trestle board, stored under the ladder to the upstairs room, for them all to eat at. Large bowls of red earthenware appeared from a cupboard—the one piece of furniture larger than a stool that the room boasted, with the exception of the fire settle.

Anne and Joan sat with Mary and Jennet squashed between them on the backless plank form, while on the other side of the board, Bernard had the smallest, little Bernard, on his knee while Alice, an exquisite three-year-old whose tangled black curls clustered like grapes around a face of ivory and rose, cuddled up to his side.

Margery busied herself shuttling food from the fire to the table. There was a huge wooden bowl of good soup packed with pieces of white fish; a large, solid flour-covered loaf of barley bread; butter made from goat's milk: almost white, rather than yellow; and a mound of small neaps, turnips, topped with crumbled goat's cheese. It was substantial bounty from the sea and the small gardens that the villagers kept in sheltered places at the top of the cliffs.

"Will you bless our meal, Sisters?" Anne was embarrassed and flicked her eyes toward Joan, but the nun smiled, nodded at her friend, encouraging her.

"Father, Mother, bless us all. Guard this family and this house; keep them safe from all harm. May your sea and your sky be their friends, their garden, their farm. We are grateful for safe harbor here, and for this food."

Anne spoke the words softly and for a moment the world receded into peace. She was hungry, so hungry, that food had never, ever tasted this good, this rich, or been so filling.

That night as they all slept together—crammed in the one large box bed nearly the size of the room above on a ticking mattress stuffed with heather—Anne lay awake, little Bernard cuddled, breathing softly, against her body.

In the fitful moonlight, as the clouds came and went outside the one small window with its panes of horn, she could almost mistake this baby for Edward. Oh, let Edward be safe. Man and child both.

Eventually she slept, as the room filled up with the sound of the sea and all of them breathed as one.

# Chapter Forty-six

Worrying dispatches had arrived from York. The threat previously reported by Elizabeth to Edward the king, in Brugge, was real once more: the north was beginning to rise.

Edward paced impatiently as his secretary droned on, laboriously translating the cipher of the letter from Richard as he read.

" . . . and they have money from France. The rebels are being run . . . out of the Borders; a French spy has been sighted . . . hiding at a convent near here; the old queen is massing men in France and . . . I need an army if we are to hold . . . what we have now. Come quickly or all may be lost."

The secretary could not help himself; he looked up fearfully as he read the last words. The king fixed him with a glance.

"Be careful, Malcolm, very careful."

The man fought fear with pride. The king must be worried indeed if he thought for one moment that he, Malcolm de Gracey, might betray the trust he held—that of utter silence on all he heard and saw in this the king's own private closet: the room from which he effectively ruled the kingdom.

Malcolm was stoic. "What would Your Majesty prefer I do with this?" He held up the parchment with the duke's cipher on it, wriggling black symbols that seemed unnaturally bold on the cream calf skin.

"Here." The king held out one hand and as he was given the document, waved toward the door.

"Go. But I will need you at first light tomorrow."

Edward was not normally suspicious or unkind to his servants, but the times were making him shorter, less instinctively polite. Turning his back on his secretary, who bowed himself from the room, Edward tossed the document on the fire, and as the flames consumed the dried skin, the smell of burning flesh filled the room though the calf itself, origin of the vellum, was long, long since dead.

The king turned to William Hastings, quietly nursing a beaker of honeyed wine beside the fire.

"Well, what do you think?"

With a sigh, William stood and joined the king, looking deeply into the heart of the coals.

"There must be real need or Richard would not ask. We will move as fast as we can."

The two men were silent for a moment, each thinking of what must be done.

"The queen will have to be told." Edward said it almost absently, as William kicked a log that was threatening to roll out onto the hearth. The chamberlain nodded. "She will understand." It was an optimistic statement. Elizabeth, the mother-to-be, would be most unhappy when she heard the king had left for the north. The queen, who had brought news to Brugge of the mischief being wrought in the Borders earlier in the year, would know the king had to act. Yet pregnancy changed things—a woman wanted protection and reassurance at such a time from the father of her baby, even if he was a king, and even if they, man and wife, were estranged.

Unspoken, the thought hovered. Thus far Elizabeth had had only girl children. The king dearly loved his little daughters, but they would be useful to the kingdom only at a marriageable age. The country needed a male heir, especially now. Edward's thoughts went to the little boy riding for York. And then he saw Anne's face in the coals of the fire, laughing. The intensity took him still—the pain, the fear, did not dull with time. Abruptly he shook his head hard.

Hastings watched covertly, but the king caught his eye, even grinned ruefully. "You know it and I know it. I must ride north with the small band with as much speed as we can find." Edward meant the men referred to as his "riding court"—trusted friends and fighting companions from the wars who had put him on his throne. "I'll raise the standard with Richard; and you must bring me an army, parliament willing or not."

Both men grimaced; they knew that assembling a real fighting force would take time—and parliament must be convinced of the danger. Soldiers were expensive line items in the country's ledgers.

The times were nervous, though, very nervous, and Edward had taken the precaution to retain and feed the levies of men raised from the shires since before the last summer. At one time, earlier in the year before the wedding, he'd seriously considered an invasion of France itself, had even got so far as an inconclusive sea campaign, until he thought better of the expense of an all-out war.

Since August, however, the levies, underemployed, had been dwindling away as, man by man, they skulked back to their villages to help with the harvest. That would have to be stopped; it was William's task now.

The fire flared up and crackled—one last bit of vellum with its flammable ink. Again, that smell of roasting flesh; the acrid smoke energized Edward.

"Enough! I'm glad it's come, glad that the wait is behind us. Now we shall do what we know best, you and I. Let the French fear, let Warwick fear; we will catch their spies, and their deaths will be an example for all who follow traitors!"

William, saying nothing, rejoiced. The king had returned and it had taken a French spy to do it.

# Chapter Forty-seven

 The Duke of Gloucester was only rarely tired. Yes, he was young, but he had the same stamina that sustained his older brother the king and was famous in his family. It was said the Yorks could ride faster, drink deeper, and fight longer than mere mortal men. People laughed uneasily when they repeated the tired old saw: there was an uncomfortable rumor that Plantagenets—and the Yorks were Plantagenets—were descendants of the Devil and a mortal woman. Sometimes it was easy to see why.

But increasingly, as the people of York got to know their young duke, Richard, he could do no wrong. He was their good lord. Sensible, evenhanded, slow to anger, mostly, even if he was so young. And not vicious. Unmarried girls were safe at his court though he was not yet, himself, wed; it was even said he had no bastards, not one. Unlike his brother the king, well known even this far into the north for his prodigal appetites.

Edward's prodigal ways. Richard was considering them anew as the little boy was presented to him one evening in the great hall of York Castle when he'd returned from a two-day foray out to the Borders and back and was reading, amazed, the letter he'd been handed about the child.

*Brother, guard this child very well and staunchly, of your love for me. His name is Edward, he is my son and very dear to my heart. More shall follow this, when all is made safe. Edward R*

Short. To the point, though enigmatic, yet it was signed with Edward's seal—a signet ring that never left his finger and that Richard knew well: it had been their father's. Yes, the letter certainly came from the king.

"Have my people served you well, Mistress, in my absence?"

The child and his—what was she, governess? serving woman?—had arrived the day before Richard had returned, and now the boy himself was fidgeting, bored with being made to sit still on Deborah's lap. The youth sitting in the great chair—little Edward's uncle, the duke—looked the child over from the crown of his head to his small red boots, searching for likeness to his brother.

He was a strong little boy, well set up, well nourished, forward for his age: already keen to explore the strange new world he found himself in. No sign of rickets and all his milk teeth seemed good, as was the quality of his clothes. His confidence, too—being unawed in strange surroundings—marked him out as a child who had been well loved. How old was he? Ten months? A year? Where had Edward been—more to the point, whom had he been with, apart from the queen—something less than two years ago?

"Edward. That is your name?" The child looked up and smiled at the duke. Bright, bright blue eyes, corn-silk hair.

Then, quicker than thought, the little boy wriggled out of Deborah's arms and toddled on uncertain legs towards the duke. Holding up one small, fat hand, he patted Richard's steel-mailed foot because, it seemed, he liked its sharply pointed shape, admired the spurs. Then he giggled and tottered back to the safety of Deborah's skirts, where he hid, peeping out mischievously. Everyone in the chamber tried not to smile. Even the duke's lips were seen to quirk; the child was certainly charming.

Richard nodded slowly. Edward's son? Yes, that was easy to see, but who was his mother?

"Where is your mother, child?"

It was a rhetorical question but Deborah dropped a hurried curtsy and dared to speak. "Edward's mother is not with us, sir." It was said with an instant prayer to Aine, the Mother Goddess herself. *Protect her, defend her. Let her live.* And suddenly a warm rush of feeling swept through her chest so intense it was hard not to cry out. And an image. She saw Anne, alive! Somewhere within sound of the sea.

Richard looked curiously at the old woman holding the boy's hand: would she faint? Her face had drained of color and then flushed red.

"Madame, are you well?" He nodded for a stool to be brought, but Deborah breathed deep and smilingly refused to sit. "All is well, sir, all is well." It was odd, that phrase, when he thought about it afterward, but Duke Richard shook his head impatiently. There was much to accomplish yet tonight, and though there was a story here, he had other more pressing issues to attend to.

He beckoned his steward, Roger de Liversey, forward.

"Steward, see that the Lord Edward here," he added the courtesy title, "is lodged by my rooms with his guardian"; he gave Deborah the courtesy title also. "They are to have two rooms, one to sleep in, one for the day. He is to have his own guardsman at all times, and Mistress?"

Deborah curtsied again. "Deborah, Your Grace."

"Mistress Deborah, does the child need a wet nurse still?"

Deborah shook her head. "No, my lord, he drinks from a beaker now. He was weaned just recently." The duke had no need to know that little Edward had refused his wet nurse not long after Anne went missing. Perhaps he sensed the upset in the house; blessed be, he'd still thrived in the days and weeks since, drinking goat's milk from his own horn cup.

"Very well, then you shall have a girl who will work hard and assist with the care of Lord Edward. Perhaps, since it is late, it is time he was in his bed."

He bowed slightly from the waist to Deborah and Edward as they were escorted from the Presence hall. He would know more of the mystery, the boy whom his brother acknowledged as his son, later. The child could be important in the struggle he knew was coming to England—especially so if the queen were to give birth to another girl. For now, he would do as he was asked, guard him, and keep him safe. Discreetly.

Now, where was Henry Hardwell and, more important, where was the girl who might be a French spy?

Margery's kindness to Anne and Joan did not end with food and shelter. As the next day seeped in with sullen rain, she heard Anne whispering to Joan that they must be on their way, much to the other woman's dismay.

"But, Anne, it's so foul out there. We shall be soaked."

"Indeed you will, ladies—washed away, more like! But this will only last the day; tomorrow, by the time the sun is level with the top of our wall"—she meant the great cliff behind the village—"the rain will stop. You can be on your way with little pain; meantime you can stay here with us. And if you choose it, there will be company. Fish must go to Whitby with my man—you could keep him company when he sets out tomorrow."

And so it was decided, but neither girl had realized that "going to Whitby with Bernard" meant going on the sea road: sailing with Margery's husband in his little fishing smack up the coast to Whitby Harbor.

"But what about Brendan?"

"Will you pass this way again, Sisters?" Uncertainly, Joan and Anne looked at each other.

"It would depend on which road we take back south, after we have made our oblations to the saint," said Joan.

"Well then, I'm suggesting we keep your donkey with us here until you return or we receive word from you. If you are not long in Whitby, you could come back with another of the men from this bay perhaps. We take it in turns to take the catch to Whitby, and all the families divide the proceeds when the boats return."

Joan closed her eyes for a moment. The thought that she might for the moment escape climbing back up the cliff which sat so ominously above Margery and Bernard's good little house was an intense, giddying relief. But she'd never been on a boat either. Would that be worse?

"Sister Anne, what should we do?"

Anne thought for a moment. Sailing up the coast to Whitby

would be much quicker than walking the remaining way, especially in this weather. "If Bernard will have us, we would be most grateful. Brendan will like it here. He would be pleased to be useful."

Anne smiled warmly at their squat little hostess, who beamed in return, exposing healthy red gums and gaps from missing teeth, with unconscious charm.

"Well, Sisters, it's settled then. Just one piece of advice when you're in the boat: try to keep the hems of your robes out of the scuppers or you'll reek of fish for many a month. Very difficult to get the smell out of wool, they say, though I don't notice it myself."

So it was that next day Anne and Joan sat huddled together in the prow of the little fishing smack as Bernard pushed away from the sea wall and raised his one large square sail, which the wind took and bellied.

It was a fresh breeze that found them, and the women barely had time to wave to the small number of fisher families standing outside Margery's house, her children among them, as the little craft slipped out through the gap in the harbor wall and pointed her nose to the north.

Margery's prediction was true, for the rain had stopped this morning, after a sodden day and night that the girls passed playing with the children in the tiny spaces of the fisher house. Now the dank wind made Anne and Joan shiver convulsively as cold air fluttered their cloaks and veils.

Bernard helmed his boat from the stern as David, his young apprentice from the village, trimmed up the sail so that it strained tight, gathering the wind. He smiled broadly at Anne.

"Easy today, Sister. Easy passage. Good driving wind this—we'll be inside the harbor underneath the Abbey before you've had time to say 'tierce'!"

He had to shout against the crack of the wind in his rigging, and they could only just see his face behind the great mound of fish caught yesterday and stored in wicker creels on the deck of his boat.

She was named *The Porpoise,* Bernard's little fishing smack, and he was justly proud of her. She'd been keeled and built in

Robin Hod's Bay by his own father when Bernard himself had been a tiny boy, and she was the source of his family's modest prosperity for two generations now.

As he adjusted the tiller of his boat, pointing her nose slightly across the wind to drive her faster, Anne saw Margery's man turn his head and stare ahead of them, north, and it came lurching back to her. That other sea voyage up this same coast, that other sea voyage to Whitby less than two years since . . .

Leif Molnar. He'd been the captain of the *Lady Mary*. Why were there so many adventurers in her life? Would there ever be a time when she would sit and spin, as other women did? Grayhaired, respectable? Married, with her children, her legitimate children, around her knees?

She shook her head, sweeping the comforting image away. How could that be when she had to find them both again, Edward, and her son? His son.

"Oh Anne! Look!" Ahead of them, where the bow cut through the water, a school of silver fish had divided around the little fishing smack.

"Herring, Master. They're running!"

It was the boy, David, who yelled to Bernard against the slap and groan of the rigging, the slipping rush of the water.

"More's the pity, boy. More's the pity." There was nothing to be done. The little smack was loaded deep with yesterday's catch from the whole village. Full to capacity, she had no way of accepting even an extra ounce of the bounty God was offering today.

Regretfully Bernard watched as the silvered mass of fish churned the water, boiling beneath the surface of the waves in the wake of his boat. Here's hoping he'd find that same great school again; it would stand them all in such good stead for the last of the autumn fishing, before the great gales sealed them down for the long dark months ahead.

But that was the luck of the sea and a capricious God.

# Chapter Forty-eight

 It had taken Edward's riding court four days and most of each night of relentless galloping with five changes of horse to reach the ferry on the banks of the Humber. Once across, they would make York in less than half a day. Ordinarily, in good weather London to York should only take a troop of horse five days, but they had not had good weather and this had been a testing, brutally fast ride.

Only some sixty chosen men made up the king's companions, but each man would count in the battle to come: that was what Edward expected, and that is what they would give him. It was for this, the bond they shared, that he had driven them all without pity—none for them, none for himself.

Now, standing beside his sweat-flecked, drooping mount, Edward was detached, being so tired, as he watched men and horses loading onto the punt that would take them across the Humber. Fifteen men, fifteen horses, that was enough in each trip—more was dangerous. He must be careful; exhaustion must not distort his judgment now they were so close.

"No more than fifteen each time, Geoffrey—tell them." One of his riding companions, Geoffrey Luttrell, a long-term member of his affinity—even from a Lancastrian family—touched a finger cheerfully to his riding bonnet as he scrambled down the small hillock to the punt's loading ramp.

"Only fifteen men and horses at one time; those are orders."
The king grimaced; he would have to control his impatience,

for this crossing would take the time it took. They'd be on the far-ther bank by dawn if the ferryman could be persuaded to punt all night back and forth across the river. Fortunately the storm they'd ridden through had blown itself out with the evening and the river was calm, under a waning moon. It should be possible. It would be possible.

"Geoffrey!" Below him, the man looked up, face a white disk in the silvery light. "For the ferryman. We thank him and value his service." The small skin bag arced down into Geoffrey's wait-ing hands, the definite chink of coins clearly heard as he caught it.

One more night and half a day tomorrow and they would be in York.

Edward yawned mightily and eased his neck, letting his head relax from side to side. He could feel the sinews in his shoulders and his arms; they were tight from all the riding. He'd have to warm and loosen them if he was to be any good with a sword in his hand when the time came.

At least all the hard riding, the willing horse beneath him, the sky above him, and the utter pressing need as time slipped by, day after day, had dulled and distanced his fears for Anne.

He'd hear nothing more before he'd left London, but now, as he waited for his turn on board the punt, time slowed, time stopped, and she walked back into his mind. He frowned, only half awake. There was another woman there as well.

Then he saw them both, two faces side by side: Anne and Elizabeth; one dark, one glitteringly fair. They held out their arms to him, unlikely sisters, but when Anne smiled, a radiant smile, the queen turned away and he saw again, with a lurch, her proud pregnant belly.

He was shackled to Elizabeth, and perhaps she carried an heir to the kingdom within her body. Only perhaps; and then he saw that Anne was holding little Edward, undoubtedly his son . . . but she was walking away from him, away into shadow, into darkness!

"Holla, Your Majesty!" Edward was startled from his odd half-dream and straightened his aching back as his weary eyes opened. "Yes, Geoffrey?"

"We are ready for you now, sire."

Edward gathered up his reins and encouraged his mount down the slope with his knees, to where the punt was tied, waiting for him, sullen black water lapping at its sides.

At the water's edge, Edward slipped down from the horse's back and led the nervous animal up the ramp to stand close beside the other nine horses and their riders. Geoffrey called out, almost cheerfully, "Cast off, boatman. We have the king safe."

Safe? There was no safety. Anywhere. Edward crossed himself. All he asked was that they be in time for Richard, or the urgent need for an heir, legitimate or otherwise, would have passed since there'd be no throne for him to occupy.

*Help me through what I must now do, dear Lord, for the good of us all in my kingdom.* Edward was not devout, but his prayer was fervent. *And God, if it be your will, let me not die before I meet with Anne once more. Please let that not be.*

He was only a mortal king but perhaps the god of Solomon, of David, would understand his need and forgive his frailty.

For God was also Love, was he not?


*The Porpoise* slipped around the southern arm of Whitby's sea wall, running before the sudden storm as the evening blew into dark. But the tide was on the turn and the boat was difficult to steer as tidewater tried to run the harbor mouth, fighting the fearsome wind. Thus, two mighty forces came against each other in a great cloud of spume, leaving the two women in the prow of the little smack soaked and frozen. At last, however, the vessel caught a sudden gust in its sail and was driven with a grinding crunch into the dock.

Deftly, ignoring the solid rain that had replaced the wind, David and Bernard rapidly worked to lash *The Porpoise* to the sizable iron rings set in the dock wall, fearful that at any minute another buffet might force the boat away, back toward the harbor mouth.

Huddled together, Anne and Joan tried to wipe the rain from their eyes, both tense as the dock heaved in and out of vision above them.

At last it was done. Now the women must climb the swaying

rope ladder that Bernard and David had already scrambled up to get to the quay. The rings alone would not hold *The Porpoise* in this wind—she must be secured to stone bollards fore and aft as well.

"Come now, Sisters, just hold tight and don't look down as you climb."

Anne gulped and she caught Joan eyeing her fearfully.

She smiled with a confidence she did not feel. "You go first—I'll be behind to catch you."

It was shouted above the howl of the returning gale as she helped Joan to her feet and placed her hands on the slimy ropes above her head.

"I'll hold it—you climb."

Joan looked fearfully at the dock—so far away in the wild semidarkness. Anne nudged her friend firmly in the back. "Go. Now!" Finally Joan nodded and began to haul herself up the narrow ladder, sodden skirts and wet cloak impeding every step.

Anne watched as Joan, hand over hand, rung after rung, got closer, closer to the lip of the dock—a looming shape above in the howling dark. Her own arms ached: it was hard anchoring the ladder to compensate for Joan's weight as the wind tried to swing the nun against the stone sea wall while she climbed.

"Concentrate. Hold on. Concentrate. Hold on." It became a prayer, and just when it seemed her arms must give out as the pain burned and her muscles shook, a red veil blocked sound and sight.

"Anne, Anne." Was the storm speaking to her? "You are not the sacrifice." It was the Sword Mother's voice, harsh and direct, as she heard very distantly the sound of steel meeting steel. Swords, swordplay, Anne had heard it often enough at tournaments—and in her dreams.

There was screaming on the wind and, the veil suddenly gone, Anne looked up to see a red-cloaked woman, wild hair flying in the storm, standing behind Bernard and David as they finally hauled Joan up from the ladder to the dock.

"Lash the ladder, lash it. There's rope by the mast."

Bernard waved his lantern to catch Anne's attention, and his great voice cut through the wind that drove Anne's wet cloak out behind her like a sail.

"Lash the ladder and climb toward my light!"

But Anne did not hear him; she was looking at the lines, the black lines, tattoos, drawn all over the Sword Mother's cheeks, her throat, and shoulders—curving, writhing, looped, and spiraled patterns. Under her red cloak, she was naked to the waist—Anne saw that when the Sword Mother held one arm high in salute—one great ring of gold clamped around a muscled upperarm. Then she was gone, into the dark.

"Sister Anne?" Bernard was calling down to her, increasingly anxious. The storm was gathering force again.

"I hear you!" Anne screamed back, nodding, agreeing.

*Lash the ladder down, lash the ladder now;* this was her task if she was ever to leave the lurching, straining *Porpoise*.

Fumbling her way among the wicker creels of fish fastened to the sides of the deck, Anne searched for rope—and was rewarded. Near the mast there was a spare coil neatly stowed in case the sail needed extra staying. Stumbling as the boat bucked beneath her, groaning as it rubbed against the stone wall that was close, so close, Anne found her way back to the rope ladder somehow as it slapped and swung against the harbor wall.

Catching the ladder as she would a restive horse, Anne shucked the sodden nun's cloak. Better be as wet as a seal than blinded by flapping cloth. And finally, too, she ripped off her novice's veiling, leaving only the wimple covering her head.

Somewhere, deep in her mind, burned the image of the Sword Mother. It had force, that last salute: it was a message. Anne was not to be a victim—not anyone's victim.

Quickly, deftly, Anne lashed the ladder to the deck and then she began to climb, slick rung by slick rung up, up toward the light, toward the men's faces looming down as the lantern swayed and swayed: shadow and light, shadow and light.

She was in Whitby. She had come this far. When she'd had the vision in Brugge, the Sword Mother had said, "I guard, I guard." Anne was not alone.

# Chapter Forty-nine

Edward, like his brother, mostly enjoyed being in York. So many family associations—and the good memories outweighed the bad, just.

Now he was comfortably sprawled inside an enormous butt of good oak, previously used to hold wine, filled with scalding water as he tried to soak some of the pain out of his arms and back after the long ride north.

Richard's men had carried the open-topped tun to the duke's sleeping quarters, placing it in front of the raging fire as relays of servants carried pail after pail of water into the room. Such was their haste that more than one or two slopped the contents of their buckets on the slate floor and were roundly cursed by the duke. An unusual occurrence.

Perhaps the brothers were just over-worried, and God knew they had cause; so thought Warrington as he chivied the last relay of kitchen hands with empty buckets out of his master's sleeping quarters.

"Your Grace, shall we return with more?" He didn't even get the last words out as the duke closed the door in his valet's face with an abrupt snap. From the other side of three inches of good, solid oak, he heard his master's muffled "No. You will be called."

"Shortly, Warrington. We'll call you shortly!" Edward called out loudly also, less abrupt than his brother. If he was going to all the trouble of having a bath, he wanted hot water and lots of it.

Richard didn't understand why himself. All this washing could not be healthful could it? "You'll smell of malmsey out of this, Edward."

That made the king smile. He liked malmsey. "I can think of worse things, brother. You should try this, you know. It relaxes the muscles; much less pain after a hard ride."

Richard was pacing restlessly and he interrupted his brother. "Pain! It's more than stiff backs will pain us soon."

Edward smiled mirthlessly. "No, brother, it is not we who will suffer, believe me."

Richard looked at the king as he sat back in what was, effectively, a great wooden bucket. His magnificent muscled torso was picked out by the light from the fire; mighty arms draped casually over the edge of the butt. He looked relaxed, quite certain of what he was about.

Richard sighed and Edward smiled. "There's no point, you know, getting so worried. You've done well; planned well, now all we have to do is frighten them for five, maybe seven days. That's all. Then William will join us. We'll crush them if they go too far, I promise you."

Richard kicked at the fire moodily. "I wish I had your confidence, I really do."

"Come, brother, we've been here before." But Richard looked uncertain still. Edward sighed and a moment later began, regretfully, to clamber out of the water. "I've changed my mind. Let's eat, and you can tell me about my son. That will be more cheerful."

Richard twitched the bath sheet, which had been warming before the fire, in the king's direction. "A likable boy, that one. Who's his mother, did you say?"

Edward, lazily drying himself before the fire, stretching newly supple muscles, one by one, smiled craftily. "I did not. And I will not." As he dried himself, a different, bleaker look crept over his face as he stared deep into the fire.

"For all he's a bastard, he's well descended, very well descended, on his mother's side. Better than you or I. And England needs a boy, an heir."

Richard said nothing, though he was intrigued. He heard the purpose in his brother's voice. Elizabeth had not given Edward a son, but someone else, another woman, had. Who was she? Who could she be? Well enough descended to be the mother of a potential king? He mentally reviewed the very few likely court women as Edward turned with sudden purpose toward Richard's bed, on which was arrayed a new suit of clothes. Pulling a soft muslin shirt over his head—he liked soft clothes, his little brother must have remembered—he shot a penetrating glance at Richard.

"And so, did you find the girl, this French spy?"

The duke shook his head as he strode to the door and flung it open. "Bring food. And wine." The guardsman hurried away as Richard turned back into the room again. "Not yet but we will."

"Dressed as a novice, you say? A good disguise, if you needed one." Edward was nearly dressed again, in the quick way that a soldier has before battle.

"Yes. I have a man on her trail, however. A man with an interest."

Edward observed the slight grimace as his brother said the words. "A good man?"

Richard shrugged. "You could say that. Relentless rather. He's been made a fool of." A faint smile lingered in his eyes. It piqued the king's interest "Really? By whom?"

"His father. It seems the old man fell in love—or lust—with the girl. I've heard word that the father now pursues the son and I wait to see who will find her first. Two men on a mission for us, brother—we cannot fail."

The king laughed. "All this fuss about one silly little girl! Is there any proof that she actually is a spy, by the way?"

Richard shrugged, slightly sulky. "She ran from her hiding place, which seems suspicious; and she caused me, personally, a mighty lot of trouble in so doing."

The king grinned. "Ah yes, the archbishop. I heard."

Annoyed, Richard flung himself into a Venetian chair drawn up to the fire. "That man is impossible, Edward. Impossible! He thwarts me at every turn."

A discreet knock at the door signaled Warrington's entrance

accompanied by two boys, all loaded with platters of food and an enormous jug of wine.

"On the table, Warrington." The king nodded to Richard's worktable and pensively held his peace until the servants had deposited their burdens and left once more.

"Seems to me there's been a great deal of needless bother about this girl, Richard. She's hardly important enough to fight with George Neville about, is she?"

Richard flared in sudden defense. "You were not here, brother! I did what I considered best, for us all. You would not have ignored a rumored spy, Edward, not if information came from a trusted man."

Edward smiled slightly; he liked Richard's spirit, but there was a lesson in this, a valuable one in *réal-politique* for his passionate younger brother.

"But Richard, your 'spy' caused you to waste much time and energy, it seems to me, when the main game is clearly elsewhere."

Richard refused to look at Edward, moodily kicking at the fire with one boot-clad foot as the king went on. "Oh, I know the archbishop's a difficult man, stubborn, but we need him, and you, to at least pretend amity in this city; you don't want to scare your people here more than we need. We've got much more than Warwick's brother to think about—we've got Warwick himself."

Edward sauntered over to the fire and offered his brother a beaker of wine. "Here, let's drink to your reconciliation with the archbishop—and to someone, anyone, catching that silly girl so we can make an end of this overblown nonsense!"

# Chapter Fifty

Stephen Hardwell was consumed by an unexpected emotion: a sense of loss.

How could it be that someone he'd seen only once, to whom he'd only ever addressed so few words, could have come to obsess his every waking thought?

He pondered the mystery of the missing girl as he paused, surrounded by his small party, to view the way forward.

Things had come to a pretty pass indeed when a man had to track his son as if the boy were a thief and he the thief taker! But that was the way of it; he'd committed himself and he would see this through. Things had gone too far now between Henry and himself for him to even consider backing away, for his son would kill that girl even though she was no spy—just to earn favor with his duke.

Stephen shook his head sorrowfully as he thought on it; he was deeply ashamed that his son, knighted on the field of battle—as he himself had been—should so seek to dishonor his vows to protect all women so he could reap political advantage.

"Ale, Sir Stephen?" The baron grunted distractedly as Liam Fellowes handed his master a leather flask of good ale brewed in the manor kitchens of Hardwell Hall; the baron was very particular about his ale—no muddy alehouse slop for him on this journey!

"How far d'you make Whitby, Liam?"

Liam, a Whitby man by birth, cheered up considerably. "We'll be there well before noon, Baron."

"Looking forward to it are you, Liam, after this cold journey of ours?" Liam was astonished. Normally his self-obsessed old master thought of nothing and no one but himself and his own comfort. Something odd was going on, and not just this mad pursuit of a girl, and his son.

The steward nodded. "Aye, sir. I am. My old ma's still alive, or she was last I heard."

The old baron nodded and then sighed as he waved the steward away. Filial piety, family bonds: nothing was more important, nothing. His own son now, when had he last felt for him, his own father as Liam did for his mother? Stephen Hardwell sighed gustily. He'd failed, failed as a father with that boy. Now all that linked them was mutual suspicion—and blood, though blood was not to be slighted, ever.

Perhaps he felt so touched by the plight of the castaway girl because she, too, was bereft and alone in the world, as he felt he truly was. And, when he came to think of it, she'd also come to symbolize the hope of a new start; a new start so that he, Sir Stephen, might yet have children again, proper, grateful children this time—children who loved him as they should rather than plotting and scheming to take what was still rightfully his own patrimony. As Henry had, and did . . .

Wat Brewster was holding Liam's horse and he nudged the steward from long acquaintance as he clambered back onto his sturdy cob.

"His brain's gone soft; what d'you reckon?"

Liam gathered up the reins, hauling Polly's head up just as she found a particularly nice and unexpected clump of grass hiding near some gorse. The horse objected, and in the moment of scuffle when Liam, taking no nonsense, dug his heels into Polly's flanks—which caused her to snort and dance—he avoided an answer.

If he was honest, he thought Wat was right. This was a fool's errand they were all on, but if he, Liam Fellowes, was to best that slimy reeve Simon—and protect his master's interests and his own from Henry—he had to find a way to make it work.

Spies! Since when did dangerous spies end up in poxy little convents in the very midst of nowhere?

It was a measure of the times, this nonsense they were about—and the uneasy family politics of the Hardwells, of course. Not many a man liked to yield place to his son in his own lifetime, when it came right down to it, and if Henry were *his* son, well, he could understand how double hard that might be.

The baron was waving to him again, and Liam raised a hand in acknowledgment. "Right, men, lively now, follow the baron."

Follow the baron; Liam wondered if they would, if the time came to stick in a dirty fight. He shook his head; things got bad when family fell out.

The baron, riding at the head of the party, called back over his shoulder, "Liam! Ride with me."

Liam sighed and kicked the reluctant Polly up into a canter; he liked Polly but she was far too fond of food.

"That horse blown, is she?" The baron looked with disfavor on Liam's mount.

"No, Sir Stephen, she's enjoying it, aren't you, Polly? Good long ride, just what you like, eh girl?" The horse responded with a loud, luxuriant fart and a torrent of manure, which unexpectedly made the baron laugh. That was surprising—the baron never laughed.

"Ah, Liam, Liam, what I would not give for my son to see sense."

Liam said nothing—there was little point.

"He cannot understand, to my lasting shame, what our duty, the duty of knights, is in this matter. God's will is ever stronger than that of man."

Oh yes, and what would the king think of that, thought Liam cynically.

"Yes, man is driven by vice and sin, yet, if we will only listen, God is always there to guide us, protect us; to set our feet back on the straight and narrow path. And bring us the peace we deserve." The baron felt happy tears well in his eyes, so certain was he that God approved of the nobility of his actions in seeking to protect this girl from his son. And, too, it must please him that in this, in

his honorable intentions toward this girl, he could make repara-
tion for all the less-than-gallant relations he'd had with women at
other times in his life.

"There, Baron, do you see it?" Liam's abrupt shout brought
Stephen Hardwell back to the present as the little party crested a
rise. There was the sea, and with it, the stone-gray town of
Whitby huddled around its harbor under the Abbey. The wind
off the restless sea hit them in the face and for the first time they
could smell salt in the air.

"We'll be there in time for tierce, Baron, what did I tell you?"
There was a lift in Liam's voice as he said it—if he looked very
hard from this height, he could almost make out the house he'd
been born in, his mother's house in a lane behind the market
square . . .


Whitby was calm at last, having endured three days of battering
storm, three nights of fearsome, howling wind.

After that first night spent in a noisome harborside tavern,
The Two Tunns, in a tiny, freezing space up under the tiles, Joan
and Anne had struggled up the steep road from the harbor that
led to the Abbey on the cliff. Anything, anything at all had been
preferable to a day spent huddled around the sulking fire in the
common room of the tavern, where strangers, men who came
for the sailor's women who frequented the Two Tunns, eyed the
two nuns and their companions, and were tempted to ask questions.

Now, as the day dawned with a dying wind, Anne and Joan
whispered together in the women strangers' dorter of the
monastery.

" . . . but I cannot leave you here. It's not safe." Joan was going
over old ground, old arguments, but Anne was clear.

"Dearest Joan, I am so grateful for your kindness, for your
companionship. But this is more than enough. You must go back
with Bernard. You will be missed at the convent—I'm sure that
he will be happy to take you home, or find someone to accompany
you there."

"But what will happen to you?" Joan shivered; a woman alone in the world was never safe.

"You forget, dear friend, I have resources. I will purchase an escort, an armed escort."

Somewhere, from deep within the Abbey, the sound of a bell could be heard, coming and going on the wind.

"Come, or we shall be missed." Hurriedly both women swaddled cloaks around their bodies—their winter cloaks rescued from *The Porpoise* and dried in the Abbey's hot room, its caldarium—over darned but clean nuns' habits. The nuns who ran the women strangers' dorter, for the monks had taken pity on Anne and Joan when the two girls arrived at the Abbey—particularly Anne, since her habit was in such a state. Out of charity, she'd been supplied with a postulant's white veil and a decent black habit as a temporary substitute until, it was presumed, she returned to her mother house and proper clothing.

That had not been an end to the Abbey's kindness to them. As pilgrims, they would never have been expected to stay in the women's dorter for three days, but the weather had shut the clifftop community in on itself and there were no other pilgrim women currently staying.

With the exception of the one professed nun and two lay sisters whose service was specifically to wait on the women strangers who came to pray at Saint Hilda's great Abbey, they had the women's dormitory to themselves, and that was just as well. Anne lived in daily terror that she would be recognized, for as the two women hurried down the stairs and across the Abbey garth, Anne could not help remembering how it had been the last time she stayed within this place. She'd been a fugitive then as well.

Nearly two years had passed since that time, but her transformation from a servant girl into a lady of wealth, of quality, had begun here in this place with her friend Jane Shore.

Rags to riches; and now, riches to rags. What was left to her that was important, truly important? She'd lost that proud independence she'd worked for, risked all for, but she did not miss it now. She missed Edward—and their son—with a dull ache that was nearly always there, unsleeping. Perhaps once she found little

Edward again, she should go to the king as his mistress. Could she do it, would that be best, after all? She would have him whenever he could give her time, and perhaps they would have other children, children he would protect—especially from the queen—and most especially, she would have little Edward.

Tears filled Anne's eyes as she saw the ivory-and-rose Christ child, held by his beautiful mother, as she and Joan hurried into the darkened church, and to the side aisle where pilgrims were permitted to worship while observing the brothers on the other side of the rood screen.

All the power of the king had not been enough to protect her from kidnap in Brugge—how, then, would Edward protect her in England if she came home?

Anne pondered her choices: there were really only two that were practical.

Find someone within the town who was rich enough to buy one of her two remaining gems, and thereafter try for a ship's place to a port on the continent, thence on to Brugge; or, more safely, wait out the winter storms in Whitby, taking lodging with some respectable family, if she could bear it.

But how to transform herself from nun to, say, widow? Would that do to explain her being alone, once Joan went on her way?

A most difficult choice, for each was fraught with risk. But if she wanted to see them again—Deborah, little Edward and his father—she must make up her mind. She must choose, and very soon.

# Chapter Fifty-one

Edward and Richard were off on sortie with the members of the king's riding court plus one hundred well-armed men of the duke's own affinity, archers and swordsmen, all decked bravely in the duke's livery, the white boar badge prominent.

Since Edward had arrived at York, plans had been talked through extensively, and today the first of them was carefully set in motion by the king and his brother.

Officially, the brothers were on a progress to visit and hunt at one of the Crown's lodges within easy ride of York.

Unofficially, it was the intention that they should make a good show of military preparedness so that word would travel to the Border country that the king was in residence at his brother's palace and backed by fighters.

Archbishop George Neville himself had been cajoled into blessing the riding party before it set out at dawn on a cutting, frosty morning. He and Richard loftily ignored each other while Edward was a charming but implacable conduit between the two—listening patiently to the archbishop before the service as he bemoaned the lack of respect for the church within the barbarian north. Then, Edward nodded wisely in agreement as George proffered advice on how to ward off the ills of this changeable season with boar's fat and salt regularly rubbed into the skin of the chest and throat, and smiled genially as he accepted the bishop's prayers for the queen's safe delivery of a prince . . .

As ever, the king had the larger game of politics in mind. He knew that permitting George Neville to see him among his fighters would be the same as sending a personal letter to Earl Warwick. The king meant business, that was the message. And it was a true one.

Now Edward looked magnificent as he sat astride his formidable destrier Mallon, the horse shifting from hoof to hoof as the "riding party" assembled in plain view of the townspeople who had gathered to see them off.

There was a great whoop from the crowd as this goodly mass of fighters, or hunters—though they looked more like the former than the latter—started up on their way.

The people of York were proud—and felt a little less uneasy. They, too, had heard the rumors of the she-wolf of Anjou massing troops in France and hoping to land them in the north before the worst of the winter gales. Many said she would join with her supporters in the Border country and sweep down from Scotland to harry them all.

A butcher on his way to work in the shambles summed up the common feeling as they watched Edward and Richard ride out: "Hope their hounds bring down a bit of game today; hope they hunt well for all our sakes . . ."

It was still early when Bernard arrived at the Abbey to escort Joan down to the dock and thence south to Robin Hod's bay once more.

Despite all the last-minute entreaties, all the prayers, Anne would not be swayed. Joan had been her kind friend and companion but now the time had come for the nun to return to her convent. Anne had made plans, daring plans, and the fewer who knew what she was about, the safer it would be for them all.

With great reluctance, Joan was persuaded to leave with Bernard, and Anne stood waving at the gate of the women strangers' dorter as the couple walked away from the Abbey on the road down to the harbor.

Then she was alone. But not friendless.

During her three days at the Abbey, Anne had been kind to the smallest, youngest, and most harried of the two lay sisters responsible for the cleanliness of the women strangers' dorter. The monastery, while it provided lodging freely to all pilgrims who asked for it, looked for guests' donations to contribute to the running of the Abbey itself; a building that was ever hungry for repairs since the salt wind took such toll on the fabric.

Anne told her new friend that she'd been instructed by her mother house to leave a large donation for the Abbey but needed first to find a money changer who could discreetly change some of the large coins she had been given by her "convent" for smaller ones.

Little Sister Agatha knew of only one money changer, or rather, a family of them. They were Jews who had grown wealthy brokering wool for local growers yet were quite liked by the townspeople of Whitby—an unusual thing for the outsiders they'd always been.

"Would it not look odd if a nun were to visit the house of Jews, though, Sister? They were the enemies of Christ." Agatha was genuinely worried for Anne.

Anne pretended to think for a moment. "Well, perhaps it would, but I could not ask anyone else to complete this task."

If Agatha had been older, a little more experienced in the world, perhaps she might have questioned why Anne was not given smaller money in the first place. However, though she was an honest girl, she was quite naïve; and she was pleased with herself when she came up with a solution to Anne's problem.

"I have something for you! Wait here!"

It took the nun only a few moments to whisk out of Anne's cell and return carrying a dark blue dress and a long, forest-green winter cloak. Both were old, and the cloak was patched, but having been fashioned from good cloth that had been well treated over its long life, they were in respectable condition.

"These were left here when the lady who owned them died," Agatha hurried on, seeing Anne's uncertain look. "No, really, she was a lovely lady and the Lord took her to him from inside the Abbey itself; she just keeled over in front of the rood screen one day while she was praying. The abbot says it was a good death, a holy death, and her family didn't want the clothes when they came to get the body. I'm sure she'd have wanted them put to a good, Christian use."

The little speech was breathlessly delivered but the idea was bold, even a little shocking. A postulant dressing in worldly clothes so that she could do business with a Jew?

Anne nodded, impressed. Never underestimate a church mouse. "A very clever, and serviceable idea, Sister. I am grateful to you. Very grateful, and so is my mother house."

The "church mouse" blushed with pleasure. It was rare in her comfortless life to receive a compliment. Smiling quickly, she left pretty Sister Anne to her own devices, hurrying away as she remembered the numberless chores assigned to her by Sister superior.

Anne's heart hammered as she stripped off the black postulant's habit and the trailing white veil, shaking out her hair with relief as the hot, constricting wimple came off her head. Then, trying not to hurry, she slipped the dead pilgrim's prickly wool dress over her naked body—shivering as she felt the coarse weave against her skin—and strained to lace the back without help, no easy task.

Agatha, ever resourceful, had thought to supply Anne with a long sacking apron as well, to help gather the dress in a little since it was the garment of a much larger woman. The combined voluminous folds were a blessing as the two garments, plus the cloak, would be thick enough to keep Anne warm in the bleak weather—an important consideration as she walked down the long hill from the Abbey to the town.

Finally Anne was ready, with the green cloak swaddled closely around her, hair pulled back out of sight inside the hood, which now shadowed her face.

The extra material in the dress and apron made Anne look stouter than she would ever be, and the basket that Agatha had lent completed the picture. To the world she would look like any other respectable goodwife intent on this morning's marketing. Even the lay brother at the Abbey's great gate was fooled when he was asked to let "Agatha's aunt" out so she could go down to the town. The man saw nothing amiss in the stout little woman who kept her head modestly bent, so he waved Sister Agatha's aunt through cheerfully enough, being careful, however, not to speak to her directly lest he pollute himself by exchanging words with one of Eve's sisters.

And so, on a clearing late autumn morning, Anne walked down toward the town of Whitby intent on one thing: changing at least one of her remaining gems into money, money that would buy her a passage to France, and thence to Brugge.

Keeping her head down as she walked, she exchanged greetings with no one and was careful to draw to one side of the narrow road with the hood of her cloak covering her face as a party of armed, mail-wearing men cantered past toward the Abbey buildings, driving their horses at a great pace for such a slippery, rain-mired road.

Anne would not have recognized Henry Hardwell if she had seen him, but if she'd looked up, she would have remembered Simon the Reeve, having known his face from the baron's visit to the convent.

But she kept her eyes on the road and the men ignored her. They were after a young girl posing as a novice. Local housewives were of no interest, no interest at all.

# Chapter Fifty-two

The Whitby market was very busy as Anne sauntered between the stalls, seeming to carefully inspect the dried cod, the barrels of salt herring, the flitches of bacon, and the woolen cloth on sale against the coming winter.

People in the north took full advantage of anything that resembled a fine day at any time of the year, so even if it was cool, with a biting wind off the sea, all of Whitby had things to sell and things to buy, and they were telling everyone and his wife all about it at the tops of their lungs.

But Anne needed information and was uncertain where to find it. Agatha had told her that Master Cohen was to be found in Silver Lane, but her directions had proved confusing. She'd said that Silver Lane ran off Conduit Street, itself a small alley behind the quarter where animals were butchered, close to the market square.

Anne found the butchers and poulterers easily enough, for even on a cold day the stink was impossible to avoid, but Conduit Street she just could not locate in the maze of little alleys filled with shouting men and herds of terrified beasts.

Time was pressing and she had no choice; she must ask directions.

Anne grimaced in sympathy as she passed a small mob of bullock calves, backed up and blocking the street in wide-eyed confusion as they smelled blood from the slaughter yards, and stopped by the first shop she came to. It was a poulterers' stall and the trestle board in front of the open shop front was piled high with plucked bird carcasses of all kinds: chickens, ducks, and geese, plus the smaller corpses of larks, linnets, blackbirds, plovers, and many water birds she could not name—waders with long legs somehow pathetic in death.

"Yes? What can we give you today, mistress? We have wonderful fresh chickens, well fed, see? Fine and yellow from last summer's corn. Plump, really plump. Or duck? Goose? No need for lard when you cook these birds. Then we have teal, and wood pigeon, doves by the brace, and the sweet flesh of songbirds."

It was hard to stop the girl—the poulterer's daughter—in her singsong patter, so Anne smiled, said nothing, and waited for her to stop.

"Lark, linnet, starling, blackbird. Or there's black gull, and I can even get you pheasant, if you want something a bit special—legally obtained, of course. We have rights to a certain quantity, which we buy from the monks' game preserves."

The girl guttered to a halt, perplexed and a bit annoyed. Market day was busy, they did their best trading of the whole week; she didn't have time for a customer who didn't know what she wanted.

"Thank you. It all sounds excellent, but what I really need is direction. I'm trying to find someone."

"So, did she buy?" The poulterer's daughter shook her head as she watched the woman in the green cloak walk away. "No, Father, she didn't."

The poulterer frowned and his daughter was immediately defensive. "I did my best—she was just a looker and a toucher. Wanted to know the way to Silver Lane. Yes, Mistress Rafe, what can I do you for? I mean, do for you?" Customer and shop attendant laughed; they knew each other well, and with this goodwife, money certainly would change hands to everyone's advantage.

But the poulterer watched the woman in the green cloak for a moment as she disappeared up the street outside his shop. Silver Lane? Only one reason to go to Silver Lane—the money changer, the Jew, lived there. No good ever came from moneylenders or changers. Or Jews for that matter. Christ knew that.

Impatient with his idle thoughts, the poulterer turned his attention to reaching down a brace of the birds from the carcass curtain above his daughter's head. "What about a nice fat duck, Mistress Rafe? Nothing like a juicy bit of duck at the end of the day, that's what I always say."

The noise from the market receded as Anne turned a corner beneath the overhung first floor of a large half-timbered house. There were no signs, nothing to say she'd found Silver Lane, but it was a dark, dead-end street and very narrow: black-and-white houses crowded tightly together, tops almost touching—that had been part of the poultry girl's directions.

And there, at the very end of the short street, was the façade of a house, again black and white, but it looked secretive somehow; that, too, was how the Jew's house had been described.

Anne stopped hesitantly. Should she knock on a door and ask someone else if this was the place, just to be sure? But then above the blackened front door of the house at the end of the street, Anne just made out a faded checker-painted board hanging from an iron bracket on which was a crude depiction of gold and silver coins and, above them, a scale.

She had come to the right place; this was the money changer's house.

Nervously she clenched the fingers of her right hand tighter around the two remaining gems. If she was clever and careful, perhaps they could bring her old life back; her son, and Deborah. But not Edward, not the king. She dearly hoped they would meet again, just once—*let that be, Sword Mother, of your pity*—but her path lay away from his. She knew it now, could not avoid that knowledge. She ached, she ached deeply when she thought of life, years and years to come, without Edward, but she must find the strength she had found before when she'd left England, an exile.

Sacrifice. Perhaps these stones were the last sacrifice. Perhaps she had not yet paid enough and must be left with nothing.

Then an odd thing happened: the jewels shifted within her folded palm—they moved. As if they were alive.

Startled, she opened her hand. The last diamond, with its companion ruby, tumbled out and lay on the street where some stray gleam of light from the sky above caught the clarity in both stones among the dirt: one bloody, one clear as water. Anne dropped to her knees, scuffling desperately to retrieve the gems. Then she felt a hand drop to her shoulder.

"These are very fine, very fine indeed. Let me help you."

Anne scooped up her treasures with one hand, eyes wide with fear. The man stepped back quickly.

"Hola! I will not hurt you."

Anne's heart was pounding, but then, slowly, she relaxed. No, he would not hurt her. He had kind, dark brown eyes and was respectably dressed in a well-made ankle-length woolen gown of a pleasing dense black. Snowy linen, beautifully goffered, formed a high fluted collar under his chin and peeped through beneath the front fastenings of his robe. He could have been a well-dressed court functionary except for the curls dangling from his forehead and his skull cap. That marked him.

"Are you Master Cohen?"

"Yes, mistress, I am he. But we have not met. Will you tell me your name?"

"I am a customer, perhaps that will suffice?"

The old man smiled, a surprisingly sweet sight. "Well then, Mistress Customer, let us go into my house and let me be what service I can to you."

Anne dared for a moment to hope. Soon she would leave this place and this man was the means, the means to that end.


"Sister, this is very serious for you and for the Abbey. A matter of treason. A burning matter."

Sister Agatha, terrified of the grim soldier in front of her, looked pleadingly at the abbot and her own immediate supervisor, the Sister superior, mistress of the women strangers' dorter. What should she say?

"The novice we seek. You spoke to her? Helped her?"

An imperceptible nod from the abbot gave Agatha courage to speak.

"Yes, sir."

Henry Hardwell was angry; he had no time to waste on this nonsense. With good fortune, and an annoyingly large expenditure of pennies and even thruppences, he'd tracked the two errant "nuns' to the inn at the Whitby waterfront, the Two Tunns, only to be told they'd gone as pilgrims to this Abbey, but now, again, the girl had fled ahead of him!

This was sweaty work—and much was at stake. His father's lusts were a minor consideration now that the duke expected him to deal with the matter of the supposed spy promptly and efficiently on behalf of the king his brother. And he would do that, by God, so he would. It was a priceless opportunity to gain influence and advancement at court.

And perhaps when he found the girl, he could just tear her tongue out. That way, he'd have a "spy" to exhibit to the duke, but she'd not be able to speak. Excellent! An excellent solution. He thrust his face close to the mewling child who was the key to the mystery, hissing his question, "Where is she? Answer!"

Poor Agatha was torn. Sir Henry was a grim man with a harsh, red face and he meant no good to Sister Anne, of that she was certain. Nervously, she bowed to avoid his gimlet eye.

"Delay is dangerous, girl, very dangerous."

The abbot cleared his throat. He was a compassionate man and he did not enjoy the sight of this little poor scrap being bullied so mercilessly, but he was also a pragmatist and he had the welfare of the Abbey to think of. To have harbored a spy running from the king's justice was a serious matter; and this man, unpleasant as he was, had warrants from the Duke of Gloucester himself.

"Sister Agatha, you must speak. If you have knowledge of where our sister might be, you must tell Sir Henry."

Poor Sister Agatha. She closed her eyes and quickly asked for guidance. None came. Tremulously, she opened them to find Sir Henry glaring directly into her eyes, so close she could smell his breath. It was a shock; she'd never been this close to a man, any man, before. The words babbled out of her mouth in a terrified stream and forever after, when she smelled garlic on another's breath, unconscious terror would make her bowels run.

"The Jew's house in Silver Lane. She's gone there to change

money so that she can return and make a donation to the Abbey."

"Moneylenders? Jews?!" Henry Hardwell's rage, never far from the surface, ignited. He hated them, hated them! They were a scourge on the face of the earth, and it had nothing to do with religion. His father had mortgaged the manor, Henry's patrimony, to Jews who'd kept the Hardwells in debt for years.

It would give him pleasure indeed to go to the moneylender's house and find that girl. Great pleasure!

"We know where she is, Edward. My man tells me the French spy is definitely in Whitby. He'll have her back here in the next few days."

The duke delivered his news defiantly, very pleased. He'd just had the dispatch from Henry Hardwell, delivered by an interesting new innovation: a trained pigeon had flown from Whitby to York, the coded message attached to one leg in a tiny lead canister.

Edward grunted as he watched his little son with fascination, totally absorbed. The boy was sitting on the floor doodling with a stick of charcoal on scraps of vellum.

"Edward?"

Reluctantly the king looked up. "Yes?"

"Yes. And Hastings is close to York now: about a day's march, I'm told." The duke rubbed his hands together with relish. Things were starting to come right. Happily, he picked up a freshly picked apple from a silver bowl—he relished the fruits of autumn—and began to peel it with a dagger from his belt, the oiled steel very black against the rosy skin.

"It's worked, it's all worked. That's very pleasing." The peel dropped in a long spiral from his knife now as he cut a sliver of the apple's flesh and chewed it vigorously. "New season's, brother. Delicious!" Humming, he cut another piece and considered their situation. "The hunt" had indeed put the fear of God into the Lowland counties north of York and talk of the imminent arrival of Margaret of Anjou had died away. It was true, then, by the Grace of God, that the wild autumn weather had prevented her embarkation. They were safe for the nonce. Unreflectively, just to ward off bad luck, the duke crossed himself.

Edward was amused. "Superstitious, brother, or devout? Either seems unlikely."

Richard grinned. "Come, brother, I'm more devout than you've ever been. And much less superstitious, if it comes to that."

Edward laughed out loud but then scoffed.

"Oh ho, then why do you wear the relic ring, Richard, and the wolf's claw at your throat? Dusty old beliefs mean nothing to me, never have. Do you think they will protect you in battle—or from sorcery?"

Abruptly the laughter died. Sorcery. The word had power when the king's own wife was still called a witch in some quarters. And Edward had never told his brother about the interview he'd had with a certain bishop in Brugge about Anne. And he never would.

Briskly, the duke changed the subject to familiar concerns. "So, what do we do about Hastings's levies, brother?"

Edward tousled his son's head. Little Edward hardly noticed, so absorbing was his task—he was trying to draw a tree.

"Does this look like a tree to you, Richard?"

Impatiently, the duke rolled his eyes. God's bones! The boy was only a baby still; how could he possibly draw a tree, at his age? Mary save them all from the idiot fondness of parents!

"It will be good to have the levies on hand, Edward. I think we'll just garrison them here for a short time."

"A very short time, brother."

The king's tone was a warning. The townsfolk of York, while they might welcome the presence of five thousand men as a protection in these uncertain times, would not appreciate having them garrisoned on the town for very long. Troops with nothing to do tended to get out of control very fast, and who knew what rapine and slaughter, not to mention looting, might result if men from the foreign south got too much ale into them?

"Very well, a short time. Then I think we should march toward the Borders, let them loose a bit, and send them home when the Lowlanders have learned a lesson."

Edward nodded agreement, but his grin was wolfish. They both knew what "turn them loose" meant. These desperate times called for blunt action. Fear and sword were potent weapons in the Borders and if they didn't apply them first, others might, to their own people here in York.

"Therefore, let us eat, drink, and be merry tonight, brother Richard, for I feel the tide is turning."

Brave words, but each man knew that while the Earl of Warwick lived, the conflict was not over. Could never be over. Edward kissed his son on the top of his head as the little boy turned to him, clamoring to be hauled up on the king's knee.

The father looked deep into the blue, blue eyes of his son. Was his mother lost to them both for good, lost in that other, undeclared war he'd been waging with his wife, the queen? Would they ever see Anne again, together?

He shivered, suddenly cold. Something was nudging at the margins of his mind, something strange. He watched his brother pick up his black steel knife, watched him begin to peel another rosy apple . . .

And then he had it. A black knife, another black knife, months and months ago, that he'd placed so carefully close to the hand of a corpse. The corpse of the man who'd died the triple death in Loki's cave where he and Richard might have died themselves.

A sacrifice for the good of the tribe—was that what the man had been? And might he, Edward, be another for the good of his kingdom? Perhaps his life must be made forfeit in battle to come so that this little boy could reign after him—if he survived childhood.

The king shook himself like a dog, startling the duke.

"Brother?"

The king grinned mirthlessly. "Fanciful notions, Richard. Your superstitious ways are catching!"

Richard laughed as Edward gently cradled his drowsy son, carrying him toward the door of the chamber murmuring.

"Time for a little sleep, my friend. Just a little sleep."

The baby stirred and his father soothed him, cuddled him. What morbid thoughts he was prey to because he was tired! Particularly this nonsense, all this rubbish, about sorcerers—and witchcraft!

He had the great misfortune to be married to a woman he now mistrusted, and to be deeply in love with another whom he might never see again.

But the game was not over yet, not remotely over, because he was the king!

What seemed complicated, mysterious, and frightening was easy enough to deal with if each problem was broken down into small enough pieces.

That is what he would do.

Win the war in the borders, find Anne, and get on with ruling his kingdom.

But meanwhile his son needed his bed and his nurse.

The king kissed his sleeping baby. If only all life were this simple.

# Chapter Fifty-three

Master Cohen's counting room was enough like her own in Brugge to make Anne melancholy.

The Jew himself was puzzled, and not just by the sheen of tears in the eyes of the unknown Gentile girl now sitting on the other side of his worktable. Something was badly awry and his instincts, the instincts that still functioned so well to protect his family and all their commercial interests, were well roused. There was a mystery here; he'd seen the jewels lying in the dirt, jewels this girl looked much too poor to own.

"The jewels are mine, Master Cohen. I cannot prove it, but I swear that it is so."

Benjamin Cohen jumped in his seat; then he was fearful. His eyes hooded and hardened. Perhaps something here was unclean.

Anne sighed and shook her head. "Oh, Master Cohen, I have come such a long way, such a long way. I have lost everyone and everything that I love and these," she had the gems in the palm of one hand now, holding them up to the meager light from the one small window in his room, "these are all that are left to me. I am willing to trade one of them, whichever you shall tell me is worth the most, for it will give me the chance to start again, to find my son."

She could not help herself. Silent tears slid down her face and she was shaking so much, the jewels almost slipped from her hand.

Reaching over, Benjamin Cohen closed Anne's fingers over her palm. He was touched. Such depth of feeling, even from a Gentile, could not be ignored or explained away.

"I shall weigh them, each of them, shortly, but I can already see they are very fine. I am glad you wish only to change one for coin. I do not think I could afford to buy both of them from you."

Anne, deeply relieved, took a shuddering breath and allowed herself to glance around the room they were in. From recently learned habit, she placed where the doors were, where the windows were, should she need to escape.

"Thank you for your honesty, Master Cohen. Believe me when I say that I am grateful for your kind treatment of me. My gratitude, one day, may be useful to you."

Again there was a strange moment between them, yet he, man of affairs, man of the book, did not doubt her. And that was odd for she was just a girl in an old blue dress.

"Refreshments, while we conduct our business together."

The Jew picked up a little silver bell that was placed on his elm-wood table, and rang it. It had a shiveringly clear sound, melodious, like water falling, and instantly a door opened at the back of his room.

A girl slipped through and stood there in the shadows.

"Yes, Father?"

"Hephzibah, bring refreshment for our guest, if you please."

The girl nodded silently and as quietly closed the door behind her. Though the room was deeply shadowed, Anne had the impression of an ivory skin and a good face: warm brown eyes like her father, and a flow of very black hair falling loose down her back. A pretty girl, no more than fifteen at most.

"Your daughter is very pretty, Master Cohen."

The Jew had risen and, bowing respectfully, held out his own hand for Anne's gems. He smiled, pleased. "You are very kind. We are thinking, my wife and I, that it is time she should be married." Unconsciously he frowned as he said the words. He was preoccupied in the task of assessing each stone with a powerful crystal lens as he held it over a candle to check for flaws.

Anne said nothing but she was slightly startled; the girl seemed so young. Master Cohen glanced up from his work and caught her expression. He smiled ruefully.

"Yes, you are right. She is very young." Now it was Anne's turn to laugh: he was reading her thoughts.

"It seems we understand each other, mistress." The girl before him looked too young, just as his daughter did, to be married, yet she had mentioned a son. "Yet I must think of her welfare. Her future. We are the only people of the Torah in Whitby; a suitable husband for Hephzibah must be found elsewhere. But we shall miss her when she goes. Very much." He sighed heavily and for a moment, great sadness formed deep lines in his face.

"Perhaps in York you will find someone acceptable."

Master Cohen concentrated on weighing each one of the jewels very carefully. It was a distraction from the pain, when he thought of York. "No. Not in York. There have been few of my people in York for many, many generations."

Anne, who knew almost nothing of the history of the north, felt great pain behind his words. Then it hit her like a physical blow. Anguish. Flames. She heard screams, loud, terrified screams. Women, children, even men.

Horrified, she gasped and stood suddenly, desperate to run from the room, run from the terror. Master Cohen looked at her in astonishment. "Mistress? Mistress, are you well?"

Anne thought she would vomit from horror. She could smell burning flesh as hot coals rained down. The roof was going, the roof of the cellar! She could feel the agony, smell the loosened bowels, hear the babies wailing for their mothers as they died.

She collapsed onto the floor where she lay, sobbing uncontrollably "They died, they all died. Aaah, Dear God, how could they let it happen?"

Blood filled her mind, clogged her heart. All she breathed was pain, all she saw was covered by anguish too deep for words.

"Hephzibah, Hephzibah!! Call your mother, run!"

The Whitby market was at its busiest as the baron and his escort picked their way through the crowd, being heartily cursed for trying to force their horses through such confined spaces.

But Liam didn't care. How was it that smells took you back so far? Fish. And sea-coal smoke. It was all so familiar, as if it were yesterday.

"Liam, Liam Fellowes, is it really you?" A woman of about his own age, early thirties, was peering up at him with an expression of such joy on her face that all the world stopped. Mary Gardiner. His own first love. Until she married Tom Fletcher.

"Mary!" He was lost in the sight of her face and unconsciously leaned down from his horse to grab the outstretched hand she offered.

"Liam!" It was the baron and he was not pleased.

"Yes, Baron?" Reluctantly, Liam turned in his saddle to answer his master.

"Information, that's what we need. We have little time if this is not to be a fool's errand."

Liam composed his face with one sad shake of the head to Mary; that shake said, not now, later. She nodded. She understood. She'd always understood him. She smiled at him saucily, curtsied to the baron, and was about to go her ways when Liam called out, "Mary, wait!" Before the baron could object, Liam put his case. "Mary's married to an innkeeper, aren't you, Mary? Tom Fletcher?"

Reluctantly, Mary nodded. It was true, she was married to Tom. "Innkeepers know who's about, know who comes and goes; we should ask Tom if he's seen them."

The baron weighed the man's words suspiciously. It was true an innkeeper would be most likely to know about strangers in town. "Very well, where is this woman's husband? I shall speak to him."

Mary looked up into Liam's eyes and licked her lips quickly. He felt himself stiffen against the pommel. He'd have to watch how he got off Polly, at this rate!

"The inn is this way, sir." It was said with a certain saucy lift—she'd seen the effect she had on Liam. So she still had the power. She led the party of armed men toward her husband's inn, the White Boar, while she walked beside his horse's head.

"Are you here for long, Liam?"

He shook his head. "Not if we find what we're looking for."

"And what might that be?" The look she flashed him was open provocation. Unconsciously he clenched his thighs as he felt the heat mount his belly. Polly snorted in protest; she was already nervous among all these people, so she didn't like being confused by such strange commands. Normally Liam's thighs, when they clenched, were telling her to canter.

"Liam, do you still like apples?"

It was as if she had touched Liam on his naked flesh. Like apples? He remembered that afternoon and closed his eyes, breathing deeply. He'd watched Mary eat a new pippin, white teeth against red flesh. She'd let him lift her skirts and he'd slipped himself between her legs as if coming home while she went on eating that apple, went on enjoying it and him together. And now, eating a new season's apple always had a nostalgic, erotic charge.

"The White Boar, sir." They were there, outside Tom's inn. Liam wanted to shout aloud with happiness: he knew he'd find a way to have Mary again, perhaps even later today. She knew it too: she winked up at him, and swung her hips deliberately as she walked away, conducting the baron into the taproom.

And she knew he'd have God's trouble getting off that horse and that pleased her mightily.

"Mistress, mistress, can you hear me? You must come back. Come back to us."

But it took a long time for Anne to hear Master Cohen and return from the world of pain. And when, finally, this other world, that of the present, began to make sense once more, it came with terrible loss.

Benjamin Cohen was very frightened. This odd young woman was a messenger, he was sure of it, a messenger of disaster to his house. Why else had she had the strange fit when he spoke of the Jews of York? She had screamed and screamed. Sobbing, crying, she'd spoke of burning, of people dying, dying in the cellar! For his people, the passed-down knowledge of long centuries ago was pitiful, too terrible to speak of. The sadness compounded also of disgust and rage: so many had died in York, and one of the worst of the pogroms had caught his people, innocent families, as they sought shelter in the cellar of a Christian church. And this girl had known; she'd seen it. It was an omen, a most terrible omen. Perhaps the pogroms would start again.

Hephzibah was as terrified as he was and so was his wife, Rachael. But his wife was a sensible woman; she was wiping the stranger's face with dampened linen, wiping the tears.

"Yes, Master Cohen, I can hear you." Anne's voice was a reedy whisper as she left the horror slowly, obedient to the urgency of his words.

"You see, I have weighed and assayed both the stones." Better not to say the words he so wanted to say, better not to ask her how she knew. "As you said, each is very fine. I will buy the diamond for five angels. It is the most I can afford."

Five angels, that was enough—more than enough. It would buy her passage, and clothes, and take her back to Brugge. Anne felt energy return as the thought warmed her being. She would go home! She would begin again, she would find them, the people she loved. She didn't care about anything else, the money, the possessions: they alone would be enough.

Waving to his wife and daughter to leave them, the Jew went to a curtained cupboard at the back of his workroom and extracted an iron-bound box. Carefully he unlocked the three locks with three different keys and pulled out a tray of coins, bright gold.

"See now, five angels, we agreed."

He was counting the coins out into her palm with shaking fingers when she stopped him. "I will need change, Master Cohen. Please give me the worth of two angels in pennies, farthings, and groats, I think. And a bag, or a belt. A money belt?"

She spoke hurriedly for urgency was driving them both now. They were both fearful of something close, something coming.

Liam had a warm feeling in his gut as he headed toward Silver Lane. He'd persuaded the baron—happily ensconced in the taproom of the White Boar eating fish pie and drinking tolerable

new ale, brewed by Mary herself—to let him seek out more information about the girl. His local knowledge and contacts might
serve to shorten the time they would have to spend in Whitby. Or
that was how he sold it, anyway.

He had no conscience, of course, about slipping off to see his
old ma first. She was local and her sources of good gossip had always been impeccable, hadn't they? Then he heard the noise before he saw the source. Men yelling and a woman shouting.

"Away! Leave me!"

He rounded the corner into the familiar old street, Silver
Lane, at something of a run because he had an instinct, and saw
them!

Henry Hardwell was pulling a dark-haired girl onto his
horse, and she was resisting: scratching, biting, screaming!
Around Henry milled his men, swords drawn, bellowing, filling
the dark little street with booming sound. Fear and chaos!

His old ma was standing in her doorway, transfixed, because
on her doorstep, just beside the dancing hooves of the horses, lay
the body of an old man, gray hair stuck to his face with blood.

"Stop!" but it was too late, too late.

Henry Hardwell was charging back down the street toward
Liam with his sword held high as the son ran toward his mother.
A well-timed slashing blow from the berserk knight caught Liam
in passing and gashed his chest deeply so that bright blood sprang
out, splashing to the cobbles, the black, pounded earth.

Before the world went black, all Liam heard was shouting
and screaming, and the endless, anguished cries of women; and he
was puzzled, very puzzled—why would Henry Hardwell want
to kill him for helping his old mum? But then he smelled the
burning.

Burning ice was lodged in Anne's throat, but all she felt was
red rage.

Henry Hardwell himself had shattered the Jew's front door
with his iron-spiked cudgel, then burst through, surrounded by
his thugs, all braying like hunting dogs and screaming insults at
the old man and her as they were dragged out to the street.

Now she had a rope around her throat, the ends in Henry

Hardwell's mailed fist. He'd sliced under her chin too in the mad
mêlée he caused, so that blood flowed down and stained the
bodice of the old blue dress.

The rest was blur and fury as Henry charged out of the lane,
screaming like an eagle, she lying winded across his saddle bow,
followed by his yelling men all hopped up on the smell of blood
and burning—one of them had tried to torch Master Cohen's
house, throwing the Jew's own lighted candles into the heavy curtains lining the windows of his workroom.

Panic followed them like companions of war as the armed,
mailed men galloped down the steep shopping streets of the town,
scattering the market-day crowd, before bursting out into the
square itself, yelling like ravaging Norsemen as they spurred their
horses, iron-shod hooves striking sparks from the cobbles as the
people ran, snatching screaming children as they fled from the
armed terror suddenly among them.

Some things never go, and memory stored in muscle is one of
them.

Years and years of practice with a sword slumbered in
Stephen Hardwell's biceps, knees, and thighs; it was long indeed
since they'd been used to fight, but as the noise of the screaming,
outraged crowd grew closer and closer to the White Boar, old
instincts stirred.

Before he understood it, the baron was on his feet and shouting, too, yelling for his men, and his sword was in his hand without thought. Many things Stephen Hardwell had been accused of
in a long life, but cowardice was not one of them.

It was chaos in the market square as the baron ran outside,
searching for the attacker. There must be an attacker—people
yelled that loud only from terror or invasion.

He was right! There they were!

"Yaaaaaaaaagh!" The knight braced himself, roaring defiance,
and swung his sword high to the right and above his head, but
there was little time to find a proper stance as the mailed man on
the destrier bore down on him. The baron was in his way!

At the last moment Stephen saw the body of the woman
slung over the saddle boy. Rapine! But a knight never struck a

woman—so with long and painfully learned dexterity, the baron pivoted neatly to one side and swung the sword in a long graceful arc as the mail-clad rider galloped past.

The sword caught the armed man on the shoulder, just enough to unhorse him as the panicked destrier tried to blunder on. The rider hit the ground hard, and the girl, suddenly unbraced, fell down from the saddle bow, too, hitting her head on the cobbles as the riderless horse cannoned off into the screaming, milling crowd.

It was over quickly once Baron Hardwell ran to the downed man, sword high and ready for the coup de grace. Then, unbelievably, he saw his own son's unconscious face; saw the blood, his own son's blood. And understood.

Instantly he spewed into the gutter in the center of the carnage; and as he turned away, shaking, to wipe his mouth, there was the girl he sought, lying among all the mire of the marketplace, the girl from the sea. Wonderingly, before he vomited again, he saw that she had a rope around her throat, a rope that had nearly strangled her as she fell from the horse, and someone had slashed her throat: but she was alive, her chest rising and and falling. Joy warred with shame and terror for what he had done.

He had nearly killed his son, his own son, and now he didn't care.

# Chapter Fifty-four

"He's leaving? What do you mean? Where will he go?" Elizabeth, Queen of England, was very, very frightened.

The dark-skinned woman pointed to two of the large, crudely colored cards and shrugged nervously. "I do not know, Your Majesty, but it is true. See, here, this card. The King of Cups. And here, the journey card beside it. The king will leave York very soon."

Fearfully she flicked a glance toward the queen as Elizabeth paced the dark little room. Irina had not wanted to come to the palace—it was too dangerous, too many people knew of her visits, but she had not been given a choice.

"More. Tell me more."

Irina was silent. "Speak, woman. What do you see!" Suddenly the queen was towering over the girl, the words delivered in a venomous whisper. The two women were hidden away in a part of the Palace of Westminster that was virtually ruinous, a warren of little shadowed rooms, but it was necessary to be careful.

"There is a woman; and a child. They are important to the future of your house." Irina tried to be cheerful, but dread crawled up her spine as she said the words.

"A child. Is the woman me?"

"No." Irina could barely breathe the word, but it was true. The woman she saw in the cards was not the queen.

Red rage flooded the body of the queen—of course, there was

always someone else! Even now, especially now, that Edward was away in the north without her.

"Who? Tell me who?"

Irina felt sudden peace surround her, against all likelihood; she had never asked for this gift, but she knew that what she said was the truth. She did not flinch this time when she looked up into the face of the queen.

"I cannot tell you her name, but she has hair the color of bronze and eyes like sea topaz."

Elizabeth Wydeville felt the gorge rise in her throat. Of all that she thought, of all that she believed, surely this could not be true.

"This woman. Is she the mother of the child you see?"

Deliberately, slowly, Irina reshuffled the thick pieces of pasteboard and laid them out in the pattern of a six-pointed star, with one card placed in the middle. She was relaxed now, no longer afraid. One by one, she turned each card over as she spoke.

"Here we have the Queen of Cups above, and here, at the bottom, the Page of Cups. Yes, she is the mother of the boy. This is not your child."

Elizabeth gasped. Queen and Page: mother and son. Anne, this was about Anne. Her nemesis. But surely the slut was fittingly swallowed up in the slave markets of the Barbary Coast by now.

"Do you see my child—my son?"

Irina shook her head "No, great queen. There is no son of yours here, in these cards, but here," Irina hurried on, fearful of the effect of her words as she turned over each of the remaining cards, "God in his heaven; and the Devil." The girl's voice faltered as she said the last word.

"Go on, tell me. What do you see?" Elizabeth had to know, had to. Why else risk scandal, and much more than scandal, if the church ever found out, by bringing this woman to the palace?

Irina was still, head bowed, as if she prayed, and she did not answer immediately. In a monotone, finally, she said, "I must turn the other cards, then I can tell you." She shivered as she looked up, but it was not at the queen she gazed. No, she was looking past the queen into the darkness behind her.

The queen looked over her shoulder fearfully. Then she

shook herself: there was little time now, she must return to her rooms to dress for the evening.

"Quickly then, do it quickly!"

One by one, stoically, Irina turned the cards. A ragged man, hurrying away from a castle, a thunderbolt splitting a great tower so that it shattered and fell, and then the final card in the center of the star. Death: a dancing skeleton with a scythe.

Elizabeth was not without courage. She forced calm into her voice. "Therefore, tell me. What do the cards mean?"

Irina tried hard to swallow the fear, which had returned, but she would not lie, could not lie. That would be a betrayal of herself and her people, the little dark people whose land this once had been, or so their songs said.

"Great queen, there is great loss and there is lust. And the avenging hand of God in these cards." Against her will, Elizabeth's eyes found their way to the image of God, implacable on His throne.

"Great wrong has been done, and it must be paid for, atoned for, or much will be lost." Irina pointed at the man hurrying away from the castle, the sores of poverty on his face, his thin arms and naked feet, his rags all telling the same story of destitution.

"God on His throne tells me this, and here," she tapped the card of the tower crumbling into the sea, "This card warns me that everything you know, everything you take as yours, may be broken and destroyed. You are in peril. And if this card"—now she had picked up the grinning Devil, gazed at it with a sigh, and then carefully put it back in its original place in the spread—"is ignored, the jeopardy is further increased. You must not ignore the Devil. He does not like it. He means lust, the flesh, all that is treacherous and mean-spirited in each one of us. He would like to see the tower fall; he would enjoy that."

"And this?" Elizabeth could not bring herself to say the name; she would not speak of Death.

"Change. He means change but, allied with these others." Irina couldn't help it, she shook her head.

There was silence in the room now as the women gazed at the cards. Irina had done her best, she had spoken the truth, but perhaps not all of it. No, perhaps there was more, but she would not speak unless questioned directly.

"One last card?" In the past, in times when Irina had read cards that seemed more hopeful, Elizabeth had always enjoyed pulling one final card from the pack. So often they'd portended luck—the Ten of Cups, the Nine of Cups—happy cards, prosperous cards.

Irina nodded; there was no choice if she wanted this to end. Ever since this morning, even before she'd received the summons to come to the palace, she'd been oppressed with a gloom so palpable it was like a dress laced too tight across her chest. She ached as a woman does whose breasts are full of milk for the child she has lost.

Silently she shuffled the cards one long, last time. The queen held out her hand to pull her card from the pack.

"No, I cannot!" Irina suddenly held the cards away.

Elizabeth was shocked, then angry. Never before had Irina been so direct. There was a moment's cold silence.

"Do as I ask, Irina." The queen's voice was calm.

Irina had tears in her eyes and her hands were shaking as she finally held out the pack. It was as if her body tried to do what her heart would not permit.

"Ah, lady, please, everything I feel, everything I am, asks that you do not do this."

Elizabeth stood suddenly, her face white with rage. Violently she ripped the cards out of Irina's hands and scattered them.

All but two fell to the floor beneath the table, but these final two fell directly onto the trestle's surface, face up: the Wheel of Fortune—with helpless, hopeless souls clinging to the iron-shod rim as it turned and crushed some, while others rode high above them—and the Death card. Again.

"They're only cards. Just cards!" But both women had seen it: one of the tiny figures clinging desperately to the rim of the wheel as it turned, one of the figures that could not escape being crushed, had yellow hair and a dress of imperial purple; this little figure was wearing a crown. Today the queen was wearing a purple dress and her hair, bound high and crownlike on her head, was blond. Incontestably it was blond.

# Chapter Fifty-five

She was a good-looking piece, all right, but she didn't talk to anyone. Just sat in the back of the cart they'd hired in Whitby market, as far away as she could manage from the delirious Henry, and continually looked out over the moors, back toward the sea with the saddest expression in her eyes.

Wat watched her, watched it all, rolling his eyes at the vain attempts the baron made to get the girl to speak to him. He shook his head in disgust as he kicked the jennet up, to speed her past the cart on this sadly mired road. They deserved each other, Henry Hardwell and his loonlike father. Well-bred idiots!

The baron himself refused to acknowledge Wat's contemptuous pity, for he was weighted down by the consequences of that one blurred moment in the marketplace. Some might say that lust had driven him to that mad action, lust for this silent girl, but that was untrue. He had acted from instinct, unaware of his assailant, or the identity of the girl on the saddle bow. He was a knight; no matter what they said, it had been for duty that he'd nearly murdered the only son he had.

Stephen sighed gustily as he looked at Anne huddled in the back of the cart and always gazing out toward the sea. Perhaps no one would ever understand this tragedy. It was certain he did not, for over the last two days' journey from Whitby, his chosen lady, the girl for whom he had risked and lost so much, had refused to entertain his suit, even out of courtesy, the courtesy she owed him as her rescuer.

Perhaps it was the ropes. Perhaps he should untie her now. He'd first tethered her to the backboard of the cart for her own protection, since she was unconscious when the cart jolted its way out of Whitby. Then, opening her eyes again, she'd said not one word to him, her rescuer, and turned her face away!

Perhaps she really was as mad as she'd seemed that day at the convent when she'd collapsed. Or the fall from Henry's horse, the loss of blood from the wound to her throat—could these explain the oddness of her behavior, her apparent contempt of him?

For Anne, the hallucinogenic miles jolted on and on as the foolish man at her side warbled distractingly of chivalry and honor. She hardly heard him or took in the sense of what he said. The rope that burned her wrists burned her heart as well. She ached all over, and fever from the wound to her throat deepened her despair at the loss of her purse of coins in the fight in Silver Lane—now all that remained was the one single ruby. If she lost that, or if it was found by the mob of ruffians she'd been forced to join, she would be lost indeed.

In her misery, she hardly noticed that the cart had creaked to a stop until she heard Wat yell out, "Defend yourselves!" at that same moment the baron roared, "To me, Wat, to me!"

Only presence of mind saved Anne's life as an arrow fleeced the air between her face and the backboard of the cart. Hunching down as much as the ropes allowed, Anne huddled into a corner as the shouting and screaming began. Head down, hidden as much as she could, she did not see but she heard. A mêlée engulfed the baron's party as men and horses screamed, swords rang, grunt and clang, and arrows flew through the last of the light.

It was moments, moments that stretched to hours, before they found her, but find her they did.

"Captain. There's a woman."

No use burying her head. No use for anything anymore. Deliberately Anne straightened her spine and dragged herself up to a sitting position. Time to face death—it had truly found her at last.

*    *    *

Deborah cried in her sleep that night. In her distress she called out, "Anne? Anne!"

Her anguish woke little Edward and he began to wail.

That lonely little cry woke Deborah properly, and in a moment she had flung a cloak around her naked body and hurried over to the sobbing child, scooped him up, and held him tight, rocking him, kissing his wet cheeks, until the sobs subsided into gulps and he was silent once more.

Quietly soothing him as she walked, Deborah carried the little boy over to her own box bed and put him between the covers, climbing in beside him, pulling him close. She thought he'd gone to sleep, but then she heard his forlorn whisper.

"Wissy?" It was one of his few words—the word he used for Anne.

"Ah my lamb, she'll come back, she will. You'll see. Our Wissy . . . we'll find her."

Yet as she kissed the little boy and sang to him, felt him snuggle up against her, heard his breathing even out until he slept deeply, Deborah did not allow the thought to take form or substance.

But then it was impossible to hold back as the floodtide of fear lapped higher and sharper. Loneliness and death. There was a black, black ring around Anne and no matter how hard Deborah tried to shake the feeling of doom that swaddled her like a cloak, she did not have the strength. *Let it be dawn soon, let the night pass. May the darkness lift, may it lift.*

Deborah was not alone in her prayers, for the king, too, in the bleak, silent hours before dawn, found he could not stop his mind from roiling and roiling over the events of the last few days. At last he gave up trying.

Padding to the fireplace, he shivered as he felt the dank, icy breath of night against his naked skin.

It was grave quiet. There was not even the rustle of a mouse or a rat to disturb the suffocating black blanket of the night. Edward grimaced. He needed warmth and he needed light. Flint; there was some here, somewhere.

Feeling around the hearthstone of the fireplace, Edward

found the flint box. And, yes, pieces of pitch pine and a heap of wood shavings lying ready for the morning. He would restart the ashes and bring some warmth into this tomb of a bedchamber.

The sound of the flint as it struck sparks was alien in the quiet: too sharp, too metallic for the smooth darkness that clogged the room. It did its work, though: the white sparks fell among the wood shavings and soon a sharp crackle gave promise of warmth as the banked ashes brought assistance to the first tiny flames.

Edward moved quietly around his room looking for his cloak. He did not want to wake the guard who was sleeping outside across the chamber door—he needed this moment of solitude; there were so few in his life and they were precious.

It was in solitude like this that he thought best and most constructively, without the clamor of others' advice, without the distraction of competing obligations.

The fire had caught well now, generating light as well as heat, a red cave in the darkness. In the ruddy glimmer he saw the branch of candles on the gateleg table standing beside the fireplace; more light flared in the gloom. There it was! His riding cloak was thrown on the end of his bed. He picked it up then, sighing, the king turned to look at the scrolls heaped up on a chest standing against one wall. Each one of them demanded his attention. But there were other things to think about. More important things. Anne.

Edward, King of England, sank down into a cathedra that had been placed for him in front of the fireplace the night before.

It was a good chair, substantial. It even had a padded cushion stuffed with horsehair and goose down on its unforgiving plank seat. A rare luxury, one he liked. He grimaced as he shifted around to get comfortable. Even used to riding the distances he did out hunting and on campaign, the last days had been a marathon and he was still sore, despite the daily hot baths.

Anne. Panic gripped him. Could he remember her face? Could he summon it if he tried? Deliberately he closed his eyes and breathed deeply, thinking of her, thinking of their time together in Brugge. Imagining her body—her feet, her legs, then her belly, her breasts, her hair. Her face.

Yes. Her face. He could see her face. She was smiling at him lovingly. Then she pulled him down to her so that her mouth was against his; he was lying with her, so warm and smooth, so . . .

A knock at the door tore the fabric of the fantasy. He ignored it, trying to hold the feel of her skin in his mind, the softness.

"Edward?" His brother's urgent voice.

The king stood and wrapped himself in the cloak, trying to ignore the ache in his belly as he strode to the door, wrenching it open.

"What?"

Richard was ashen: the light of the sconces in the passage outside the room showed the pallor of his face. Silently he held out a vellum packet, sealed with an extravagant amount of red wax. "This has come for you just now. From Warwick." Edward hurried back inside his room, Richard at his heels, as he tore the seal and opened the document, holding it up to the candles to read.

*To Edward, King of England, from Richard, Earl of Warwick, greetings. Know that today I was presented with something of value to your majesty. Lady Anne de Bohun. I have her safe in my care. A most charming lady and with such a surprising past.*

Richard saw the look on his brother's face and swallowed fearfully. Edward was staring into the fire, his lips drawn back from his canine teeth. In the flickering and uncertain light it was as if he'd been transformed from a man to a wolf. "Richard." It was a whisper.

"Yes, Edward?"

"Get the horses saddled."

# Chapter Fifty-six

Middleham Castle was said to be a fair place, in happier times.

As it was now, Warwick's favorite castle was reduced from a home to a garrison stuffed with armed men, men who ate too much and quarreled, and got in one another's way when the rain stopped practice at the butts, or training with horses in the fields.

Anne looked down from the window seat in her room in the Round Tower onto the seething inner wards below. Even in the driving rain, which turned the sky into a brooding leaden mass, the men worked with all the industry of ants. Preparations were everywhere; preparations for war, preparations for the death of innocent people. That was the meaning of war. Always.

How strange, then, that she who knew death so intimately, who'd expected to die even so little time ago as yesterday, should feel so calm. Perhaps she was feeling less after feeling so much.

Wearily the girl closed her eyes. She would think more clearly after a little sleep; just a few moments of rest and then she would assess what she must do. So tired, so very tired . . .

Behind her, an iron-bound door opened silently and a man stood looking into the room, looking at the girl in the window.

Richard Neville, the Earl of Warwick, was a courtier to his fingers' ends, a competent general, and a good lord to his tenants, but above all, he understood politics and played at them like chess.

Every instinct he had said that, in the fortuitous advent of this girl's being picked up on the moors by men out on routine patrol of his lands, he had the queen piece in this current game.

Edward would not just be checked in the war of nerves they were waging on each other, he would be swept off the board.

For he remembered all the rumors, the mystery, the scandal of less than two years ago when it was said the king had found a new love, his greatest love, and that the queen knew. And yes, he remembered the tournament vividly, the tournament of Saint Valentine's Day, when a veiled girl, riding into the lists on a donkey, had made her own challenge to the king. Now he knew it was this same girl, Anne de Bohun, the girl who'd been in sanctuary at the Abbey, evading Edward.

He'd never seen her face then, of course, but he'd known her name, oh yes, he'd known her name. And now, here she was. And she wasn't going anywhere.

Unconsciously his hand tightened on the pommel of the dagger in his belt. Then he relaxed. Gently he coughed, and Anne slewed around, instantly awake, unable to completely suppress the wariness of the captive.

"And so, lady, I hope my people treat you well?" He smiled charmingly, sweeping her a deep bow.

She refused to rise when he addressed her; he noted that with wry approval. He rather enjoyed women with mettle, though of course, in the end, it was a useless quality, irrelevant in their sex.

Anne nodded graciously and he watched one white hand smooth the pretty surface of the gown she'd been given. It was one of his own daughter's, kept in readiness for when the family was in residence—deep, almost night-blue velvet; it suited Anne de Bohun well. He saw, too, that the wound on her throat had cleaned well and was healing. It would leave only a faint scar on her throat, a white necklace. That pleased him: he did not like beauty to be needlessly destroyed.

"I am well housed, Earl Warwick, but I should be most grateful if you could arrange for me to journey on to my home as quickly as can be arranged."

The earl nodded sagely, maintaining the polite fiction that she was his guest. "Ah yes, to your lands in Somerset?" Anne smiled and, as if the thing did not have stakes, looked away idly and yawned delicately.

"Yes, I am expected these last ten days. My people will be most concerned."

The earl sauntered over to the window seat and gently sat at the farthest end, facing her.

"But the ways are foul, lady. Very deep with all the recent storms. I could not, in all conscience, allow you to leave us. Even with an escort, there are far too many wolvesheads about. You should consider yourself my guest until at least the spring."

He looked regretful and sincere. Anne controlled her voice with effort, replying evenly, "Ah yes, I do understand, sir. But I see so many men about you, surely you could spare, say, ten to escort me south. I would be delighted to pay you for their services."

She turned toward him fully and smiled brilliantly.

"But, lady, you have no baggage; nothing for such a journey at this time of the year."

Anne nodded gravely in turn. "Alas no, Sir Earl. It was most inconvenient that I was robbed as well as kidnapped by the baron and his son."

Both fell silent for a moment. After the fight on the moor, the fight in which Baron Stephen Hardwell had fallen as a knight should, sword in hand, and his son dispatched also by a zealous member of the Neville affinity, there was no one to contradict Anne's story.

The earl sighed. "Truly, lady, a most terrible ordeal, but it will not be possible to send you back to your people, not with all the rumors of invasion from France. I should be failing in my duty to an unmarried lady, alone in the world." Anne, wound tight, smiled, though her teeth clenched and her breathing quickened.

"Then, sir, perhaps I can help you change your thought in this matter." Reaching into a little pocket bag attached to the high belt of the velvet gown, Anne brought out her last hope—the ruby. It lay in the palm of her hand like a drop of blood.

The earl smiled mirthlessly. "Ah lady, a stone such as this might buy much more than an armed escort."

"But I would be pleased to give it to you, Lord Warwick. A trifle to thank you for a service well rendered." She said it carelessly, with just the right degree of finesse. The man and the woman locked glances and Richard Warwick found he respected Anne de Bohun—a surprising development. Clearly she understood he had the power to take the stone, perhaps she was daring him to do it. And now he could not. Not if he was a knight.

"A pleasingly bold move, Lady Anne."

She smiled at him. "Are we players in a game, Earl Warwick?"

The earl laughed genuinely, openly, as he rose and extended his hand to the girl. "Well now, I have always considered life is but a game of chance. For now, as we consider its meaning, I find myself hungry. Will you break your fast with me?"

George, the young Duke of Clarence, was hungry also, and annoyed. He could not go into the great hall to eat without his host, but his gut was rumbling from lack of food, and fragrant smells were wafting up from the kitchens below. Altogether he was sick of roosting with Warwick in this drafty castle when it was clear that the decisive action they had planned might need to be abandoned, for all that Middleham was stuffed with soldiers.

Secretly, though, a part of him was relieved that the weather was so foul and that dispatches from France had confirmed that Margaret, the old queen, would not now bring men into the country in this season. No sane man likes entering into a fight that cannot be won, and the old queen's presence with troops was vital if they were to have a quick, sharp, successful war with Edward's troops in the border country.

He shivered. Successful. Yes, that was the rub. He didn't like to acknowledge it, but he was afraid of Edward, even with Warwick there to lead the fight. Hard to forget, after all, that he was the king's brother.

He shook his head to distract him from the prickle of fear as he stalked over to a window embrasure with a grumpy sigh. But the fear seeped back, the fear inherent in this current situation, siding against Edward and Richard.

Privately, when he thought about it even for a moment, he'd been stunned to hear that the French woman, the old queen, was even interested in supporting Warwick and him against his brothers.

There was much bad blood, much bitterness between Margaret of Anjou and the earl because Warwick had engineered Edward's usurpation of her own husband's throne. She'd not loved Henry VI, ever, but she had loved being his queen—the Queen of England. The fact that the earl was now courting her for his own good ends, that of toppling Edward and putting him, Clarence, on the throne in his place, would not endear the earl to her at all; she'd never trust either the earl or himself, surely?

George, Duke of Clarence, sighed. He hated politics. Hated all the waiting and the compromise, yet he knew that he must play this part, the disloyal brother, if his dream of ascending the throne were not to disappear like mist in the morning.

The duke snorted as he looked out into the miserable, driving rain that obscured the vale of Wensleydale; they could all think what they liked, plot all they liked. He didn't trust any of them, or any of the promises. He'd use the earl as he needed to, and he'd take the throne, with or without him, just as Edward had.

George of Clarence bit his nails, moody and petulant. Life was so unfair sometimes; he hadn't asked for all this bad feeling in the family, but Edward knew quite well that Clarence had more than enough reason to feel unfairly treated. The king had blocked his marriage to Isabelle, Warwick's daughter, more than once and if that wasn't unkind, unbrotherly, what was? Yes, he had good reason to challenge his brother for the kingdom. He'd always been treated like a child, always been laughed at for perfectly reasonable ambition, but they'd see, they'd all see—and they'd sneer at their peril when he was crowned in Westminster!

"George?"

Clarence wheeled and saw to his surprise that the earl was approaching with a good-looking girl on his arm—a very good-looking girl of about his own age. Clarence smiled brilliantly and sauntered toward them, pulling down his doublet so that it sat well and squaring his shoulders. He bowed charmingly at the girl. Things were looking up!

"Lady de Bohun, may I present George, Duke of Clarence." The duke made another, even deeper and more graceful bow; not for nothing was he Edward's brother. "Perhaps you knew one another formerly, at court?"

There was the smallest pause before the girl shook her head shyly, blushing becomingly as the duke discreetly looked her up and down.

"Lady de Bohun and I have never met. A great loss but now repaired." George gazed shamelessly into Anne's eyes until, embarrassed, she dropped her gaze to the foor.

The earl frowned. George, who professed to love his own daughter Isabelle, showed far too much interest in his "guest." The Yorks were like that, any woman was fair game; he would have to be careful. Briskly, he took the initiative.

"Come, we are all famished. If you would, Your Grace?"

Bowing, the earl resigned the lady's arm to the ranking duke, and George gracefully led Anne into Warwick's hall, where the Neville household waited obediently to begin the breakfast. Solemnly, with a suitably impassive face, George led Anne to a place of honor at the high board, where she was to sit beside her "host," chatting loudly to her as they processed past the assembled ranks of the Neville retainers as if the other people in the hall did not exist.

A pretty girl always gave you confidence, George found, and he was getting on with Anne splendidly, almost as if they'd known each other since childhood. Yet though he was positive he'd never met this charming girl before, there was a familiarity about her face he found disquieting. It was like a word lost on the tip of the tongue . . .

For Anne's part, the physical similarity that George had to his elder brother was deeply disconcerting. If she half-closed her eyes, if she listened to the timbre of his voice, it was almost possible to believe they were the same man. But then he spoiled the impression by letting his eyes flick too clearly to the breast of her gown— he was entirely unsubtle, something his brother never was—and by his loud laugh, a laugh with some similarity to a donkey's bray.

As Anne took her place between the duke and the earl at the high board on the dais, a discreet buzz ran around the hall as all eyes focused on the trio.

The castle people were avid for gossip; they'd all heard how the girl had been rescued from kidnappers on the moor and were agog to see if she lived up to the reports of her physical attraction. George, too, was intrigued when the earl described the events of the day before. "Stephen Hardwell and his son? I'd not heard they'd turned outlaw. So how did this all happen, lady?"

Anne calmly told her story once more. "I was in York, transacting business on behalf of my partner, Sir Mathew Cuttifer, and myself, with Master Cohen of Silver Lane—we have wool-growing interests at Burning Norton—when Sir Henry burst into the house and abducted me. Later he was joined by his father." She shook her head, apparently deeply overcome by the terrible things she had suffered.

The earl, tut-tutting, patted her hand and finished the story for her. "And since we had received a report that a party of armed men was loose on my lands, I sent to find out what was afoot. Unfortunately, or fortunately for Lady Anne—who was tied into the back of a cart—my servants met resistance when they sought to question Sir Stephen and his son, and well, here she is, safe and sound!"

Certainly it was best to be economical with the truth in front of this witless, vain boy; best not to speak of the directive he'd given his men that all unfamiliars found on Neville land were to be stopped and challenged in these times.

Unfortunate that his men had exceeded orders, unfortunate that Sir Stephen had drawn his sword before asking even one question—though the earl knew well his men were overzealous in their approach—but that was the price one paid for vigilance in these times.

The duke was astonished and outraged on Anne's behalf. "I must speak to my brother, I really must! The kingdom is becoming entirely lawless if a lady is to be treated in this way. Tied into the back of a cart! Outrageous, truly outrageous!" The earl suppressed a smile at this unconscious hypocrisy from George. "For a lady of quality to be dragged from a private house and kidnapped in the full light of day is appalling."

Anne closed her eyes quickly. She hated to lie, and the image of Henry Hardwell, disemboweled as he lay dying in the cart beside her, was a horrible one. Quickly she said a silent prayer for the peace of the knight's soul to Mary, the mother of his God, but she opened her eyes as a cold draft shifted the hangings behind the high table.

Warwick and Clarence, oblivious to the sudden chill, were talking of supplies for the men in the castle, but Anne felt the flesh of her arms prickle as she looked around to see where the icy breeze was coming from. The doorway into the hall was covered by drawn curtains but a hand appeared between them, a hand holding a plain, naked sword. A woman's hand.

The curtains fluttered, blowing aside for a moment, and Anne glimpsed a cowled figure behind them. The cowl dropped back from the face as the unexpected guest at the feast strode forward.

The Sword Mother advanced some steps and, staring full at Anne, took up a position standing guard at the entrance to the hall, both hands resting on the pommel of her sword as she grounded the tip on the flags.

Anne's mouth was dry as she stared back.

"Lady Anne? More bread for this excellent saffron sauce? You look quite pale. We must feed you well if you're not to sicken after your ordeal." The duke smiled encouragingly at Warwick's charming guest as the busy servants came and went, adding more and more food to the table.

"Thank you, Your Grace. Yes, strength is just what I need."

Only Anne saw the Sword Mother smile as the chill wind sighed through the hall. And Anne smiled back, smiled at the empty air and then at the duke as she dipped bread into the saffron sauce on their shared pewter trencher.

# Chapter Fifty-seven

"What does she look like, your son's mother? Her hair, for instance?"

Edward stirred the meager fire with the toe of his riding boot. "I'm not telling you, Richard." His brother was persistent, although ordinarily the king liked that.

"But why not?"

Edward laughed. He couldn't help himself, and that eased the tension. God knew, after the last two days, that was a relief in itself.

The brothers were camped out on the moors two days' journey from York with a small party of hand-picked men, and it was a cold night.

"How long has the scout been gone?"

The duke shrugged. "Five minutes longer then when you last asked, Edward."

He sat squatting to feed the flames with heather; it was wet, and smoke billowed into their eyes from a sudden gust of wind. Edward cursed heartily. "God's bowels and arse! What're you doing?" Richard coughed and leaped up, eyes streaming.

"It was going out."

Edward turned away, choking, but Richard wouldn't be swayed from his obsession. "You've got to tell me more about your lady love, Edward. How will I know her in the fight if you don't describe her to me? We could end up with the wrong girl."

Edward punched his brother hard in the shoulder so that the duke fell, arse first, into a wet gorse bush.

"Oy! *Aaargh*—get me out! Come on!"

"That's for being nosy. And I'm not letting you near her, fight or no fight." But the king reached down a hand and hauled his brother, half-laughing, half-snarling, out of the bush just as they both heard hooves approaching at speed.

Geoffrey Luttrell reached the man first as he rode into the little camp, horse wild-eyed, man breathing hard. Geoffrey helped the scout from his horse and, throwing the reins to a bystander, hurried the man to Edward and Richard.

"Therefore, tell me about Middleham."

The scout, Walter Ferrars, made a sketchy bow as the words fell out of his mouth. The king was famously impatient before a battle and he didn't want to provoke the Plantagenet wrath unnecessarily. "Stuffed tight with troops, liege. Too many of them— at least a thousand, I'm thinking."

Richard had spent several years at Middleham, sent there as a boy by his father, the old Duke of York, to learn the civilizing arts from the Nevilles. He shook his head grimly. "Middleham can accommodate twice that number, if it has to. They'll be primed and ready for a fight. We should have kept the levies by us, brother." Edward shook his head; that was all too late now. "Well supplied, are they?"

The scout nodded. "Wensleydale's alive with the talk. They've enough provisions, enough armament to survive a six-month siege. Warwick's there. And it's said he has a guest; a lady who answers your description, sire,"—Richard flashed an outraged look at his brother, who shrugged—"though she's not much seen. Gossip says she's not so much a guest as a captive. The earl's family, though, is away at Warwick Castle—or so I was told." The man guttered to a halt. Plainly there was more to say.

"And? What else, Ferrars? What do you know?" Richard stared so intensely at the scout that the man dropped his eyes, abashed.

"Well, Walter?" The king's tone was calmer. No sense in making Walter feel as if his last day had come; it was not easy being the messenger.

"The Duke of Clarence, sire. He's known to be in residence with the earl."

Richard made a disgusted noise and glared savagely at the fire, now almost out thanks to his previous attentions. "There, look at that now! Wood! We must have wood—for the sake of Christ's sorrows!"

Edward ignored his brother. "Thank you, Walter. Get some food; and you, Geoffrey."

Geoffrey Luttrell sprang to his feet. "Yes, sire?"

"Wood. See if you can find some wood."

The two hurried away leaving the king and Richard together contemplating the ruins of their wretched fire. "I didn't say it was going to be easy, Richard."

The duke said nothing, merely slung his cloak tighter around his body against the cold. An eloquent action that said, and so, what now?

The king sighed. "Listen, my hot young friend. This has to be done and there's more to it than you know, than I can tell you."

The duke spoke furiously.

"Don't patronize me, Edward. If you can't tell me, who can you tell? Why do we have to retrieve your doxy when there's so much that's important to do?"

Just the merest ghost of a smile touched Edward's mouth, but he was grim, very grim. "My doxy, as you call her, has more of a right to the throne of England than I do. Or you. Or Clarence for that matter. That's why."

Richard's mouth hung open for a moment and then he gulped. Edward was serious. "Well then, isn't it time you told me the truth? Who is she?"


The Earl of Warwick was uneasy. He'd sent the letter concerning Anne to Edward more than five nights since, but as yet nothing, no word, had come from York.

He was puzzled; the king was still at York Castle with his brother—that's what his trusted people, his intelligencers, were telling him.

Richard and Edward were seen at chapel, and holding some state together within the hall. True, they'd been closeted for the last two days or so within Richard's rooms, but food was regularly sent in and consumed, clothes were dirtied and washed, audiences were held, with Hastings in attendance.

It was strange, therefore, most strange, that there had been no response. Then, thinking of the case, the earl brightened. Edward must dance to his own good pleasure for he, Warwick, was in possession of the girl. Like the spider on his web calmly waiting for the hapless fly to approach, that must be his course of action: watch carefully, and wait.

Meanwhile, there was chess to play with the charming Anne de Bohun.

"Your move, Earl Warwick." There was a certain edge of triumph to that slightly husky voice—it gave him pleasure to hear it, though, of course, her certainty would not survive this next move.

"Ah, yes, so it is. I think my bishop must move to take your castle, thus." His turn to smile into those long green-blue eyes. Really, if he were not a well-married man he might be tempted.

"Ah, then my knight will take your bishop, so." She was smiling at him, damn her. Smiling quite saucily and, truth to tell, he had not seen the possibility of the move. He must concentrate, for this was not like him; he always won at chess!

She chuckled. "But I'm sure you always win, Your Grace." He looked at her sharply, but there was such innocence in her eyes that the odd timing of her remark dissolved.

He held her glance for one moment before she looked down modestly. He approved of that. Women who gazed at men boldly were nearly always overreaching trollops—as most women were, of course, at heart. Sisters of Eve, all of them, sisters of Eve, under the skin.

He studied the board. Had she trapped him?

"Your Grace?"

"Hmmm?" He was distracted, finding it harder and harder to think his way out of the puzzle she'd set him.

"I should like to ride out a little later today. I feel the need for exercise."

He looked up, smiling, from the board, though a certain tension stiffened his spine.

"Alas, I fear that all this rain would make the going difficult. Not safe, Lady Anne, not safe at all."

She laughed. "But I ride very well, Earl Warwick. Come with me, if you're so concerned. We've all been immured too long!"

"Well said, Lady Anne. Excellently said!"

The earl swiveled in his seat, annoyed; Clarence had just strolled into Anne's solar, arriving in time to hear her last words.

"Fresh meat, cousin. I swear my teeth are coming loose from the lack of it after all this salt pork we're eating. Just one or two bucks? The whole castle will thank us."

Earl Warwick narrowed his eyes at the young duke and George felt suddenly uncertain. For a moment, it almost appeared as if the earl might hate him; then it was gone. George shook his head. He'd been mistaken; the earl was smiling broadly, after all.

"Ah, you young people. You think of nothing but pleasure."

Clarence was like a puppy now, so happy to be smiled at by his master he was positively panting. Yet Anne observed the unconscious contest between the two men dispassionately—she saw the rivalry between them, even if they did not. That could be, would be, useful to her.

"Where's the harm, cousin? Lady Anne, help me change his mind!" Anne smiled graciously. "Indeed, Your Grace, there could be no harm, could there? Healthful exercise?" The earl contemplated the chess board in rapt concentration, then, having essayed a move toward Anne's queen—and rejected it—sat back and smiled a rueful smile.

"Perhaps not. It might be good for us all." In truth, he too would be happy to get across a horse after days and days of voluntary incarceration. And there was no threat to Middleham; he'd made sure of that. His lands bristled with his affinity on careful, attentive patrol. Yes, they could hunt safely if he made sure the girl was well guarded as they rode. It might be a pleasant little lull before what must come, eventually.

"Very well." He rose and made a nonchalant little bow to the girl. "Let us hunt. Afterward, perhaps I will think more clearly"—he grinned as he nodded toward the board—"since you are such a very good strategist."

Anne smiled at the compliment as George whooped with delight. "Oh ho, Lady Anne! You've bested him—that's a first! So now, we must see if you hunt as well as you play. Who knows, you might even beat our host to the kill!"

The earl frowned quellingly at this unnecessarily noisy display before turning back to Anne. "Lady, we must see to finding you a hunting dress. I'll get the housekeeper to give you something of Isabelle's." The light stress he placed on the name of his daughter was enough to curb George. He fell into a sulk and didn't bother to hide it as he stalked out.

Isabelle! It had been a month since Warwick had permitted him to see his daughter. For the life of him, he had no idea what game Warwick was playing at—didn't the earl want him to marry his daughter? In token of his displeasure he slammed the door at his exit.

Anne suddenly found the view from her window immensely interesting, but the earl was unperturbed. "My daughter keeps a spare riding habit at Middleham, I believe." He sauntered to the door and smiled charmingly at his guest as she turned back to him. "I shall have it sent to you."

The door closed behind Richard of Warwick and Anne counted to five deliberately, taking slow, deep breaths. If will could make her heart beat less fast, then she would will it so. She had a knife hidden, an eating knife she'd filched one night at dinner in the hall; she'd sharpened it well on the stone windowsill and she would bind it carefully to her forearm, just as she'd been shown by Ivan such a long time ago, it seemed, in Brugge.

Today she would find a way to use it, for this ride felt like a last chance to cut free from the politics she'd been caught up in. And she still had her ruby.

Freedom and her son, and Brugge, still beckoned and there

was nothing—nothing!—she would not do to claim her life back once more.

Edward's men had done very well to penetrate so deeply into Warwick's lands without being spotted. Walter Ferrars had done his work carefully, guiding the king and his brother with their men up moorland streams—so that the horses left no trace for dogs—and taking little-known sheep ways toward the Wensleydale hills; and now, at last, after a morning's tough, concentrated ride, Edward and Richard could see Middleham below them.

"A very fair castle, brother." Richard sounded wistful as he looked down from his perch on the fell beside his brother; he'd been happy there, as a boy. "Well situated, as you see."

Edward grunted, studying the place. Unfortunately Richard was right. Earl Warwick was famously protected by massive, carefully built walls—some of the thickest in England—and the ancient, grim central keep was well defended by inner and outer wards, a formidable gatehouse, and a moat.

The only way into Middleham was through the mighty East Gate and once through that, a visitor to the castle passed beneath a further two inner gates, each including a portcullis, each one guarded by its own troops.

"And so?"

Edward gritted his teeth. What did his brother expect him to say? That they should just stroll down, knock on the door and . . .

Edward laughed. Of course, that's just what had been done on another celebrated occasion at Warwick Castle. Their brother Clarence had been staying with the earl, about to marry his daughter, though Edward and Hastings had interrupted that little liaison. And here, in this castle, George was once more keeping company with the earl. Did nothing change?

"I'm game to have a go—just knock on the door and ask for breakfast." Richard sounded remarkably cheerful and that made Edward laugh as he slithered back from the edge of their aerie on his belly, followed by his brother. Once beneath the line of sight from the castle below, he stood up and joined the small group of men waiting for instructions.

"We will watch and ward, relays of two men each: two hours on, two hours off. I'll want reports of movement over the next eight hours: we'll time by quarters of the sun. Duke Richard and I will watch first, you are to rest."

Walter Ferrars had done his work well in finding this place—a small blind valley behind the summit of a high fell with, at its end, an abandoned salt mine that went some way back into the hill itself—an artificial cave, large enough for men and horses both.

"Here, Geoffrey, take Mallon." The king tossed Geoffrey Luttrell the reins of his destrier and Richard did the same for his own stallion, Hautboys.

Silently, for they were well trained, the band of young men led their horses into the mouth of the salt mine, disappearing one by one into darkness like wraiths, leaving the king and his brother alone in the quiet green valley.

Richard smiled. "I look forward to meeting her, you know. Meeting this nameless girl. And I hope she's worth it to you."

Edward did not reply, but as he reached the lip of the fell once more and lay down—careful to make sure that his sword was covered by a fold of his cloak and that he'd removed his metal helm so that the sun should not find it and give away their position to the castle below them—he caught his brother's eye.

"I'm here, aren't I? What does that tell you?"

# Chapter Fifty-eight

The inner ward of Middleham Castle was a roiling mass of horses and people as the earl's party mounted for the hunt. Anne was the sole woman, surrounded by more than twenty of the earl's closest affinity, with the addition of the Duke of Clarence.

What had promised to become a fair day was changing, the sun partly obscured by clouds—pretty clouds, many shades of gray and silver, but clouds nonetheless.

Anne was settling herself onto the back of a delicate mare—finely made and full of energy, dancing from foot to foot—as Warwick rode over.

"Now, lady, I hope you will forgive me, but if the weather turns, we will abandon the hunt. The ground is already so wet that more rain will make our efforts pointless; the scent will be destroyed."

Confidently Anne gathered up the reins of her mare in borrowed red leather gloves and smiled brightly. "But I am certain we'll have good sport, Your Grace. The sun will return, you'll see."

The tremendous noise of baying dogs caught their attention as the earl's pack of hounds streamed out from their kennels.

"Well then, let us see what this day brings." Signaling the dogs to be whipped in, the earl led the party of horses out through the raised portcullis of the gate between the inner and outer wards, the dogs massed in a yelping, trotting pack ahead of them.

Now they were past the second gate leading on to the last ob-

stacle, the great East Gate, and Anne held her breath, only daring
to breathe again as she passed beneath the last and third raised
portcullis, her horse clattering over the wooden bridge that
spanned the moat, until finally they were out into the fields beyond the castle. There, in front of her horse's hooves, lay freedom,
the freedom of the green dales.

She still had her ruby, and the knife, and a good horse beneath her; there was hope. There was always hope.

"Edward, do you ever wish things had turned out differently?"

Richard was lying on his back, gazing up at the sky. His
brother glanced at him for a moment, distracted from scanning
the plain below, the plain that lay before the castle.

Edward sighed. "We do what we do, what we were born to
do, and there's no help for it." Against his will, Richard nodded.
Sometimes it felt as if he and his brother were caught in the toils
of some great mill-working and the only way to escape being
crushed was to control the mechanism that turned the mill wheel.
The role of a king, to be the miller for his kingdom; perhaps there
was comfort in that homely thought.

"Look—there!" Richard's musings stopped abruptly; he
flipped back onto his belly to see what his brother was pointing at.

Beneath them, there was movement around the East Gate of
Middleham—a mounted party and a pack of dogs issuing forth.
Distantly, very distantly, the belling of the hounds reached them
on the damp, uncertain wind.

"Hunting party—how does that help us?" Richard was disappointed.

"Look again, brother."

Richard squinted, but his long sight was not as famously good
as his brother's. "What am I looking for?" It was just a hunting
party, a group of men.

"Use your eyes, Richard! It's not all men. There's a woman
among them. Yes!" Now both made out the bright red of the
hunting dress among the group of men in their darker, more
somber jackets and cloaks.

"Anne." Edward breathed the word, eyes locked to that distant, red-clad little figure.

Richard looked at his brother. "Anne is her name?" Edward nodded distractedly. "But you can't know it's the girl you seek. Could be anyone. Edward?"

But Edward was already slithering back down the bank of the hill "Edward?" With a swallowed curse, Richard scrambled down after his brother, already hurrying toward the salt mine's mouth; but Edward called back over his shoulder as he ran.

"No! Stay there! Keep watch while I get the others; we need to know which way they go."


"Into the trees, into the forest, Your Grace!" Anne had spotted the hounds as they took the scent and began to bell loudly as they ran. Deliberately she sank her heels into the mare's flanks and the horse responded, leaping forward, leading the riders ahead of the earl himself as Anne galloped for the densely packed trees at the meadow's edge.

The earl, caught off guard, was furious. "Pursue, now!" He meant pursue Anne, and Alan of Braydon caught his angry eye. He was ambitious, Alan, and didn't want to betray the trust that the earl had placed in him. In all of them. *Keep sight of the girl, guard the girl.*

But if Anne's mare was small, she was very nimble and willing—as if she sensed her rider's passionate desire for freedom and shared it—and Anne was so much lighter than the men. Soon she had well outstripped the others on their heavier horses, riding alone by a length, two lengths, three lengths, racing on as clouds slid over the sun and the day darkened.

"Hah!" Alan had spurs—vicious, bright slashers with barbed wheels; he used them mercilessly and his gelding surged forward. A big horse, the gelding, plenty of heart, and soon he was out from the pack of hunters by a neck, by a length, gaining on the girl, gaining on the hounds as the other riders, screamed at by the earl, charged on hard, neck or nothing.

"First to find wins a crown!" The earl's words slid on the

wind—prophetic did he but know it—but many of the men around him heard, and it was enough, more than enough because their blood was up. Two quarries today, it seemed: the stag and the girl. Up ahead, the red dress flashed between the trees, deeper and deeper in the forest among the dark trunks as Alan's gelding gained even more pace on the fleeing girl.

"Into the forest, they've gone into the forest!"

Richard, catching up, yelled to his brother as the king let Mallon find his own way down the hillside path, sure-footed as a goat, the men scrambling after him, the horses spooked and sliding on the wet ground.

"We'll run to the west, come in to the trees from that side: we'll surprise them."

Gallant optimism; there was no telling where the Middleham party would be by the time Edward's men came to the forest; they were losing precious time in the treacherous terrain.

"Where is she?" The earl hauled his horse up very short, bellowing; searching for the girl as he scanned the trees, willing himself to see that flash of red. He spurred his horse as he wheeled it, urging the animal on with his whip, his heels.

"Don't think much of your hounds, cousin—don't seem to have put up the stag yet for all the noise." Clarence was suddenly racing beside him. "Anne's outridden us all, come on!" And the young man forced his horse past the earl as he galloped in the direction of the belling hounds.

Clarence was a fool, young and stupid, and if he weren't so valuable as a piece on the board it would have given the earl much, much pleasure to scream out what he really thought behind the retreating royal back. He wasn't even bright enough to understand that Anne was now the object of the hunt.

But Alan of Braydon hadn't lost Anne. He'd settled into wary but hot pursuit: dodging the trees, ducking the branches, keeping his horse close reined.

There she was! Red, blood red, among the stark black trees. Clever girl, she was running away from the hounds but not fast enough, not nearly fast enough.

The king's party was galloping too, flat-galloping, across the meadow toward the west as the fence of trees came closer and closer. Shouts and halloos could be heard from the castle battlements behind them—they'd been spotted!

"Go! Go!" Edward urged his followers, "Find the girl, red dress!"

Behind them, the outer ward of the castle came alive as men rushed to arm and find horse. The pursuit would take minutes, cursed minutes, to organize, but it was worth their heads when the earl found out that armed strangers were on his land, in his own forest! Terror put salt on the tails of the garrison of Middleham Castle.

The little mare was courageous and she smelled the urgency, but she was close to the end of her reserves and Anne knew it. The man behind her was crashing nearer and nearer on his bigger, stronger horse, but there, up ahead was a forest ride, a long straight swathe of grass cut through the heart of the trees. A pleasure ride. At least the little horse could run flat, not use energy dodging trees.

"Come up, up!" Anne screamed the words and the mare responded, one last gallant time. Together girl and horse flew from the protecting trees into the ride, faster and faster.

Alan could not believe his luck; only desperation could make her think she could outrun his gelding on open ground. Again he slashed the spurs to the blood-running sides of his horse as he, too, broke cover from the trees.

The earl saw Alan head for the ride as he came hard up behind him; he'd sent some of his men off with Clarence, riding in hot pursuit of the hounds in an entirely different direction.

Warwick swerved out of the trees, into the ride. Ahead was the fleeing girl, the skirt of his daughter's long red dress flying like a banner, like a flag, but Alan was gaining, gaining, three lengths back, two . . .

"To me, to me!" The earl yelled out to his men, elated as he gouged the sides of his destrier. He had her now, they would run her down—check!

"Saint George! To me, to me!" Mallon had a fighting heart, so too did Hautboys, and both horses answered the call—they'd been in too many battles, they knew what it meant. Bellowing, Mallon put his head down and charged into the ride as the mare and the girl in the red dress ran full tilt toward them, pursued, closer and closer, by one lone rider with a pack of men behind him.

Then Anne saw the king and his men. Ye Gods!

At full gallop, swords were drawn and arrows knocked. "On my word—divide!" Edward roared the command, his eyes locked to Anne's, as his troop peeled into two neat halves, and the girl and her mare charged through their midst and out beyond.

Richard had one wild impression of flying hair and a glorious face, while his brother screamed another command, "And chaaaaaaaarge!"

Now the knights, white boar badge so plain on their chests, formed a dense wall around their king and his brother, spurring their horses faster, faster. A tournament with no tilt yard, no lance, just naked swords and bows . . .

And the earl and his men were upon them, howling for blood, and the crash when they met, the screaming of the horses, was immense.

Anne pulled her mare to a shuddering stop, just yards beyond the fighting, and ripped the sharpened knife from its straps, terrified for the king. Though personal fear had left her and her heart beat like a hammer, the energy, the blind-red exhaltation of battle, was roaring, screaming at her, praying for her—*let him live! Oh let him live, Mother of all Battles.* The little mare was baying like a destrier too, head up, all exhaustion banished as she curvetted, Anne barely holding her.

It was brutal, swift, and drenched with blood, Anne's first exposure to men fighting to win. Alan, her pursuer, was down and trampled, neck sliced open to the spine, dreams of glory gone as the gelding, spooked by the gore, blundered riderless from the fray, running for its stable; and there, in the heart of the battle she could see Edward on his great horse, thigh to thigh with his brother as they swung their swords in wheels, in flashing arcs, swords that rang and rang again as they met those of the earl's men pressed thick around them.

And in the center of the howling mass, the blade-flashing fury, the earl was edging closer, ever closer to the king—now they were fighting, hand to hand, both off their horses as the fight formed and re-formed around them.

Anne had a knife, only a knife, but she would use it, make it count. Standing in her stirrups, she took aim without thought and hurled the blade.

It ran true and straight, and found its mark—Earl Warwick's sword arm—and that was enough. With a scream, Richard of Warwick dropped his blade and the king's own sword was at his neck in a blur.

"Hold. Now. Or the earl dies!"

Edward's roar cut through the tumult; the moment was extraordinary. Frozen. The berserk fury on the king's face spoke the truth. Haltingly, swords and men disengaged. The slithering sound of steel sliding from steel. It was very strange.

Richard of Gloucester, voice hoarse and harsh, bellowed, "Kneel. This is your king!"

Edward pressed the sword's edge deeper into the earl's throat, a thread of blood appearing. That scarlet line did its work. One by one, the earl's men dropped their swords as they knelt.

"Geoffrey, Walter—disarm them!"

Minutes later, as the men of Middleham's garrison burst out into the forest ride, they saw an odd sight and, at a signal from their captain, reigned in their horses, confused and fearful.

Riderless horses careered past as the earl, their master, rode one-handed toward them at a sedate pace; he was wounded in his sword arm and the blood could be seen dripping from the unstaunched wound. Beside him was the king, accompanied by the Lady Anne, shocked and white, and Duke Richard, the king's brother.

On foot behind them walked only some of their comrades from Middleham as, close behind, came a party of armed men, swords drawn, wearing the white boar of Gloucester on their chest, the archers among them with arrows knocking as they rode. And there were bodies farther down the ride, dead men, men they knew.

The captain of the Middleham garrison was not a fool and he was not a coward. His first instinct was to form his men up and charge, but that was the king himself beside his master, and Duke Richard, the boy he'd once known as a page serving in the earl's own great hall of the castle behind them.

"Hold, Eamonn. There's been a misunderstanding, just a misunderstanding. Lady Anne's horse bolted." The earl still had his voice, though it was hoarse from shouting in the battle and had an iron edge. The words were hard to say, after all.

At that moment, preceded by an enthusiastic pack of hunting dogs, the Duke of Clarence and the earl's remaining men issued forth from out of the forest. The duke, very proud, was leading a horse with a stag of a good size slung across the saddle bow.

"Earl Warwick, just see," he paused, doubt, and then horror. "Brother? And Richard."

It was an awkward moment, worse than awkward, but Edward broke it calmly.

"Yes, brother I am here. What a pleasant meeting! The earl was kind enough to invite us here to Middleham. Something was borrowed I believe, Earl Warwick? Property of the Crown you wished to return?"

The earl remained quite impassive. "Perhaps it can be restored as we feast on the fine stag the duke has brought down for us, Your Majesty."

Anne spoke up. "Alas, Earl Warwick, I fear that I have trespassed far too long on your hospitality. Now that the weather is fine"—the first fat drops of rain made clear nonsense of her words—"I truly believe I must be on my way home. As I explained, Your Grace, those I love must be so worried by my continued absence."

Edward smiled graciously. "Ah, Lady, truly it is not safe for you to travel without an escort through my kingdom, ashamed though I am to say it. It happens that my brother, Duke Richard, and I have pressing business in York, which will not permit us to join Earl Warwick and our brother in their feast. We would be most pleased, therefore, to provide an escort for you; and then we can see you on your way farther, should you wish it."

Her eyes met his, and it was a long look. And though she smiled, the sadness in her eyes broke Edward's heart.

"I should be glad of your escort to York, my lord king. As to where I may go after that time, those I love will help me find the road home, of this I am certain."

# Chapter Fifty-nine

It was night, very late, and Edward's room in York Castle was lit by candles and light from the fire.

"Are you hungry, Anne?"

The king looked at the girl standing in the great oriel window of his private quarters in York Castle gazing out into the darkness, still dressed in the now-filthy red hunting habit. She had her back to him. Outside, the world was black and quiet, though wind nudged the cold glass of the window, sighing.

Anne shook her head though she did not turn to look at him. She could not speak, could not form the words.

"I'm sorry we could not rest on our way home," he grimaced as he said the word. So did she, though he could not see it. "But it seemed best to be out of Warwick lands and away here as soon as possible; I hope the ride was not too much for you."

He was trying to find the words to reach her, and all he could talk about was riding. "Would you like to wash or sleep?"

Now Anne turned to face him and he could see the glimmer of tears in her eyes. On all the long, mad ride back to York through a wet day and most of a freezing night, they'd barely spoken, though he had tried every way he knew to get her to talk to him.

"No, Your Majesty. I do not think I could sleep. If it were not so late I would ask to see my son."

There was such a gulf between them. She did not know how

to cross it and yet each ached to touch the other. He knew it and she knew it too.

"Ah, sweet Anne," his voice broke and so did her resolution. All she could see was his face, all she could hear was his voice as he crossed the room toward her. "I thought you were dead." The words were wrenched from him.

He never cried, he never cried, not in all the battles, all the wars, but to say the words, as he pulled her against his chest, was agony and the salt of his tears was a blessing.

She whispered, "I thought I would never see you again, never see our son again." It was the staunching of a wound for both of them.

"Or I you." Pain like madness, the memories, for both of them. Now he was kissing her, kissing her mouth as she clung to him and he to her as if they were both drowning.

"But fate sent you back to me." She heard the words, but they made no sense. She found herself laughing, and absurdly, he was laughing too, great whoops, his whole body shaking with it, as was hers.

Then, gently, subsiding into choked sobs, she wiped his tears away—tears of loss, tears of longing, tears of joy, heedless of her own.

"Edward, bide with me here." She sank down onto the floor, because her legs would not hold her any longer, onto the rug that lay before the fire, a rug made from silk, very soft and variously colored.

He joined her there and the two sat cuddled against one another, looking into the flames. Like children. She was the first to break the silence between them, the silence that comes after tears.

"Oh, King, I will ask you three questions and you must answer, for I command it." Anne's voice was very soft and low.

"The first is this. What would you wish for, if you could have anything in the world?"

He looked at her quizzically. "You know what I want, you've known since we first met."

Anne closed her eyes and leaned her head into his shoulder.

When she answered it was a whisper, almost a prayer. "Great King, I cannot give my life to you. And you cannot give yours to me. No." He had tried to protest, but she kissed his mouth sweetly, deeply, stopping the words. "But there are other things. Valuable things that you may have. Some have called me a sorceress, even a witch. And I may have some little power to grant other requests," she kissed him again, "but only a little."

Edward laughed as his arms tightened around her. "You? A witch? I do not believe in such things. I only believe in you. And you are a mortal woman," he was breathing faster, "but I should like my wishes granted, lady."

That breathy whisper came again. "There are two more questions liege, before I do."

He was turning her face toward him with one hand, seeking her mouth; gently pushing her backward, down onto the rug so that soon he lay beside her, holding her body so tight to his that she spoke into the base of his throat, the words shivering through him, down into his belly.

"Edward, this is my next question. Do you want to be king?"

He spoke without thinking. "No. Not if I cannot have you." Words from the heart. He groaned. It was the truth. "I cannot bear this, to lose you again." She could hardly breathe, pinioned against his chest.

"There is one more question, Edward, and you must let me ask it."

Suddenly he rolled, flipping Anne onto his belly so that she straddled him, the red hunting dress, so crushed, so mud spattered, riding up her thighs. He lay looking up at her. Her face was in shadow, though the warm glow rimmed the shape of her body in rosy light, finding an answering glimmer in the ruined scarlet velvet.

"Ask me, then. Whether I can answer you . . ." He trailed away into silence as his hands slid down her back looking for the point where the laces of her dress were tied.

Anne was not indifferent; she wanted this man as much as he wanted her. She could feel him. He was hard, only the soft leather of his riding britches between them.

"What will you sacrifice so that your children, all your children, can be safe?"

He grimaced and his hands paused for a moment. "I do not know the answer to that question."

"I do." Briefly she turned her head and he saw the tracks of fresh tears. Her sorrow tore at his heart.

"We can be together, Anne. We will be together."

This was Edward Plantagenet now. Not asking. Demanding. "I am the king of this country and you are my subject. So, too, is the queen."

The fire flamed up and sparks flew into the room blown by a cold wind down the chimney. It was as if Elizabeth Wydeville were in the room with them.

"Edward, nothing has changed. Twice in my life I've broken faith with myself. My love for you has been the cause each time. But there is too much danger—for all of us."

It was true, they both knew it, but Edward was not listening now; his hands were too busy, impatience building as he eased the tight lacing of the back of her dress apart. She closed her eyes as she felt the first touch of those strong, bone-hard fingers on the soft naked skin of her back.

They were silent together for a moment, just a moment; then she stopped his hands, found the laces herself, breathing as fast as he was. "You make me shameless." She laughed a little tremulously as she found and pulled the last lacing cord loose and the bodice of the dress dropped from her shoulders exposing her breasts.

"Let me look at you." Edward's voice was husky and his mouth dry from desire as, slowly, caressingly, his eyes roamed her body, the architecture of her shoulders, her breasts, as the firelight found sumptuous shadows, delicate tendrils of hair, the whorl of an ear as she turned her head to look into his eyes.

He did not touch her, waiting; he would not make the first move now. She must agree freely to what they would do together.

"Help me, Anne." It was a husky plea for deliverance.

"Yes." She breathed one word in reply as she gathered the material of the riding habit and eased it off completely over her head.

She was naked now, straddling his lap. He groaned as she leaned toward him teasingly, allowing her breasts to touch his chest through his muslin shirt.

He shivered, aching to touch her, but restrained himself as she pulled the soft material from the points on his britches, so slowly, one by one.

Then his chest was naked and she leaned forward to kiss the base of his pulsing throat. He could bear it no longer; roughly he pulled her to him, skin to skin as his fingers fumbled between them, tearing at the lacing of his riding breeches.

"Take me into you," he spoke into her mouth as she kissed him, deeper, deeper, gently moving her hips against his, sliding against him as he freed himself from the soft buckskin.

Breathing as one, slowly, so exquisitely; she straddled him for one unbearable moment and then sank her body over his so that her weight pushed him high inside her belly. Holding his breath, allowing himself to be encompassed, he and she both gasped with that first deep sense of his heat inside her body; she embracing him as he held her, breasts flattened against his chest. And then she began to move.

They were both silent because the alternative was to scream, but as she knelt, parted thighs on either side of him, moving slowly at first then faster and faster—sliding on him, whimpering, mewing—he cupped his palms beneath her soft buttocks, guiding her, half sitting to hold her tighter to him so that he could take himself ever deeper into her belly. He wanted her, wanted every particle of her slick, soft body, breasts and belly and legs and . . .

He had her on her back now, so fast she did not feel him move until he lay on top of her, his weight pinning her as now he moved faster, faster, and deeper, deeper and harder . . . and she felt helpless, boneless, open . . .

"I am hungry, therefore feed me." She said it to his chest, but he heard it in his groin. He growled deeply, breath more and more ragged, and the bliss, the hot, slick almost-pain building and building between them—their own fire, greater than the oak wood burning to ash in the fireplace behind them—that it had to end, must end.

*"Aaaaaah."* Now it was a scream, a scream that built from the pit of her belly, from between her legs where he filled her and forced her ever more deeply open, and traveled from her chest to her mouth where he ate it with a savage kiss as the sweet explosion took them both and he collapsed onto her, holding her, holding her, holding her.

He would think about tomorrow when tomorrow came.

# Chapter Sixty

The little boy woke in his new bed—the bed that the duke had caused to be made for him alone. It was a good bed, this one, painted dark green with horses drawn on it, and curling tendrils with leaves and red apples among the horses. He liked the bed, liked waking up in it.

This morning, however, was different, and for the very good reason that he awoke to kisses and tears: that was what woke him, saltwater falling onto his face.

He was awake properly now and so happy; here was Wissy, back again! He was clinging to her and she smelled so good, like flowers. She held him fiercely tight against her body, feeling his small heart beating.

"Hello, my darling. Oh, my lamb."

She looked up from her son's embrace at the people she loved, the king, Deborah, even Richard, all watching as she was reunited with her son.

The duke, standing beside his brother the king, was amazed. *See the three of them together, Anne, little Edward, and the king, and you would never, ever mistake them for anything but mother, son, and father.*

Pain and happiness. Such a potent combination.

Anne looked at the king. "Time to go home, Your Majesty, time for us to journey south." She smiled with her mouth, though it did not reach her eyes.

The little boy touched the wet that came from his aunt's eyes and tasted it. Salt. He giggled, and she laughed, she couldn't help it.

"Edward, the king has brought you a present. Haven't you, sire?"

Somewhat helplessly, she turned to the king, eyes appealing for help.

"Yes, it's very special." Edward smiled cheerfully at his son as he strode over to the little boy's bed, though his chest ached as if from a blow.

The little boy was very excited. People kept giving him presents these days; that was one of the good things about being here in Duke Richard's castle—but not as good as being at home, of course.

Edward revealed what he'd been concealing: a small wooden dagger in its own embroidered doeskin scabbard.

"You liked my dagger, so I had a copy made for you from ebony. It's just the right size for you, and see"—he lifted the little boy from Anne's lap and stood him on a stool, so that the two of them were nearer in height—"it has its own belt. You must look after it very well, keep the blade well oiled."

The little boy's eyes were saucer large as the king buckled the belt, with its knife and keeper, over the child's nightdress.

"Do you like it, Edward?" Richard smiled as he asked the question—but his nephew was speechless as, very carefully, he withdrew the knife from its scabbard, one stubby little finger gently tracing the delicate carving on the blade.

Anne smiled at her small son, standing so proudly on the stool in front of them all. She caught Deborah's eye—they had not yet spoken and there was much to say and tell between them, but not now.

"So now, perhaps Deborah can dress you, for there is much to do and we have little time."

Anne was practical now, useful camouflage for inner turmoil that she could only just control. But the boy was not listening, jigging up and down, waving his own little dagger, flourishing it!

Over the head of the dancing child, as Deborah tried to scoop him up to be dressed in the garderobe, Anne and Edward gazed at each other, glance locked to glance. Then, after one long moment, Anne broke the silence between them as their son bellowed with outrage at being washed by Deborah in cold water.

"My liege, I thank you and your brother the duke for everything that you have done to reunite us all." The words had levels of meaning known only to Edward and herself, but Anne curtsied formally to Edward, subject to king, and then to Richard, who bowed in return, from the waist, equal to equal. "Lord Duke, I gratefully accept your kind offer of an escort for we must be away home."

Edward found it hard to speak. "Would you break your fast here, before you leave?"

Anne sighed. And shook her head.

"We will breakfast on the road. Fair weather does not last long at this season."

There was a catch in her voice as she said it. It was a bright, blue day today outside, and the freeze last night would have set the roads better than they had been for many days. But that would not last and the ways would again be deep and treacherous before the journey was done—for all of them.

He stood on the battlements and watched the party of his soldiers surrounding the two women and the boy leave.

He had given her the best: Walter was with her, and Geoffrey Luttrell. They were well armed and well provided for, and Anne was riding the little mare the earl had given her on the hunt. It was a measure of the horse's quality that one night's rest and good barley and bran mash had restored her well enough for the long journey south, the journey that would take Anne away from him, out of his life. But she was alive; at least she was alive.

Richard silently joined his brother and waved to the girl below. She waved in return, once, then turned her face, turned her back, riding beside her son and Deborah, into the future.

"She's doing the right thing, Edward. You need to let her go. We know who she is, others will in time. Warwick." He fell silent. The stakes would be heightened far too much if Warwick ever found out that the girl he'd let slip through his fingers was a daughter of the old king.

Edward said nothing. An iron band was clamped around his chest, an iron band that would not let him speak, for if he tried, he would howl like an animal.

Something moved in his hand, moved within one clenched fist; it felt like a trapped insect, scrabbling at his palm. He was startled and, distracted momentarily, uncurled his fingers; he was holding the ruby, the ruby Anne had given him. He shook his head, puzzled—he must have imagined the movement, and yet there was a scratch on his palm, blood welling where one sharp edge of the gem must have cut him slightly.

He willed the distraction away, gazing down the road below as the group slowly retreated into the rags of morning mist. He closed his burning eyes, determined to imprint the image of the girl riding away from him on his mind, for all time, while he lived.

Her words of this morning, as she mounted the mare and held out her hand to touch his face, covertly, one last time, came back like a sigh. "You gave me a ruby once. This is mine now to give to you. It is my love, and my blood. And my blood is yours."

It was then she gave him the stone.

Blood. His heart's blood, on her ruby. He looked down at it again, startled, and when he glanced up, the party of horses was nearly too far away for even his famous long sight to make her out, buried among the forest of male bodies around her horse, and the mist.

But Anne did look back, one last time, though he did not see it. She saw the two men standing on the battlements, saw his cloak flying out behind him emblazoned with the leopards and the lilies—the leopards and the lilies that belonged to him, and to her, as emblems of the country that was jointly theirs by right—and was jolted by fear when she saw the figure who now stood behind them.

A woman with wild, tangled red hair and a gold torque gleaming at her throat in the pale morning light, thick bands of gold on each of her muscular arms. Silently the Sword Mother raised her arm, her shield arm, and spread it wide. In her other hand there was a sword; this, too, she held out, high above her head, and shook it, once, twice, three times.

And Anne lost her fear for she saw that the Sword Mother stood between the two men; she was protecting them—Edward and Richard—but they gave no sign of knowing she was there, too intent on watching Anne ride away with her son, and Deborah.

Anne turned her head away and set her face for home and Brugge. She would not turn back; it was not her right, but for days after, as the jolting miles to Dover were consumed on good roads and bad, as the sun rose and set, she dwelled on that last image, the goddess protecting the king and his brother. She had been given this one last comforting vision; it was hers to cherish.

The presence of the Sword Mother said battle was yet to come, but all might still be well for she would be there. Would Anne?

# Epilogue

 The scar on Anne's throat from Henry Hardwell's knife had faded to a white line by spring of the following year, and the bad dreams of pursuit, of blood, had nearly stopped.

In Brugge, happy people flung open their windows—it was warmer, assuredly it was a warm wind! Summer, surely they could smell summer coming.

Anne could feel the season changing too—the casement open to the heber allowed a flood of perfume from the blossom on the apple trees into Mathew Cuttifer's parlor in the house near the Kruispoort, and she could feel her heart lifting at last.

"Careful! Oh, gently now!" Deborah was terrified; she was doing her best to supervise Ivan and Maxim. The steward refused help from anyone else in taking down Hans Memlinc's master-work from its place on the wall.

Anne watched herself descending from the wall, watched Saint George—and remembering Edward, their last time to-gether—saw the dragon freshly, so real it seemed to squirm within the frame. Did its glittering scales, its insatiable mouth remind her of the queen, her enemy? She smiled ruefully. *Foolishness!* she could hear Edward say it, *Superstitious nonsense!*

"There! Now . . . careful Ivan! You nearly dropped it!" Anne had to turn away; she'd nearly laughed out loud through the pain, which would not have helped. Pain to leave, pain to stay. Change, radical change, burned away the dross. Perhaps she would be at peace later.

"Deborah, where's Edward?" Her foster mother, distracted, nodded to the heber as the two men, red-faced with the effort, lowered the huge painting with muscle-burning effort into its specially made case packed with loose wool. There! It would travel safely now.

"I think I'll just . . ." Anne couldn't bear to watch them pack up the rest of her things. She slipped out of the room into the tiled hall and hurried through the dark passage, unlatching the door that led out into the scented, walled garden.

She heard her son before she saw him: wild giggles and gleeful shouts.

"Edward? Edward? Oh, there you are. Hello, Father!"

Father Giorgio was staggering around, arms out, blindfolded, doing his best to catch the laughing child as he dived in and out of the priest's legs. Then the boy saw Anne and ran toward her, his few words chasing each other. "Wissy, wissy, baw, baw!"

Laughing, Anne picked up the brightly painted pigskin bladder stuffed with rags and threw it to her son, who overreached himself trying to catch it and tumbled into the new grass beneath the blossoming trees.

Laughing, Anne joined him, and mother and son rolled together, over and over, as Father Giorgio, strolled toward them, removing his blindfold.

"And so, Mistress Anne. You found it?"

Anne spat blossom petals from her mouth, tickling the little boy, who squealed joyfully.

She nodded "Yes, Father. A house of my own."

The priest sat beside her in the grass, frowning slightly. "You are sure then that this is right?"

His friend looked at him, smiling. "I shall have a house and a farm and a physic garden for Deborah, Father Giorgio. I've missed, oh so much, having somewhere that I belong, properly belong—my own home. Edward will have space and green fields to play in, and none of the noise, the stink of this city."

"And you, what will you have, my child?"

Anne looked up at the spring sky, fingered the scar on her throat. "I will have peace, and the knowledge that I am not the sacrifice."

The priest looked at her curiously.

"The triple death, Father. Have you heard of it?"

The worldly Italian shrugged uneasily. "No, my child, I have not." The intensity of her glance unsettled him. Suddenly the day was still, very quiet. Even the little boy lay quietly in Anne's lap, suddenly drowsy.

"In the old times, the old world, sometimes they made a sacrifice of someone for the good of the tribe, or the village. Or if the people were afraid."

The priest, sophisticated though he was, felt the hair on his neck move as Anne spoke, almost chanting.

"First they hanged them, then cut the throat while the sacrifice still lived," she touched her neck gently where the faint silver line of the scar caught the spring light, "then they drowned them, or buried them underfoot at the crossroads."

She smiled at him, but her eyes were very far away.

"Sometimes, I have felt as if I were that sacrifice, Father. As if I must die so that others could live." The boy stirred in his sleep, muttering something. "But now, I know that is not true."

The priest, discomforted, jumped up to break the mood, vigorously brushing white petals from his finely woven habit.

"Anne, sweet child, you've been upset by all that has happened to you—which I understand; we all do. But to speak of such things, on such a lovely day, when you are just beginning the next great adventure of your life . . ."

He leaned down to help her with the sleeping child.

"Now all I need for you is a husband—a dear man who understands you and all your strange little ways." He was determined to make light of what she had said, and because he was her friend, such a good friend, she made it easy for him.

"Of course! And he should be rich, and handsome, and sing as well as you do!"

Delighted she had responded, the priest led Anne back into the house, caroling, in English, "The Nut Brown Maid," Anne

joining in, descant, on the chorus. But as they reached the door that led into the house, Anne said, "Did you know, by the way that Elizabeth Wydeville has had another daughter?"

Startled, the priest held open the door, his look asking the question.

"Well now, that changes everything."

"Again." Anne smiled as she cradled her sleeping son, stepping into the shadows of the doorway, leaving the warm light behind. The door closed, but ahead of her the great door to the street itself was wide open, allowing the brightness of spring into Mathew Cuttifer's hall, into her heart.

There were leaves on the trees again, and they were green, emerald green.